MW00879316

THE ACCIDENTAL ORIGIN

KOS PLAY

aethonbooks.com

THE ACCIDENTAL ORIGIN
©2023 KOS PLAY

Aethon Books
www.aethonbooks.com

Print and eBook formatting by Josh Hayes. Artwork provided by Cyan Gorilla.

Published by Aethon Books LLC.

ALSO IN SERIES

The Accidental Summoning

The Accidental Education

The Accidental Contract

The Accidental Corruption

The Accidental Origin

Check out the series here! (tap or scan)

[1]

PANIC FLOODED through me as I stumbled into another throne room. It was just as crowded as I remembered it, with alcoves filled with women sitting at luxurious tables. The dark man from my dream sat on his throne watching me with a bored expression on his face while resting his head in his hand.

"Where's Kalli?" I shouted, hoping Kalli would pop up somewhere.

When she didn't answer, I teleported again only to arrive in the same place as the first time. The second trip down the red carpet was much quicker as I jogged over to the man on the throne. He didn't move or say anything, though he looked slightly amused by my antics.

"Where's Kalli?" I asked again as I gasped for breath.

The man stood to get a better look at me. "That's strange. Were both of your eyes always red?"

Kalli!

"Kalli?" I echoed my thought out loud.

The man let out a protracted sigh. "I'm sorry, Melvin. No human can exist without a body. I'm afraid your girlfriend is gone."

My legs chose that moment to fail me. I dropped like a puppet with its strings cut and sobbed on the floor. My worst nightmare was coming true. Kalli was missing. It felt like she'd been ripped away from me. Not only could I not hear her, but I also couldn't feel her.

"I can see you're upset," the man said, patting me softly on the head. "I think it's best you sleep it off."

It was hard to tell what was going on with my eyes squeezed shut, but the man's voice slowly faded as my mind slipped away from me.

Congratulations. You have reached level 44.
Congratulations. You have reached level 45.

I shot to my feet, ignoring what should have been a pleasant feeling while I looked desperately for Kalli. "Kalli! Where are you? Can you hear me?"

It felt odd shouting in my dream. Especially when I was alone. Then again, why was a dream still a place if I was all alone? Wouldn't I dream normally if Kalli was gone?

Deciding she must be around somewhere, I decided to look for her. The problem was, while it wasn't exactly a dream, the world behaved as dreams did. Everywhere I looked, I found what I thought I would. At first, I believed it was a coincidence. I walked toward what I assumed should be a basketball court, and that's exactly what I found. Then, I decided to check out the pool, and I found the pool.

After that, I tried to get creative. I imagined I'd find Kalli the next place I looked. While the area was a video game arcade like I predicted, Kalli wasn't waiting there for me in a two-piece bikini. While she would have been mad at me if it worked, I would have given anything to see that scowl on her face.

I gave up after what felt like forever. There was no telling how much time passed. In the end, I sat there on top of a bridge and replayed the events of the previous day. "Fight Rasputin, check!"

What happened after that? I knew most of the TGB had been lost. They were good distractions, but they were pretty worthless when fighting toe-to-toe with an awakened like Rasputin. Zofia hadn't lasted more than a second. Truthfully, she was scrawny, so it made sense that he took her out in one hit. I felt a twinge of regret when I remembered Gulliver and his lifeless eyes. Then, Rasputin produced those horrific heads in the sack. Kalli's scream still haunted me when she discovered her parents' demise through our bond. Her grief had been paralyzing.

It came crashing back in on me. Kalli was dead. She'd blown herself up in an attempt to kill Rasputin. Why hadn't I just sucked it up and put him in the ring? For that matter, why didn't I kill him the first time I grabbed him? Then, we wouldn't have lost Gulliver. I wouldn't have lost Kalli…

She was gone.

Even though I knew it was a dream, I didn't know how to wake myself up. Fog flooded my brain, and it felt like I'd just awakened again and didn't understand the world at all.

Was the entire adventure just a dream?

———

Eventually, as all dreams do, mine came to an end. I blinked away the sleep from my eyes as a fancy textured ceiling came into focus. What looked like Egyptian hieroglyphics covered the ceiling.

I rolled over to get out of bed and yelped when I saw two women standing quietly by the door. One of them came over and waited patiently while I calmed down. "Good morning, my Lord. Is there anything I can get for you?"

A quick inventory check told me I was hungry, and I had to go to the bathroom. Starting with the more urgent need, I muttered. "Toilet."

The woman gave me a knowing smile and pointed to a door at the end of the room. "Just this way, my Lord."

Was I still in the empire? Why was she calling me lord? I was pretty sure I'd never seen the room I was in before, not even in Celestea Castle.

Noticing I wasn't getting up right away, the woman asked, "Do you require assistance, my Lord?"

I shook my head, feeling myself blush at the thought of someone helping me relieve myself. "No, thank you. I can manage."

It was only when I tried to get up that I realized I might not be okay. My legs felt like jelly, and I found myself falling back down to the bed. The woman looked concerned. "Are you certain you wouldn't like just a little help, my Lord? We have a wheelchair prepared just in case…"

"Why can't I walk?" I asked, already starting to massage my legs with mana.

"You've been asleep for two weeks, my Lord," The woman explained, motioning for the other girl to ready the wheelchair.

I waved her off and stood a second time. The mana had done its job, and my legs were back in commission. "I got it! Thanks anyway."

The facilities reminded me of the magic commodes from Shaw Manor back on Earth. While looking incredibly medieval, it was actually more effective than modern plumbing. Not only did it dispose of my waste, but it also cleaned itself when I was done, and the magic erupted from the bowl to clean me. I discovered how it worked when I was forced to dodge a waterspout that rose from the toilet bowl and attempted to give me a wet wipe.

I only realized the women had followed me when I heard one giggle in the background. The other shushed her and said, "I'm sorry, my Lord. This one is still in training."

At a second glance, I realized the girl who giggled was significantly younger than the other one. Perhaps even younger than me. I decided to pull up their menus to at least see what their names were.

Access to the system is being blocked by Parental Controls.

I stared at the words for a few seconds before trying some other commands. Not only could I not inspect people, but I couldn't even inspect myself. Also unavailable was the ability to edit. Strangely, I still felt my mana and was fairly confident I could use it.

Deciding there was no helping it, I looked at the older woman and asked, "Who are you, and where exactly am I?"

The woman smiled and bowed. "My name is Marcelle, and this is Ulli. We have been assigned to serve you. As for where you are, welcome to Origin, my Lord, the planet of beginnings."

"Isn't that the forbidden planet?" I asked, vaguely remembering a lesson about it from The Academy.

Marcelle smiled. "If you're referring to the fact that nobody comes here without permission, then you're absolutely correct, my Lord."

"Why is it called the planet of beginnings?" I asked, slightly curious.

Marcelle continued the lecture, "Origin is the planet where human life began in this universe. Many legends from the other worlds originate here."

The way she said that made me wonder just how many universes there were. Regardless, I had bigger fish to fry. "Who is that guy on the throne?"

Ulli gasped, and even Marcelle seemed taken aback by my question. She leaned in and asked, "That's The Creator. Isn't he your father?"

I shrugged. While I knew that much from my bloodline, I wasn't one hundred percent sure he was the man on the throne. Then again, I'd expected a name and not just a title. "What is his name?"

Marcelle covered her mouth with her hand. "I'm afraid I'm not worthy of saying his name. Only those he chooses are allowed. Well, and you, my Lord. You're the first offspring he's invited to Origin from off planet since I've been alive."

The only way I was going to get some answers was probably going to be from Dad directly, so I said, "Take me to him."

———

"Ah, you're awake," my dad pointed out from the throne. I wondered if he'd moved in the weeks I'd been asleep. "I knew you'd be on your feet in no time."

"Who exactly are you?" I asked, wanting more than just the revelation that we were related. "Why did I end up here when I teleported to Kalli?"

One of the servants behind the throne fed him a grape, which he enjoyed before replying, "You probably know me as Michael. That's what your mother called me for most of our relationship. However, the name I am most known by is Merlin. Your mother chose to name you Melvin as a nod to that name. There was some drama during the Middle Ages, and I got caught up with a certain legend. The truth is, I've gone by many names over the years. The longer you live, the more you grow bored with the mundane. If you like, I'll let you choose my next name. Just make sure it starts with an M since I'd hate to have to rename the entire bloodline."

"Um, I think I'll just call you Dad," I decided. "You didn't answer my second question, though. Where is Kalli? I teleported here to be with her."

"I'm sorry, son," he said soothingly. "Your girlfriend is dead. She sacrificed herself to save you. You teleported here because of your connection to me."

"Is Mom here?" I asked, not believing him for a second. "She was looking for you."

Dad frowned. "I haven't heard from Sam in years. Don't worry. Now that I know she's looking for me, I will be sure to find her and bring her here."

"Why is my magic blocked?" I asked. "And what are parental controls?"

Dad chuckled and nearly choked as his servant fed him another grape. She recoiled as he glared at her. "I couldn't exactly have you deleting things around the tower. Don't worry. You'll have access to your magic when you need it. We just need to go over a few ground rules first before you begin your training."

"Training?" I asked. "I need to get back to Gaia."

"In due time," Dad replied, waving me off. "As I'm sure you're painfully aware from your recent battle with Rasputin, you have a lot of power, but you don't know how to wield it properly. If you're going to be a champion of the people, you are in desperate need of training."

"Are you going to turn me into an animal?" I asked, remembering Merlin's training methods from a book I read one time.

He snickered, obviously having read the same book. "Do I need to do that? Don't try to edit yourself into one. That's how the Dark Ages began. Why don't you take today to get acclimated to the palace? We can begin your training tomorrow."

[2]

I LEFT the throne room after my sudden dismissal. The revelation of who he was swirled through my brain like a maelstrom. My dad was *that* Merlin. The one from the legend. In hindsight, it made perfect sense. That was what M stood for. Of course, there were probably thousands of other notable M names throughout history I could have been related to. When it came to magic, it was even possible the M could have meant I belonged to The House of Mouse. It was a growing empire slowly taking over the Earth, after all. I think they even owned the name Merlin.

Marcelle and Ulli guided me down the vast halls of the palace that I was just starting to take in for the first time. Glowing runes lined the walls like fancy art that moved. That's what I would have taken them for had I not known about the magic making them grow and shrink as though they had a heartbeat.

The carpet that lined the hall was similarly interesting, changing colors as I walked on it, as though it wanted me to go somewhere. Marcelle stopped in front of a large set of double doors. "This is where we eat. You can eat here as well, though you can request food be brought to you anywhere you are. Simply tell anybody you see that you're hungry, and food will be brought for you on the spot. When it comes to any special *needs* you have. Just ask me, and we will take care of you."

The way she said the word needs was very specific, leaving no room for doubt about exactly what she meant. Ulli still hadn't said a word since I met her. Under normal circumstances, I might have tried talking to her to see if I could get her to open up, but the only thing I had on my mind at the moment was Kalli. I needed to find her.

"I'm sorry," I said, feeling bad for making Marcelle's job harder. "I have to find a way to get out of here."

Folding mana over myself, I decided to go to the one place I knew I could. I used the gate spell to send myself home. The trip through the void was quicker than normal. The world between worlds looked different, too. The myriad paths of light I was accustomed to wasn't visible. It felt like I was cut off from the cosmos. My suspicions were confirmed when I landed in the lobby outside of the throne room. I was still on Origin.

Moments later, Marcelle came skidding around the corner dragging Ulli behind her. "Please, don't do that, my Lord. It is my job to know your whereabouts at all times. If you intend to teleport back here, at least give me a heads-up."

"Why is this considered my home point?" I asked, ignoring her request. "I need to go home and check on things. I need to find Kalli."

To Marcelle's credit, at least she looked sorry when she replied. "I'm sorry, my Lord. Nobody gets off this planet. Didn't The Creator tell you that?"

Seeing red again, I turned and stormed back into the throne room. Conversations all around me died as I stomped up to my father. "Dad! Am I…uh…am I…grounded?"

He smirked at my childish outburst and replied, "You're free to go anywhere in the world you want, son. However, I do ask that you show your old man at least a little respect. I am protecting you from yourself."

"What are you talking about?" I growled the question, not quite ready to give the father I'd just met any respect at all.

He sighed, waving off his attendants and climbing to his feet again.

"Perhaps I need to put you down for another nap. I saved you from doing something stupid and getting yourself killed. Look, son, I'm sorry your girlfriend died, and I know how much she meant to you. It filled my heart with joy watching the two of you together. Not many of my children find true love like that. You're more like me than you know. I am saving you from doing something reckless when you can't find her. I want you to stay here with me for a while so you can grieve properly. During this time, we can focus on your training so you won't be as vulnerable when you go back out there."

"Training?" I asked. That was the last thing on my mind. All I could think about was getting Kalli back. I knew she wasn't dead. I could feel it in my core.

When I opened my mouth to speak, Dad knelt in front of me. "Meet me halfway, please. Give it a few months to clear your head. I promise you'll feel better with time."

"I'll make you a deal," I said, grasping at straws. "If I agree, you need to help me, too. I need to figure out where Kalli's soul went, as well as what happened on Gaia. I need to make sure my friends are okay."

"I assure you, the ones who weren't dead before you left are still alive," my dad said. "As for Kalliphae's soul, there are several paths it can take after death. When a person finds themselves in a state of completion when they die, they ascend beyond the mortal plane. There are many rumors as to what lies in the great beyond, but as we've both been there, I won't bother sugarcoating things. That place is typically called Heaven.

"While there is a place for those who weren't exactly the best of people, I wouldn't call that ascending. That falls under the purview of reincarnation. A soul that has been reincarnated is virtually impossible to track. Basic reincarnation involves a spent soul seeking new life to attach itself to and grow into a new being.

"While these souls occasionally get flashes of previous lives, it's unlikely that they carry anything solid from one life to the next. That leaves complicated situations. Occasionally, souls find ways to bypass basic reincarnation. This usually happens when someone with great power is very bored.

"I happen to know the guy who decided it would be a great idea to turn random people into dungeons. While it's amusing to watch for the first thousand years or so, the souls who populate the dungeons eventually descend into madness."

I gaped at the man who went from being quiet and mysterious to a walking wiki. "I didn't need to know all that. Just tell me where Kalli's soul went so I can go to her."

He sighed, shaking his head sadly. "I don't think you understand, son. She's gone. In the best case, she's moved on. If she's up there, the worst thing you can do is try to pry her out. Your best bet is to live your life and hope to join her when you die. If she reincarnated, the odds of finding her are almost infinitesimal. Don't torture yourself by looking for her. You're still young. Give yourself time to grieve, and then move on."

"I need to speak with her," I continued, refusing to give up. "Take me to Elysiana so I can go check the afterlife. If she's up there, I need to—"

He cut me off. "She isn't up there."

"So, you do know where she is!" I barked, probably a little more cruelly than I intended. "Tell me where she is so I can go to her."

Dad shook his head. "I'm sorry, son. I don't know where she is. For all we know, she's a baby right now and won't even recognize you. How cruel would that be to go to every family in the cosmos and demand to see their infant? Besides, we can't even be certain she's human."

"She might be an animal baby?" I groaned as I asked the question, feeling like my head was going to explode.

He chuckled and shook his head again. "No, that's unlikely. Do you remember when I mentioned a place other than Heaven for those who haven't exactly led a good life? Well, the sea of fire and brimstone isn't the only destination for such folks. Some come back as animals, or worse, monsters."

"Kalli's a monster?" I asked, feeling like I was going to be sick.

He sat on the throne again. "Relax, Melvin. Kalliphae was a good kid. There is every indication she's come back as a human. Hopefully in a better life than the last one. I am sure she will always remember the love you showed her during your short time together. Your bond is proof of that."

"That's right!" I yelled, jumping to my feet. "We're bound together! Surely, the bond will lead me to her, right?"

He shook his head again. Something told me my dad would have been an excellent god of bad news. "Sorry, kiddo. You made that bond expire upon death. If it persisted, you might have died right along with her. Don't worry. The important thing is that you're alive."

"I'll never give up on Kalli!" I screamed, turning and running from the throne room.

It wasn't lost on me that I was behaving like a child. The problem was, I didn't know what to do without Kalli. She had been my world. I wanted to scream and cry all at once. The last thing I wanted was to be around other people. For that reason, I ignored Marcelle and Ulli as I sprinted past them.

———

The palace was an incredible place. If not for my grief, I would have found exploring it a great deal of fun. Every turn I made led to interesting rooms. There were guards stationed everywhere, but nothing was off-limits. Guards in bright red uniforms opened doors as I approached and bowed reverently to me as I passed. They didn't speak or make eye contact while they did their duty.

Marcelle caught up after a while but kept her distance when I told her to go away. She sent Ulli off somewhere but refused to let me out of her sight. At that point, I just didn't care anymore, so I pretended she didn't exist.

After a bit of exploring, I discovered an outdoor garden through a set of glass doors. It was only then that I discovered Origin for the first time. The blue sky and solitary moon in the sky strongly reminded me of Earth. The second thing that stuck out was that I was nowhere near the ground.

The outdoor garden hung from the side of a tall tower, and I was so high up that I was looking down on the clouds. Colorful patterns stretched out on the ground in patches below the clouds in what I could only assume were blocks of houses and other buildings. Looking up, I realized the throne room in the palace was somewhat close to the top floor. Only about five or six levels existed above me.

Finding a nice patch of grass, I did my best to make myself comfortable. I needed to think. Dad wasn't going to be any help at all. The first thing I needed to do was find a way through the magic that was keeping me on Origin. From there I could go back to Dabia and retrace my steps. Surely, there would be a clue there or something to help me figure out where Kalli had gone. Then I could find her and… and… Well, that was a problem.

If Kalli was a baby, what would I do, then? Move in next door and be that creepy guy that waited for her to grow up? Would I have to let her go? Even if I couldn't be her lover, I'd still want to make sure she was happy. Would she be awakened? Should I awaken her again?

I sighed, sitting up. There was no way I'd ever be able to sleep. I cringed at the thought of having to go ask dad to put me to sleep every night.

There was only one solution. I wouldn't rest until I found her. Having a plan in place made things easier. I walked back to the tower where Marcelle stood waiting by the door. She started to back away when I approached, but I stopped her. "Wait. I think I'm ready for that tour now."

She blinked in surprise. "Um, okay, where would you like to go first?"

"Show me everything," I replied.

[3]

THE TOUR WAS BORING for the most part. Marcelle showed me all around the floor that contained my bedroom as well as the throne room. There were a lot of public areas, all of which were populated by beautiful women.

"Who are these people?" I asked as we passed the third room. "Are they my sisters? And why don't my menus work?"

It would have been an easy task to identify them if I could pull up their traits and look for the M bloodline. Marcelle steered me through the door to yet another room. "These women aren't related to you. They were chosen to be consorts for your father."

"That reminds me," I muttered. "Why does Dad need so many girl-friends in the first place?"

Marcelle froze, which caused Ulli to crash into her. She cleared her throat and started walking again, not bothering to look back. "We don't talk about that. Let me show you the bathhouse. While there are usually no men up this high outside of your father, you have unre-stricted access to all facilities on this floor."

Steam leaked into the hall as we approached the sprawling bathhouse. My eyes bugged out of my head when I ducked through the curtain that served as a door. Inside the crowded bath were dozens of women all in various states of undress. Some looked up at me before going about their business, apparently oblivious to the fact that I had entered the room.

I beat a hasty retreat, my head spinning. Ulli giggled, and Marcelle had to shush her before moving on to the next location. "I would have thought you'd be more excited about the bath. Perhaps you aren't *his* son after all."

I had a feeling I knew what she meant. Dad was a player. The concubine suites, as I'd taken to calling them, consisted of four major parts. The main section contained the throne room where he sat on his throne surrounded by what I guessed were his favorite women. Then, there were the lounges for the rest of the women.

The third looked like a large restaurant, big enough to seat hundreds. It was the first time I saw another man since I arrived. He stood behind an army of comparatively plain women in white outfits and aprons barking orders like he was Gordon Ramsey. Everyone hustled to prepare meals with systematic haste.

Marcelle weaved a path through the room to a grand table raised on a dais. "This table is always reserved for you. All you need to do is take a seat, and the head chef, Achemes, will make you anything you desire."

"Even Earth food?" I asked as my stomach rumbled noisily. If I wasn't going to be able to edit up some food, I was likely going to have to learn the system if I wanted to eat.

Marcelle nodded, holding out a chair and inviting me to sit. "He can make food from every known world in every known dimension. Some of it isn't suited for humans, though, so I'd advise caution when looking at the menu."

Achemes, who had been watching me as I made my way through the room, waded over the moment my butt hit the seat. Both Marcelle and Ulli stood quietly behind me. When Ulli's stomach rumbled, I laughed. "If you're that hungry, take a seat. Eat with me."

She hesitated, but Marcelle answered for her, "Go on, you can sit. The young lord invited you."

"You, too," I said, motioning to one of the empty chairs. The table itself was a full-sized banquet table with enough seating for twenty.

"If you insist," she replied, her tone sounding much more pleased than her words.

Achemes ignored them when he arrived. "Welcome, my Lord. It is an honor to serve you this evening. Tell me, what is your pleasure?"

I looked at Marcelle and Ulli, hoping one of them had conjured up a menu from somewhere. They both hesitated. Not getting any help from either of them, I said, "Ladies first. I'll order after."

Marcelle smirked at me and said, "I'll take an Ulvian Special."

Ulli fidgeted and whispered, "I'd like the taco plate."

That gave me some options. I could take the safe route and order Earth food or live on the edge and try something new. I locked eyes with Marcelle and said, "I'll take an Ulvian Special, too."

Achemes lip curled up in a smile. "Very good, sir. And to drink?"

Again, both girls turned to me. I grinned back and replied, "Give me a type of soda I've never tasted before."

The smile grew wider. "Consider it done."

Marcelle ordered some wine I'd never heard of, but Ulli surprised me by saying, "I'll have what Lord Melvin is having."

We sat in silence for a while after the chef left. Finally, when I could take it no more, I asked, "What exactly is the Ulvian Special?"

Marcelle's mouth fell open. "You mean to say you ordered it not knowing what it was? I hate to tell you this, but it's not exactly for everyone."

"What do you mean?" I asked.

Ulli whispered, "She means it's spicy."

Marcelle decided to make it a teaching moment, "The people of Ulvar have very weak taste buds and can only taste extremely strong flavors. Their favorite taste is heat. Don't worry. Surely, you have ways of handling spicy food. The Creator certainly enjoyed it the one time he dined with me."

"You had dinner with my dad?" I asked, wondering what kind of relationship they shared.

The look of dejection on her face told me it hadn't gone as well as she'd hoped. "Yes. I was invited to brunch with him once on my birthday."

After an awkward few minutes of silence, Ulli leaned over and whispered in Marcelle's ear, "You never told me you ate with The Creator."

Fortunately for me, my hearing was still enhanced enough to make out what she was saying. Marcelle shook her head urgently at Ulli and said, "It doesn't matter. We're with Lord Melvin now. He's our priority."

I wasn't sure how I felt about being someone's second choice. Fortunately, I didn't have time to dwell on it when three platters were delivered to our table along with a variety of beverages. While the food scared me, the drinks looked delicious. Achemes went overboard, lining the table with glass bottles filled with various colors of carbonated beverages. Ulli hesitated, but I could see her excitement as she looked over the selection. I motioned to them and said, "You pick first."

"Can I?" she asked, reaching for a purple bottle that I decided must be grape.

"Sure," I replied, hesitating between a red and a blue one. While blue was my favorite color, red reminded me of Kalli.

I picked up the red bottle and nursed it for a minute while the other two started to eat. The red soda had a sweet flavor that kind of reminded me of strawberry, but there was something bitter in it, too. It helped the fruity beverage not be too sweet.

Marcelle explained, "That's raddiberry soda. From the planet Herschwind. It's quite popular."

Deciding I could hold out no longer, I hoisted the domed top off my platter and was met by a wave of steam. Immediately, I knew I'd made a mistake. My nose burned like I'd just taken a mouthful of wasabi. I slammed the lid down and wiped my eyes, which were already watering from the heat. Ulli let out a giggle and, somewhere on the edge of my consciousness, I heard Marcelle try to silence her while I fought to regain control of my senses.

After several bottles of soda and half a pitcher of water that was hastily brought out, I finally felt normal again. We agreed to give my plate to Marcelle. Ulli switched places with her to sit between us, and shared a taco with me while I had the chef make me a plate of my own.

"What's Earth like?" she asked as I savored the taco. "The food is so good that I imagine it must be wonderful."

"You've never been to Earth?" I asked her. "What planet are you from?"

"I was born here," she explained. "I'm not one of his kids, so I managed to work my way up the tower. Marcy tells me I did pretty good to make it this far even if you claim me."

"Claim you?" I asked. Ulli seemed like she was about to reply when Marcelle elbowed her. She made a show of choking on a taco and didn't answer.

I had a strong feeling Dad was trying to set me up with replacements for Kalli. It was too bad he didn't realize Kalli was irreplaceable, and I had every intention of finding her. Death wasn't going to stand in the way of that.

———

After dinner, we concluded the tour and arrived back at my room. I realized I hadn't seen any other bedrooms. "Where do all of those women sleep?"

Marcelle answered, "That depends. Most of them sleep on the floors below this one. They are good enough to visit this floor during the day but must sleep elsewhere. The floors above this are reserved for The Creator and the lucky few he chooses to claim. Those who ascend are typically only there for less than a year. Nobody knows why, but he usually doesn't settle on a single woman for very long.

"While it's not uncommon for chosen women to be with child, nobody knows what happens to them after that. They usually vanish. The popular rumor is that they move off-world. We know his children lead privileged lives, so it's assumed the mothers do as well. This is the reason so many women aspire to gain his favor. It's rare for his children to ascend. Some say he intends to train you to be his heir. That's just a rumor, though."

I sat on one of the many chairs in my room as I took it all in. Was I being groomed to take over for my old man? Was that why he brought me to Origin? There was one thing that was confusing. "Why did you call him The Creator? Are you saying he creates life like some kind of god?"

"Not exactly," she explained. "He doesn't create life. He created the system."

While I knew my dad had something to do with it, I didn't know he created it. I was overwhelmed and needed time to think. There was so much new info to digest, not to mention I needed to come up with a plan to rescue Kalli.

"I think I'd like to take a bath and go to bed," I said as I rose from my chair. "Can the two of you come back later?"

Marcelle shook her head. "We're assigned to you. I'd be more than happy to wash your back if you'd like to enjoy a bath. As for the two of us, we live with you, so we don't have anywhere else to go."

My shoulders slumped as it dawned on me what my dad had planned for the two of them. "I can bathe myself thank you very much. Just make yourselves comfortable, I guess."

"As you wish, Lord Melvin," she said dutifully, standing by the door.

I stared at the two of them for a moment. "If you're going to live here, you can't just stand guard all the time. Relax, both of you. Consider it an order."

Ulli heaved a sigh of relief and made her way to the nearest couch, where she slumped over. Marcelle sat daintily in a nearby chair. "Very well. We will be here when you return."

[4]

MY PERSONAL BATH rivaled any tub I'd ever bathed in before. About the size of an Olympic swimming pool, it had nooks around the edges with seating for four or five people in the water. In the center of the tub was a fully stocked bar.

It reminded me of the one time my mother, and I had gone on vacation. She'd told me she'd received a coupon for an all-expense paid trip to a resort. While it was only in San Diego, it might as well have been Hawaii for us. We never went anywhere.

I floated around for a while, thinking about how much fun it would be to share a bath with Kalli again. Having a moment to myself for the first time since the incident, I closed my eyes and tried to remember what exactly happened. I couldn't forget the look in her eyes as she clung to Rasputin's back.

The explosion was strange. It wasn't something I knew she was capable of. Then, I felt it. Kalli was just as confused as I was when it happened. She hadn't meant to do it. And she was gone. There was no pain or agony or any of the thousands of other things I associated with death. She was just gone.

Kalli, can you hear me?

I called out to her again even though I somehow knew she couldn't answer. It still made me feel good to have hope. Were the parental controls keeping me from her? I closed my eyes and searched for traces of her within myself. The chains of my vow were oddly soothing as they dug almost painfully into my core. Their existence meant she had to exist somewhere. She just had to.

I pushed mana along the connection, flooding it with emotion in hopes she would feel me and reciprocate. While the tether between us was strong, it cut off suddenly, disappearing into nothingness.

I didn't understand. How could the vow and the connection still exist if there was nothing on the other end? Was it some kind of phantom illusion? An echo of what once was? Why was I able to feel it at all if the system was blocked?

Wait a second...the system?

I thought out loud in my head. It was a bad habit. Was my core perhaps not part of the system? Or was the way I felt mana outside of it? What I wouldn't give for someone to explain things to me. One of the big three from the ring would have been ideal teachers. Malric, Longinus, and Nirvana all claimed to exist before the system and would know what to do.

Could I get off the planet without the system? Teleportation seemed to be locked to the throne room. Deciding to test my abilities outside of the system, I focused on a spot at the other end of the pool and wrapped mana around myself.

SPLASH.

I arrived in the lobby outside of the throne room along with what felt like half the water from the pool. On top of that, I was buck-naked. Since there wasn't really anything to do about it, I covered myself and began the walk of shame back to my room. Fortunately, it wasn't far, and only a few women saw me, giggling and whispering to each other as I slunk past.

"Oh, my!" Marcelle gasped when I walked into the room. "What happened to you?"

Not bothering with an answer, I marched back to the bath. Only once I was back in the relative safety of the warm water did I feel comfortable.

So, teleporting is off the table? What about other things I can do with my mana?

There was no response from Kalli, not that I expected it. The first thing I tried was infusing the bath water with mana. Adding elements to my mana was still working. Bubbles rose from the water when I gave it a fresh infusion of air. Next, I tried spells by chanting Kalli's favorite.

"Pvruzth."

Nothing happened.

"Pvruzth."

"Pvruzth."

Still, nothing happened. The magic wasn't responding to words, so I tried doing it manually. I went through the motions of altering my element to fire and letting it form in a wave over my hand. Then, I pushed it around, letting the fire flow through the air as though it were seeking a target.

That works. I guess words of magic are part of the system. Why doesn't teleportation work? I definitely don't have a skill for that, and I clearly didn't use a spell.

I stewed over the dilemma for a while before eventually lying on my back and enjoying the bath. The water was the perfect temperature. It felt as though it was alive and knew just how hot I liked it. Either that or it was slowly getting hotter in an attempt to boil me alive.

Another thing I noticed was the intoxicating flavor the water had. Whoever enchanted my bath has incidentally flavored the water as well. It was kind of like magic chlorine, only it tasted good and probably wouldn't poison me. It also removed impurities from the water, which I made sure to test thoroughly.

It was only when I started to prune up that I climbed out of the tub and got dressed. Rather than putting my old clothes on, which smelled of Rasputin and death, I chose to put on one of the robes that lined the walls of the bath chamber on conveniently placed hooks.

Both Marcelle and Ulli looked up when I emerged. Ulli blushed and looked away, and Marcelle smiled. "I see you decided to exit the normal way this time. Are you all refreshed? Is there anything I can get for you?"

I shook my head. "No, thank you. I'm fine. So, what happens now? You said you live here with me, but I only see one bed. Where are the two of you supposed to sleep?"

Ulli continued to look away while Marcelle answered, "Where do you think your father expects us to sleep? Don't worry, though. All these couches are comfortable enough. Just tell us how you'd like to arrange your room, and I'll see to it that it's done."

"I guess it wouldn't help if I asked you to find a room elsewhere, would it?" I asked, looking around the spacious chamber for a way to make them more comfortable. "Would it be okay to have someone bring in beds for the two of you?"

"We could do that," Marcelle replied. "I don't have any problem sharing your bed if you wish. Perhaps just a bed for Ulli?"

I shook my head. "I'm sorry, but there's only one person I want to share a bed with, and she's not here."

The thought of Kalli was threatening to overwhelm me again, so I cleared my throat to change the subject. "So, about those beds? If we can't get you some right away, you two can take my bed, and I'll figure something out."

It was then that I remembered my trusty fanny pack. It was still clinging to my waist. It was so unobtrusive, I often forgot it was there. After digging through it for a while, I found what I was looking for.

Both girls stared at me as I pulled a hammock out of a bag that was far too small to contain it. It didn't take me long to find a place to hang it. After making myself comfortable, I looked through the bag again for a second item.

There it is. The M-Phone!

I powered the device on and fed it some mana to make sure it was fully charged.

Connection lost. Please, go to a planet or dimension with a better signal and try again.

I groaned at the phone. What was the point of magic phones if there was almost no service? Two of the three planets I'd visited had none whatsoever. Deciding to take what I could get, I pulled up the magi-wiki app and looked up Origin. The first thing that popped up was an advertisement.

As you know, we strive to keep this wiki free of charge. However, mana costs money, and money is something we desperately need. lease, consider making a donation to keep this app free.

I declined and clicked **NEXT**.

Origin - Little is known about the forbidden planet. Placed on the restricted list of hostile planets in 2014, the planet is best known for the disappearance of the Credence Expedition in late 2013. Since then, the governing bodies of 314 guilded worlds have issued decrees banning further exploration of the mysterious planet.

I glanced over at Marcelle and Ulli to see what they had gotten up to. While Marcelle hadn't moved from the chair she was sitting on, Ulli made herself right at home on the bed and was snoring loudly. Deciding I probably wouldn't wake her by talking, I asked, "Marcelle, have you ever heard of someone called Credence?"

"Credence?" she asked in reply. "What are you talking about?"

I held up the phone to show her. "The wiki about this planet says they disappeared here almost ten years ago. That's why the planet is off limits."

She got up and walked over, taking the phone out of my hands. "Hm, this says almost nothing about Origin. If anybody tried to get in, I'm fairly certain The Creator would deal with them. It's not something we would ever hear about."

I rolled over on my back, placing my hands behind my head. "I want to know more about this place. Specifically, how to get out of here."

"Have you tried asking The Creator?" she asked. "He is the only one who can grant that request. I don't see why you'd want to leave, though. People on this planet would give everything to have what you have. They would be willing to share your bed just to get a taste of what is essentially your birthright."

That didn't make sense to me. "Why me? How is it my birthright? Don't I have thousands of brothers and sisters? What about them?"

"Nobody knows," she admitted with a shrug. "The Creator only admits a few of his children. Nobody knows why."

"Then, why am I the only one here?" I asked, knowing she was just in the dark as I was.

She hesitated, handing the phone back to me. "There have been others in the past. I believe this room has been vacant for half a century before you arrived."

That just added to the list of questions I had for my dad. Sitting up in the hammock, I grinned at Marcelle. "No time like the present. Let's go see the old man."

Marcelle gasped. "Are you referring to The Creator as a common old man? That's blasphemy."

I laughed. "But he's still my dad."

———

My third entrance of the day into the throne room drew a series of gasps from the women in the alcoves. I'd teleported directly from my room, leaving Marcelle behind. I was still wearing just a bathrobe, which seemed strangely fitting for the atmosphere my father kept in his audience chamber.

He watched me approach with a bored expression as one of his servants attempted to feed him cheese on a cracker. I waited patiently until his mouth was full to ask, "Can I get a grape?"

The servant behind him froze, and I watched my dad become off balance for the first time as he struggled to swallow. "Erm, don't you have your own servant for that? Why don't you go back to your room and ask one of them."

I laughed, pleased that my words were having an effect on him. It was a tactic I occasionally employed on my mother when I wanted her to answer questions about something she was hiding. "Am I grounded, Dad?"

"Dad?" he asked, clearly uncomfortable with the informality. "You're free to go anywhere you like, son. Have any of the servants been rude to you?"

"Only you," I replied with a smirk. His face darkened at my remark. "I want to go to Earth real quick. Maybe bring Mom back so she can see all your concubines."

"Do you know where your mother is?" he asked, ignoring my taunt.

I shook my head. "I'm pretty sure she is looking for you. Just let me go back, and I'll—"

"Don't worry about that," he replied, brushing me off. "I already have people out looking for her. She is precious to me, so I assure you no harm will come to her."

"What about my magic?" I asked. "Why am I cut off from the system?"

"That," he replied with a big smile forming on his face. "Is for your benefit. Your training begins tomorrow."

[5]

THERE WASN'T much to do after being dismissed. I was exhausted but couldn't sleep. Nobody seemed to be doing anything except lounging and socializing in the many lounges I had access to. To top matters off, I wasn't entirely convinced Dad ever left his throne considering he was always there every time I visited.

Without anything productive to do, I made my way back to my room to be greeted by a fuming Marcelle and a snoring Ulli. At first, I thought Marcelle was going to punch me in the nose when she stomped up, but she stopped short just a few inches from my face and glared. I was pleasantly surprised by the sweet smell of strawberries on her breath, but it reminded me of Kalli, and I took a step back.

Marcelle noticed my mood and stopped scowling. She gave an exasperated sigh and said, "Can you please stop doing that? It makes me look incompetent when you leave me behind all the time. I get that you might not want me, but don't make me undesirable to anyone else in the process. I can't go back to the bottom. I've come too far."

"What are you talking about?" I grumbled as I flopped on one of the couches. "You're not the one stuck here. What's so good about this place, anyway?"

"Where do I start?" she asked. "No crime? No empty bellies. Whatever we need is essentially provided. With the number of consorts your father takes, we hardly have to do any work. Sure, I got assigned to you, but I don't mind. The perks will be the same if you accept me."

"Accept you?" I asked.

"You know…" She trailed off.

"Ugh," I groaned, refusing to think of anyone but Kalli. "Can I just reject you now so you can get back in line for my dad?"

Marcelle shook her head. "Unfortunately, it's not that easy. Sure, once you complete your training, you will be free to do as you wish. For now, and until you officially choose your first consort, you're stuck with us."

"I'm tired," I lied. "I want to get some sleep."

"Understood," she droned, making herself comfortable on a couch opposite me. "Please, let me know if you decide to go out again."

———

I lost track of time staring at the ceiling before sleep finally claimed me. The world of dreams that I used to share with Kalli was as desolate as ever. No blissful dream took over to guide me through the night. I found myself sitting in the room Kalli and I had crafted for ourselves to hang out. It was spooky how quiet my head became in Kalli's absence.

Sulking over it didn't do any good, so I sat and closed my eyes to meditate. Infusing mana with emotion was second nature by that point. The only difference was the essence of my mana changed. No longer did I feel any sense of curiosity. The rage I'd felt when I overwhelmed Rasputin was gone as well. The only thing left in my core with a sense of sorrow that threatened to consume me.

I took this raw emotion and infused it into my mana, letting it permeate my body until I shivered uncontrollably. I focused on the feeling and what I was going to do to make it go away.

I made another vow and added a thread to my core. "I will find you."

Nothing happened. I waited a few seconds and tried again. Again, there was no change to the vow or my mana. Was it because I was locked out of the system? Could I no longer use powerful magic?

I knew I could use elemental magic. I'd managed flames already. I had to figure out what else I could do. Remastering teleportation was going to be key if I wanted to find a way off Origin.

"Wake up!" Marcelle's voice echoed through the dream.

I tried to focus on what I needed to do. The last thing I needed was to be distracted by an annoying would-be suitor.

"Wake up! Wake up! Wake up!" Ulli's slightly more cheerful voice chanted. The dream world shook.

———

I opened my eyes to find Ulli bouncing around me and shaking me vigorously. When she saw I was awake, she squealed, "He's up! He's up! He's up!"

Behind her, Marcelle grumbled. "Great. Now, get ready. Your father wants you in the arena by first light."

"First light?" I moaned, trying to roll over with little success. Ulli wouldn't let go. "I just went to sleep. Bug me in the morning."

"It is morning," Ulli chirped. "You slept for ten hours."

My eyes shot open. Ten hours? I'd just entered the dream world minutes ago, hadn't I? Nights seemed normal length when I spent my dreams with Kalli. Why was solo dreaming different? The only thing I could think of was focusing on my emotions.

Groaning, I pulled myself up to a seated position and rubbed the sleep from my eyes. "I need a few minutes."

"Well, you don't have them," Marcelle said, crossing her arms. "The Creator summoned you personally. You do not want to make him wait."

"Do I have time for a bath?" I grumbled, staggering to my feet.

"You'd better take a bath," Marcelle ordered, pushing me toward the bathroom. "You can't meet The Creator at anything less than your best. Just hurry."

I grumbled something about being forced to bathe. Then again, I

29

did ask to take one, so I wasted no time stripping off my robe and jumping in. After a quick scrub, I made my way back to my room to find Marcelle and Ulli standing next to a plate of food and a change of clothes.

The clothes looked like a karate Gi and were very brightly colored. I frowned at the yellow-and-white outfit and asked, "What's wrong with my clothes?"

Marcelle sniffed at me as if she didn't trust me to wash properly. "You arrived with a single outfit, and it was tattered and filthy. I sent it off to be repaired. In the meantime, wear this training outfit. It will make The Creator happy."

I stared at the two girls until Marcelle realized my problem and forced Ulli to turn around with her. After which, I quickly shucked the robe I'd been wearing and pulled on the gaudy outfit. Surprisingly, it fit perfectly, as though it was made for me. Then again, it probably was. I cleared my throat, which informed Marcelle and Ulli that it was safe to turn around.

"We ordered you a selection of food for breakfast," Marcelle explained, holding up a tray of food. "Help yourself."

I looked down at the plate. It was filled with sausage, bacon, and a variety of other meats I didn't recognize along with eggs, bagels, and donuts. It was way too much for just one person. I looked up to see Ulli licking her lips as she watched in silence.

"Would you two like to join me?" I asked, offering Ulli a donut.

She reached out but didn't take it, looking to Marcelle for permission. She nodded, and Ulli smiled, helping herself to a donut and a slice of bacon. Marcelle made herself a plate as well, and we quickly ate breakfast.

———

"Why do you have to wait for me to eat?" I asked while following Marcelle and Ulli down the hall.

"You're our master," Ulli explained. "We only eat when you say we can eat."

Marcelle cleared her throat, and Ulli stiffened. "That's not exactly how it works. We are allowed to eat, but we must do so discreetly unless invited to join you. The same goes for sleeping and relieving ourselves."

"And you said this was a good life?" I asked, wondering how anyone could live like that, let alone want to.

Marcelle gave me a knowing smile. "It sounds bad on the surface, but life up here is typically pleasant. We live happy lives if we devote ourselves to service."

"Only women?" I asked.

Marcelle rubbed her chin for a moment. "At the moment, you're the only lord up here aside from The Creator. That's also why it's a good deal for us. Most of us spend our entire lives waiting to be chosen. An unattached lady enjoys a life of privilege. It is a thousand times better than—"

"Than what?" I asked when she trailed off.

"Life outside of the tower," she replied reluctantly. "Life for the unrecognized is little more than existence. Nothing is provided in the streets. Nothing at all."

I wondered why Dad would let something like that happen if he truly controlled the system. Even as a manipulator, I was able to make food out of pebbles. Couldn't Dad do better than that? And why was he infatuated with women?

Before I had a chance to ask any more questions, we arrived at an open-air courtyard with a circle painted on the ground. Merlin stood waiting for me with an angry look on his face. He spoke in a low voice, "Leave us."

I looked back just in time to see Marcelle and Ulli slink around a corner and out of sight. When I didn't come any closer, he spoke again, "You nearly died because you're weak. That's not to say you don't have potential. It just means you've never trained properly. We are going to remedy that. Come, step inside the circle."

"What is this?" I asked, hesitating. "If you want to see how strong I am, take off the parental block, and I'll show you what I can do."

"That's the problem," he explained. "You shouldn't rely on the system. We are above that. Get over here, now."

My legs complied before my mind did. Did he just use a mind control skill on me? Since there wasn't much I could do about it, I decided to go with the flow. However, that didn't mean I couldn't ask questions. "Why did you bring me here? It can't be a coincidence that I ended up here when I tried to teleport to Kalli."

Dad shrugged. "Do I need a reason? Now, get down on the ground and give me fifty sit-ups."

I frowned, not understanding why he was treating this like a gym class. "Yeah, you do need a reason. I can't just pause my life because you want to be my dad all of a sudden."

"Now," he commanded, and I found myself on my butt, straining to do sit-ups. Exercising was never my strong point. After watching me struggle for a while, he continued the lecture, "You are continually getting yourself in trouble out there. I've been watching ever since you appeared that day. You have a strong grasp of your powers, yet you continue to squander them."

"I, ugh, use, oof, my, ah, powers, argh, just, oof, fine!" I managed to say as I completed my third sit-up.

Dad groaned as he watched me struggle. "What is wrong with you, boy? Use your mana. Stop acting like a peasant."

Mana? Why did it never occur to me to use mana for mundane daily activities before? A simple application of mana to my abdomen, and I was a machine. "Four, five, six, seven, eight, nine, ten … forty-nine, fifty."

Dad gave me a nod of approval before saying, "Okay, now push-ups. Same thing. Give me fifty."

Having gotten my wind back, I asked more questions as I flipped over and did as he asked. "If you've been watching me all this time, why didn't you help when I was in trouble? For that matter, why are adults so scared to help when people try to take over the world?"

"You aren't just any people," he replied. "You are my children. Those in power know that to invoke the wrath of my children is to suffer a painful death."

"Lots of people tried to kill me," I complained. "I don't remember you going postal on any of them."

Dad laughed. "You were beneath my notice until recently. Then, you picked a fight with your brother."

"He picked the fight," I corrected. "You just sat back and watched while he killed Kalli."

He watched me finish with his arms crossed. "He didn't kill her, she killed herself trying to save you. It was quite noble. Now, do squats."

"It wasn't noble!" I roared, already standing to do squats. "And you could have stopped it. She didn't have to die."

"Everything happens for a reason," he said flippantly. "Look on the bright side. Perhaps she will reincarnate, and you will find her in a couple hundred years. Or perhaps she's moved on, and you can be reunited with her when you cross over. Don't look at death as a bad thing. Be happy for those who've made the transition."

Even with mana to assist me, I still felt the burn in my muscles. Sending light-element mana to soothe them helped a little, but it was obvious that, physically, I was out of shape.

Then, there was the fact that I didn't have an answer for my dad. I'd never given much thought to life after death except that I'd met two death gods and helped two people cross over. Was Kalli there? If she was, why couldn't I visit her?

I looked up at my dad and asked, "Why can't I leave Origin?"

"You will," he replied. "In time. Now, I want you to repeat what you did ten times, and then run."

"How far?" I asked.

"Until I say you can stop," he replied before teleporting away with a *pop* and a puff of smoke.

[6]

I WAS EXHAUSTED when Merlin finally returned. He looked me up and down, shaking his head at the sweaty mess I'd become. "You look like you haven't exercised a day in your life. Do you understand what it takes to be strong?"

While it was true I didn't get into physical exercise as much as the next guy, I was far from weak. I was the manipulator who slayed vampires, dragons, and gods. Technically, the dragon was the god, but I also dealt with other mages who were significantly higher level than I was. The problem was finding the words to express that.

After I failed to reply, he continued, "The body is the foundation of any good mage. Forsaking it as you have will make you weak in the end no matter how much you refine your magic."

"I'm not weak," I mumbled. "I train every—"

He cut me off, standing behind me and waving his hand in the air. My status window appeared midair like a holographic PowerPoint presentation.

Name: Melvin Murphy
Class: ??? (Locked)
Level: 45

Hitpoints: 4,500
Mana: 135,000
Stamina: 4,500
Strength: 25
Dexterity: 25
Agility: 25
Constitution: 50
Intelligence: 85
Wisdom: 30
Charisma: 10
Luck: 20

He tapped his foot impatiently and asked, "Do you see a problem with this?"

"Yeah," I replied, turning to scowl at him. "You locked my class to something unknown."

"No, don't play dumb!" He barked, glaring back. "Your base stats are pathetic. If you had been training your mind and body since awakening, all your core stats would be closer to one hundred right now. This means training keeping up with basic exercises every day. It also means thinking before you act.

"You're a bright kid, as your intellect will attest, but you have no common sense, which is reflected in your wisdom score. That means you think you're so smart you don't pay attention to the details. Your body is still that of a child. You've only survived combat as long as you have because of the protection my blood provides for you. The one thing I give you credit for is that your mana capacity is exceptional."

"How do I even train that?" I asked incredulously. "You can't train common sense, can you?"

"Think about it, my boy," Dad said, tapping his skull so loud it made a *thunk*. "A little reflection goes a long way. If you think before you act, your wisdom will go up. Physical stats go up with training and exercise. You can use your mana to compensate for that which you lack, but always remember to put your body through its paces."

"What about luck?" I asked. "How do I train my luck?"

He rubbed the stubble on his chin thoughtfully. "Have you ever heard the saying, you make your own luck? Luck is a combination of a bunch of things. Some of it is outside of your control, but the rest is just a combination of who you are. Train everything else, and your luck will rise naturally."

While I didn't understand the explanation, I nodded anyway. "Did you just bring me here so you could be my personal fitness advisor?"

Merlin shook his head. "No. I brought you here to be my apprentice. I am training you to be my successor. I won't always be around."

"So, you're Willy Wonka, then," I suggested with a snigger.

He groaned, closing the status window with a clap of his hands. "Okay, that's enough question-and-answer time. You will continue these exercises every morning until I decide you're ready for the next step. Trust me, I'll know if you slack off."

Before I could complain, he vanished in a puff of smoke. My chuckle at the thought of him appearing where I always did when I teleported vanished when my muscles screamed at me for trying to stand up.

Marcelle and Ulli both came running when I staggered and struggled to stay on my feet. After helping me sit on a bench, Marcelle pulled out a device that looked like a phone and said, "Please, deliver a wheelchair to Private Garden One."

I gaped at her until she put the device away before asking, "Were the two of you spying on me the whole time?"

She shook her head. "It's not spying if we're assigned to watch over you, my Lord."

"I'm fine," I said, groaning and rubbing my sore thighs while infusing even more mana. "I don't think a wheelchair is necessary. I can walk."

"Are you sure?" Ulli asked. "We don't mind pushing you."

I forced myself to stand, biting my lip to push back the pain. "Call them off. I want to explore some more before going back. I don't think I can do that in a wheelchair."

"But we already showed you the entire floor," Ulli said.

Marcelle eyed me suspiciously and asked, "Where are you thinking about exploring?"

"I think I'll start with one of the other floors," I replied, hobbling toward the door before adding, "You don't have to come."

"You're wrong there," Marcelle muttered as the two of them plodded after me. "We do."

"Up or down?" I asked, resigning myself to being followed as we reached an elevator.

"Down!" Marcelle said emphatically. "The upper floors are out of bounds. Those belong to those chosen exclusively by The Creator. We are forbidden from going up there without an express invitation."

While I wanted to ask if an invitation from me would work, I really didn't want to meet more of Dad's mistresses. What I wanted to see was how the rest of the planet lived. Since leaving the tower seemed like a lot of work, I decided to make my way down one floor at a time.

The floors below mine were fairly similar. Marcelle preceded me out of the stairwell and started another tour. "This is the top floor of ranked housing. This floor and the one hundred below it contains rooms of women hoping to gain The Creator's favor. He rarely chooses any below the top twenty, though and only the top five are allowed to loiter on the throne level. You are free to select any woman you wish on the throne level or below. If you see someone you like, just point her out, and I'll make the necessary arrangements."

It would have been a dream come true in another life, but the only person I wanted to choose was currently lost. "Is there anything else on these floors?"

Marcelle blinked. "What do you mean? They are just living quarters. Is there something specific you're looking for?"

I sighed, not wanting to let on that I was looking for an exit. "I don't know. How does someone move up from one floor to the next?"

We walked as Marcelle explained, "Girls are nominated for service in the tower at a young age. The first twenty floors are all children. When they come of age, they progress by showing promise. While you don't have to be awakened to be in the tower, almost all are."

"What about men?" I asked. "Is there a male tower?"

Marcelle laughed. "The Creator isn't interested in men."

"Why does he need so many women?" I asked, wondering about my father's motives.

She stopped walking, a frown forming on her face. "That's the thing. Nobody knows why your father is doing this. You'd think it was obvious, but he doesn't often do that. As a matter of fact, I don't think a single woman currently in the tower has had the honor of sharing his bed. He sits on that throne every day. It's almost like he's waiting for something."

"Or someone," I muttered, thinking of the rumors I'd heard about Ms on both Earth and Gaia. "Why do I have so many brothers and sisters?"

"Well, he has...in the past," Marcelle stammered. "I don't think what he's doing here is just about sex."

I looked at Ulli to see what she thought of the whole thing. She was blushing and acting very interested in the embroidery on the carpet. We walked in silence for a while, Marcelle not even bothering to tell me about the rooms we passed. Not that she needed to. The floor was littered with bedrooms with open doors. Beautiful women, some of whom I recognized from the concubine floor, glanced at me as we walked past. A couple of them got up and closed the door when they saw it was me walking by.

"Don't worry about them," Marcelle explained. "They are just worried your father won't want them if they catch your eye."

"You can tell them all they don't have to worry about that," I said, probably a little too loudly. "I don't want any of these women."

Ulli touched me for the first time by clamping a hand over my mouth, whispering anxiously. "Are you trying to make everyone mad?"

She stared at me for a moment before realizing I couldn't answer with her hands over my mouth. She removed them and said, "Sorry."

"It's okay," I replied. "I just can't love anyone but Kalli. I'm going to find her and—"

My eyes watered, and I stopped walking. There was a part of me that wanted to find a hole in the wall and hide, but the other part told me I needed to keep moving so it wouldn't catch up to me. "Ahem, what's below the hundred floors?"

"The basement," Marcelle replied, trying her best to ignore my sudden burst of emotions. "There are several floors under the tower, but they are mainly for workers. There's nothing of interest down there."

"What about outside of the tower?" I asked. "Can we go outside?"

The two exchanged worried glances. Ulli answered in a little over a whisper, "You don't want to go out there. It's not safe."

"What do you mean?" I asked.

"Never mind," Marcelle replied in a stern voice. "We aren't allowed out there without The Creator's permission."

I grinned at her, feeling a little more like myself. "That just makes me want to go even more. Didn't you hear my old man? He says I lack common sense. I suppose I'm just living up to his expectations."

Since both of the girls refused to tell me where the elevator was, we took the stairs. I was still sore from the morning workout regimen, but my mana was more than up to the task of keeping my muscles functioning for the descent. Marcelle and Ulli, on the other hand, were both drenched in sweat by the time we made it to the ground floor.

Marcelle stood in front of me, holding both arms out to bar my path. "I can't let you do this. The Creator forbids it."

"Doesn't he see everything?" I asked. "If he wants to stop me, he can come down here himself. He doesn't need you to tell me what I can and can't do."

"Yes, he does," she barked. "He assigned me specifically to make sure nothing untoward happens to you."

"And how did he expect you to stop me?" I asked, raising an eyebrow.

She fidgeted, her face turning red. "Well, he, um, he told me to distract you."

"How?" I asked, only realizing what my dad meant when she looked away and turned a deeper shade of red. "No! I refuse. If I didn't do that with Kalli, there's no way I'm doing it with you."

I raced around her and made my way to the doors of the tower that reminded me of the automatic glass doors of a grocery store. A blast of air slammed into me as I made my way outside in Origin for the first time. The deserted entrance didn't seem like it saw that much traffic.

Once I was outside, the reality of what the planet was like hit me all at once. A stench assaulted my nostrils like that of rotting garbage. While the streets immediately around the tower were relatively free of clutter, it was surrounded by old, dilapidated warehouses.

"Now do you see why we fight to live in the tower?" Marcelle asked from the doorway.

[7]

"It can't all be like this," I observed more to myself than anyone else.

Marcelle and Ulli both followed, though I could tell they were nervous. Marcelle looked down the alleys between buildings as we passed. "It isn't all like this. You arrange transport from your father before you travel? It isn't safe to explore on foot."

"What do you mean?" I asked, wondering if my low wisdom score was getting the best of me again. "Is there a lot of crime on Origin?"

"Not exactly," she admitted, still scanning the shadows for some hidden threat. "Still, it's not a good idea to wander around outside of your designated city on foot. If we run into anyone out here, it's not going to be the pleasant sort."

She had a point. The area around the tower looked like a ghost town. Large warehouses and factories lined the empty streets. The tower seemed out of place, rising above the derelict buildings like a shimmering oasis in a desert.

"Why is all of this around my dad's tower?" I asked, wondering if Merlin knew the neighborhood was bringing down the property value.

"He chose this area because it's abandoned," Marcelle explained. "The Creator made this tower to house the chosen. We are protected so long as we stay within its walls."

"You can go back if you like," I offered, still not sure I wanted to give up. "I'll just teleport back if I run into anything dangerous."

"Unfortunately, we cannot do that," Marcelle sighed. "If The Creator found out we abandoned you, the outcome would be worse than death. If you stay, we stay."

That wasn't fair. Not only was I trapped on Origin by my dad, but now I was responsible for the safety and wellbeing of my two attendants, further confining me to the tower. Deciding to compromise, I asked, "Fine. Please, arrange transportation to one of the cities?"

"I'd have to ask permission," Marcelle replied, looking at me with hope in her eyes for the first time. "We can probably visit my hometown. That should be allowed."

"Or mine," Ulli squealed, speaking for the first time since we left the tower.

Since both girls were scared, I decided to call it a day. "Come here. I'm going to take us back to the tower."

I wasn't sure either of them teleported before. Once they were close enough, I said, "I'd hold your breath if I were you."

Then, I wrapped my mana around the three of us and teleported. For old times' sake, I attempted to take us to Kalli, though I knew the end result would be the foyer outside of the throne room. I wasn't surprised when that's where we ended up. It did come as a shock to both Marcelle and Ulli though as they both fell to their knees, losing the contents of their lunch on the waxed floor.

"I did tell you to hold your breath," I said with a chuckle, regretting the fact that I couldn't just **DELETE** the mess.

Then, I remembered. I did have skills that could be used to clean things. A skill Kalli taught me.

"Pvruzth."

I frowned when nothing happened. Then, I remembered the words were tied to the system and summoned my mana. Ulli yelped when flames erupted from my hands and started incinerating the vomit while she was still in the process of making more of it. My flames caught the spray in midair, making it look like she was breathing fire.

Marcelle reached for my hand. "Careful, Lord Murphy. You don't want to hurt her."

"Don't worry," I replied, shifting the flame over to the mess Marcelle made. "I'm very good at this spell. Kalli taught me."

———

My daily routine for the next several weeks consisted mostly of physical exercise. Merlin didn't bother to show up and turned me away the few times I went to see him in the throne room. Marcelle told me the earliest transportation heading to Ulli's hometown was two weeks away. I didn't question it as I was having a rough time moving after pushing myself to level my base stats. While I couldn't pull up my menu anymore, I felt like I was getting stronger.

When it came to leveling things like luck and wisdom, I didn't have the first clue what to do. I guessed it had something to do with making better life choices, but there was hardly any decision-making in Merlin's tower of women. It usually boiled down to what to eat and how late to stay up.

I searched for Kalli every night while I slept. The severed bond between us provided just enough solace to allow me to sleep. While I was cut off from her, the tether that combined our souls was still there, wrapped around my core. I traced it and applied mana to it in a sort of morse code every night. I wished and hoped that something would come back, but nothing ever did.

Other than that, my dream world became another place to train. Rather than focusing on my body, I trained my core by further refining my mana and imbuing it with the purest emotion I could muster. With everything else lost, the one thing that remained was hope. Hope that I would find Kalli. I fed that into my core constantly, sustaining my life force with the hope that Kalli was still out there somewhere.

While I couldn't see my traits, there were some things I still felt. I retained my vision skills from the God Eye trait as well as the Mantis Style Kung Fu. I still knew how to form a mana blade, so I wasn't exactly defenseless.

One thing that was missing was the artifact armor. I cringed when I realized it was missing. Thinking back to the last time I saw it, I realized to my horror that I fed it to Rasputin. It was probably sitting in his stomach wondering why I abandoned it. Fortunately, I still had the ring. Even though I couldn't see it due to Lavender's enchantment, I felt it resting snugly on my ring finger.

A part of me regretted freeing Maya from the ring. It would have been comforting to have her to talk to during my imprisonment on Origin. She probably would have been just as surprised that I'd met my dad. He was hers, too, after all, right?

Even without her there, I still visited the ring. It was the one place I could hide from Marcelle. I made a private bedroom in Maya's old cell. I'd given her a good amount of furniture and only had to clean the bed five times before I was confident I'd washed all of the love stains out.

It wasn't until the third visit that anyone acknowledged my presence. Mardella, who hadn't spoken in quite some time, called out to me right when I was about to leave, "Melvin, is that you?"

———

Meanwhile, in Japan…

Joe Reid tinkered with his latest creation while he sat on the top of a mountain. The wind-powered drone was just big enough for a single rider. He wanted to make it seat two, but Wendy assured him it wasn't necessary. She was the wind. Joe was still somewhat in shock that his girlfriend was a demi-god.

Her mother—or was it her father—was a wind god called Fujin. Joe couldn't be sure because they seemed to be interchangeable. From what he could tell, one or both of them could be gods. Sometimes, at the same time. The only thing they couldn't be at the same time was human. Wendy explained that to him. "Then, there would be no wind."

Like her parents, Wendy had the ability to become the wind. Unlike her parents, she could do this in her human form, which looked very cool in Joe's eyes. Of course, everything she did was amazing to him. He decided long ago that he would marry this girl. There was no one like Wendy in the world, and Joe wasn't the type of person to let a good thing pass him by.

He just had to wait for the right time. The first step was to get her father's blessing. The problem was that ever since he mustered the courage to ask, Wendy's father hadn't come down from the clouds. There was no way Joe was doing to ask the god dad for his daughter's hand, so he was forced to wait patiently until he decided to become human again. He sat on the mountain passing the time by tinkering with his creation.

"Good afternoon, Joe," a strange voice called from behind him.

Joe spun on the spot, dropping his wrench over the side of the mountain. "Aw, crap. I mean, who are you?"

His wrench appeared magically in the hand of a beautiful blonde woman. She held it out to him. "Hello, Joe. Your friend is in trouble and needs your help. I need you and Wendy to come with me so we can rescue him."

"What?" Joe stammered, taking the wrench and looking over the edge of the cliff where it had just fallen. "What friend? And again, who are you?"

She sighed, sitting next to him. "My name is Lavender, and the friend I'm referring to is Melvin Murphy. He's been taken to a planet called Origin, and I need your help to get there so we can break him out."

Joe wasn't sure he trusted this strange woman who appeared out of nowhere, but if there was one thing Joe knew, it was that he would always be there for his friends. "I want to help Melvin, but I need to discuss this with Wendy first. She should be back soon."

"She is here," Lavender said with a soft smile. Joe felt it, too, the soft breeze that kissed his cheek, signifying his girlfriend's arrival.

Moments later, she materialized beside him and asked, "Who's this?"

Joe introduced them, "This is Lavender. She says she's a friend of Melvin's, and he's in trouble."

"That sounds about right for Melvin," Wendy giggled. "How's Kalli doing?"

"That's complicated," Lavender replied. "Are the two of you ready to go?"

Joe frowned. "The last time Melvin was in trouble, we all nearly died. This isn't like that, is it?"

Lavender shrugged. Joe had a bad feeling.

———

Joe had been expecting a trip to the airport, followed by an eleven-hour flight. What he got was a magic door on a mountain that led to a rather lavish house. They were greeted by a couple of children.

Lavender introduced them, "This is Eddie and Sylvie. Eddie is a warlock in training, and Sylvie here is in training to be my successor. Kids, this is Joe and Wendy, friends of Melvin's."

They seemed nice enough, greeting Joe and Wendy with friendly smiles. Joe idly wondered if Lavender planned to assemble a group of children to help them rescue Melvin. Fortunately, she sent them off before showing Joe and Wendy to their rooms. She gave Wendy a sly smile and asked, "Would you like one room or two?"

Wendy blushed when she answered, "Two, please."

Joe raised an eyebrow at his girlfriend. They'd been sharing a single bedroom for months at that point. Little did he know, Lavender knew everything.

"I'll let the two of you settle in for the night," she explained. "Your rooms connect through that door. Tomorrow, I'll fill you in on my plan."

———

The next morning, following a lavish breakfast, Lavender sat the two of them down. "Melvin has been taken to Origin by his father. If we don't get to him soon, he will be warped when he comes back."

"His father?" Joe asked. "I didn't think he knew his dad."

Lavender sighed. "He does now. His father is arguably the most dangerous man in the universe."

"Who is he?" Wendy asked.

"You know the name." Lavender began. "But his father is not the lovable old guy with the beard anymore. Melvin's father is Merlin, the wizard of legend."

"No way!" Joe exclaimed, letting out a long whistle. "I guess that explains why he's always doing the impossible and why the gods all seem to love him."

"So, how are we going to rescue him?" Wendy asked, looking concerned.

"Don't worry," Lavender said. "I've got a plan."

[8]

"MARDELLA?" I asked, both nervous she might be crazy and a little excited to speak to someone I knew outside of Origin. "Are you sane again?"

"Bah!" she spat in outrage. "I was always sane. I was simply mourning the fact I let myself be defeated by a whelp of a boy."

"You realize you're speaking to the whelp of a boy right now, right?" I asked, wondering if it wouldn't be better to just leave her to rot. "How about you try being nice to me for once?"

"Will you let me out if I do?" she asked in a silky voice.

"Let's not get ahead of ourselves," I replied, walking over to her door. Mardella peeked out through the window slit. "How are you holding up? Is there anything I can do to make you more comfortable?"

I didn't know why, but I felt friendly toward her. Mardella looked around for a moment as though she was scouring the hall for a way out. Finally, she heaved a sigh and said, "I wouldn't say no to some more furniture and perhaps a tasty cake. While I've grown accustomed to not eating or using the toilet, I still crave those things. It's like my mind doesn't know it's been separated from my body and wants to do all the things it did before."

"Ah," I hesitated, not sure how to broach the subject of my skills being locked down by my father. "Unfortunately, I can't do anything about your living situation at the moment."

She disappeared from the slit, dropping out of sight. It only then occurred to me that she was shorter than the window on the door. While she'd always seemed imposing in battle, it probably had a lot to do with the suit of armor she always wore.

She sighed. "Very well. I suppose I can hold out for the time being. So, what brings you in here today without your girlfriend? Did the two of you have a fight?"

Without knowing it, she managed to hit me in yet another sore spot. I felt a strange need to tell someone, and Mardella wasn't exactly in a position to tell anyone my secrets. "Kalli exploded when we fought an M class man from Earth, and I don't know what happened to her after that. When I tried to teleport to her, I ended up on a planet called Origin and met my dad. Everyone there calls him The Creator, and he sort of grounded me."

I wanted to add "from my powers" but I was worried she might try to use that info against me. After realizing I wasn't going to continue speaking, Mardella snickered. "It would appear life hasn't been entirely pleasant for you either. I would have assumed it would be my mother who did you in. She can be nasty like that."

"We met her," I admitted. "We snuck into her castle when we were looking for the cure to that poison you used on me."

"She let you go?" Mardella asked incredulously.

"No," I replied. "She followed us back to Celestea. She didn't do anything, though. She just left."

Mardella cackled from the darkness in her room. "That sounds like her. She never makes a move until she's ready. She told me it was a bad idea to try to marry you off to Alariel. How is she by the way? Is she still with that harlot?"

"Do you mean Kiki?" I asked. "I don't know. The last time I heard from her, she was taking Kiki and one of the ancients to meet your mother."

"I'd love to meet them," Mardella said softly, almost lovingly. "I can't believe they were still alive up there. The stories my mother told me said they were all killed by the Celesteans."

"Maybe someday you will meet them," I said. There was a part of me that wanted to help her, that wanted to forgive and forget. Still, there was no denying the fact that she was dangerous.

"I'll come see you again," I found myself telling her. "Maybe next time I'll be able to fix up your cell."

I cast a glance into the other four cells on the way out. The other prisoners were strangely quiet.

———

"Ayee!" I yelped as I fell over when I discovered Ulli sitting in front of me so close I could feel her breath on my face.

She jumped, startled by my sudden movement. I shook my head to clear it as she scampered for the door. "Marcelle! Come quick. He's back."

I'd just managed to get back to my feet when she reappeared with Marcelle in tow. After taking a few minutes to appraise me, she sighed. "I'm glad you woke up. The Creator would have been quite cross with us if you'd died."

"Yeah," Ulli agreed. "You didn't tell us you can freeze yourself."

"Thanks," I said, realizing I needed a better hiding spot than the bathroom when I used the ring. "I'd rather my dad not find out that I can do that."

"What were you doing anyway?" Ulli asked.

Thinking fast, I lied, "I was meditating. It might have looked like I was frozen, but I was just sitting very still."

"So still your heart stopped?" Marcelle asked, raising an eyebrow.

"It stopped?" I blanched at the news, starting to wonder if going into the ring was bad for my health.

"I may not be awakened, but I know at least that much," she assured me.

"Let's eat now," Ulli cried, tugging my arm.

"She wanted to wait for you," Marcelle explained as I let myself be pulled out the door.

————

I didn't see Merlin again until the day we planned to visit Ulli's hometown. He showed up right when I was about to finish my daily exercise regimen.

"It looks like you're getting the hang of that," he began. "I think you're about ready for the next phase in your training."

I stopped mid-push-up and climbed to my feet. "What is that exactly?"

"You've worked hard these past few weeks," Merlin explained, squeezing my bicep for emphasis. "This type of exercise builds your strength, dexterity, and agility. In other words, it makes you stronger, more flexible, and it gives you a solid foundation. The next step is to work magic into your training. Now, I know you're very skilled at mana manipulation, so I won't bother giving you exercises for that, but you've been going about your day-to-day life without using magic at all."

"But you took away my magic," I began, wondering if Merlin was going senile. "How am I supposed to use skills and traits if you've blocked them."

He shook his head, holding his hand out and manifesting a fireball. "No, I blocked your system access privileges. Let me see. How do I explain this to a youngster who's addicted to the system? Let's say I took away your computer when you have to write an essay for school. What do you do?"

I knew where he was going with his analogy, but I didn't feel like playing along. "Oh, I know! This is an easy one. I'd type it up on my cell phone and submit it by email."

That earned me a groan from my old man. Part of me wondered if this was what it was like to have a dad. "Wrong! You'd write it out on paper like a normal kid. That's what you have to do with magic. Stop relying on the system for spells and skills. Anything you could do with the system, you can also do without it. I'm just taking off the training wheels."

"Are you saying, I can edit reality and make things out of pebbles in real life?" I asked, daring to believe I was actually that powerful.

Merlin sighed and shook his head. "No. That is the one thing you cannot do. You can learn to make things out of nothing, but your manipulation skills are a sort of cheat on reality. Everything you manipulate has a cost. If you want to make food or something edible, the ingredients have to come from somewhere. The system obtains them and provides them for you when you create something. The same goes for deletion. When you delete things, the system is just moving it around somewhere you won't notice it."

"Wait," I started, thinking about all the things I'd deleted since I got the skill. "Are you saying every time I deleted poop, I was just moving it somewhere else?"

Merlin actually laughed. "Hah, yes, that was a fun one. Who other than my son would decide to use such powerful magic for something so crude? The good news is, those times you summoned a toilet, the system was able to replace it where it took it from once you deleted it."

"Well, that's a relief," I said, wiping the sweat from my brow. "Though Kalli is probably going to be mad when I tell her I didn't actually delete her…"

The thought of Kalli sent a surge of sadness through me, causing me to trail off. Merlin noticed and quickly said, "The next part of your training is to learn to use magic in every aspect of your life. You think your core is made up of only light elemental mana but that's just the way it manifests. The truth is, your mana is un-aspected and perfectly suited to host all of the elements. That is why you've been able to filter different elements through your core in the past. While it's amusing that you kept assigning yourself affinities through manipulation, I will teach you to do that on the fly by changing your element at a core level. With practice, you'll even learn to combine elements for surprising results."

"How do I train that?" I asked, eager to learn despite myself.

Merlin sat on a rock and directed me to sit across from him. "For starters, you're going to practice changing the element of your core to as many different forms as possible. I don't care what element you choose, just make sure the element completely takes hold and then move on to the next one."

"What about emotions?" I asked, wondering how much Merlin knew about the ancients and their techniques.

"Don't get bored," was the cryptic answer I got. I couldn't tell if Merlin had no clue what I was talking about or if he was messing with me.

Simple elements like fire and wind were easy. I'd done them before while back at The Academy. Had it really been so long since I practiced basic things? Kalli, and I had jumped from one adventure to the next so much I'd forsaken most of the things I learned in school.

Merlin watched quietly while I let my core catch fire. It reminded me of Kalli's core as it burned like a supernova in my chest. He gave me a nod of approval, and I moved on to wind. Soon enough, I had a whirling tornado raging where the star had been previously.

From there, I switched to void. The dark element intrigued me because it was basically the absence of an element. Even though I couldn't see anything, I felt it swirling around in my chest, both feeding and drawing from my mana channels as it circulated through my system.

"Try it," Merlin said, stepping a few feet back. "Destroy this rock."

I looked down at the rock, imagining it was a monster or an enemy. Rage flooded me when I saw Rasputin's face and Kalli clinging to his back, ready to explode. I stretched out my hands, not sure what was about to happen. Invisible mana came out, causing the air around me to burst outward in every direction. The void mana created a vacuum as it traveled through the gap to the rock. The moment it touched the surface, the rock collapsed in on itself. It grew smaller and smaller into a glowing red ball that sunk into the ground.

"Excellent," Merlin said while clapping and backing farther away. "I suggest you move back, quickly."

I barely had time to jump out of the way as the ball exploded violently. Merlin held up a hand, and a shimmering barrier appeared around the explosion, forcing the blast upward, where it harmlessly dissipated in the sky above us.

"That was a good sample of void magic," he began. "You truly are my son. However, I need to warn you. Always be mindful of your surroundings when you try a new spell for the first time. As you've seen here, the aftereffects can be unpredictable."

"You should teach me how to make a shield," I said in awe after witnessing Merlin's magic.

He laughed. "In due time. Focus on the basics. Oh, and don't forget your exercises. While you have grown stronger, you're still weak for an awakened."

Then, he left. I glanced over at Ulli and Marcelle, who were both standing at attention as Merlin vanished in a puff of smoke. Now that he was gone, we could finally leave the tower.

[9]

"Wow, we don't have to go down to the first floor?" I asked as we stepped out onto a large hangar built into the side of the tower. The wide opening in the wall with the shimmering blue force field reminded me of a spaceship.

Open-topped shuttles that looked like convertible cars with no wheels lined the bay. As we entered the hangar, a man in a black suit with well-polished shoes approached. "Greetings, Lord Melvin. It is my great pleasure to transport you to Sevaar today. We are prepared to depart any time you wish."

"Wait," Ulli squealed. "We aren't taking the public shuttle?"

He answered without taking his eyes off me, "No. Lord Melvin will not be using public transportation. The Creator sent instructions to take the young master anywhere he wishes to go. Are you prepared to depart, my Lord?"

So much for keeping my destination a secret from Merlin. I nodded and followed as he turned to guide me to one of the fancier vehicles. Unlike the other shuttles, ours was stretched like a limo and had a hot tub in the back.

"What's your name?" I asked as he held the door open for us.

"My name is of no consequence," he replied. I waited for the girls to get in, but they lined up alongside him and looked back at me expectantly.

"Ladies first," I insisted before turning back to the man. "Your name is of consequence to me. If I'm going to travel with you a lot, I'd prefer to get to know you."

Marcelle gave Ulli a discreet nod, and the girl hopped into the vehicle and scooted all the way toward the front. Marcelle slid in after her, leaving plenty of room for me to sit.

"It's Alfred, my Lord," he replied with a deep bow. "It will be my utmost pleasure to serve you."

"Sweet! It's like I'm Batman," I exclaimed with a grin, hopping into the strange shuttle much the same way Ulli had. "With an awesome name like Alfred, you should shout it from the rooftops."

"Very good, sir," he replied. I couldn't tell if he was mimicking Alfred from the movie or if all chauffeurs were just trained to act that way. Either way, he shut the door and walked around the shuttle to take his seat up front.

I watched him, waiting for the tell-tale sign of an engine firing up, but nothing happened. Instead, mana flowed out of Alfred and was quickly sucked up by the shuttle. The entire thing vibrated, and a shimmering shield, much like the one on the hanger, hummed to life around us.

The shuttle steadily rose off the ground until it was hovering a foot above the ground. It then lurched into motion and built up speed as it approached the barrier at the end of the hangar.

I braced myself for impact, but it never came. The shield around the outer wall flickered just long enough for the shuttle to pass through into the open air. And then we were flying. Ulli leaned over the edge, looking down at the clouds as we sailed over. She had obviously done this before as she had absolutely no fear of falling out.

I looked around, hoping to find a seatbelt or something to secure myself...just in case Alfred decided to do a barrel roll. Not finding any, I clutched at the seat back as I joined Ulli in admiring the view. She noticed and giggled. "You don't have to worry about falling out. There's magic in place that prevents that."

Looking back at Alfred, I focused mana on my eyes to get a better idea of how he was powering the shuttle. Not only did his mana flow into the vehicle, but it also formed a bubble around it, protecting us from not only the air speeding past us but also potentially falling out. I crawled over to the front of the shuttle so I could speak to him. "I didn't know you were awakened."

Alfred laughed but kept his eyes on the sky in front of him. "You have to be to pilot one of these things. They don't exactly come fueled."

"Oh," I replied, rethinking how I thought of Origin. "Are most of the workers here awakened?"

"Everyone you've met so far is awakened," Marcelle said from my other side, sitting with her legs crossed and a bored expression on her face.

"Everyone?" I echoed, imagining all the people in the tower having magical powers.

"Pretty much," Marcelle replied. "Some of the girls aren't, but they have to possess outstanding qualities to be considered. All the workers are awakened."

"How long does it take to get to Sevaar?" I asked. The fact that everyone was awakened played heavily on my mind. "Why don't any of you ever use your powers?"

Ulli turned her head to look at me. "We aren't allowed to use them. Well, we can, but only in very special circumstances."

"Like what?" I asked, wondering why people weren't allowed to use their powers. Were they dangerous?

Marcelle tugged Ulli back into the shuttle. "We use our powers during our training and when they are beneficial. Powers aren't to be used recklessly."

"Is that why Merlin blocked me from the system?" I asked out loud.

Marcelle shook her head, cringing when I said the name. "You're different from us. You're free to do whatever you like. The laws don't apply to you. Everyone knows that."

"Anything I like?" I asked, wondering what exactly she meant.

"Anything at all," she replied.

I looked over at Ulli, and she looked away but said nothing. I sighed. "I just want you both to know I'm not like my father. I think there are some laws that should apply to everyone, especially those in charge."

It took us about an hour to get to Ulli's hometown of Sevaar. A group of people stood on the landing platform when we arrived. Ulli perked up and leaned over the side of the shuttle again to wave at them.

"That's her family," Marcelle informed me when I gave her a curious look. "She's been looking forward to this visit for weeks. Thank you for choosing this town to visit."

"Can't you go home when you want?" I asked.

She shook her head. "Once we start training in the tower, we can only go home for certain things such as funerals."

We landed before I had a chance to ask any more questions. The landing zone looked like a parking lot. It was a paved area next to a three-story building. There were no other vehicles or any parking spaces marked. I soon found myself surrounded by a small family, who wasted no time surrounding Ulli. Marcelle tried to hold them back, but I stopped her. "I'd like to meet them."

It looked like the whole family turned up. Her mother and father hugged her while an older couple, who I assumed were her grandparents, stood quietly behind waiting for their turn. Three little girls raced over to Marcelle and gave her a hug. They were all smiles until Ulli told them who I was. "This is Lord Melvin, The Creator's son. Marcy, and I are assigned to him.

Her parents and grandparents dropped to their knees and didn't look at me after that. I rushed over to help her grandmother when I noticed she struggled. "Don't worry about that. You don't need to kneel for me."

"Of course, we do," her mother cried out. "You honor us with your presence."

"No, I insist," I said, turning to help her up as well. "Please. Call me Melvin."

She looked away. "I couldn't possibly. Thank you for honoring our humble town with your presence, Lord Melvin."

I sighed. There was no way I was going to be able to learn anything in town with Ulli's family fawning over me. I turned to Ulli, who had made her way back to Marcelle after greeting her family. "You can take the day off. I'll send Marcelle for you when I'm ready to head back."

She looked hesitantly at Marcelle. The older woman nodded and said, "It's okay. Lord Melvin says you can, so go."

Ulli hesitated but, eventually, she left with her family. Alfred stayed with the shuttle as Marcelle, and I left the parking lot. We walked for a while before Marcelle turned to face me. "What is the purpose of coming here?"

I gave her a hard stare. "Are you spying for my dad?"

"What? No!" she bellowed, folding her arms defensively. "I'm loyal to you. I just don't understand why you'd want to come out here. This is just a town. It's not even a good one. There are much better places you could visit, like Camelot."

"*The* Camelot?" I asked. "Does King Arthur live there?

She giggled and shook her head. "No, my Lord. He's been dead for centuries. Camelot Castle still stands, though. It's actually a very nice castle town. When you said you wanted to come here, I figured you were doing it for Ulli, but then you dismissed her. So, why are we here? What do you want to do?"

I took a few more steps, looking around as I walked. Marcelle was right. It looked like a normal town back on Earth. Rows of houses stretched out in every direction, and I saw some apartments and businesses in the distance. After flying in a shuttle, I expected to see vehicles whizzing by in the sky, but there was none of that. Actually, there weren't any vehicles. Or people for that matter.

"Where is everyone?" I asked. "Why are there no cars anywhere."

She frowned, rubbing her chin. "They probably were informed of your arrival and told to stay off the streets. It isn't every day royalty visits small towns."

"How did they know?" I asked, groaning in frustration. "The whole idea of coming here was to see what daily life is like on Origin."

Marcelle shrugged. "I don't think you're ever going to see daily life. Not on this planet. Your arrival was broadcast the moment you arrived."

"Why would they do that?" I grumbled, frustrated that my plans were essentially ruined.

"So nobody would hurt you," Marcelle explained. "This way, you'll be respected no matter where you go."

I wasn't sure how I felt about that. It was one thing to be coddled by everyone, but to be told that the reason for it was because I was so weak I needed to be protected was downright infuriating. "I can take care of myself!"

Marcelle backpedaled. "That's not what I meant. I'm just saying that nobody would dare even try anything with the son of The Creator."

We walked together in silence down a street lined with houses. Back on Earth, I would have called the neighborhood middle-class. Well-cared-for lawns and cookie-cutter two-story homes stood about ten feet apart from each other, separated by white picket fences.

Most of the homes had their curtains drawn but, a few times, I spied children peeking out at me as we walked past. It wasn't so much that I wanted to meet people, I wanted to talk to the citizens of Origin as a mysterious outsider, not the son of the local god. It was hard for people to be honest about life on the planet when they had to fear death by deletion if they said something wrong.

It soon became apparent I was going to have to get creative when I left the tower, but I was stuck in Sevaar for at least the day if I wanted to give Ulli time with her family. Then, I had an idea. Double-timing it back to the shuttle, I pulled Alfred and Marcelle into a huddle. "If I teleport back to the tower, will the two of you give Ulli at least a day with her family?"

"Absolutely not," Marcelle said firmly. "Where you go, I go. However, I don't see why Alfred can't hang around and give Ulli some time off. It's a kind thing you're doing for her. It will help her warm up to you."

"What?" I asked, giving her a wounded look. "Are you saying she doesn't like me yet?"

Marcelle let out a long sigh. "Face it, Lord Melvin. You are kind of intimidating."

[10]

FOR ONCE, when we arrived back at the lobby outside of the throne room, I was exactly where I wanted to be. Even though Merlin told me he didn't want to be disturbed, I pushed the double doors open that led to his chamber and marched the distance over to the throne while ignoring the many women in the alcoves.

"Dad, we need to talk," I barked, not bothering to say hello.

"What is it this time?" he asked. "Was your little field trip not to your liking?"

I frowned. "I want to see what this planet of yours is like, and I can't do that until you inform everyone that I'm coming."

"Then, do something about it," he shot back. "You have my blessing to do whatever you like, so long as you don't try to leave Origin."

"And you'll stop interfering?" I asked hopefully.

"Nope," he replied smugly. "You are free to do what you like, and I will do what I'm going to do. Consider it part of your training."

"They say it's dangerous to wander outside of the tower," I countered. "Why don't you put an end to that?"

He rested his head on his hand with a bored expression on his face. "People who commit crimes are punished accordingly."

"Aren't you all-powerful?" I asked. "Can't you make the streets safer?"

Merlin laughed. "The fact that you would even suggest that shows how naive you still are. Only tyrants try to stomp out crime by punishing would-be criminals before they commit a crime."

"What does that mean?" I asked.

He let out a heavy sigh, "It means, son, that I do not intend to punish someone for a crime I think they may commit. It is not a crime to lurk in the old town outside of the tower. However, do not think I am heartless. I provide safe transportation to any of the tower's many residents who wish to visit their hometowns. All they need to do is ask, as you've seen."

"And what if I choose to leave the tower on foot?" I asked. "What if I am attacked?"

Merlin stomped his foot on the floor for emphasis. It was only then that I noticed there had been chatter in the alcoves because it suddenly stopped. Everyone was listening to what my father said next, "If someone is foolish enough to attack you, there would be no place they could hide from me. Besides, you are more than capable of defending yourself."

I thought about that for a moment. While I had managed to survive against countless powerful enemies, the victories hadn't been without a cost. My defeat of Carmella Shaw nearly killed me. I could argue that my victory over the god Kur had been without loss, but he had kidnapped and threatened to eat me before my friends came to the rescue. Mardella stabbed and poisoned me. Without the ring, she likely would have won. Then, there was Rasputin. He had killed...had killed...

I couldn't think about it without my eyes watering. Instead, I sniffled loudly and glared at my father through bleary eyes. "I'm still weak."

I couldn't bear to be seen by anyone anymore, so I teleported away. Walking the short distance probably would have been more efficient, but I didn't care. It got me away from my father. His voice followed me, echoing through the chamber. "Don't worry, son. You will grow stronger. I guarantee it."

The tone of Merlin's voice was softer than I'd ever heard it. It was almost as though he cared.

———

"You didn't have to come home today," I sighed as Ulli slid in through the door. "You could have stayed with your family as long as you wanted."

"That would be inappropriate," Marcelle explained from her spot by the door. "She has a job to do."

I walked over to one of the couches and motioned for the two girls to sit across from me. After waiting for them to sit, I began, "This has got to change. I know you've been assigned to me and have to be here. Can you do me a favor and try not to be so formal all the time? Can we just be friends?"

"If you command it," Marcelle said, a hint of a smile forming on her face. "We will obey anything you order us to do."

I groaned. "You can't order someone to be your friend. If you do, they aren't really your friend."

"I'll be your friend, my Lord," Ulli said hesitantly. "You don't have to ask me to."

It was my turn to blush, quickly followed by a feeling of shame when I realized I found Ulli attractive. Just a little shorter than Kalli, she had golden curls that flowed freely down her back. Her fair skin was complemented by cute dimples and rosy cheeks. She reminded me of a famous actress from the nineteen twenties.

"For starters, don't call me my lord, I said. "Or Lord Melvin for that matter. Just Melvin or Mel will do."

"Yes...Mel," she giggled when she said the word. Marcelle frowned at Ulli but didn't admonish her.

"So, is Ulli short for something?" I asked, wanting to get her to open up to me. "Do you have a last name?"

Ulli fidgeted, rubbing her fingers together and looking down at the floor as she answered, "My full name is Ullrisa. It's supposed to mean rich and powerful, but my parents are neither. We can't even afford a surname."

"You have to buy those?" I asked, curious about how the world worked.

"You can purchase them," Marcelle corrected. "Noble families are born with surnames. Peasants may purchase status if they accumulate enough money. Many families save for generations just to rise a single rank."

"Do you have a surname?" I asked, realizing how much I'd have to ask without the system to provide information. "Does my father?"

Marcelle gasped. "The Creator doesn't require a name. He's the most powerful man in the universe. Everyone knows him without having to mention his name. He's on an entirely different level."

"You didn't answer my question," I persisted. "Do you have a last name?"

Ulli giggled, and Marcelle glared at her. "I, ahem, I do have one. I'm not a direct descendant but close enough to use the name. My full name is Marcelle Friedman."

"Her third cousin twice removed was a famous chef," Ulli announced, looking smug.

Marcelle slumped in the chair and grumbled, "I never even got to taste her cooking, but I'm saddled with the name. My parents hope I'll earn a better one working here in the tower."

"We all want that," Ulli added. "If I'm selected, my parent's family won't have to work for ten generations."

"Selected?" I asked. "Weren't you already selected?"

They both turned bright red. Ulli gave a casual glance at the bed, and Marcelle said, "She means if you select one of us to, ahem—"

"Oh!" I gasped, feeling my face start to burn. "Can I just say I chose you? That way you can get the reward without having to do anything."

"No!" Marcelle practically screamed, cutting me off. "They check that kind of thing. It would look bad for both of us if you did that."

"How do they check?" I asked before deciding I probably didn't want to know. "I mean, *why* do they check? Isn't my word good enough?"

"For you, it is," Marcelle replied. "You can say whatever you like and only your father can challenge it. We must provide proof to claim any perks of status."

It felt wrong. I had all the power and none of it at the same time. What was the purpose of being The Creator's son if I couldn't even get my direct reports a proper raise? Then, it dawned on me. I didn't have to lie. "I got it! How about I just give you both last names? That would count just as much as, you know, right?"

I waited in silence as the two of them looked at one another. Finally, Marcelle rubbed her chin thoughtfully. "That could work. I don't think it's ever been done before. The Creator only hands out titles based on merits. People like us who don't have specialties usually wind up in the tower. Once you get here, there's really only one path to glory."

"It's settled, then," I said with a grin. "Do either of you have a last name in mind?"

More silence. Ulli finally said something. "You can't expect us to choose our own surnames. What if I gave myself something ridiculous like Superior?"

"Ulli Superior," I sounded it out. "Now that Ulli's is settled, what about you Marcelle?"

"No, no, no, no!" Ulli cried. "I can't give myself that name. What will people say?"

I shrugged. "Just tell people I did it. You'll be blameless."

Marcelle surprised me when she told me her choice. "I've always wanted a simple name like Jones or Smith."

"Very well," I said, a sinister grin appearing on my face. "We will call you Marcelle Masters."

"What?" Marcelle asked, staring at me.

———

Meanwhile, on a planet called Bloodmoon…

Shara stared at the last of her sample. It was late, but she was anxious to try it again while the experience of the last failure was still fresh. The corrupted blood she acquired from Melvin Murphy turned out to be an enigma she just couldn't solve. Sure, she had no issues alleviating the pain of those afflicted, but blood was her specialty, and she refused to believe there was something she couldn't do with it.

She activated the contraption by pushing mana through a tube and the process was in motion. The blood swirled rapidly, slowly turning from red to clear and finally to black. Shara found herself holding her breath while hoping fervently that the experiment would have a different result for once. Steam rose through a trap and, for a moment, she thought she'd done it. Then, the whole thing exploded… again.

Shara collected herself as a knock came at the door. She struggled to a chair and shouted to be heard over the still hissing mess, "Not now. Come back in the morning. I'm in no mood."

"You have a guest, Lady Shaw," the voice of her servant came back.

That was new. *Who would visit this late at night?*

She groaned, pushing herself to her feet and looking at her ruined lab coat. "I'll be down in a short while. I need to freshen up."

"I'm sorry, my Lady," her servant replied, sounding worried. "I'm afraid your father sent your guest up."

A familiar voice asked, "Are you decent, Shara?"

"Lavender?" Shara squealed, worried that something happened to her mother. She rushed to the door, no longer worried about how she looked.

"Ah," Lavender said with a warm smile. "Perhaps you'd like a moment."

"Is Mother okay?" Shara cried, ignoring her.

Lavender nodded, finally realizing what the commotion was. "Your mother is fine. Still without a body but fine in Homestead, nonetheless. I've come today on an unrelated matter. May I trouble you for a moment of your time?"

"Sure," Shara mumbled, at a loss for what could possibly be so urgent to require a midnight visit. "Shall I have Bianca prepare the study for us?"

"That won't be necessary," Lavender said, stepping past Shara. "Here will do."

Shara scrambled back into her room, kicking some dirty clothes under the bed before making her way over to the lounge where Lavender was already seated. She sat across from the woman and asked, "What do you want exactly?"

Lavender looked over her shoulder at the wreckage in Shara's lab with a worried expression on her face. "Do you have some of the blood samples left?"

Shara shook her head. "That was the last of it."

Lavender looked crestfallen. "Then, all is lost."

"What?" Shara asked, not understanding what Lavender needed. "Why is Melvin Murphy's corrupted blood so important?"

Lavender's head swung back to look at Shara. "What of Kalliphae's? Do you have any of her blood?"

"Yes," Shara replied. "Not much, but—"

"I need you to gather all of it and come with me."

[11]

"I don't like my name," Ulli whined.

"Me neither," Marcelle joined her, showing child-like defiance for the first time since I'd met the woman.

I laughed. "I never said I was any good at name-choosing. Feel free to choose your own names. Then, I'll make it official."

Faced with choosing a name or going with one of my ridiculous suggestions, the two retreated to a corner to brainstorm. I found an open area on the floor and started exercising. It was a good way to clear my mind. I'd just admitted to Merlin that I was weak. No! I admitted it to myself. It was on me to do something about it. Strengthening my body was only a part of it.

I listened to the chirping girls as they threw out one name after another. My muscles began to burn steadily as I worked them systematically. I did all of the exercises Dad ordered me to do along with some of the ones I remembered from gym class. It was also a lesson in mana control.

If I added too much mana to a muscle, it went into overdrive, twitching madly when the exertion didn't match the power the mana was providing. Too little, and I might as well not have used any. While it did have some effect the trade-off made me more fatigued than when I used none.

I'd just gotten up to go for a run when Marcelle and Ulli approached. "Okay. We've decided."

"What'll it be?" I asked, wondering if I needed to fill out some paperwork to make it official.

Ulli went first, "I've chosen the surname Cyprus. What do you think? Isn't it cute?"

I smiled. She was so proud of her name. I'd never thought about Murphy. I was born with it. "I love it! How about you, Marcelle? What did you come up with?"

Marcelle was the opposite of Ulli. Rather than showing excitement, she listed off her last name like she'd just completed a business trans-action. "I've decided on Barlow. You will need to inform the registrar for them to take effect. I believe there is some paperwork involved."

"Ugh, paperwork?" I grumbled. "Is that something I can make you do?"

Marcelle nodded curtly. "Yes. However, as this business pertains to me directly, you will have to sign off on it."

"Sure thing," I replied. "Now, who's ready for dinner?"

———

I have no way of knowing if I was leveling up. While I didn't get any messages or the crazy good feelings that went along with the experi-ence, I knew I had to be making progress. Merlin didn't show up again for several days after he promised to help me get stronger. I continued my daily exercise regimen every morning.

After that was done, I practiced mana control. To do that, I focused on performing acrobatics while enhancing the necessary muscles with mana. While regular mana infused into my legs would help me jump higher, infusing my entire body with wind mana made me lighter and greatly increased the height I could jump. I was also able to float to the ground by expelling the wind as I descended.

It was during one of those sessions that Merlin showed up again.

He nodded his approval when I touched down in front of him. "If you do that right, you'll be able to fly. Don't think wind is the best element just because it makes you lighter. Other elements can have surprising results when used creatively. Consider infusing different parts of your body with various elements at the same time. The earth element can help your feet gain stability with the ground and fire will fill your legs with explosive energy."

Trying his advice was a recipe for disaster. Infusing multiple body parts with different kinds of mana was significantly more complicated than patting your head and rubbing your belly at the same time. Multiple types of mana fused together created a murky burnt concoction that knotted any muscle it came into contact with.

Marcelle was ready. She raced into the arena with a stretcher. She and Ulli carted me off to a room that hadn't been included in the tour. A beautiful redhead in a nurse's outfit that reminded me strongly of Kalli approached as Marcelle unceremoniously dumped me on an examination table. "What happened here?"

"Training with The Creator," Marcelle explained. "Mana-related injury."

"Understood," the nurse replied, moving over and running her hands over my legs. She wasn't wearing gloves.

"Hey," I complained. "That's cold. Uh, ooh. Never mind, that feels good. Keep doing that."

It felt like a betrayal, but I squeezed my eyes shut and told myself it was medicinal. The nurse didn't hesitate to strip me to get better access to bare skin. The good feelings that were spreading through my body were just a byproduct of the healing. The nurse worked in silence, methodically examining and treating every inch of my body. I kept chanting the mantra in my head.

She knows what she's doing. She knows what she's doing. She knows—Hey!

"I didn't injure that!" I screamed, trying to roll over but trapped by the nurse's viselike grip. "You don't need to treat… Aaaah, okay, then."

When I opened my eyes, I saw her staring at me with one eyebrow raised. "Young master. You suffered chaotic feedback when your mana had an adverse reaction in your body. There is residual damage everywhere. If I don't treat the problem, you are going to feel it the next time you attempt to use your mana."

"Trust her, Melvin," Marcelle lectured from several feet away. I turned my head to see her and Ulli standing guard by the room's only exit. "She is one of the most skilled medics on the planet."

I was painfully aware of the fact both of my servants were staring at parts of my body that I hadn't even revealed to Kalli yet. Well, not intentionally in any case. I was just getting used to the spectacle when the nurse said, "Okay, all done. You're good as new. Try to take it easy with the mana next time. You may be The Creator's son, but even you have your limit."

The way she said that made me wonder. "Have you ever treated my father?"

The nurse busied herself with a clipboard and pretended not to hear me as she walked into an office and closed the door. Marcelle draped me with a robe and smiled coyly. "Are you ready to leave, Melvin?"

Swinging my legs over the edge of the table, I said, "I think I need more practice."

"You're going to do that again?" Ulli asked. "It looked painful."

I shrugged, hopping to my feet and walking through the door as Marcelle opened it for me. "There's only one way to get better. Practice, practice, practice."

I used the walk back to my room to take baby steps with my mana. Rather than risking my muscles again, I formed fire above one hand and wind above the other. I held my arms out to either side and focused on feeding the appropriate mana to each. It took a while but, eventually, it felt less awkward to produce two different types of mana at the same time.

"I don't get it," Ulli said after a while. "What's the benefit of using two different types of mana?"

"That's right," I replied. "You're both awakened. What class are you?"

Ulli puffed out her chest with pride. "I'm a dancer. You should see my dancing. I've got moves."

I thought about it. While it would be interesting to see Ulli dance, could she use it in a fight? Some video games had dancers that fought. Then again, were all classes designed to be useful in fights? There had to be awakened with skills and traits just for creating things. I turned my attention to Marcelle, wondering if her class would answer the question. "What class are you?"

She gave me a sidelong glance. "I am a strategist. My skill is to come up with ways of accomplishing goals."

"Do either of you fight?" I asked.

Ulli shook her head. "It's easier to run away than to fight."

Marcelle added, "We all know how to fight to a certain extent. Life outside the tower often means learning to defend yourself. Just like in your world, there are weapons that can aid us."

"Like guns, you mean?" I asked.

Marcelle got a sickened look on her face. "Such crude weapons. Guns are forbidden on Origin. The system would flag them if anybody tried to make one. The intended function of a gun isn't what's illegal, though. It's the fact that you can miss your target and hit someone unintended. That is what's not allowed."

"What about intentionally attacking the innocent?" I asked.

"The innocent?" she asked. "I suppose everyone is innocent until they aren't. If you're speaking about children, the system has safe-guards in place. Harming children goes against the rules of the system, and thus is blocked. Additionally, children are blocked from commit-ting acts of aggression by the system. They are deemed too immature to understand the weight of their actions."

"But I'm still a child," I muttered.

Marcelle shook her head. "By the laws of this world, you became an adult the moment you turned sixteen. All parental locks would have been disabled at midnight on the day of your birthday. You are free to do all of the things children are forbidden from doing."

"And not just violence," Ulli added cheerfully, her cheeks turning a rosy red.

"Do you mean children can't…" I trailed off. It wasn't like I'd gotten any action as a kid. Well, Kalli, and I did come close, though she never wanted to do anything more than make out. My heart twinged at the possibility of never seeing her again.

Ulli giggled, oblivious to my internal turmoil. "No, we can't, but you'd be surprised how creative some kids can get. The problem is, any girl who crosses a certain line can never get work in the tower. That doesn't stop boys from trying, though."

"Did you have a boyfriend growing up?" I asked Ulli, curious about life outside of the tower.

She turned an even deeper shade of red. "I-I don't want to talk about that."

"What about you, Marcelle?" I asked. "Is there someone special back home?"

"No," she stated. "I knew from a young age that I wanted to aspire to the tower. The best way to do that was to focus on my studies and hope to get noticed."

"A true strategist," I complimented. "So, how do you get noticed anyway?"

She smirked. "It isn't just about beauty. The truth is, most people on Origin are beautiful. Some say our ancestors were selected and brought here because of their beauty. The tower selects the brightest minds and the most unique of the population. If you don't graduate at the top of your class, you have no hope of making it in."

"Wow, the two of you must be pretty smart," I mused. "It's a shame you got assigned to me."

"Why is that?" Ulli asked.

I shrugged, nearly at a loss for words. "The two of you could do so much better than me."

Ulli shook her head and whispered, "I'm happy I got assigned to you. I don't think I could go through with the other path."

It took me a second to figure out what she was talking about. Then, it dawned on me. All the other women in the tower were walking a path that led to Merlin. Deciding I didn't want to think about my dad's love life, I resumed my focus on mana training.

[12]

"WHERE ARE WE GOING, MEL?" Ulli gave me pause when she used the nickname Kalli made up for me. I couldn't be mad considering I'd asked her to call me that. "You passed the garden."

"We're not working out today," I explained, doubling my pace.

Both girls hustled to keep up. Marcelle frowned as she jogged alongside me. "Then, what are we going to do?"

"It's a secret," I announced triumphantly.

"Why do I have a bad feeling about this?" Marcelle groaned as they followed me.

I rounded the corner into the hangar as I called over my shoulder. "You don't have to come if you don't want to."

"You know that's not an option," Marcelle continued the lecture as I spotted Alfred preparing the limo shuttle. "If it were discovered that you wandered off without me, they would throw me out of the tower."

I stopped and turned to face her. "I doubt that. The way I see it, you belong to me. Nobody but my dad can do anything to you without my permission. That means you're safe."

She stopped in her tracks, pondering my words for a second before turning to Ulli. "Go back to the room. As Melvin said, you don't have to come."

"I'm going!" Ulli said defiantly with her arms crossed. "I never said I didn't want to go. You can go back if you want."

Marcelle heaved an exasperated sigh. "Fine. It looks like we're going along with whatever scheme you're up to. The least you can do is tell us what that is."

"We're going out," I replied, careful not to say anything else in case one of the girls was actually a spy for Merlin.

Alfred looked up as we approached. "Can I help you, Lord Melvin? I wasn't aware you were scheduled to be here today. I have other plans, but I can rearrange—"

I cut him off, motioning to a row of shuttles. "Can you teach me how to fly one of these?"

He gaped at me. "You want to fly a hover chariot?"

"Hover chariot?" I replied. "Why didn't anyone tell me they had such an awesome name? I was thinking of them as floating limos this whole time."

I worried he wasn't going to help me when he didn't move right away, but he laughed. "Floating limo, eh? Is that what they call them where you're from?"

"They don't have flying cars where I'm from," I replied. "Well, they do but only in movies. My second world has airships, but I've never been able to fly one of those either. You said I can pilot one with mana, right?"

"Well, yes, in theory," he answered slowly. "You can probably turn the chariot on, but controlling it required a bit more skill."

"That's where you come in," I informed him. "I need you to show me how to work the controls."

"This isn't safe," Marcelle said, pleading with me. "Please, just tell Alfred where you want to go, I'm sure he'll—"

I cut her off with a wave of my hand. "The fewer people who know what I'm up to the better. Unless you want to explore on foot again. I have to warn you, though, I won't turn back this time."

"Fine," she groaned, her shoulders sagging in defeat. "Let's get this over with."

———

Alfred chose a smaller chariot than the limo he'd transported us in on our first trip. Marcelle and Ulli climbed in the back seat, which was just big enough for the two of them while Alfred led me to the driver's seat.

I felt a plate on the seat make contact with the small of my back the moment I sat down. There were also similar plates on the controls as well. Rather than a steering wheel of a car that I was used to, the shuttle had a pair of joystick controls. Each had multiple buttons on top and a trigger that made me wonder if the chariot had guns.

"Grip each control firmly in your hands, and it will draw out your mana," Alfred instructed from the passenger seat. "You will feel a slight tug at your back as well. That exists to keep the chariot from crashing in case you lose contact with the controls. I can only assume you have more mana than me, but the chariot will descend when it senses you getting low."

I gripped each control, careful not to push anything, and looked over to Alfred. "Okay, now what?"

He smiled. "Give it a moment."

I felt a jolt run up my spine as it started to siphon mana through my back. The sensation was odd but not altogether unpleasant, kind of like a premonition that something bad was going to happen. I hoped that was just the mana talking.

One by one, the displays in front of me illuminated. I knew I'd done it right when I felt the chariot vibrate. Slowly, we rose about a foot off the ground. The problem was there were no pedals like I'd seen my mother use in cars all my life. I looked over at Alfred and asked, "How do I make it go?"

He let out a good-natured chuckle and replied, "Perhaps we can leave that lesson for another day. How about I tell you what the various displays mean? The first one is— Argh!"

He groaned as the chariot lurched backward when I pulled back on the controls. So much for the tutorial. I shoved both joysticks forward, and several people were forced to dive out of the way as our chariot barreled toward the portal window.

Crap! I think I just felt my wisdom score go down again.

It was a shame Kalli wasn't there to admonish me, though I would have given anything to hear her voice. Alfred reached over and pushed a button on the console just before we reached the portal, and it flickered, allowing us to pass through.

"You were going to tell me about that, right?" I asked, heaving a sigh of relief as we hit the open air. "Did my father ask you to keep me from going out?"

"It's not that, my Lord," Alfred said, holding onto his seatbelt for dear life. "My only instruction is to keep you safe."

"Great!" I replied, perhaps a little too forcefully. "Then, you can teach me how to safely fly this thing."

After that, he was much more cooperative. He went over the various displays and what I needed to pay attention to. The buttons on the joystick didn't turn out to be a weapon system, though the chariot was armed with some interesting features like a tractor beam.

"The shuttles are designed for industrial use as well as search and rescue in case of accidents," he explained as I pushed the right stick forward to descend over a farmhouse. "There are a lot of functions you won't use for day-to-day flight, but they come in handy in the event of an emergency."

"How fast does it go?" I asked, wondering if I should test it.

Alfred frowned. "These chariots are rated at one hundred miles per hour. While it is possible to go significantly faster-using mana travel, you would have to take out one of the sonic chariots for that. To do it in one of these, you would have to bypass the safety features and risk a malfunction."

"Got it," I replied. "This is the top speed. Now, is there any kind of GPS in this thing, or perhaps a map in the glovebox?"

"Glovebox?" Alfred asked, looking confused.

"Never mind," I replied. "Tell me how to get to Camelot."

Alfred punched a few buttons on one of the consoles he hadn't told me about, and a shimmering blue road appeared in the sky in front of me. Alfred laughed when I tried to look over the windshield to see if it was real. "That's just a hologram projected on the windshield. Follow it, and you will reach Camelot."

"In how long?" I asked.

He punched a few more buttons, and a timer appeared on the display.

3:24:13

It began ticking down, and I knew we would be there in just over three hours. Alfred punched a few more buttons before saying, "I've set the auto-pilot function. You can release the controls for now, but please do not leave your seat. You are effectively the battery for this chariot. While it retains a charge, it will immediately begin to descend if you get up."

"Got it," I replied. "Now, let's go over all these displays while we fly.

———

Camelot was exactly like I imagined it would be. A large castle on a hill surrounded by a great city. The whole place bustled with activity, even though I wasn't sure if they were locals or tourists. Did Origin even have tourists? Ulli made it sound like it did.

"You are permitted to land at the castle," Alfred began, pointing at a large flat space in a courtyard of the castle.

I shook my head. "Where would a normal chariot have to land?"

He looked at me and sighed. "Why on Origin would you want to do that?"

Not wanting to answer that particular question, I lied, "I just want to meet people. As me, you know, not as The Creator's son."

"But everybody knows what you look like," he replied. "There is no place on this planet where you wouldn't be recognized."

I closed my eyes and mentally crossed my fingers. How had we done it before? I pushed mana over myself, envisioning what I had done to Kalli and I when we snuck into Wrotor, home of the trolls. I transformed my appearance into that of a man a few years older than me with short curly locks of crimson hair the same color as Kalli's. The only thing that really needed to change was my face. I altered it just enough so I wouldn't be recognized. I changed my red eyes back to blue, and I added Kalli's freckles for good measure.

Alfred gasped. He had a front-row seat for the transformation. "You truly are powerful, my Lord."

"It's just an illusion," I replied. "Now, where can I land this thing?"

Alfred pointed at a nearby hill. "You won't be allowed to land anywhere near the city without authorization. It's different for The Creator's son but, as a random nobody, you'll have to land outside of town and walk in. There is also the issue of your identification. The guards aren't going to allow you in without it. You can pull this plan off, but you're going to have to do a lot more preparation than this."

"Can I count on you to keep my secret?" I asked, turning to the girls in the back. "All of you? None of this will work if it gets back to my father."

I got a round of nods from everyone but Marcelle. She gave me a hard stare and asked, "I'll only agree to it if you tell me what you're up to."

It was a pleasant surprise that she was standing up to me more than when I first met her. I tried my best to explain. "Since I've been here, I've only met people who worship me as my father's son. I want to meet people and see what Origin is really like, and not through the filter of power. If I'm going to live here from now on, I need to do this."

I didn't bother to tell them that I was secretly looking for a way out. A way back to Kalli.

[13]

"WHAT ARE WE GOING TO DO?" Marcelle asked after I landed the chariot behind a small hill.

"I don't know," I admitted. "It feels like a shame to not even try now that we came all this way."

Marcelle folded her arms. "You could have saved yourself a lot of trouble if you'd just told us what you intended to do."

"I'm sorry," I replied. "It's hard to trust anybody on this planet. It feels like everyone I meet is reporting to my father."

"You can count on us," Ulli replied. "We are loyal to you."

"I want to trust you," I sighed. It that I wanted to lie to any of them. Marcelle and Ulli were the closest things I had to friends on Origin. It felt like the moment I put my true objective to words, it would find its way to Merlin.

We walked halfway around the hill before I got an idea. "Can I see what identification looks like?"

"Sure," Marcelle replied, reaching into a pocket and pulling out a purse that was way too big to fit. When she noticed my look of surprise, she said, "Pocket dimension. Everyone in the tower gets one."

The ID card she handed me looked similar to an Adventurer's Guild ID card.

Marcelle Friedman
Class: Strategist
Job: Tower Ascendant
Current Floor: 101
Age: 20
Restrictions: Upper Floors

Taking out my Guild ID Card, I used the same illusion magic I had on my face to make a few alterations.

Mel Hellquist
Class: Blacksmith
Job: Apprentice
Age: 17

"Would this pass?" I asked, handing my newly doctored card around.

Alfred pointed out my mistakes by showing me his card. "Non-ascendants use a different form of identification."

Alfred
Class: Aviator
Job: Tower Chauffeur
Rank: B Class
Age: 47

"What does B Class mean?" I asked after looking over his card.

"It's his rank," Marcelle explained. "Everyone gets a rank except those who live in the tower."

"What kind of life does B rank live?" I asked, not sure I liked Merlin's system very much.

Marcelle was on a roll, explaining the way the world worked. "B rank is the minimum rank allowed tower access. Ulli and I were automatically A ranked the day we were admitted into the tower program. Our families can claim some benefits from our status but, for the most part, each person gets ranked individually. That way everyone is on even footing no matter what family they come from. If you're a dead-beat, you'll be ranked F even if you come from a top family."

I considered how to make my ID while Ulli asked questions. "Why did you choose that surname? Isn't your surname Murphy?"

"It used to be the last name of someone special," I replied, feeling a bit melodramatic. "She hated that name, though. It was the only thing that came to mind.

Mel Hellquist
Class: Blacksmith
Job: Apprentice
Rank: D Class
Age: 17

"That won't work," Marcelle said, shaking her head. "Rank D isn't allowed to travel outside of their hometown. If someone sees that, you'll be detained while they try to figure out how to send you home."

In the end, I settled on rank B and no surname. While C technically would have worked, I'd probably still be asked questions about my reason for traveling. Apparently, C rankers were only allowed to travel in certain circumstances.

"I'd hate to see what F rank people go through," I said as I slid my newly minted ID into my pocket.

"You really would," Ulli replied, making a gagging sound after she said it. "They are mostly homeless. When someone drops to F rank, their families usually disown them. You have to be very lazy or very naughty to drop that low."

Marcelle added, "You don't have to worry about most F ranks being criminals. If they get re-ranked for that reason, they usually wind up in prison."

We stopped talking when we approached the bridge leading into Camelot. It was a mechanical draw bridge over a wide moat with green water. A pair of eyeballs of a monster I didn't recognize looked up at me from the depths. Alfred took all of our IDs to present at the guard shack built into the side of the gate. We decided he would do the speaking as he was the oldest.

A pair of guards looked at him as he approached. "State your business."

"Tourists," Alfred replied, his face a mask of professionalism.

One of the guards accepted our IDs while the other stared at Ulli and said, "Those are some mighty attractive daughters you got there. Have you considered allowing them to court a guard? I assure you, I am quite well-endowed."

"Forget it, Gerard," the first guard said. "They are both tower maidens. Highly ranked at that."

"Well, that's a shame," the second guard said, sitting down. "All the pretty ones get claimed. It's just my luck."

I could tell Marcelle wanted to say something, but she bit her tongue. The first guard handed the IDs back to Alfred, and the gate creaked open. "It looks like everything is in order here. If you plan on staying for more than a day, you will need to check in at the visitor's office."

Alfred nodded and accepted our ID cards, handing them back to us. Once we were out of earshot, I asked, "Do guards hit on you like that often?"

Marcelle rolled her eyes. "Not really. Those two were just creeps. It also helps once they know who we are. Nobody messes with a tower maiden. While not guaranteed, harassing us can incur The Creator's wrath. It has happened in the past."

"So, Dad steps in from time to time, eh?" I thought out loud, wondering if Merlin had a magic prison somewhere for people who annoyed him.

Ulli poked Marcelle in the side. "I don't recall The Creator ever getting involved in events outside of the tower."

"It has happened!" Marcelle barked, catching herself when her voice drew attention from passersby.

The presence of futuristic technology like chariot shuttles and the flashing lights of businesses was all that kept Camelot from being the fantasy kingdom I'd read about in books. Old brick-and-mortar buildings lined the busy street that led up the hill to the castle. The roads were clogged with a mix of horse-drawn wagons and magically powered vehicles. People walked the sidewalks oblivious to the clashing of two worlds around them.

I pressed my face to the windows of several shops as we passed. Chain restaurants were sprinkled in between weapon and armor shops. One of the weapons shops caught my eye.

KING ARTHUR'S ANVIL
GET YOUR REPLICA EXCALIBUR HERE

I tugged on Marcelle's sleeve. "I want one."

Her eyebrow twitched. "Then, go buy one."

It dawned on me that I didn't have any local currency. Would gold work? I decided to find out and walked into the shop. A man wearing a blue Merlin robe and a fake beard stood behind a counter. "Can I help you today, sir?"

He was addressing Alfred, not me. Alfred pointed to me, and I said, "I'd like to see Excalibur, please."

He pointed at the glass case in front of him, where a shiny sword with runes etched in the blade was on display. Again, ignoring me, he turned to Alfred and said, "The blade costs ten thousand credits. You can take it today and pay installments if your credit rating is high enough."

"Don't look at me," Alfred said. "This is your customer."

The smile that had been plastered on the salesman's mouth suddenly vanished. "Do you have money, boy?"

I looked over at the others imploringly. Ulli looked away and Marcelle shrugged. "That's a lot of credits for a souvenir."

"If you're looking for cheap, you're in the wrong place," the man said. "The price is the price. Can you afford it? If not, I would be more than happy to show you our miniatures, though those aren't exactly cheap either."

"Do you take gold from other worlds?" I asked, patting my fanny pack.

The man shook his head, holding out a small device. "Sorry, kid. No trades."

I reached out and placed my hand on the device. A small burst of mana went out of me as my finger made contact with the smooth surface. The device made a satisfying *ding*, causing the man to look down in surprise. "Oh! Well, I guess that's that, then. Would you like me to wrap it for you?"

I watched in shock as he removed the blade from the case and set it on the counter. From there, I could read the writing etched into its surface.

Who so pulleth out this sword of this stone and anvil is rightwise king born of Albion.

"Albion?" I questioned. "Shouldn't that say Camelot."

The shopkeeper shook his head. "It wasn't always called Camelot. Before the days of Arthur, it was known as Albion. The true sword vanished centuries ago. Some say it was reclaimed by the Lady of the Lake. This here is as accurate of a copy as you'll ever see. It was created based on testimony provided by some of our most ancient Camelotian scholars."

"Ooh, I'd like to meet them," I said, excited to learn more about one of my favorite folktales. Or was it just world history on Origin?

"Fat chance of that happening," the shopkeeper replied. "They aren't part of the tour."

Rather than wrapping the blade, I forced it into my fanny back. Ulli gave me a curious look as we left the shop. "What are you going to do with that thing?"

"Well, it's pretty big," I explained. "I think I'm going to use it as the basis for my mana blade from now on. How cool would it be to have a mana Excalibur? A Manascalibur."

"I was surprised you could afford that," Marcelle said. "That was expensive, even for us."

"Do you make a lot?" I asked.

She shook her head. "Not really. It's just that we don't have any expenses in the tower so it's easy to save."

"How do I find out how much money I have?" I asked, becoming curious.

"You can check at a bank," Marcelle replied. "There's one over there."

First Bank of Camelot, where every account is the top priority.

I headed for the door, but Marcelle stopped me. "Just use the machine. It's quicker if you just want to check your balance."

I laughed when I saw what looked like an ATM. It had the same tiny screen and darkened window where a camera would go. Instead of a card reader, I discovered another one of the flat surfaces. I looked back at Marcelle. "What are these things anyway? How does it know who I was? Is it a magic fingerprint reader?"

She shook her head. "It's an aura scanner. It reads your mana. No two people have the same imprint, so it's an ideal way of identifying yourself. It's used everywhere on Origin."

I reached down to touch the aura scanner.

Welcome, Melvin Murphy

1. Withdrawal
2. Deposit
3. Transfer
4. Account Balance

I pressed the four that appeared on the screen.

Account Balance: Unlimited
Would you like to make another transaction? Y/N?

We all stared at my balance for a few seconds before Alfred let out a low whistle. "Well, you are The Creator's son, after all, Lord Melvin. It would only make sense that you'd be set financially."

"I guess that means he predicted I'd go out," I sighed, looking around at people in the area to see if they'd noticed Alfred call me The Creator's son. "Also, remember, I'm just Mel today."

Alfred stiffened. "Oh, right, sorry, sir...uh...Mel."

"No problem," I replied, hitting cancel on the ATM before leaving. We wandered through the busy streets, Ulli giving me a tour of the various cuisines offered by the chain restaurants. "This restaurant hails from a planet called Quackalot, where a race of duck men called the Pouldarians hail from. They eat a mostly vegetarian diet, but you can find some interesting dishes from their world at The Duckish Delight."

"I know a duck man!" I bellowed. "His name was, um...Howie! That's right, Howie McDuckenStein. He was my teacher. He's the one who taught me of Origin's existence actually."

Before anyone could answer, a commotion broke out at a nearby building. A man shouted at a young woman, who had fallen in the street clutching a thick blanket to her chest. "I've told you before! We don't treat filth. If you want help, go to the church."

"Please!" the girl begged. She had dirty blonde hair like me and a defiant look on her face that reminded me of Kalli. The girl continued, "You have to help him. He's going to bleed to death."

Before I knew it, I was sprinting over to the commotion with the rest of the group in hot pursuit. The man from the building, which I realized was a clinic, asked, "Who are you?"

[14]

"WHAT HAPPENED?" I asked, ignoring the man's question.

The girl looked up at me with a wild look in her eyes. "He fell. Please! He's going to die."

I gently peeled the blood-soaked blanket back to see a bone sticking out of the kid's leg. While I'd never done any bone setting, I instinctively knew to apply my mana directly to the wound. It permeated the boy's leg, giving me an instant picture of just how the two bones in his shin had broken and why it broke through the skin. I also knew I couldn't begin healing him without setting the bone first.

"This is going to hurt," I said, rubbing the kid's arm for comfort. He didn't reply as he whimpered with his eyes squeezed shut.

"If you can help him, hurry up and do it," the girl barked, shaking my arm for emphasis.

"Give me a second," I replied. "I've never done this before."

"You've never—" she began right when I made my move. Her voice was drowned out by the kid screaming in agony as my mana forced his bone back into his body. It snapped together, causing more damage to the soft tissue as it passed through.

I went to work on both the bone and the surrounding wounds. Somebody gasped as the external wound closed, leaving blood as the only outward proof he'd been injured. The bone was another matter. Not only did I need to mend the bone but parts of it had splintered off and needed to be eliminated. I knew there was bone marrow as well, but as I wasn't a medical professional, I had to trust the magic knew what it was doing.

I spent a few more minutes working on him and gave his whole body a fresh infusion of mana to make sure he wouldn't die on me. The girl shook him violently. "William? Stay awake! Oh."

She heaved a sigh of relief when he groaned and tried to roll over. The man from the clinic stared at me. "What did you just do?"

I stood, looking down at my bloody clothes. "The question is, who are you, and why didn't you help him yourself?"

The man huffed. "You should know we don't treat strays. They have to go to the church."

I looked at the girl. "Why didn't you take him to the church?"

She rolled her eyes at me and scooped up the kid. "You've obviously never been to the church. Thanks for your help. We will get out of your way now."

"What are you going to do about all this blood outside of my clinic?" the man barked after her as she slipped into an alley.

I spoke the words as I used the familiar spell manually.

"Pvruzth."

Nothing happened.

"Pvruzth."

I cursed inwardly at the parental block and altered my mana to fire manually. Flames shot out of my fingers and incinerated the blood like a power washer. The man stared at me and asked, "Who are you?"

"None of your business," I snapped, racing into the alley after the girl.

The others struggled to keep up while I looked around desperately. "Where did they go?"

There was nowhere a normal person could have gone other than crawling up the side of the wall to the roof. A flicker of movement caught my eye, and I looked at the ground. A pair of eyes stared at me through a mesh grate that was mostly obscured by debris.

The man from the clinic poked his head into the alley and shouted, "What are you guys doing back there? Don't make me call the guard."

I sighed and walked back toward the man, careful not to draw any attention to the grate. Casting an angry look at the man as we passed, I said, "We were just leaving."

———

I couldn't stop thinking about what I'd just seen as I stomped through town. We passed by many stores and attractions I normally would have geeked out over. "I can't believe that just happened."

"Yeah," Marcelle sighed. "That poor kid. The girl should have known where to take him. The church would have helped."

I skidded to a stop. "Would they?"

"Sure," Marcelle replied. "Just because they are F ranked doesn't mean they don't have resources. The church always keeps healers on staff specifically for situations like this."

"What I don't get is how a kid becomes F ranked," I muttered.

Marcelle shrugged. "They were born into it most likely. Kids don't want to be separated from their parents and refuse to rank up. It happens more than you'd think."

Looking at a group of people passing by, I leaned in close to Marcelle and whispered, "Is there a way of telling what rank people are?"

She frowned. "Generally, it's rude to ask someone what their rank is. It's only obvious in the lower ranks. Otherwise, you can really only tell by where a person lives or what they do for a living."

"Don't forget about surnames," Ulli supplied, holding up a finger.

"Right," Marcelle gave her an approving smile. "And surnames, though they could have been born into it like I was."

Scanning the houses in the distance, I asked, "Where would the D and F ranked people live?"

Marcelle looked around for a while until she spotted a series of large buildings in the distance. "There, and there. Standard apartment buildings that are out of the way. You can expect to find mostly D and

C ranked people living there. You will occasionally find an F, but they usually rise to D when they decide to take jobs. It's hard to afford a place to live without a job."

"Where do F ranks live?" I asked.

Marcelle sighed. "Wherever they can. It's different for every town. Sometimes, there is a designated shelter for them to stay. Other times, it's under a bridge."

"They live in a cave just outside of the gates," a passing woman said. "I saw what you did for that boy earlier. Thank you for that. There isn't enough kindness in the world."

Alfred waited until the woman was out of earshot to say, "I think we should take this conversation elsewhere. It's not exactly a discussion we should be having out in the open."

We stopped for a late lunch. Alfred guided us to one of the fancier restaurants in Camelot.

King Arthur's Steakhouse and Tentacles

I cringed as we made our way in the door, asking the waitress, "Can't you just call it surf and turf?"

She gave me a curious look. "Why would we call it that?"

I shrugged, and Alfred spoke to the waitress, "Do you have anything with a sound barrier?"

The waitress nodded. "We do, but it requires a deposit."

Alfred stopped aside when she produced a payment reader. I raised an eyebrow. "Why do I have to pay?"

He tutted at me and motioned to the reader. "I'm the help, right, Mr. Unlimited?"

We were led to a booth in the back after I paid the deposit to a booth surrounded by a translucent blue bubble. The ambient noise from the restaurant died the instant I pushed my way through. Ulli slid in next to me before either of the others had a chance, so Alfred and Marcelle took seats opposite us.

A waiter arrived quickly to take our order, poking his head inside the bubble to speak. I scanned the steaks on the list and quickly determined none of them came from cows. Alfred pointed to an item called Riftwalker Steak. "Try this one. It's delicious."

I nodded, and Alfred ordered one as well. To our surprise, Ulli decided to have one, too. Marcelle surprised nobody when she ordered a dish called Tentacular and requested it to be prepared extra spicy.

Once our food was ordered, we started the discussion. Marcelle looked me in the eye and asked, "What is the true purpose of this outing? You said you want to meet the people, but you seem fixated on the lower class. If it's not too much to ask, what exactly is your goal?"

I rested my head in my hands, still not ready to trust anyone with my mission to get back to Kalli. "I don't know. When I got here, I wanted to see the world and meet people. Then, I saw what we saw at the clinic, and I can't get it out of my head. Did you see they went underground from that alley?"

"I suspected as much," she replied. "We have something similar where I'm from. It's not uncommon for those people to find lost caves and structures to live in."

I sighed. "I want to see this for myself. You don't have to come with me. I'll teleport back if I get in trouble."

"When are you going to learn?" Marcelle asked. "You don't get to make that decision. If you go, I'm going."

"I want to go," Ulli added, bouncing up and down beside me. "It's kind of like an adventure seeing what you're gonna do next. I didn't know you could use healing magic."

I held up a hand in front of my face. "I learned with Kalli. It all started when she was sore after working out."

A lump formed in my throat. I had to get back to her. Alfred saved me from the awkward moment when he cleared his throat. "Driving for you is never boring. I'll come along as well."

Marcelle had to stop me from trying to shovel food down my throat so we could get out of there. Alfred chuckled and said, "You don't want to rush this. The Riftwalker is quite delicious when prepared properly."

"But can't we get this back at the tower?" I asked, dipping a slice of steak in a thick green paste. It was gamier than beef but melted in my mouth. The sauce had a tart flavor that enhanced the natural juices of the steak.

"Yes, you can," Marcelle replied. "Alfred is not permitted to use the kitchen on your level. I'm afraid the food he has access to in the tower is nowhere near as good as this restaurant."

"That sucks," I said. "You now have a standing invitation to join us for dinner every night."

Marcelle gave me a stern look. "You do realize that means you'll have to eat dinner every night now, right?"

"I can make the sacrifice," I replied, realizing there was a whole universe worth of food I had yet to try. "Alfred can tell me what's good."

"What's wrong with my suggestions?" Marcelle asked with a smirk. To emphasize her joke, she sucked a tentacle into her mouth with a loud smack.

———

We snuck into the alley beside the clinic. It was the only access point to the underground that I knew of. Fortunately, no eyes peeked up at me when we got to the grate. Reaching down, I grasped it in both hands. It didn't budge at first, so I was forced to infuse my body with mana. Using Merlin's advice, I went with the flame element for a burst of strength. To my surprise, the grate not only lifted but went flying into the air.

"Oops," I said as it landed on the roof of the clinic with a *clang*. "Let's go quickly before that doctor comes out to see what the noise was."

Alfred went first, and then I lowered the girls one at a time into the darkness. I went last, dropping several feet into running water. At least I hoped it was water. It didn't smell bad in any case.

"Which way?" Marcelle asked, looking both ways down a long, round tunnel.

While I still had the God Eye trait active, I was starting to wish I'd given myself God Ear as well. I could see perfectly well in either direction, but both paths turned, and I couldn't tell what lay beyond. As far as sound went, all I could hear was the running water beneath my feet.

"Let's go this way," I suggested, deciding to travel against the flow of water.

We trudged through the path for a while before the tunnel opened into a wider chamber. At the far side was a set of stairs leading up. At least it was dry up there. We made our way up the stairs and entered another long hall. About halfway down the hall, we heard it.

CLANK!

The door behind us slammed shut. Ahead of us, a group of men entered the hall. The one in the front wielded a crudely made spear. I summoned my mana blade.

[15]

"WAIT!" a familiar female voice echoed through the hall.

The man with the spear lowered it, looking back over his shoulder. "Not now! We have an intruder. Go back to your room."

"But he's just following me," the female replied urgently. "He's the one who saved Ollie."

Several of the men behind the man with the spear gasped and lowered their weapons. The man leveled his spear at my chest and took a couple of steps forward. Marcelle stepped in front of me protectively while Ulli clutched my arm, shaking uncontrollably.

"Is it true?" the man asked, ignoring Marcelle and staring at me. "Are you some sort of healer? That doesn't explain what you're doing down here."

"I wanted…" I began, changing my mind before amending, "I needed to see this place for myself."

"What for?" the man asked. While he still pointed the spear at me, he did stop moving. "Who sent you?"

I hesitated to reply. His question confused me. "I, um, well, nobody sent me. I just wanted to see where the F ranked people live. I never heard about them before today."

"Have you been living under a rock?" the man asked incredulously.

"I don't believe you. You're all going to have to come with me while we sort this out."

I placed a hand over Ulli's to comfort her and spoke with as much conviction as I could muster. "The one living under a rock is you. You can take me, but you'll have to let my friends go."

"No!" Marcelle whispered urgently. "I'm not leaving you alone down here."

"Keep Ulli safe," I croaked back.

"Everyone, shut up," the man with the spear said, taking another step toward me. "We aren't letting any of you go."

Feeling fire in my core, I felt like Kalli was with me. Flames of pure mana bled from every pore in my body, making it look like I was on fire. "I recently lost someone very close to me because I failed to kill people who threatened her. Listen carefully. If you don't want to die, never threaten my friends."

"Stop it!" the girl from the clinic screamed and shoved her way past the men. "This acting tough is going to get people killed. They obviously aren't here to do a purge. In what world would the police send children?"

"Hey!" I grumbled, offended at being called a child even though the girl was trying to help. "I'm of age."

"Do you want to fight the entire underground?" she asked, raising an eyebrow in a way that reminded me of Kalli. "Why did you follow me?"

I shrugged. "I couldn't believe people lived down here. I didn't realize it was off-limits."

"Do you mind waiting for just a few more minutes?" the girl asked. "My mom is in charge, and I'm sure she would like to meet you. She was checking on Ollie to make sure he is okay."

"That's the boy I healed, right?" I asked.

The eyebrow shot up again. "Why did you do that anyway?"

"Do I need a reason?" I asked with a shrug. "We were visiting because I, er, we wanted to see Camelot, and then I saw a dying kid. It seemed like the right thing to do."

"He's suspicious," the man with the spear said, turning his attention to the girl instead of us. "How can we trust someone who doesn't even know about us?"

She moved closer until she was within arm's reach, not appearing concerned about the mana blade in my hand. "It is curious, you know. First, you come to save one of us, and then you claim to not even know what we are. Either you're a major idiot, or you have some kind of savior complex. So, tell me, which is it?"

"I'm not from around here," I replied. "And I'd appreciate it if you didn't call me an idiot."

"Sorry, sorry," she said with a grin. "I'm just trying to figure you out."

"Get away from him, Mika," a woman said from behind the guards. "Can't you see he's armed?"

"Don't worry, Mom," Mika replied, flashing a lopsided grin over her shoulder. "I had a premonition."

The woman looked a lot like her daughter. She stood about a foot shorter than me and had blonde hair, tied back in a braid. She wore overalls that were already dirty before recently being caked in blood. The woman pulled Mika back before appraising us. "What do we have here?"

I felt Ulli pressing against my back, doing her best to hide. I felt her through the flaming mana that surrounded my body like an aura. She was still shaking but only slightly. I lowered my sword to the ground and snuffed out the flame. "Can we put the weapons away, please? You're scaring my friend."

Mika's mother looked over my shoulder and motioned to the man with the spear to back off. Reluctantly, he put the spear behind his back and motioned for his men to stand down. The woman approached and held out a hand. "My name is Viola. I run all things underground in Camelot. Government sanctioned."

"I'm, Melv…Mel," I stammered as I shook her hand, nearly forgetting my secret identity. "Mel Hellquist."

"And your reason for visiting our lovely resort?" Viola prodded me.

I replied. "I wanted to make sure the boy was okay. I believe Mika called him Ollie."

"This is the boy who saved him," Mika informed her mother.

"Really?" Viola asked, appraising me with newfound respect. "Are you a healer?"

"I am," I replied flatly.

"Would you be willing to do it again?" she asked.

A small laugh escaped my lips. "Did he already hurt himself again?"

Viola let out a small laugh. "No, not at all. I put him down for a nap. There are others among us who aren't well. Could I perhaps persuade you to do what you can for them? We don't have much down here, but we will do what we can to compensate you."

I glanced back at the others momentarily. "I need to get these guys to safety, but then I can—"

"No!" Ulli cried. She was still shaking, but she made a brave face and stepped out from behind me. "If you go, I go."

Marcelle said, "She's right. You aren't going anywhere without us."

Alfred nodded. Viola noticed the look on Ulli's face and took a tentative step toward the girl. "I am sorry about Brogus, honey. He should not have threatened you."

"Why does he have a spear?" Ulli asked defiantly.

"I ask myself that every day," Viola replied, rolling her eyes and earning a giggle from Ulli.

Mika walked over to Ulli and reached out, taking her hand. "Please, be my guest. I promise I won't let anyone hurt you. This is a peaceful place."

Even without the system, I knew there was something up with Viola. Mana emanated off her in waves. It was subtle, but my eyes could see it. It wasn't as controlled as Merlin or some of the ancient mages I'd met, but she was strong, likely high-level.

I took a step forward and said, "If you can guarantee the safety of my friends, I'll take a look at your sick. I can't make any promises, though. I've already had one person die when I tried to heal them."

Viola frowned. "Hm, well, maybe only heal the ones you can, and let me know if any are beyond your skillset."

"That's fine," I replied, trying to sound like I knew what I was doing. "The one I lost died the moment I went inside them."

"Went…inside…them?" Mika asked, a look of revulsion on her face. "Please, don't do that."

"Not literally inside them," I corrected, cringing at the thought of attempting surgery. "Ollie is the most I've ever done with a physical wound. Most of the people I helped were sick. Well, there were a few internal injuries I dealt with, but none of them broke the skin."

By then, we were following Viola through a series of halls. She looked back over her shoulder and asked, "What kind of healer are you, exactly? What is your class?"

I couldn't tell them I was a manipulator. Not that I was anymore with my system blocked by Dad. "I'm a cleric."

"A holy man?" Mika spat the words with a sneer on her face. "Are you from the church?"

"No," I replied, not sure if I was giving myself away.

"Mel is specialized," Marcelle supplied. "He heals with the touch of mana not faith."

"Do you mean like the Lay on Hands skill?" Viola asked. "I've never seen it before. Not that I'm much of a believer."

"It's true, though," Mika told her. "I watched him do it to Ollie. He touched his leg, and the bone went back inside."

Viola walked with purpose through what reminded me of sewers. There was no foul smell, though, so I assumed they must not have been in use for quite some time. The tunnel emerged into a large chamber that looked to have had a special purpose at some point in the past. It was filled with tents and crude dwellings built into the remnants of buildings.

While there were some nooks that could have led to private rooms, most of the people underground congregated in the main area. I estimated there must have been hundreds of people milling about.

Violet led us to a large tent in the back. Inside were rows of cots with people laid out on them. Many were coughing and wheezing. She looked expectantly at me and asked, "Can you do anything for them?"

"Sure," I replied, kneeling in front of the first cot.

———

Most of the people underground were just sick which was easy enough to cure. The only ones with any physical issues were the elderly who had arthritis and other issues that came with age. By the time I finished, I was sporting a one hundred percent success rate. I refrained from awakening anyone because I didn't want to draw attention to myself.

Viola let out an appreciative whistle and said, "I'm impressed. I don't even think the hospital could have done better. The church definitely couldn't."

"Is the church really that bad?" I asked.

"Have you ever been there?" she answered with a question. "I think some of them mean well but aren't staffed to handle many people and usually only admit severe cases. Often, they give us painkillers and tell us to go home to die quietly."

"That's horrible," Ulli spoke in a quiet voice. Mika had wanted to take her somewhere, but Marcelle refused, saying she wasn't to leave our sight.

"It really is," Mika confirmed. "That's why I took Ollie to the clinic. It was the only way to save him. Thank The Creator you showed up when you did."

"That was fortunate," Viola said, her arms crossed. "Now, would you care to tell me who you really are? I know enough to know you're not a cleric. However, I can't read you at all."

"I can't answer that question," I replied. "However, there is a question I'd like to ask you in private if possible."

[16]

"THERE IS no way that's going to happen," both Marcelle and the man with the spear protested at once.

"Seriously, it's a trap," the man with the spear continued. "This man is clearly dangerous, and you cannot be alone with him."

Alfred added, "I agree. Splitting up will do none of us any good. We should stick together."

Viola, who had been silent since I asked to speak in private, pointed to a door and said, "Come with me. This should be close enough for both of us to come back if there are any problems."

I gave Ulli a reassuring nod and said, "I'll be right back. Don't worry."

Marcelle shook her head but said nothing. After walking through the door, Viola shut it and said, "Nobody should overhear you if you speak quietly. I'll answer your questions to the best of my ability and would like you to do the same with mine."

"Thanks," I replied. "I'll try to answer your questions, too. Have you ever heard of anyone getting off Origin? Or anybody getting in from outside?"

"Getting out?" she echoed, sounding startled. "I'm not aware of anyone coming or going from this planet. If you're looking to travel, you probably want to try the tower."

"That's not really an option for me," I muttered, slightly dejected.

Viola offered a kind smile. "Are you from Origin, originally?"

"No," I replied. "Are the people who live down here rebels against the tower?"

"Heavens, no," she laughed. "Nothing of the sort. The people under my care don't exactly fit in. Where are you from, and how did you get here?"

"Earth," I said. "I teleported here. The problem is, I can't teleport back out. Do you know anyone who might know a way out?"

Viola paced for a bit while she thought. "The Creator is the obvious person to ask, though it is true he might not give you an audience. There are few people outside of the tower who might have that kind of knowledge. Most won't give you the time of day. There is one place though. I would pay a visit to Atlantis if I were you."

"Atlantis exists?" I asked, not grasping the significance of the fact that I was standing in a sewer under Camelot.

She laughed. "Why would I tell you to go to a place that doesn't exist? I assume you have some form of transportation. Otherwise, it will take you a month to walk there. Why did you come down here? Wouldn't it make better sense to ask over at the castle?"

"Something tells me leaving Origin isn't exactly legal," I replied.

"We aren't criminals," Viola snapped. "Everyone here are law-abiding citizens."

"What did you mean when you said people don't fit in down here?" I asked. "Is that why you are all F ranked?"

She laughed. "Not everyone is F ranked but, yes, people move down here because there is nowhere else for them. Sometimes, we do what we have to. Sometimes that is frowned upon."

"What about the church?" I asked. "How does that fit in?"

"The church accepts everyone," she explained. "Anyone who seeks assistance will find it at the church, whether it be lodging or health care. The problem is, they don't have unlimited resources. Often, people slip through the cracks."

"That's why Mika brought Ollie to the clinic," I said, piecing the events together.

Viola nodded. "Most likely. It was probably closer. The boy fell off a roof. I am going to have to have words with Mika about that when this is over. Thank you for saving him, and for healing the others. How do you have such powerful magic, by the way?"

"I'd rather not say," I answered truthfully.

She sighed. "Very well. Would dinner be an acceptable payment for your services?"

Always eager to try something new, I nodded. "Sure!"

———

The food wasn't great. I wanted to try everything while Marcelle, Ulli, and Alfred insisted they had just eaten. The plate I was served consisted of slightly charred meat with not enough seasoning, a dry potato, and green mush Viola insisted was nutritious.

"It's not as good as eating out," Mika insisted as she shoveled a spoonful of the green stuff into her mouth. "You get used to it, though."

"What is this meat from?" I asked, trying to place the gamey texture.

"You don't want to know," she replied, stifling a giggle by taking another bite.

"We should be getting back," Alfred said, looking at his watch.

Mika swallowed, giving me a curious glance. "Are you ever going to come back?"

"Did you want me to?" I asked, looking over her shoulder at the man with the spear who stood guard by the door.

"Sure," she said. "Next time, I'll give you a real tour of Camelot. There's a lot you don't see if you just explore downtown. I can show you where the real legends took place."

I grinned at her. "That sounds fun. I'll be back for sure."

"You know where to find me," she replied.

"Let's go," Ulli yipped, tugging at my sleeve.

———

Mika led us through the underground to a cave outside of the city walls, saying, "It's easier to leave this way. Otherwise, you have to wait in line while the guards examine everything you have on you."

"Thanks," I replied as she led us through foot deep steadily flowing water.

From there, it was a short hike to the small hill where we'd parked the chariot. Realizing it was getting late, I turned to Alfred and suggested, "I can teleport us all back to the tower if you'd like?"

He gave me a hopeful look. "What about the chariot?"

As funny as it would have been to drop a chariot outside of Merlin's throne room, I ultimately decided it would raise too much suspicion. "Can we send somebody back for it tomorrow?"

He shook his head. "Somebody would notice. If you command it, anything is allowed, but that will get back to your father."

"Good point," I replied. "I guess we're flying back, then."

"You can go back ahead of me," Alfred replied, climbing into the driver's seat. "I don't mind flying back alone."

I was about to turn him down when I noticed how worn out Ulli looked. "Thanks, Alfred. Do you mind taking me out again?"

He bowed his head slightly. "Off the books again, I take it?"

"That's right," I replied with a smile. "Thanks."

Moments later, the three of us appeared in the lobby outside of the throne room. I cast a glance at the pedestal where the ring prison once sat and asked, "Why are all of these artifacts on display out here?"

"The Creator displays these," she replied. "Each represents one of the great wizards and warlocks before the dawn of the system."

"What about this one?" I asked, pointing at the empty pedestal where the ring used to sit.

Marcelle frowned. "That was stolen. The tower was in quite an uproar immediately after until the culprit was caught."

"What happened to them?" I asked, hoping I didn't get anybody in trouble.

Ulli yawned while Marcelle replied, "The same thing that always happens when somebody breaks one of the rules. The suspects disappeared."

"There was more than one?" I asked.

Marcelle nodded. "Three to be exact. The Creator questioned a lot of people, and three were accused. I don't know more after that because it was dealt with."

"You mean they disappeared?" I asked.

Marcelle nodded, looking at the floor. "Let's return to your room."

Once we got there, Marcelle took a seat on her favorite couch. Ulli fidgeted and followed me around instead of going to the bed like I thought she would. I gave her a curious look. "Do you need to use the restroom?"

She gave me an urgent look and whispered, "Did you mean what you said today? Were you going to kill all those people if they tried to hurt us?"

I was taken aback. Was she scared of me? "I'm sorry. I didn't mean to frighten you."

"No!" she squealed, causing Marcelle to look up. "It's not that. I, um, I think that was so brave. You were protecting me. Thank you."

"Uh, no problem," I replied, feeling nervous all of a sudden. "I meant it. I won't let anybody hurt you."

"I don't think it would be so bad, you know," she hedged. "If you wanted to claim me, that is."

"C-c-c-claim?" I asked, looking desperately at Marcelle for translation.

Marcelle was less than amused by our interaction. She rolled her eyes and explained. "She's saying she wants you to bed her and make her yours."

"Marcy!" Ulli shrieked, burying her blushing face in her hands. "That's not what I meant. Well, not exactly. I'm just saying, I like—"

While she kept mumbling, I couldn't understand what she was saying through her hands. What I did notice, however, is that she was rubbing her knees together. "Are you sure you don't need to use the restroom?"

She stopped fidgeting, and Marcelle sighed. "We are trained to do things like that discreetly. She isn't allowed to use your toilet and is supposed to only go when you're asleep or distracted."

"Well, that's a dumb rule," I replied. "You can go whenever you need to, and feel free to use my restroom. There's no sense having to leave every time you need to go."

Ulli looked conflicted for a few seconds before the urgency got the better of her. She darted off into my restroom and closed the door. Marcelle's eyes followed me as I paced around the room. "Are you going to claim her?"

"I can't," I sighed. "The only girl I'll ever love is Kalli. I can't even think about that."

She sighed and spoke in a soft voice, "She's gone, Melvin. I can only imagine how that makes you feel. If you need someone to talk to, I'm here."

I refused to believe Kalli was gone, even if the whole universe told me so. Changing the subject, I said, "Order some beds and anything else you need to be more comfortable."

"It will be done," she replied.

———

I woke in my hammock to discover both Ulli and Marcelle were already awake. I stumbled into the restroom to freshen up and take a bath, and then we all went to the garden for my morning exercise.

I just finished the physical part of my training when Merlin showed up. "Good morning, son. Did you have a pleasant adventure yesterday?"

I glanced over at Marcelle, who shook her head. Merlin laughed and said, "Relax, boy. Nobody informed me. Did you think you could sneak out of the tower without my knowledge? I know you went to Camelot. Did you have a good time? Did you check out the round table? It matters not. You are free to explore Origin to your heart's content. Alfred will be available to you at your whim from now on."

"Tell me something, Dad," I said, changing the subject. "What is the purpose of the system?"

He gave me a hard stare as I shifted my core from light to fire. "I created the system to restore balance. When left unchecked, strong awakened can ascend to levels that threaten reality. The system restricts that growth, preventing any one person from becoming all-powerful. In exchange, every living being in the universe feeds mana to the system and gives it power."

"What about people alive before the system?" I asked, thinking of the ancients. "They aren't fully controlled by the system, are they? The same goes for artifacts."

Merlin gave me an approving nod. "That is true. There are some beings out there who are not a part of the system. We have come to an unspoken accord. They don't interfere with the system, and I allow them to exist. Artifacts are different. That is going to be your next lesson.

"An artifact is something that a wizard creates over a lifetime. It can be anything. A child's favorite blanket or a knight's first sword. Awakened spend a lifetime infusing an item with so much mana that it takes on a life of its own. Your next lesson is to choose an item you cherish and bond it with your mana. You will create an artifact of your very own. As my son, I expect to you do this within a month."

Without waiting for me to reply, he vanished.

[17]

I COULDN'T INSPECT the item I chose for my artifact. There were no menus with the parental controls in place. My search for the perfect item led to a source of comfort. Even though it didn't say what it was, I already knew. Kalliphae's First Wand. She'd gifted it to me the day I bought her an upgrade.

Originally little more than a stick, it soaked up mana as she used it to learn magic. The instant I connected to the wand, I felt Kalli for the first time since arriving on Origin. Her mana had a familiar feeling to it that reminded me every time of her cleansing flames.

I sat cross-legged on the floor in my room trying to push as much mana into the wand as possible. Kalli's mana embraced my offering and fused with it. While I couldn't be sure, it sure felt like it was growing.

Merlin sought me out the next day to make sure I was keeping up with my exercises and to check the progress of the wand. Holding it up to the light, he sighed. "At this rate, you'll have a functional artifact in about fifty years."

"How long does it take you to make one?" I asked in a defiant voice.

He rubbed his chin, possibly in an attempt to twirl a beard he'd long since shaved. "That all depends on the item. The more personal it is to you, the quicker it will accept your essence. Are you sure of this stick?"

"Yes!" I barked, causing Ulli to jump.

Merlin glanced at her and tutted, causing her to go rigid. Turning his attention back to me, he handed me back the wand. "If you're sure, how about you try different things."

"Like what?" I asked. "I'm already infusing it with as much mana as I can."

"Is that all you know how to do?" he asked with a smirk. "Did you already forget how to change your element?"

"Does that make a difference?" I asked, staring at the wand in my hands.

"Of course, it does," he replied. "With a bit of trial and error, you'll discover that every artifact has a distinct taste for mana. While you can force it to grow, you will find far better results by being in tune with the item you're trying to infuse."

As usual, Merlin left once the lesson was done. I stared at the wand for a long time.

How do I make your wand grow?

While I didn't expect her to answer, the idea hit me almost immediately. Flame. I had no doubt that Kalli fed countless amounts of fire through the wand. Shifting my core to an element that closely matched Kalli's ever-burning soul, I clutched the wand in both hands and fed it.

The wand hummed in my hands and devoured my mana. It was immediately apparent that Merlin was right. The subtle change increased the rate at which the wand accepted my mana tenfold.

Ulli came over and sat across from me while I worked. She gasped when the flame surged for a moment when I pushed too hard. "Is that hot?"

"No," I replied with a chuckle. "It just looks that way. Do you want to see a trick?"

"Sure," she replied, looking eager.

Remembering the first time Kalli "washed" me, I spread my hands out in front of the girl and released a wave of fire over her. Things immediately became awkward when I realized what I was doing. I'd never done it with anyone but Kalli, and the thought of touching another girl even with magic made me feel guilty.

Ulli let out a high-pitched scream as the fire ran through her hair. I stuck to her arms and legs and other not-private parts. Once she realized she wasn't in any danger, she started giggling profusely. "Oh, my gods, stop, stop. It tickles. Oh, no, not my feet, too!"

She propped herself up on her arms when I retracted the flames, breathing heavily. "Wow, that was intense."

"I cleaned you," I replied with a smile.

"But I wasn't dirty," she whined.

I laughed, remembering Kalli's explanation the first time she did it. "This fire can clean everything, even sweat and grime."

Ulli ran her fingers through her hair. "It does feel clean. Why wasn't the fire hot?"

"It is," I explained. "I only make it burn what I want. It's magic fire."

"Do me next," Marcelle said, plopping down next to Ulli. It was the first time I ever saw her excited about something.

"Are you sure?" I asked, feeling uneasy showing off Kalli's spell.

She closed her eyes and held her hands out, expecting me to do it. I heaved a defeated sigh and did the same thing to her. Ulli squealed in delight as Marcelle's hair lit up when my flame passed through it.

When I retracted my flame, Marcelle rubbed her wrist and said, "You avoided my body just like you did with Ulli. Is there a reason for that? Can you feel things through the flame?"

"Yes," I admitted quietly. "The flame becomes an extension of me. That's why it doesn't hurt you. I control what it consumes. I can make it clean the sweat off your arm while leaving the hair alone."

"That's interesting," she said. "Do you use that spell in battle?"

"Kalli used it all the time," I chuckled, feeling sad saying it in the past tense. "She was a master of fire. A true pyromancer."

"She sounds like an incredible person," Marcelle said.

I nodded, wiping away a tear from my eye. The girls pretended not to notice. "If you like, I can awaken you further than you already are."

"What do you mean?" Marcelle asked.

"I can connect your core to your mana channels," I explained. "It will enable you to do things like I just did."

"Do it!" Ulli shouted, surprising both of us. She cleared her throat. "I mean, I'd like to try it."

Marcelle sighed. "By all means, age before beauty."

Ulli stuck out her tongue at Marcelle and took my hand in hers. "What do I have to do?"

"Nothing," I explained. "Just relax, and I'll do everything."

She smiled and closed her eyes. Taking a deep breath to calm myself, I pushed my mana into her. It was the first time since we cleansed ourselves of corruption. However, I was confident I had no afflictions as I couldn't sense any foreign emotions in my mana. As expected, Ulli's mana channels were completely closed off. I pried them open with my mana as I made my way to her core.

Ulli's oblong core shed sparkles as it twirled and dissipated in the darkness. I reached out to touch it with my mana. The instant I made contact, the core pulsed, and mana flooded out, following the path I'd laid out through her passages. I found myself spinning as I flew back-ward across the room, expelled by her core.

I opened my eyes to find myself cradled in someone's arms. "Are you okay?"

I groaned. "Kalli?"

She stroked my face. "No, sorry. It's me, Marcy."

"Oh," I replied, quickly sitting up. "Sorry, I must have blacked out for a second."

Marcelle smiled. "You crashed into the wall headfirst."

"That explains it," I replied, probing myself with my mana.

I felt the damage and soothed it with mana. Heaving a sigh of relief, I pushed myself to my feet and walked back to the newly awak-ened Ulli. "How do you feel?"

She was on her feet, ruffling her dress. "I feel weightless. I don't know how else to describe it."

Ulli rose on one foot, then one toe as she spun in place. Her other leg swung around, propelling her faster and faster as she twirled. Then, she skipped from one foot to the next before ending with a double flip and landing in a perfect bow.

We clapped while she smiled and blew kisses. Marcelle took my hand and led me over to a bench. "Now, it's my turn."

Marcelle's mana channels were similar to Ulli's. Her core, however, was a different story. When I first saw it, I thought it was damaged. Her glowing ruby core looked cracked. Perfectly symmetrical lines segmented her core into even-sized pieces. On closer inspection, I realized she had somehow compartmentalized her core.

Bracing myself for another concussion, I gingerly connected my mana to her core. To my surprise, her mana flowed out in a measured capacity and filled her channels. I rode it like a wave until I reached her extremities and allowed myself to be gently expelled from her body.

Looking up, I saw Merlin looking down at me with a stern look. He waited patiently for Marcelle to come out of it before saying, "Would you mind giving us a moment? I need to have a word with my son."

"Yes, my Lord," they both stammered before speed-walking out of the room.

"That's taboo," he chastised me as I stood up, dusting myself off. "Do you know what you're doing?"

"Helping them?" I suggested nervously.

He sighed motioning for me to sit. "You shouldn't experiment with the human body. Any time you make alterations, you run the risk of causing damage."

"I wasn't altering anything," I replied. "All I did was connect their mana to—"

He cut me off. "It doesn't matter what your intentions are. Let me tell you a story. There was a man, another manipulator, who decided he wanted to create exotic humans. He experimented with different animals like fish, birds, and snakes. While the results have been romanticized over the years, mermaids, gorgons, and harpies are abominations. Due to their human origin, they bred with humans and infested most of Europe. In the end, it took the Dark Ages to eradicate them all."

"Did you cause the Dark Ages?" I asked, slightly appalled.

"Not exactly," he replied with a chuckle. "The Dark Ages are what became of the world when the abominations began preying on the humans. The plague was a mercy compared to where the world was heading. While most records of that time were lost, the myth persists."

"I don't think what I did is the same," I said, trying to convince Merlin. "I didn't modify anything. Think of it like jump-starting a battery."

He sighed. "Look, I understand what you did. I've done it myself in the past. Just do me a favor and don't do that to anyone else in the tower. There's a reason most people's cores aren't connected."

"Why is that?" I asked, but he was already gone.

———

Meanwhile, in a strange, dark place...

Kalli rubbed the sleep from her eyes. Her dream once again had been uneventful and fruitless. She pined for Melvin. The last thing she remembered was clinging desperately to Rasputin's neck to give Melvin a fighting chance when something grabbed her. The next thing she knew, she was on a planet of perpetual night.

Rising to her feet, she slowly made her way to the privy. As she sat, she ran her finger over the toilet paper on the rack next to her. It brought back memories of her first day on the strange planet she had come to know as Scrap. After doing her business, she aimed her hands at her extremities and uttered her favorite spell.

"Pvruzth."

Nothing happened.

"Pvruzth."

"Pvruzth."

"Pvruzth."

Nothing! She started to panic. It had been years since she'd used anything but her fire to clean herself. That was when the locals showed her how to use toilet paper. After finishing her morning routine, she stretched and made her way out of her room.

"Good morning, Kalli," a young five-year-old girl greeted her as she emerged. "Are you hungry?"

"Good morning, Maribelle," Kalli said with a laugh. "You only ask me that when you're hungry. Where are your mommy and daddy this morning."

"They had to work," Maribelle explained. "Can we have ice cream?"

Kalli snorted. "Ice cream? It's a little early for that. How about a compromise? Let's have cereal with lots of stormberries."

"Stormberries!" Maribelle chanted. "I love stormberries."

"Me, too," Kalli admitted.

Kalli opened the pantry door, searching for the cereal. Maribelle sat at the table, waiting patiently. Kalli's mind was already thinking ahead to the rest of her day. She needed to train. More importantly. She needed to find a way to communicate with Melvin. If he was still alive, that was.

[18]

MERLIN INADVERTENTLY GAVE me something to think about. Why was he terrified of connecting people's mana channels to their cores? Why was it taboo? It didn't matter. Ulli and Marcelle were done, and I wasn't in a hurry to connect anyone else in the tower.

We made our way to the hangar early in the morning. Marcelle carried a plate of food for Alfred. We found him waiting next to his chariot when we arrived. He bowed when he saw me. "Good morning, Melvin. Where are we headed today?"

"Atlantis," I replied, taking a seat in the back.

"Excellent choice, sir," Alfred said, holding open the other door for the girls. "Will you be adding a trident replica to your weapon collection?"

"I think I will," I replied with a chuckle.

I spent the journey teaching the girls how to push mana around their bodies while focusing my own on Kalli's wand. While the fire element sped things up, it wasn't enough. The first thing I tried was more than one element. That took some getting used to. Many of the elements didn't want to play nice together. Fire wanted to melt ice, and water wanted to douse fire. Eventually, I discovered that certain elements paired well together while others opposed one another.

In the absence of a handy chart to explain everything, I experimented and discovered wind worked as an excellent accelerant for fire. The discovery took the form of a massive explosion that burst from the wand and penetrated the blue force field that surrounded the chariot. The wind whipped through my hair as emergency klaxons went off, and the chariot spiraled toward the ground far below.

"Hang on back there," Alfred screamed over the roaring wind as he did his best to stabilize the craft. "We're going to crash."

Deciding awkwardness was preferable to death, I wrapped mana around the chariot, and we smashed into the lobby outside of the throne room sending several artifacts to the floor. There was a commotion on the other side of the door, and heavy footsteps echoed through the air as someone approached.

The doors swept open, and Merlin stood there, looking at us in annoyance as we tried to clear ourselves of the flaming vehicle. Before I could try to explain, the chariot vanished, and the artifacts flew back to their pedestals.

"Explain yourself," he demanded, staring at me.

"Fire and wind," I replied, holding up the still-glowing wand.

"I see," he replied turning to leave. He waved his hand once over his shoulder, and we found ourselves back in my room.

———

"I don't think it's normal," Alfred said. He was still dressed in his suit even though he hadn't been able to chauffeur me anywhere in the week since the accident. "Normally, a replacement chariot it assigned to me right away."

"Yeah, you're definitely being punished," Ulli giggled.

Marcelle grunted as she struggled to keep up with me doing push-ups. "You, ugh, did, mmm, crash, ahh, the safest transportation on Origin."

With her mana awakened, she decided to train control alongside me and follow my exercise regimen. Ulli did the same, but she preferred to get her workout by dancing. Personally, I was happy she trained that way. Her dances were mesmerizing.

One thing I learned about Kalli's wand was that while it loved fire, it hated wind. The explosion in the chariot was the result of the wand amplifying and expelling the unwanted mana without absorbing any of it. After a little trial and error, it was apparent that, much like Kalli, the wand only preferred fire. I sat staring at the wand when I should have been training my core by transitioning between the elements. There had to be a quicker way to make an artifact. Something was missing.

I went over the elements in my head again. First, there was light and void. While, technically, I didn't have an element, my body seemed to default to light. Alariel was a void night, though I knew little about the element. The wand rejected it outright when I tried to infuse it with the dark element.

Kalli's sister had an affinity with ice, but this wand didn't care for it one bit. Water and wind were also a no-go. I was hopeful when I tried a wood element, thinking the fact that the wand was made of wood would somehow make it grow faster. While leaves did sprout from the wand, they quickly withered and fell to the ground. The wand rejected the mana. I tried the other elements even though there was little chance of them working. I made a chart to document my findings.

Fire: Works
Wind: Bad Idea
Wood (Nature?): Makes leaves?
Light: Works slowly
Void: Rejected
Ice: Rejected
Water: Rejected
Lightning: Rejected
Earth: Rejected
Metal: Rejected

Ulli sat next to me and watched me write. I handed her the paper and asked, "Am I missing anything?"

She shrugged. "I'm sorry. As a dancer, I don't think I have an element. If you want, I can try dancing with it. I'm pretty passionate about dancing. Maybe something will rub off."

"Passion!" I exclaimed, jumping to my feet.

Ulli flinched away from me and squealed. "What? Now? What?"

She looked confused, so I explained. "That is a great idea. I need to infuse it with passion. Well, maybe not passion but emotion for sure. I need to think of something Kalli and I shared."

I closed my eyes and focused on the wand trying to remember the emotions Kalli went through when she purged herself. The conviction in her soul burned in mine when I remembered her fiery defiance of her lot in life. I tried to funnel that into the wand but, once again, I was rejected.

Flames went everywhere as the wand spat the mana back at me. I felt as though it was telling me to try again. Images of Kalli flashed through my mind, and I went through a gamut of emotions. I felt fear for her safety, anger that she was taken from me, and pride in virtually everything she accomplished. There was one emotion at the heart of it all. I was truly, deeply, and hopelessly in love with her. That was the true feeling we shared.

At the risk of making a very sappy love wand, I armed my mana with the power of love and combined it with Kalli's fire. The wand devoured my offering, going so far as to pull it from me until I thought I was going to pass out. The experience reminded me of the first time I summoned Kalli. The ritual drained me to the point where I puked my brains out before passing out.

The tugging sensation stopped while I was lost in thought. I looked down at the wand and found it glowing with an intense aura of flame around it. The wood felt warm in my hand, and I knew I'd pulled it off.

"Are you okay?" Marcelle asked, kneeling in front of me to look at the wand. "You're covered in sweat, and you seem to be out of breath."

I'd been so caught up in what I was doing, I hadn't even realized. It took me a few minutes to calm down enough to catch my breath. Mana was no help because I was completely spent. All the mana I generated desperately struggled to refill my depleted core.

"Why is it glowing?" Ulli asked, reaching out to touch it.

"I wouldn't do that," Merlin's voice said from behind us, causing Ulli to jump off the bench and Marcelle to stiffen. "Some artifacts don't like to be handled by strangers."

"I think I did it," I said in a quiet voice as he walked around me to look at my handiwork. Ulli and Marcelle made themselves scarce while Merlin's attention was on me.

He waved his hand over the wand, causing the flame to flicker. "Do you mind if I hold it?"

"Won't it hurt you?" I asked, remembering what he just said.

He laughed, taking the wand from my hands. "An unruly artifact is no match for me. A curse, now, that can be dangerous. I haven't taught you how to do that, so we're safe."

The wand flared as Merlin held it out in front of him. I saw his mana emerge and push against the flame, having a small battle before retracting into himself. He handed the wand back to me. "You've done a good job. While I expected you to be successful, I didn't think you would do it quite this fast.

"Be warned, though, you succeeded because of the affinity you have with that wand. Affinity for an artifact is much more important than the quality of mana you infuse it with. This would not have been possible with any other combination."

"Thanks for the lesson," I said, putting the wand back in my bag. "Is it a fully grown artifact now?"

Merlin replied. "The answer to that specific question is no. An artifact never stops growing. If you use it for ten thousand years, it will continue to evolve and grow more powerful than it is now. That's why items in the system are assigned levels.

"Similar to your training, they grow through use. Even non-artifacts gain essence when mana users handle them. The silverware you eat with absorbs mana from your consumption. The clothes on your back pick up mana as you go about your day. It's usually a negligible amount but, if you focus, anything can become an artifact. It just takes time."

"Speaking of time, how long until I can have another chariot?" I asked, eager to continue my exploration.

"Soon," Merlin answered, sitting beside me. "How about I correct a flaw in your training in the meantime."

"A flaw?" I asked. "What am I doing wrong?"

"What aren't you doing wrong?" He chuckled. "Let's focus on a big one, though. Who taught you how to teleport?"

I thought back to the first time I'd teleported. It had been with The Man in Red, Nestor Bellview. It happened several times after that but, in the end, he taught me how to do it by showing me and telling me what he knew. I smiled at the memory and said, "The Man in Red taught me."

"He didn't do you any favors," Merlin sighed, taking my hand. "Just because you can step into the void doesn't mean you should. What you have been doing is the equivalent of running with your eyes closed. I know that is how a lot of people choose to do it, but that doesn't make it correct. You are so blind, you don't see the road despite treading on it."

"What do you mean?" I asked.

"Hold your breath," he replied, taking my hand.

I did as instructed and felt the familiar tug at my chest associated with teleportation. However, the feeling didn't go away. Merlin's voice echoed in the distance, "Open your eyes."

He sounded like he was far away, but he was still holding my hand. We weren't in the garden anymore. In fact, we weren't on Origin. I exhaled loudly as I realized we were floating in the void. I panicked for a moment when I thought I was going to suffocate but quickly discovered I could breathe.

Merlin saw my surprise and explained, "We are special, son. While you may find breathing a habit, you don't need to. The mana in your body will sustain you. This is the void. It is everywhere and nowhere at the same time. It exists between worlds and within them. It is outer space and inner space.

"You pass through this place every time you teleport. Dreams occur in the void. That is how you were able to visit me the first time. You passed through your dream and broke the barrier that blocks this world from reality. Only my true heir could have pulled that off."

"You said I do it wrong," I reminded him, staring in awe at the beauty of the void. Shimmering stars twinkled in the distance as a backdrop to well-formed planets that rotated around me. "Can you teach me how to do it correctly?"

He smiled, tugging my hand toward one of the planets. It enlarged as we approached. The planet in the void was too small to be real. About the size of a two-story house, I had no problem taking it all in as we floated nearer. The closer we got, the more detail I managed to make out on the planet. Merlin pointed to a tall tower. "As I am sure you've already surmised, this is Origin. The tower here is where we are now. These clusters of buildings are the various cities spread out across the planet."

"How do I use it?" I asked, my heart racing at the prospect of teleporting again.

"It's simple," he replied. "Focus."

He pointed to a castle on a hill a short distance from the tower, and the planet grew in front of us. Actually, we were shrinking. I forgot to close my eyes, and the void vanished, replaced by a crowd of startled people. They immediately recognized Merlin and fell to their knees. Merlin ignored them and turned to me. "Do you feel confident enough to take us back to the tower?"

"I can try," I said, still not sure how he did what he did.

Merlin frowned. "Do or do not, there is no try."

I groaned. 'Of course, you've watched *Star Wars*."

He waved me off. "Just do it already."

I sucked in a deep breath and folded mana around us. Suddenly, we were back in the void. Merlin waited patiently as I fumbled my way back to Origin, and then to the tower. We appeared on the ground floor, just inside the entrance doors.

He shrugged. "Close enough. One more thing you should know is that time does not pass in the void. You can spend hours deciding where to teleport only to appear instantaneously to those in reality. You have my permission to practice whenever you see fit. I'm giving you free rein of the planet. You can take your attendants with you if you so choose.

"However, I must warn you, you are not yet strong enough to pass through the barrier surrounding this planet. While the exertion of trying will not kill you, it will hurt. Your friends will not survive if they are with you when you try."

"Still stuck on this planet, check," I replied, sagging slightly.

"It's not as bad as you make it out to be," Merlin replied. "Many would kill to be trained by me. In fact, many *have*."

"But…" I started to reply before realizing he was already gone. I hated when he did that.

[19]

FREEDOM! That's what I had. Well, sort of. While Dad gave me the freedom to teleport anywhere on Origin, he warned me of excruciating pain if I tried to go off-world. It didn't help that I could see the other planets every time I set foot in the void.

The void itself was interesting when I took the time to look around. It felt kind of like a world map in a video game. The kind that let you travel from one town to another quickly. Perhaps that's where programmers got the idea for it. When I zoomed in on Camelot, I saw tiny people milling about in the streets.

The first thing I did with my newfound ability was to return to Camelot. I pretended I was going to take a bath and donned my illusion before teleporting from the privacy of the restroom, where I was sure I wouldn't be disturbed back to the street with the clinic.

———

"You again!" the man with the spear bellowed as I approached him in the underground.

"Hi there, spear dude!" I greeted him. "I'm here to see Mika."

He brandished his spear. "What for? There is no way I'm letting you—"

"Hi Mel," Mika greeted me, entering the hall. "Jasper, I can hear you from clear over at the dining tent."

"Er, I, uh," he stammered, lowering the spear. "This man is an intruder!"

"Thanks for calling her for me," I said, patting Jasper on the shoulder as I walked past.

Mika giggled. "What brings you here this time?"

"You promised me a tour," I replied. "I came to collect."

"Oh," she said, turning pink. "I didn't expect you to take me up on that. Give me a few minutes to get ready."

I found myself parked on a bench in the large chamber when a familiar-looking kid ran up to me. "Hey, mister. I'm supposed to thank you for saving my life."

"Are you going to?" I asked with a smirk.

He frowned. "Am I going to what?"

I laughed. "Are you going to thank me?"

"I just did," he replied before running off.

Mika watched him go as she returned. She'd changed into a soft green dress with flowers running up one side. "Ah, I see you've met Ollie. He wasn't rude, was he?"

"Nah," I replied. "He was fine."

———

"Um, are you sure you want to do this?" Mika asked, seeming less sure of herself now that she was actually giving the tour.

"Yep," I replied. "You promised to show me things most people don't get to see. Show me what Camelot is really like."

She groaned. "Okay, but just remember, I didn't say you were going to like it."

We walked in silence past the clinic once we emerged from the underground. Mika guided me down a series of side streets until we were close to the large apartment buildings I'd seen in the distance on my first visit. Just when I thought we were going inside, she steered me to a food cart nestled up against the side of the building. Mika introduced the stubby man behind the cart with a flair of theatrics. "This is Ruben. He makes the best food in all of Camelot."

I stared through the glass window on top of the cart. Purple lumps rotated around a heat source dripping a yellow sauce that had a sweet smell emanating off them. Mika ordered two and reached into her purse for a couple silver coins. They reminded me of the currency I was familiar with from both Earth and Gaia. I reached into my bag and took out a gold, asking, "Can I see one of your coins please?"

She licked her lips when she saw the gold coin. "Maybe I should have let you pay."

She reached into her purse and took out another silver coin. I chuckled when I took it in my hand and saw Merlin looking up at me with that serious expression he always had on his face. Flipping it over, I was surprised at the face on the back. "Mom?"

Mika gaped at me but said nothing. While the image on the back of the coin made her look medieval, it was definitely my mother. Mika ignored me as she was busy examining the gold coin in my other hand. "That's not The Creator. Forgeries are illegal, you know."

"It's real," I replied. "It's just not from this world."

"Then, where is it from?" she asked, picking up the coin and turning it over.

"Earth," I replied.

Mika gaped at me. "But that's impossible. Offworlders can't come to Origin. At least not without The Creator's permission. You don't have his permission, do you?"

I looked nervously at the food vendor who'd taken an acute interest in our conversation. Deciding I couldn't answer Mika out loud, I tried to invite her to a group.

Group access has been blocked by Parental Controls.

Silently cursing my father, I whispered in Mika's ear. "Is there somewhere we can go to be alone?"

She blushed, so I amended, "Not like that."

———

We squeezed into a stairwell built into the side of the apartment building. Mika held the dumplings protectively as she closed the door. "If you try anything, you aren't getting any of these. Now, spill. You're keeping a secret, and I want to know what it is."

I took a deep breath and said, "I'm not from Origin."

"Thank you Captain Obvious," she hissed. "You pretty much admitted that already. Now, tell me why you're here or what you want with me."

"I need to get off the planet," I admitted. "There's someone I need to get back to."

She frowned. "Then, why did you come here in the first place?"

"Well," I replied sheepishly. "I didn't come here on purpose. It was a teleport malfunction."

"A teleport malfunction?" she echoed. "How does that happen? Are you telling me you can teleport?"

"Do you want me to show you?" I asked.

She raised an eyebrow. "How do you plan on doing that?"

"Hold your breath," I said, reaching out to take her hand.

She held the dumpling away from me. "Why? Are you going to fart — Argh?"

I didn't give her a chance to opt out and wrapped mana around both of us the instant my hand touched her arm. Back in the void, I turned to find Mika frozen beside me. My voice had a metallic echo when I spoke, "Peculiar."

Deciding prolonged exposure to the void might be detrimental to anyone but an M, I quickly approached Origin and searched for Atlantis. I looked around at the various cities and picked one by an ocean. When we appeared on a pier, Mika fell to her knees and started retching. The dumplings flew a few feet away from her as she deposited the contents of her breakfast on the floor.

After composing herself, she glared at me. "What did you do? Where are we?"

"I don't know," I admitted. "I wanted to visit Atlantis, so I picked a city next to the ocean."

"The ocean?" she cried. "There is no ocean near Camelot. How did you do this?"

"Teleportation," I repeated the word.

She screamed frantically. "Take me back!"

"Fine," I said, bending over to collect the dumplings. "Five-second rule?"

"Ew!" She gagged, scrunching up her face in disgust. "I'll buy you another one. Just take me back."

She held her breath for the second trip. Since I couldn't figure out how to teleport into a building, I deposited us behind the large apartment building. Mika stumbled away from me when we arrived and glared at me. "Who are you? First, you heal Ollie like it was nothing. Then, you show up underground like it's a thing people actually do. Now, you can travel instantly all the way across the country. I thought only The Creator did that."

I sighed. "Can you keep a secret?"

Mika laughed. "Other than the fact that you're not from here and that you can teleport? Sure, what else could you possibly be hiding."

"The Creator is my dad," I replied.

Mika's mouth fell open, and she made incoherent noises for a few seconds. I waited quietly for her to compose herself. When she did, she asked more questions, "Why me? You can command literally anybody on the planet. There's nothing I can give you that you can't just take."

"I need someone who can help me without telling Merlin," I replied. She gasped when I said the name, so I hurried on. "My goal is to get off this planet, and your mom thinks someone in Atlantis can help me."

"Why can't you tell The Creator?" she asked.

I sighed. "I'm sort of grounded."

"Did you do something bad?" she asked, raising an eyebrow in an accusing manner.

"No!" I replied a little louder than I intended. "I mean, all I did was accidentally teleport here when I was trying to get to my girlfriend. She's in trouble, and she needs me."

It was easier saying she was in trouble than admitting Kalli might be dead. There was no way I could say that. Mika sighed. "Fine! I promise to keep your secret. What do you need help with?"

"I need to know who to talk to in Atlantis," I replied. "Can you talk to your mom and get more information for me? Was that Atlantis that we just teleported to?"

She shook her head. "I doubt it. They say the real Atlantis is underwater. Why can't you ask my mom yourself?"

I shrugged. "You offered to give me a tour. Also, you remind me of Kalli."

"Do I?" she asked, smiling a bit. "What part of me reminds you of her?"

I looked her up and down, not sure what it was specifically. A smile found its way to my face when it dawned on me. "You have her fire. Kalli always had this way of looking out for people."

Her smile widened. "Thanks."

We walked back to the food vendor to get some more dumplings. As we walked, she asked, "Do you have any of this world's money? As I'm sure you've figured out by now, I'm not rich."

"What is a credit?" I asked, remembering my bank account.

She dug into her pouch and pulled out a copper coin. "This is a credit. A silver is worth one hundred credits, and a gold is worth ten thousand. I've never seen one, but if you get a platinum, that's worth one million credits. They usually refer to them as credits at the bank."

"Interesting," I replied. "In that case, I have money, but I need to stop by a bank. Unless the vendor takes my mark, that is."

Mika laughed. "Fat chance of that. Street vendors are strictly cash only. Come with me. If you don't mind paying a fee, there's a machine close by where you can get cash."

———

She stared at the screen incredulously when we got to the ATM. "Unlimited? You really are The Creator's Son. Can I have some money?"

"Sure," I replied. "How much do you want?"

"A platinum!" she demanded.

Mika tried desperately to take it back when I entered the amount into the machine. I half-expected a platinum to pop out. Instead, the ATM started shooting out gold coins. Mika grabbed a bag and held it under the slot while I scooped up the ones that fell on the floor.

"I didn't mean for you to actually do it!" she barked.

I laughed, dumping a handful of coins in the bag. "Here you go. Payment for your services. Oh, and you're buying lunch by the way."

She laughed, sealing up the bag. "I need to go home after this. This is way too much money to be walking around with."

Mika paid with another silver when we returned to the vendor. Once we were out of earshot, she whispered, "He would totally be suspicious if I gave him a gold. Also, he probably wouldn't have change."

We ate lunch as I walked her home. I agreed to meet her again soon and teleported home.

[20]

"FATHER, WE NEED TO TALK," I announced, marching up to the throne where Merlin sat looking bored.

"Always with the theatrics," he announced with a yawn. "What is it this time? Do you want me to name a city after you?"

"No!" I balked. "What's your deal with Mom?"

He stared at me. "Well, now. When two people love each other very much, they do this special hug and—"

He stopped talking when I flipped him a silver coin. "I know how babies are made. What I want to know is why my mom's face is on this coin. And why does she look like she's dressing up to go to a ren faire?"

Merlin ran his finger over Mom's image. "This isn't your mother, son. Not exactly. Come take a seat. There is a story I've been meaning to tell you."

"I'm not sitting on your knee," I said when I saw there were no chairs.

Merlin chuckled, waving his hand. A chair materialized in front of me. He began his story as I sat, "My bond with your mother is special. It began nearly five thousand years ago. Your mother was my first love. When I met her, she was known as Vivien. She was as beautiful and pure as the mother you know. I was instantly smitten with her and knew she was the one I wanted to spend all of eternity with."

"Then, why do you have a tower full of women?" I asked, looking toward the alcoves where hundreds of women watched us with rapt attention.

Merlin flashed a look of annoyance when he noticed and spoke in a loud voice, "Begone."

At first, I thought he meant me, but then everyone in the alcoves exited the chamber in a rush of commotion. It turned out there were doors behind each of the alcoves. I wondered if the alcoves were actually patios connected to living quarters for the women most important to Merlin. Once he was satisfied we were alone, he turned his attention back to me. "Now, we can speak privately. I need you to know that no woman other than your mother means anything to me. I have fathered no children since you were born. Your mother is the only woman I love."

"Then, why...?" I asked, trailing off when I couldn't figure out exactly what I wanted to ask.

"Why do I have all these women here?" he asked, laughing. "Well, to explain that I need to tell you a story. Vivien and I had a love for the ages. I was enchanted with her from the moment we met. There was only one problem. I am immortal. And your mother, well, she was not. Even though I tried everything in my power to convince her, she refused to accept my gift."

"Yeah," I muttered. "She wouldn't let me awaken her either."

A tired smile appeared on his face. "I tried that many times and each time she rebuffed me. While she loved me every time, she refused anything to do with the world of magic. My world. She told me if she was meant to be awakened, she would have been born that way."

"That sure sounds like her," I lamented, chuckling at the fact that my mom was still the same even in previous lives. "That still doesn't explain why you left Mom alone to raise me while you live here with the biggest harem of all time."

Merlin laughed. "I haven't been with a single woman since I found her again."

"Then, why did you leave her?" I asked, not understanding.

Merlin seemed to age in front of me as he considered his answer. "Every time she respawns, it's the same. Sometimes, we bear children, others, we do not. In the end, she always dies. I can't bear to be there when it happens."

"So, you left her to live in poverty and raise me alone?" I replied in an accusatory tone.

Merlin groaned. "That isn't true. I offered her every luxury in life, and she turned down every single one of them. You should have wanted for nothing growing up, but she refused to let me spoil you. She says you are the only gift she ever wanted from me. Then, when you went off to Gaia, she disappeared. I don't even know where she went."

Where would Mom go? Even I had no clue. I turned my thoughts back to the tower and the situation on Origin. "I still don't understand why you keep all these women around. If you only love Mom, why not just wait for her to be reincarnated again? Better yet, why don't you spend as much time as you can with her? I would have loved to have a dad."

"I did just that for many generations," he replied. "And every time she was reborn as an unawakened. After a while, I started to wonder how I might increase the odds of her being awakened. In the end, I decided to produce heirs that will increase the chance of her being born with a magical affinity."

"But then you would be related to her," I said, trying not to look as weirded out as I felt.

He chuckled, picking up a grape from the bowl beside his chair. "When you are as old as I am, everyone is related to you."

"Only when you have as many children as you do," I replied.

"Besides," he added, quickly moving on, "there are always a couple centuries between occurrences. I'm not sure why. Perhaps her soul needs time to recharge, or maybe she comes back as an animal. There is even a chance that I miss some occurrences and only notice others. After thousands of years, I still don't have all the answers."

I wanted to ask him if he spoke to Nir Vana on the subject, but that would be admitting that I stole his ring. Not noticing the look on my face, Merlin continued, "I intend to continue down this path until your mother awakens. Then, we can live together for eternity."

"So, you have a tower of women for the sole purpose of making my mother magical?" I asked, trying to sum up my dad's ambitions.

He choked on a grape, coughing violently for a few moments. Then, with a straight face, he cleared his throat. "Ahem, pretty much. Something like that."

The idea of my dad chasing the woman he loved across time and space sounded eerily similar to my own quest. "You know, Dad, we're pretty much the same, you and me. You move Heaven and Earth to be with Mom, and I'm doing to do the same thing to be with Kalli. Do you think she's been reincarnated? How do I find her?"

Merlin shook his head sadly. "I refuse to let you walk down the same path as me. You're still young. Live a little. Enjoy your experiences. There are thousands of beautiful women here on Origin. Pick one. I've set all their affection levels to friendly."

That reminded me of Kalli's masked affection level which Lavender kindly set to "indifferent" to throw me off. Was that the reason Ulli and Marcelle were nice to me? Other than being assigned to me, that was. My voice was a little harsh when I asked, "Dad, did you edit people to make them like me? Isn't that taking away their free will?"

Merlin laughed. "You are mistaken. That part of the menu doesn't control a person's free will. It just influences emotions. I'm surprised you haven't played with it. You can make yourself feel all sorts of things."

"Why is it called Affection Level if it's something simple like that?" I asked.

He shrugged. "I don't know. It seemed like a good idea at the time. You're the first person besides me to ever see it. System sight is a mysterious thing. Even though I created it, I have no clue how some can see it and others can't. While you see them like menus in a video game, some hear voices, and others interact with it through an intermediary. While my system governs magic, magic is still mysterious."

"All the same, I'd prefer you don't mess with anyone's affection levels when it comes to me," I replied.

"Consider it done," he replied. "I'll reset everyone's affection for you to default. Is there anything else?"

I thought about it for a second. "Yeah, what is that place we go into when we teleport? I took someone with me today, and they froze."

Merlin replied. "Most people can't exist outside of reality. When you teleport, you become mana. Like that movie from your world, mana flows through everything and exists everywhere. When you teleport, you briefly become a part of that and stop existing on this plane. While you can function and direct yourself in there, others have to trust the magic to do its job and take them where they hope to go."

"So, they just freeze?" I asked incredulously.

"They cease to exist for that moment," he explained. "Speaking of which, I advise against spending too much time in there. Time will not pass in the outside world while you reside within the void."

"Can I make time stand still?" I asked.

Merlin shook his head. "Not exactly. Teleportation breaks the rules of reality. Time does not exist there. I do not advise staying in there too long. Even I don't know what might happen if you do."

I decided to take a page from my dad's book and twisted mana over myself, entering the void.

———

Inside the void, I selected Origin and zoomed in on the tower.

How do I teleport indoors? I used to do this all the time the old way.

Zooming in further, I discovered I could pass into the structure by focusing on it. Tiny figures stood frozen in miniature rooms and hallways as I scanned for the room I was looking for. Finding what I wanted, I appeared in my room right in between Ulli and Marcelle. "Surprise!"

Ulli screamed and dove onto the bed. I turned just in time to see a fist collide with my left cheek. The next thing I knew, someone stroked my hair while they whispered urgently back and forth.

"Do you think you killed him?"

"No. His head is harder than that. He might banish me, though."

"He wouldn't do that."

"I never hit him before. He might."

"Don't worry. Nobody's getting banished," I groaned, opening my eyes and sitting up. "That really hurt. Are you sure strategist isn't a combat class?"

"I am so sorry," Marcelle said stiffly. "I may have overreacted. May I implore you to not do that in the future? Also, please don't leave the tower by yourself. It reflects poorly on us. And don't tell me The Creator doesn't find out. He knows everything."

Somehow, I doubted he knew everything. The problem was determining exactly how much he knew. I had a feeling he wasn't aware of the conversations I had outside of the tower, but I had no doubts he was tracking where I teleported to. I needed to make absolutely sure I knew what to do the day I teleported to Atlantis. Something told me I wouldn't get a second chance.

Looking up at Marcelle staring me down, I sighed. "I'll try to take you with me. Give me a break, though. I need at least some privacy."

"Is there another girl?" Ulli asked in a quiet tone.

Was she jealous? I took her hand in mine. "Look, Ulli, the only girl I can think about is Kalli. The last thing I'm going to do is sneak off to find a different one. If it makes you feel better, think of everything I do as part of a plan to be reunited with her."

"I'd like to meet her," she replied.

"Me, too," Marcelle said.

I smiled. "Someday. I swear it. I am going to find her, and then I'll introduce her to you both."

[21]

Marcelle spent the time I was out, redecorating our room. Partitions had been set up, dividing the room into three private areas. Each had its own bed. Marcelle gave herself a practical bed while Ulli opted for a pink canopy with ruffles. They placed the original bed in my area along with the hammock I'd been sleeping in.

Marcelle poked her head in the flap that served as a door to my room and asked, "Do you want anything to eat, Mel? I am meeting Alfred at the dining hall."

"No thanks," I replied, still not hungry after eating the dumplings. "Is Ulli going with you?"

"She went to sleep," Marcelle replied. "Ulli's been practicing her dancing since you did that thing with the mana. She was exhausted."

"Oh," I replied, pretending to climb into bed.

"I'm going to bring you back a snack," Marcelle insisted. "You need to eat more."

Then, she was gone. I sat in bed thinking about the conversation with my dad. Was my mom really this Vivien person? My search for Kalli was quickly getting sidetracked by the mystery of my mother and her star-crossed relationship with Merlin. Thinking about it reminded me of the letter Mom left for me in the storage locker. I rummaged through my fanny pack and found it.

My Dearest Son,

First, I want to tell you not to worry about me. I didn't go off searching for you even though you forgot to check in with me when you left Earth. (I will talk to you about that later!)

There is something that I have to do. You might not hear from me for a while but please understand that I will miss you every single day. Don't worry about me.

I have left some money for you with the guild. Consider it your inheritance. I can't put a timetable on my return, so just keep living your best life until we see each other again.

Love always,
Mom

Along with the letter were a dollar bill and a black candle. The dollar bill had a message on it.

Burn only during your darkest hour.

I gaped at the message. Why hadn't I thought of that immediately after Kalli exploded? Putting the letter and dollar away, I cast a spell to light the fire.

"Pvruzth."

Oh, right. The system is blocked. No words of magic.

I changed my core to fire and pushed a tiny bit of mana out through my index finger. Gently holding the candle up to it, I lit the wick. A black flame blazed to life and enveloped me like my mana usually did before I was pulled into the void.

———

The smell of flowers on a fresh spring day invaded my nostrils. I opened my eyes and took in a vast field covered in flowers as far as the eye could see.

"Lavender?" I spoke her name out loud. Or did I? Was I real or just a projection of mana?

"That is correct," her reply came from behind me. I turned to find a young woman who looked as though she could be Lavender's daughter. Or her little sister at least. "Don't be alarmed. While I could alter my appearance to align myself with your expectations, I did not think an illusion would do me justice in this case."

"Is this real?" I asked, thinking the candle was making me hallucinate.

She smiled. "It is very real, and yet not real at the same time. Allow me to explain. Your current form is a construct made up of cursed smoke. You used a black candle to get here. While I'd like to take full credit for the curse, I cannot.

"Long ago, a witch created candles made from nightmares she extracted from the minds of the innocent. With them, she was able to become a living nightmare by becoming the smoke of the cursed candle. I altered one specific candle to send you here the first time you used it."

"I'm a nightmare?" I asked, looking down at my hands. They looked real enough.

Lavender walked toward me, the flowers parting under her feet to let her pass. "Why yes, you are a nightmare. You may take any form you wish in this dreamlike state. Since you didn't know that, you appeared as you. Next time, you may wish to choose a different form."

I gaped at her. "I can do this more than once? What is the purpose of this? There's always a purpose to everything you do, right?"

Lavender gave me the cryptic smile I'd come to expect. "Ah, you've figured me out in the end. Clever boy. Yes, you may use the candle until the last of the wax melts. The shorter the time you spend under its effects, the more uses you will get out of it. Once it's gone, it's gone."

"Do you know my mom?" I asked, trying to piece together how my mom ended up with the candle.

"Yes," Lavender replied without elaborating.

"How?" I asked, annoyed with the pointed answer. "Dad says she always shunned magic. How did she end up with a cursed candle?"

Lavender laughed. "Because I am going to give it to her."

"What do you mean, you're *going* to give it to her?" I asked. "She already gave it to me."

Lavender waved a hand, and the garden parted to reveal a pristine castle in the distance. "Welcome to the Middle Ages. It is currently the year 963 AD."

"What?" I asked, startled. "How did I travel through time?"

She smirked. "This isn't time travel. Not exactly. Let's say you bent time. You're still in the same place you were when you lit the candle. The smoke found its way through the ether where it needed to go and put you where you needed to be. In this case, that's right here. You may not be aware of this, but your family is dangerous. Your father's obsession with your mother threatens the natural balance of magic."

"Are you talking about his quest to find her?" I asked. "He is a little eccentric, but he seems harmless."

"If only it were that simple," Lavender replied. "While it is true that he is desperate for Vivien, his other endeavors are causing a distortion."

"What other endeavors?" I asked, feeling like she was guiding the conversation.

She smiled. "I *am* guiding you, child."

"Are you reading my mind?" I asked, trying to block my thoughts from the Enchanter.

Lavender placed a hand on my head. "Worry not. The contents of your mind are safe. I see everything. It's a gift and a curse. I am sure you're now aware that your father created the system. He did this for several reasons. The first is that it gives him control over traits and abilities.

140

"By governing them with a system, he controls what they do and how powerful they are. By assigning levels to people, he ensured nobody grows powerful enough to rival him. By favoring some families, he guarantees that the people he chooses stay in power. What you don't know is that the system charges a tax on all living creatures. Every time you use the system, you pay for it with mana.

"While it is true that your spells and abilities cost mana, the system takes more than what is needed. That additional mana goes into a pool. While some is needed to run the system, it takes far more than it needs. That much mana can be used to do something truly heinous. Merlin controls the amount of mana taxed by the system. If he wanted to, he could drain the mana of every awakened alive without a thought. As I said, he is dangerous."

"Are you asking me to do something about it?" I asked, worried she was about to try to make me kill my father.

Lavender laughed. "Nothing of the sort. I am simply giving you information. It will be up to you and Kalliphae to make that decision when the time comes."

"So, she is alive!" I exclaimed, feeling dizzy in my excitement.

"What do you think?" she asked, cryptic as usual. "You have a soul bond with her. You should know more than anyone. Your bond is precisely what Merlin has tried to have with your mother for millennia."

"Why can't I feel her?" I asked, reaching out before realizing I was currently made of dream smoke.

Lavender locked eyes with me. "That is one of the few things I don't know. That is a riddle you need to figure out for yourself. You need to figure it out."

"So, what am I supposed to do?" I asked, hoping she'd at least give me a solid lead.

She shook her head instead. "Prepare yourself for what is to come. That is all you can do."

"Melvin, are you still awake?" Marcelle's voice echoed across the meadow.

I blinked, and Lavender was gone, leaving me on the bed holding the black candle. The flame burnt out and a final wisp of pitch-black smoke dissipated as I watched. I turned my attention to Marcelle and replied, "I'm up. Come in."

———

Meanwhile, in Dabia...

Zofia sat on the throne. She wasn't queen or anything, but she liked the way the chair felt. It had been quite a challenge after the battle to clean up the mess. Zofia woke up hours after the fighting ended with no clue what had happened or who won. Melvin, Kalliphae, and Rasputin were all gone without a trace. When she woke up, Zofia found herself surrounded by nothing but dead bodies.

All her mercenaries and all the guards that accompanied Melvin Murphy were dead. All except one that was. The guy who looked like a butler, Orpheus, had somehow survived. She used the PING to stabilize him, but that was the extent of her ability to deal with magical injuries.

The days following the battle had been interesting. Cleaning up the remnants of Rasputin's men had been easy. They consisted of a handful of soldiers and a solitary tank. Armed with science and futuristic firepower, Zofia's men made quick work of them. The people of Dabia treated the TGB as their saviors.

Zofia used her newfound awakened powers to make subtle improvements to the infrastructure of the capital town and quickly had the populace on her side. From there, it was only a matter of time before she had the numbers to call for a vote. Thus, was the TGB made the official protector of the land, and that landed Zofia on the throne, at least temporarily.

From there, it was just a matter of moving in. A quick call to the base camp back in Meltopia and a caravan was soon underway to bring supplies, along with the portal generator to Dabia. Once everything was in place, the TGB was in business. They were the law.

She sat on the throne mulling over what to do next. In a quiet voice, she muttered to herself, "I only wish Melvin had stayed around just a bit longer so I could learn more from him."

"I might be able to help with that," a voice said from behind her.

Zofia leapt to her feet and looked around for the owner of the voice. "Who's there?"

Lavender stepped out of a door that Zofia was positive wasn't there earlier. "Greetings, child. You've been busy since the battle with Rasputin."

She wasn't alone. Accompanying the enchanter was a black man, an Asian woman, and the woman she remembered as Shara Shaw. She rested her hand on the specially modified PING at her hip as she asked, "What brings you here today?"

Lavender held her hands out. "There's no need for that. We aren't here to remove you. In fact, I think you've done quite a bit of good since you've been here. More so than the prior regime, in fact. I am here because we need something only you can do."

"What's that?" Zofia asked, her curiosity getting the better of her.

Lavender beamed at her. "We are going to break the universe."

[22]

"MARCY, DO YOU LIKE ME?" I asked tentatively as I accepted a plate of food.

She frowned. "Why are you asking that all of a sudden?"

"Sit down," I said, patting the bed next to me.

Marcelle sighed. "Are you sure you're ready for this? Also, Ulli asked if she could go first when the time came."

"Ready?" I asked. "For what? Oh, wait, that's not what I want. I told you already. Kalli is the girl for me. No. I need to tell you something, and it might upset you. So, please sit down."

This was it. I was about to test whether Merlin bugged my room. Surely, he would stop me from telling everyone his dirty secrets. Marcelle sat gently beside me and sighed. "Okay, what is it you need to tell me?"

I took a deep breath and began, "You know about the system, right?"

She nodded, so I continued, "There is a setting called Affection Level. I never knew what it did other than to tell me what someone felt about me. I never edited it even though I had the ability to do so. Well, Merlin just told me that he changed all your Affection Levels so that you like me. I asked him to change it back to whatever it was before, but now I'm worried you guys won't like me."

Marcelle sat in silence for a long while after I finished talking. Did I make a mistake? No. It was better to know how they felt. Finally, she spoke, "Do you think The Creator changed how we feel about him, too?"

I hadn't thought that. It was the obvious reason for the existence of the Affection Level in the first place. Merlin wanted everyone on Origin to love him. I couldn't say the words, so I nodded in silence.

Marcelle rubbed her chin and said, "I don't think it works. It might have worked, but I think telling me about it broke the magic. I might have had a tiny crush on The Creator before, but I think I'm over him now. I think I prefer his son."

I felt myself blush at her bluntness. At least that meant she still liked me. Perhaps a little too much. "Don't go getting any ideas now. I still belong to Kalli."

She laughed, getting up to leave. "Don't worry. I may have a thing for you, but I don't mind waiting. Take your time getting over her."

"I'm going to find her," I said in a low voice as she slipped through the door flap. "Just wait and see."

———

I missed leveling up in my sleep. It was yet another thing my father had taken from me. Was it possible to level without the system? Did I need to? My nights became mental training sessions because I still found myself unable to dream while alone in the dreams I shared with Kalli. Only she wasn't there anymore, so why was it still shared?

I pushed mana through the tether that used to lead to her. The taut connection vanished into the void with nothing at the other end. I pressed against it, getting a shock as feedback lanced through the tether to my core.

That was strange.

There was no answer. I fortified my mana with courage and tried again. It did little to insulate the shock. I transformed my core into a ball of electricity. Mixing the element with courage, I sent it back out. The painful feedback I felt was clearly not electrical. It was something else.

Next, I tried void. My soul became a black hole. It felt right considering the sense of loss I felt in my heart. I tried combining the darkness with courage, but it wasn't compatible. Dark thoughts filled my mind as I tried to find a sufficiently dark emotion. Remembering the god Lamentus and my grief over the loss of Stefanie, I infused the void with sorrow and tried again. While I could have felt sorrow over the loss of Kalli, I refused to believe I'd never see her again, and denial wasn't an emotion.

The dark mana slipped into the void where my tether cut off and vanished. The only problem was, I didn't go with it. My consciousness floated there at the terminus between my core and Kalli's, unable to proceed.

Do you feel my mana, Kalli? Send something back. Anything.

When no reply came once again, I slipped back into my dream body and sat cross-legged on the ground.

What can I do that I haven't tried?

As if to answer my question, I felt something materialize in my hand. Looking down, I found the black candle. It felt warm to the touch, as though it were alive. I looked down at it and shrugged.

If you want me to light you, I'm not going to let you down. Take me to Kalli!

———

Rain pelted my head as the wind from a strong storm buffeted against me. I was momentarily stunned as I took in my surroundings. A castle burned in the distance as explosions that definitely weren't thunder cracked in the distance.

Is that Celestea? Is Rasputin back?

I tried to pull back into the void to teleport and found myself unable to access mana.

That's right. I'm smoke right now.

Remembering what Lavender told me, I played around with my appearance. Even though I knew I wasn't real, I still felt cold and wet in the storm, so I fashioned a cloak to guard against the rain. It appeared around me, a familiar blue cloak I'd seen somewhere before.

I was about to make my way to the castle to see if I could help when I saw movement in the distance. A line of torches emerged from the city gates and began spreading out.

Are they looking for someone?

I moved toward them to see if I could help. Just when I was almost there, a pair of people emerged from the darkness a dozen feet to my left. They staggered about in the darkness, frantically trying to flee their torch-bearing pursuers.

In the distance, I heard an impossible voice yell, "Find them! We need the child alive. Kill the others."

I gasped.

Kalli's parents! This is the dream.

Like déjà vu, I knew what needed to happen. I floated after the fleeing couple, doing my best not to be seen or heard. It was easy. Armed with the knowledge that I was black smoke, I drifted through the air after them.

Suddenly, Celestea slipped in the mud. Twisting her body to protect a bundle she was carrying, she landed hard on the ground. Charles rushed over to his fallen wife, whispering, "Are you okay, my love?"

She tried to get up and cried out as her right leg buckled under her weight. Biting her tongue, she shoved the bundle, which I realized was Kalli, into Charles's arms. "Take her and run!"

"I can't leave you," Charles cried. "She'll kill you."

"Save our daughter," Celestea insisted. "She must live. Please, take her and run."

He looked stricken, but he scooped the bundle in his arms and turned to flee. He looked back as he ran. "I'll make as much noise as I can. Maybe they won't spot you."

"Don't you dare," she said loud enough for him to hear. "Forget about me."

He was silent as he disappeared into the darkness, clutching young

Kalli to his chest. She was so close. All I had to do was go to her. Just as I was about to, a sound behind me alerted me just as Mardella emerged. She stared at Celestea, a look of triumph on her face.

I didn't think as I materialized directly in front of her. A look of shock washed over Mardella's face, and I wasted no time, raising my hand and pushing dark mana infused with terror into her face.

I will never forgive you for what you put Kalli through. You can repent in that ring for a thousand years for all I care!

It wasn't like Kalli could hear me, but I still found solace in my private conversation with her. Kind of like a diary.

"Pvruzth."

Familiar flames slammed into the back of my cloak. I felt the warmth as Celestea attempted to incinerate me. Fortunately, her magic was a pale replica of what Kalli was capable of.

It dawned on me as I stood between the two stunned women. There was another person watching the scene unfold. I looked over to where I knew I was watching and pulled back my hood. In a loud firm voice to be heard over the storm, I said, "They still live. Take Kalli to a hut to the south of Celestea. Let her meet her parents."

Satisfied that I'd done a good job, I knelt in front of Celestea. She glared at me, raising her wand for another attack. I whispered, "Don't worry. I'm a friend."

Before she could object, I picked her up, enveloping us both in smoke. We passed over the landscape quickly as I flitted after her husband and Kalli. It reminded me of the time I'd become the wind and floated across Los Angeles. Only, this time, I was doing so with purpose. I had to rescue Kalli and her father.

I spotted him below us and materialized in front of the man. Celestea began coughing violently, dark smoke coming from her mouth.

Did I forget to tell her to hold her breath? Oops!

I set her down so she could puke in peace just as Charles impaled me with his sword. The blade went through me easily, though I didn't bleed. He removed the blade and gaped at me. "You're not human!"

I sighed. "I am. Sort of. Where is Kalli?"

While I knew he'd stashed her in the tree, I didn't want to let on that I was in on the plot. Kalli's part in the dream ended before that point, so I wasn't quite sure what to do next.

"Kalli?" He glared at me. "Do not dare to speak of the princess so informally."

I sighed. "Let's save the two of you first before worrying about formalities."

Celestea, done puking finally, tugged at my sleeve. "Please, my Lord. Save my daughter. It doesn't matter what happens to us."

I sighed, recalling Kalli's expression when Rasputin dumped their heads on the floor. "That isn't true. Kalli was heartbroken when you died. I am going to prevent that if possible."

"Wait, what?" Celestea asked, wincing in pain as she tried to put weight on her bad leg.

Charles looked off into the distance. The torchlight was getting closer. I dragged him down to the ground next to Celestea. "Hold your breath this time."

Neither of them listened to me. We became smoke once again and fluttered into the night sky, pushed by the wind that blew south. I hoped time stopped in smoke the same way it did in the void when I teleported. It wouldn't be good if Kalli's parents suffocated during our escape.

Somehow, I knew they wouldn't. Once enough time passed, I landed and took on a solid form. Celestea and Charles flopped to the ground beside me, heaving for breath and losing the contents of their stomachs once again.

I sat on a nearby rock and waited for them to compose themselves. Celestea recovered first, having already puked after the first time riding in my smoke. She gasped for breath and said, "You have to go back for Kalli. She's in danger."

"Don't worry," I replied. "I'll make sure she's safe."

From Kalli's memory, I knew she wouldn't be found until morning. I just needed to return before then. After that, I could take her to Hellquist Village. It made me sick to think of taking her to that place, but what choice did I have? It was all in the past.

Taking a deep breath to give a speech, I said, "Kalli is going to live, but she won't be safe with the two of you. You must wait here for her to seek you out. She is going to change this world."

"You want us to wait here?" Charles asked. "Out in the middle of nowhere. What of the queendom? Our people need us."

"Celestea has fallen," I replied glumly.

———

My eyes shot open when a loud scream echoed through the room. I looked up to see Ulli swatting at something.

Was it all a dream?

The black candle fell into my lap, slightly smaller than it had been. I sighed and rubbed the sleep from my eyes. Ulli pointed an accusing finger at the candle. "That thing was floating over you. You looked like you were dead!"

[23]

"IT'S NOT what it looks like," I pleaded, stowing the candle in my fanny pack. "Please, don't tell my father."

Ulli panicked, looking away in embarrassment. "I don't know what it was. I was just worried about you. You weren't moving. You weren't even snoring. Was that thing killing you? Is it…dark magic?"

She wasn't wrong. Becoming the smoke of some poor victim's nightmare was the very definition of dark magic. Still, I couldn't admit it. "No, it was aroma therapy. It helps me sleep."

In a way, that was the truth. I felt rested after having seen Kalli, even if it was in passing. Ulli thought about it for a moment before seeming to accept it. "Okay, I promise not to tell The Creator. What do you want to do today?"

I was a bit taken aback by the sudden shift in conversation. The truth was, I'd just woken up. "Hm, I think I'll take a bath, and then do my morning exercises. After that, I'm not sure."

Part of me wanted to teleport back to Camelot and see what Mika found out but I also recognized the need to keep up appearances in the tower. Ulli looked like she wanted something, so I asked, "What would you like to do today?"

She fidgeted. "I know you only love Kalli, but I was hoping we could go on a, um, date."

———

Meanwhile, on Scrap...

Life on the dark planet was rather mundane. Kalli learned about the inner workings of both the system and its creator since arriving. Mainly that the system was made by a man. Every person on Scrap was either discarded by The Creator or a descendant of someone who had been. They were separated into three groups.

The primary purpose of Scrap had been to house people who'd displeased The Creator and got sent there by him directly. This was the largest group. Next was Kalli's group. Some people had no clue who The Creator was or why they'd been sent to Scrap. These were called mistakes.

Finally, there were the descendants. Offspring of both groups grew up on Scrap as the only world they'd ever known. Judging by their ages, and the size of the planet's single graveyard, Scrap had been around for quite a while. Kalli had been interrogated the moment she arrived.

"What did you do to anger him?"

"Did he say anything about coming to visit?"

"Give us news from the outside world!"

It was the newcomers who dreamed of freedom she discovered. The older residents had long since given up any ambition of getting off the small planet. In fact, they'd set up a system of government. Only those who still had access to magic were allowed to run for office.

Most of the buildings on Scrap were crude, little more than the buildings in the villages Kalli helped Melvin restore in Meltopia. Still, they had four walls and functional plumbing. Kalli was grateful The Creator banished someone who knew how toilets worked. Melvin had spoiled her, and she never wanted to squat in the forest ever again.

Magic was another thing. While nobody on the planet had access to the system, some of the residents discovered ways of getting around that. Kalli was one of them. Once she understood that it was the words of magic that were holding her back, there was nothing to prevent her from summoning a friendly flame whenever she needed it. That by itself made her popular. She came to the understanding that there were two things that could raise her social standing. Magic was one of them. The other turned out to be the M Bloodline.

At first, she didn't know why that was so special. Eliza, the woman she was staying with explained it to her. "The M Bloodline signifies you are an offspring of The Creator. That is his bloodline."

"So, Melvin is related to the man who created the system?" Kalli mused. "I bet he'll be excited when he finds out."

She shook her head. "No, my dear. If you've got the bloodline, that means you are the descendant. Not your boyfriend. Unless he's also your brother."

"Ew, no!" Kalli squealed. "It's nothing like that. We, um, bonded. I think that's the word. It was the second or maybe the third time that I inherited his bloodline. The first time was just MateChat. That gave us the ability to talk to each other without being in a group. Then, he did something when he needed to get to me called Inseparable that allowed him to teleport between worlds to get to me.

"Finally, he wanted to show me what something tasted like in a dream, and we ended up with Intertwined. They just made everything we were already feeling much more intense. We also made a pact. We are bonded for life now."

Kalli left out the part where they would die without each other. Eliza rubbed her chin. "That does sound special. I never knew bloodlines could be shared like that. It must have been some bond."

"It's still a bond," Kalli corrected. "If something happened to Mel, I'd just die. He's out there, just cut off from me."

"Nobody gets off Scrap," Eliza replied softly. "You might as well get used to that."

Kalli wasn't getting used to anything. There was no way she was giving up on Melvin. She was going to find a way back to him. To do that, she needed to understand the strange planet she found herself on.

Thanks to her ability to use magic without the system, she qualified for a special job. Namely to provide electricity to Scrap.

An electrician and a scholar got together and figured out a way to convert mana into electricity. Only a few residents had direct access to their mana, and the majority had no desire to lower themselves to life as a human battery.

Kalli, on the other hand, was all too eager to do her part if it meant qualifying for perks that would give her access to information. She provided enough mana to power the local grid for a year in the first week. Even helping out with the local children in the morning, she was left to do what she liked for the majority of the day.

Kalli sighed. ***Oh, Melvin. How come you never taught me how to teleport? I'd come straight to you if I knew how. Why don't you come to me?***

He never answered. She knew she should worry. He was out there, somewhere. Something had to be blocking him the same way it did in their dreams. She explored Scrap in her first few weeks on the planet. The land situation on Scrap was strange. It was just big enough to provide homes for all the residents while not being overcrowded. The theory was that it magically grew every time a new prisoner arrived. Kalli didn't like the term prisoner even though it did seem to make sense.

Eliza's daughter, Maribelle, had been the one to explain how food worked on the first morning after her arrival. "You can get anything you want from the magic box."

She remembered the Box of Unending Food Melvin owned that created all manner of food from Earth when he fed it mana. Scrap boxes were better. They didn't require mana. Just a thought was all she needed to summon any food or drink she could think of. When she asked who made them, the reply was. "We've always had them since the beginning."

A prison. That's what everyone called the planet. Either that or a junkyard. The only thing people agreed on was that nobody got out. Ever. Even in her dreams, she couldn't escape. While Melvin wasn't there like he used to be, the tether that bound their bond still was. If

Kalli quieted her heart, she could feel him. Occasionally, tiny ripples of mana made their way through. Every time she picked up on them, she sent waves of reassurance back, hoping he would get her message and come to her.

She also spent her free time practicing magic. While she still only knew a limited number of spells, that didn't mean she couldn't get better at them. Control was never an issue, so she focused on increasing the power. More power meant more heat. She needed the power to incinerate anything. Additionally, she needed to be able to redirect her fireball spell if her target dodged. The spell was practically useless in its current form.

"Bvoomzt."

She found herself speaking the word even though it didn't work. That didn't matter, though, since she was already fluid at directing the necessary mana into the attack. The fireball leaped from her outstretched hand and rocketed toward the target fifty feet away. The target was an old oil drum that she was assured nobody would miss. Initially, it looked like Kalli was a bad shot. The fireball sailed through the air, four feet to the left of the drum. As it approached, she leaned to the right, tugging at the air like she was holding an invisible rope. The fireball shuddered and shifted its trajectory. It sailed by the target, still a good two feet off course.

Kalli cursed in frustration as the fireball exploded against a pile of rubbish, leaving a crater. Eliza whooped. "Good job, Kalli. You almost got it that time."

She sagged, heaving a heavy sigh. "But I still missed."

"But it made a bigger boom," the kid replied, trying to cheer her up.

Kalli gave a weak smile. "I suppose. I still got a way to go. Once I get control of it, I'll have to add more mana to make it even stronger. Then, I'll have to get control of it all over again."

"You can do it," the tiny child said with a fist pump.

She was determined. Melvin was going to see the new and improved Kalli when she got back to him.

———

"Kalli is going to kill me," I muttered, fidgeting as we landed the chariot. "Just to be clear, this is a fun outing as friends. This is by no means a romantic date. I only go on dates with Kalli."

Ulli insisted on traveling the old-fashioned way to get to our destination. I wasn't sure if she just disliked the queasiness of teleportation or if she actually thought the drive made her mock date more romantic. Fortunately, Marcelle insisted on tagging along despite Ulli's insistence that three's a crowd. Alfred, on the other hand, had no qualms about taking the day off. That meant I was the driver and Ulli was the navigator. Marcelle sat in the back seat of the spacious chariot, thoroughly enjoying being chauffeured around.

"Where are we going anyway?" I asked.

"It's a surprise," Ulli said with a giggle. "Don't worry, it's safe."

The destination wasn't far from the tower. Hidden behind a mountain in the opposite direction from both Camelot and Ulli's hometown was a theme park that made Disney World seem like a flea market. Magic roller coasters with tracks that looped through the clouds and disappeared underground were situated all over the park. There were huge domes nearly the size of the mountain that housed what I assumed to be more rides. A sea of people milled about at the entrance, probably lined up to go in.

I landed the chariot close to the front and looked around for a place to park. An attendant quickly ran over to the open-topped vehicle and bowed deeply. "Greetings, Young Master. It is a great honor that you decided to visit our humble establishment. Would you like me to park your chariot for you, or would you prefer to leave it here?"

"In the middle of the street?" I asked out of curiosity.

He smiled. "If you prefer, you may land anywhere you like in the park."

I shook my head. "You can park it for me. Just give me your reader so I can give you a tip."

"Oh, no, sir," he replied, waving his hands frantically. "We are forbidden from receiving money from an heir. That would be tacky."

I sighed. "Well, the offer still stands. Dad gave me unlimited funds after all."

He replaced me in the driver's seat without another word and took off. Ulli took my hand and tugged me toward the entrance. I asked, "What's this place called?"

"It used to be called The Magic Kingdom," Marcelle explained. "However, The Creator decided you might find that confusing, so it's been rebranded as Neo Happy Land."

I was still laughing when we got to the gate. "Kalli would love this place."

Ulli's expression fell. "I'm sorry I'm not Kalli. I'll try to make it fun anyway."

We just made it to the back of the massive line when a group of people pushed their way through the crowd toward us. In the lead was a black man in a golden tuxedo. "Welcome, Lord Murphy. It is both an honor and a pleasure that you've selected our humble theme park. My name is Clairvoyance Irrelevance, designer of everything you see here."

I wondered if he made all his employees say that. Ulli swooned. "It is such a pleasure to meet you, Mr. Irrelevance. I watch all your shows."

"Welcome, young lady," Mr. Irrelevance said, turning his attention to the girl. He took her hand and bent to kiss it before stopping to look at me. "With your permission, of course, my Lord."

I nodded and thought, *Perhaps I should have come in disguise.*

[24]

LET ME JUST SAY THIS. Magic rides are both more fun and more frightening than their non-magical counterparts. Roller coaster tracks were more suggestions when they didn't obey the laws of physics. I found myself floating, sinking, and even shimmering through the air at breakneck speeds as Ulli dragged me around the park, insisting that we ride everything.

A caravan of attendants led by Clairvoyance Irrelevance escorted us to every ride, pushing back crowds of park-goers that seemed eager to meet me. While we were obviously a big deal, I wondered if everyone knew who I actually was. I turned to Marcelle to ask, "Are there a lot of VIPs that get this kind of treatment?"

She rubbed her chin thoughtfully. "Well, I suppose. Every town has nobility. You can also buy the experience if you have enough money. Not Mr. Clairvoyance himself, of course. Still, it's kind of obvious who you are."

"What do you mean?" I asked.

She smiled. "You look a lot like your father, and your mother for that matter."

"How do you know what my mom looks like?" I asked, gaping at her. "Has she been here?"

Marcelle reached into her purse and withdrew a silver coin, flicking it to me. "Everyone knows what she looked like."

"How do you know that's my mom?" I asked incredulously.

A sympathetic smile crossed her lips. "It's fairly obvious."

I sighed, feeling self-conscious all of a sudden. Turning my attention to the proprietor, I asked, "Um, Mr. Irrelevant, can you tell me about how the rides work here? Do the ride operators have a carnival class or something?"

For a moment, I thought he was going to correct me on his last name, but he smiled and replied, "Please, my Lord, called me Clairvoyance. Everything you see here was designed and created by me. The Creator bestowed me with a class that allows me to use the system to bring my very dreams to life. Once they are created, they draw power directly from the system, and anyone can operate them."

"He gave you the class?" I asked. "What were you before?"

He blinked. "I was...alas, before The Creator took a shining to me, I was unawakened."

"Oh," I replied, digesting what he was saying. "Did he just decide you were going to create rides for a theme park?"

Clairvoyance laughed. "No, not at all. I had a dream and submitted a request when the time came to decide what I want to be. The Creator visited my hometown and bestowed this class upon me. This is the result. A rather wise investment, if I must say so myself."

I watched as a mascot of a monster I didn't recognize walked by what looked like a goat with a fish head. "What is that?"

Clairvoyance followed my gaze and said, "That's Frumpus the Frackas. He's just as popular as that mouse from your home world."

Slightly annoyed by how much people of Origin knew about me, I replied. "Speedy Gonzales?"

His electric smile faded for a brief moment before he covered it with a throaty laugh. "Precisely. Have you watched any holos since arriving on Origin? There is a channel dedicated to this park and its characters. I highly recommend it."

"I do!" Ulli cheered from beside him. She had somehow acquired a

Frumpus fin hat and some kind of delicacy on a stick while I was talking to Clairvoyance.

"And we love you for it," Clairvoyance replied as he ushered us toward one of the domes. "You might find this ride of particular interest. I call it 'Visions of Earth.'"

My curiosity was piqued, and I followed as the crowd parted before us. It took them a few minutes to stop the ride and usher everyone out. I felt guilty and whispered to Clairvoyance, "You don't have to do that. It probably takes longer than just waiting for it to finish."

"Nonsense," he replied. "The Creator never waits for anything. You are his son. It's one of your rights."

I sighed. A disguise definitely would have been best. Ulli was grinning from ear to ear. At least she was having a good time. I walked around Clairvoyance and stood on her other side, asking, "Are you having fun?"

She nodded emphatically. "Yes! I always wanted to come here."

"You've never been here before?"

Ulli shook her head. "No. I never got the chance before I was selected, and tower maidens are way too busy to go to theme parks. I hope you don't mind that I used you to come here. It's fun, right?"

A chuckle escaped my lips as I thought about it. Ulli used me. Strangely, I was okay with it. Since arriving on Origin, I'd done nothing but train and stress about getting back to Kalli. Taking a day off to just indulge myself was just what I needed. I leaned over and took a big bite of Ulli's snack. She scowled playfully at me, unable to suppress a giggle. "Hey!"

"This is fun," I replied with a mouth full of food. "And tasty."

The snack tasted like a churro with a spicy fruit filling surrounded by familiar cinnamon and sugar. Clairvoyance clapped and called out. "Another round of munchings and crunchings on the double, and bring some Gurgleberry Punch while you're at it."

Before I knew it, we were provided a selection of treats from nearby food carts. Ulli grabbed one of everything, making a mess on her shirt as she struggled to hold it all. Even Marcelle helped herself to something that looked like a candied apple. I tried the Gurgleberry Punch, wincing as the sour concoction slid down my throat.

"Ah hah!" Clairvoyance exclaimed. "That is the most popular beverage in the park, and it has the added advantage of making the drinker even thirstier."

"How is that an advantage?" I croaked, accepting a bottle of water from one of the vendors.

He laughed. "It makes us loads of money, that's how. People don't seem to mind though. In fact, they order more punch than any other drink in the park."

"Please, tell me water is free," I replied, gulping down half the bottle in one swig.

He laughed. "Have you never been to a theme park before? Nothing's free."

I groaned. "Some things should be."

Clairvoyance shrugged and ushered us forward as the doors swung open. We walked into a theatre designed for hundreds of people. I looked back as the doors slammed shut, allowing just our small group to enter. He led us down to the front row where attendants held devices that looked like oversized padded horseshoes. We were each handed one as we took seats in the front row. Clairvoyance settled in next to me and demonstrated by wrapping one of the devices around the back of his neck. It reminded me of a massager my mom used to own.

"Put the device on like this, and the experience will start momentarily," he explained, settling into his seat.

I wondered if the park used Cradle spray as I sunk into the comfortable padding of the chair. Slipping the device around my neck, I closed my eyes and waited for the show to start. The change was as sudden as it was intense. I heard the sounds of a bird chirping and smelled what I recognized as apple pie.

The light that hit my eyelids and the heat of the sun told me I was no longer in a dark theater but outside on a sunny day. I opened my eyes and discovered I was standing outside of a rustic house on a farm. The pie I smelt rested in an open window letting off an aroma so thick I could practically see it. Birds chirped from a nearby forest.

Beside me, Clairvoyance beamed, waving his arms around to present the scene. "Welcome to Earth, ladies, and gentlemen. While we aren't physically here, the device around your neck is feeding mana directly to your system, allowing you to experience the magic with all your senses. Go on, try the pie. I guarantee it's fresh as the day it was baked."

Ulli ran ahead and dug her finger into the pie, not bothering to hunt down a plate or utensils. The pie reformed the moment she removed her finger, looking just as whole as it was before she sampled it. She licked her fingers clean and said, "It's delicious! I don't think I've ever tried anything like it before."

I walked up beside her and did the same thing she did, scooping some out on my finger. Just like it smelled, it was indeed an apple pie. "I've had these loads of times. They are best when they are freshly made, which this one is. When we get back to the tower, I'll order you a bunch of Earth desserts so you can try them all."

"Really?" she cried, wrapping her arms around me in a hug. I cringed, expecting her fingers to be sticky. Surprisingly, they were not.

"Sure," I replied. "I sometimes forget how little you know about Earth."

"Let's continue the experience," Clairvoyance announced behind us. "There is much left to see."

The farm faded away and was replaced by a war zone. Tanks drove over uneven terrain as planes flew overhead dropping bombs on a city in the distance. I turned to Clairvoyance in shock. "What is this?"

"War," he replied with a sinister grin. "We don't have this on Origin. People are intrigued."

"I hate to break it to you," I replied. "Most people on Earth don't experience war from the battlefield. Isn't this traumatizing for people?"

He laughed. "Everybody knows you can't get hurt in a mana projection. This is all part of the show."

We stood there in the middle of the field while both sides launched artillery at each other. Bombs exploded in the distance, sounding like fireworks and lighting up the horizon. It looked like a performance to me, explosions going off all around us like an orchestra playing a rondo of destruction. I half expected a nuke to fall as the grand finale, but the scene just faded away, leaving us standing in the center of a coliseum where two sports teams prepared to start a match.

The only problem was it wasn't any sport I recognized. Did they have magic sports on Earth? I'd heard of Quidditch from *Harry Potter*, but I assumed that was fiction. The sport in front of me consisted of men and women riding various winged monsters with heavy mitts on their hands as they tried to pelt each other with balls of glowing blue energy. Ulli gasped as one of the balls made contact with a Pegasus, and the monster crumbled into dust, leaving its rider to fall to the Earth far below.

The scene faded again, and we were in an underwater aquarium. Something swam by that reminded me of an aquatic dinosaur from *Jurassic Park*, easily a hundred feet long with a mouth full of fangs. More virtual delicacies were provided, this time trays of mouth-watering sushi. Marcelle quickly became enamored with wasabi, slathering her sushi in the spicy condiment before stuffing it in her mouth. I watched her chew, prepared to laugh when she realized how intense it was. Unfortunately, she just smiled and reached for another piece, repeating the process with the wasabi.

The scene faded again, and my heart jumped in my chest as a familiar door appeared in front of us. Clairvoyance watched me intently. "Go on, open it. This is the latest addition to this attraction, and it's not open to the public yet. The house The Creator's son grew up in. It's going to be the most popular part of the experience. Please, tell me if anything is inaccurate."

I glared at him. It seemed like a massive breach of privacy for random strangers from another world to be traipsing through my apartment. I opened the door tentatively, half-expecting to find the Garcia family sitting in the living room. It was decorated exactly the way I remembered it. The dusty old couch we'd owned forever sat next to a coffee table across from a small nineteen-inch television.

"You lived here?" Ulli asked, peeking down the hall as if expecting to find more room in the back. "But it's so small."

I laughed. "Yeah. It may be small, but we got by. I wasn't rich or anything."

"How is it?" Clairvoyance asked, rubbing his hands together. "I paid a lot of money to get this recreated. We had to get a light projection from two lightyears away. That wasn't cheap."

"How did you…?" I asked, before trailing off. "Never mind. This is private. I don't think you should show this."

His smile faded, and he was suddenly all business. "Very well. We will scrap this one. What would you like us to put in its place? You are a very popular celebrity on Origin right now. We want to show the people the life you led."

I pretended to think about it for a moment, but I already knew the perfect spot. "Do the library from my high school. You can even add Mrs. Hodgins for bonus points. There was this desk in the back where I spent most of my time dreaming of worlds like this. That was before I knew it was all real."

"Perfect!" he said. "I know just the place. I'll be sure to send it to the tower once it's done so you can let us know how you like it."

The simulation ended just as Ulli was rummaging through my refrigerator. She whined when we returned to the theater. "Aww, I wanted to try that."

"No, you didn't," I replied. "Trust me, there was nothing good in there."

[25]

"Thanks for that," Ulli whispered, kissing me on the cheek. "I had a good time today. It was almost like…"

She didn't finish the sentence and ran off to her room. Marcelle smiled and said, "You did well today."

"Have you ever been on a date?" I asked, turning my attention to Marcelle.

Marcelle paused for a moment to consider the question. When she answered, she was vague, "Perhaps. I don't believe I knew what love was before entering the tower program. I still don't."

"Don't you want to find out what it is?" I asked.

She flashed a mischievous smile. "Why? Do you intend to claim me?"

"No!" I spluttered. "I was just wondering if you wanted to find someone someday."

"Sorry kid," she laughed. "It's either you or your father. That's the life of a tower maiden."

"Are you sure that's what you want?" I asked, surprised she didn't seem to care."

"Life isn't all about love," Marcelle replied. "I wanted a good life

165

for my family, and I achieved it. I was fine before regardless of whether your father chose me. It'll be the same with you."

"So, you don't like me?" I asked, wondering if it was a betrayal of Kalli to be a little upset that she didn't.

Marcelle gave me a look that one might give to a child who asked an awkward question. "Of course, I like you. Besides, it's not me you need to worry about. Ulli has a crush on you. Try to let her down gently."

"I will," I replied, not entirely sure how else to tell her that my heart belonged to Kalli. The only thing I could think of doing was make life as good as possible for both of them.

———

The candle planted me exactly where I expected it to. The rain had let up some. That told me time had passed since I saved Celestea from Mardella. Climbing trees was child's play when I could infuse my muscles with mana. I quickly made my way up to the nook Kalli's father tucked her in. She was fast asleep. I smiled, realizing she couldn't be more than three or four years old. I apologized quietly, "I'm sorry if this makes you sick."

I wrapped mana around both of us and stepped into the void. Being in the black smoke felt like being a different person altogether. It allowed me to escape not just Origin but time itself. I walked over to the small green orb orbiting the larger planet and zoomed in on Gaia until I found Hellquist village. The rundown building that served as both a monastery and an orphanage was easy to find. Most of the gray dots in the building occupied a pair of rooms. A single dot stood by itself in the kitchen. I chose that one and stepped back into the world.

A nun stood in place of the dot I'd seen on the map. She dropped a ladle into a pot she'd been stirring and screamed at me. Young Kalli began gasping for air as she struggled to wriggle out of my arms. I set her on the floor as she got sick. The nun chose that moment to find her voice. "Who are you, and what do you want?"

I offered my best smile as I tried to explain, "This is Kalliphae. I can't tell you who she is, but she's very special to me. Please, don't tell her about me and try to give her the best life you can. I promise I will make it up to you one day."

"I give all my children everything I have," she said indignantly. "This one will be no different."

"Excellent," I replied, teleporting out before I caused lasting damage to Kalli or the nun. While I wanted to teleport to the forest outside of the monastery, the smoke had other plans. I appeared in a familiar-looking room in Celestea Castle.

Wasn't this just destroyed? Did I time-hop again?

I looked around the room for clues. It was the hidden room I'd discovered before. Or was it in the future? I couldn't be sure. I looked around and decided it must be the past as there was noticeably less dust on everything. I retraced my steps from my previous expedition and ended up at one of the many boxes lining the wall. I fished through my fanny pack and withdrew the coin bearing Kalli's face. I flipped it over to make sure the inscription was still there.

IF YOU LOVE HER, YOU WILL LET HER GO.

I placed it in the box.

I wonder who made you?

Was it me?

I guess I'll never know.

I'd long since given up on ever hearing Kalli's reply through Mate-Chat. Suddenly, a shrill female voice made me jump, "You did it again!"

My eyes shot open, and the black candle fell in my lap. I sighed and looked up at Ulli. "Good morning to you, too."

"Do you want to explain that thing?" she asked, raising an eyebrow. "This can't be a coincidence. You're doing something on purpose."

"Sorry," I replied. "I can't tell you what I'm doing. Can you please keep it a secret?"

She frowned. "Is it dangerous?"

Was it? I shook my head. "I don't think so. The smoke gives me dreams of the past."

That much was true. I was pretty sure everything I'd seen so far had been from the past. The part about saving Kalli and meeting Lavender definitely had been. As for the coin, I could only hope. Ulli picked up the candle. "Can I try it?"

I snatched it defensively, causing her to flinch. "No! Uh, sorry. I mean there's not a lot left. If I ever get another one, I'll let you try it. How does that sound?"

She withdrew her hand while she thought about it. "Well, I guess that works. Yesterday was fun, by the way. What do you want to do today?"

"More training," I announced, earning a groan from Ulli. "You can take the day off if you like."

I could tell she was conflicted. While she didn't want to be left out, she also didn't seem to want to do any training. Finally, she reached a compromise with herself. "When will you be back?"

"This afternoon," I replied. It was mostly true. I had plans for the day.

———

Meanwhile, at Lavender's house…

Lavender stood at the head of a long table where an odd gathering of people was seated. She looked around the table before beginning. "I am sure you are all wondering why I've gathered you here. As you are well aware by now, Melvin and Kalliphae have been abducted by Melvin's father. By itself, that wouldn't be a big deal. However, there is something about Melvin that none of you know. More specifically, about his mother."

Everyone turned to look at Mrs. Murphy who sat next to Lavender with a bored look on her face. After a brief pause, Lavender continued. "This is Samantha Murphy. While she is Melvin's mother in this incarnation, her soul has been reincarnated numerous times. Merlin,

Melvin's father, has become increasingly obsessed with her. Several thousand years ago he began a project. His plan is to force Samantha into a unique incarnation."

"What kind of incarnation?" Wendy asked, looking alarmed.

"He wants her to be awakened," Lavender explained. "He felt that if she was born to an awakened family, she would follow the path of magic, and he could teach her to be immortal like he is."

"That doesn't sound so bad," Joe said.

Lavender nodded. "By itself, it isn't. The problem is, he isn't going to stop there. Merlin doesn't trust his beloved to do the work to become immortal, so he created the system with the ultimate purpose to gather enough mana to create a body that is immortal from conception."

Zofia perked up. "What's wrong with that? Do you think we could clone the immortal body?"

"No," Lavender replied curtly. "The problem is, this plan is doomed to fail. The immortal incarnation will become an abomination destined to destroy the universe as we know it."

"How do you know that?" Wendy asked, looking appalled.

Lavender smiled. "I see everything, child. I suppose it's time I revealed my true identity to you all. I am Gwenddydd, Merlin's sister."

"Why did you say your name was Lavender?" Shara asked, raising an eyebrow. "And that still doesn't explain how you know the future."

Gwen sighed. "I was once known as The Lavender Witch. The name resonated with me, so I chose to use it. There was a time when that name alone kept me hidden from my brother. I chose to use it with the system when he created it. He has since learned of this name, but I can still hide from him using magic. As for the future, I am a keeper of this fate."

"This fate?" Wendy asked. "Do you mean this world? Does Gaia have its own?"

Lavender shook her head. "If you look deep enough into the void, you can find other realities that look a lot like ours but are completely different. Nothing is known to me about them other than the fact that they exist. This reality is another matter. I can see threads of fate for every living being. That's why it is so important that we not allow my brother to achieve his goal. If he does, every thread in this reality will be cut."

"Why do you need us?" Joe asked. "A bunch of kids."

"I'm an adult," Zofia sighed. "But the question stands. Why us?"

Lavender sat and touched the table. A hologram came to life. It wasn't apparent if it was a product of magic or technology. Everyone present gasped, more interested in the hologram than its contents. Joe looked under the table. "Where is that coming from?"

"That's not important," Lavender replied with a sigh. "The reason I need you is we are going to break into two of the most secure planets in this reality. Merlin is usually quite guarded in his seat of power, but he has given us an opportunity when he summoned his son."

"How is it secure?" Joe asked.

Lavender smiled, pleased that he asked the question. "Merlin resides on the source of human life in this reality. It is aptly called Origin. It is shielded by a sphere of influence generated by Merlin himself. While it's in place, nobody can teleport on or off the planet without his consent. I use a similar enchantment on my home. This is why nobody can visit this place without my blessing.

Joe rubbed his chin. "I thought humans came from Earth?"

Lavender shook her head. "Humans were spread out from their home planet long ago. I believe your earliest literature documents the transition. There are also many legends on your planet where modern archeologists cannot find the cities mentioned. That's because they aren't on Earth. They are on Origin."

"What about Kalli?" Wendy asked with a look of concern on her face.

"Kalli's situation is different," Gwen explained. "I can confirm she's been placed on a planet called Scrap. When someone doesn't fit in with Merlin's plan, they end up in one of two places. Melvin relieved him of his first solution, so his only option is to imprison her on Scrap."

"What is Scrap?" Wendy asked, looking exasperated. "Is she in danger?"

Lavender tapped the table, and a hologram of a smaller planet replaced the bigger one. "She's in no danger. While I don't know much about Scrap, I sense no risk breaking in to get her. The planet seems rather tranquil."

"What about Origin?" Joe asked. "Will it be dangerous when we go there?"

"If Merlin believes we are a threat to his system, he will do everything in his power to eliminate us," Lavender explained. "So, yes, it will be dangerous to go there."

Joe stood abruptly, standing in front of Wendy. "Then there is no way I'm taking Wendy there. Melvin's a good friend, but that's not a risk I'm willing to take."

Gwen smiled. "Fortunately, of all the people gathered here today, Wendy is the one person who is not required to break this lock."

Wendy stood, giving Joe a sad smile. "I'm sorry. That isn't your decision to make, honey. Mel and Kalli are my friends, too. Besides, you didn't think I was going to let you go by yourself, did you?"

"I was afraid you were going to say that," Joe sighed.

"Excellent," Lavender said, tapping the table and changing the hologram yet again. "Now, let me tell each of you your roles in this."

[26]

I FOUND myself rushing to get through my morning training. Marcelle watched from her usual spot by the entrance to the garden. I suspected she knew I was sneaking out of the tower and wanted to insist on going when I did. I discovered I could combine my strength and elemental training if I fused the appropriate element for each type of exercise. I felt the importance of being efficient with my mana, only infusing the necessary parts of my body for each exercise.

When I did a sit-up, multiple muscles in my core worked in tandem to get the job done. While infusing the muscle with fire gave me strength, electricity gave me a jolt that made them flex automatically, requiring little effort from me directly. By infusing light mana, I could soothe the damage and make myself capable of doing nearly endless repetitions.

During my training, I had an idea.

What happens if I infuse an element and an emotion at the same time?

The first couple of tries didn't go quite as planned. Mixing the wrong emotion with an element was similar to combining the wrong elements. Fire had trouble being calm and ice didn't like heated emotions like anger. Infusing myself with certain elements also had strange effects on my body. Marcelle rushed over right in the middle of a water infusion test. "Is something wrong?"

"Yeah," I grimaced. "I need to pee."

A quick teleport to my room remedied the problem. Once I relieved myself, I was done with training for the day. As I washed my hands, I considered ditching Marcelle and Ulli again. However, they seemed sincere about keeping my secret, and I didn't have to have every conversation in front of them.

I announced, "I'm going out. Who's wants to come?"

It wasn't surprising when both girls raised their hands. Ulli had changed into a pink sun dress with white polka dots. "Where are we going today?"

"Back to Camelot," I announced, holding my hand out for them. "And we are going to be teleporting there."

"Why there again?" Ulli asked, taking a deep breath as she took my hand.

Marcelle took my other hand and braced herself. I decided not to answer the question and wrapped mana around all of us. Inside the void, I took a moment to look at the two girls. Ulli looked cute with her cheeks puffing out while she held her breath. I applied the illusion I'd been using as a disguise next. Not wanting to waste any more time, I zoomed in on the map and found the underground chamber in Camelot. I picked a spot farther in than spear guy and plopped us down next to Mika.

She wasn't prepared for us. Nor was she fully dressed. She shrieked and dove behind a shoddy-looking bed. Ulli and Marcelle were disoriented for a moment but, once they realized what was going on, Ulli jumped on me and covered my eyes while Marcelle apologized profusely.

Spear guy's voice rang out as he barged into the room, "What's going on in...um, oh, I'm so sorry. I didn't know you were... Are you safe? Do you want me to remove these people?"

I heard Mika shuffle some more before replying curtly. "I'm fine. Go away!"

I waited for what felt like an eternity with bated breath before she sighed. "Okay, you can let go of him now."

Ulli removed her hands from my eyes, and I opened them to find all three girls glaring at me. Marcelle was the first to chastise me. "It's rude to barge in on a girl while she's changing."

"Sorry," I replied. "It's hard to see where I'm going when I teleport. You looked like a dot from the void."

"From the...what?" Mika asked before thinking better of it. "Never mind. Mother gave me some info about Atlantis. I've been waiting for you to come back so we can check it out. Did you have to bring these two, um, guards?"

"We aren't guards," Marcelle said coldly.

"We're his chosen," Ulli chirped.

"You're...chosen?" she spoke the word as if she was tasting it. "Do you mean you and both of them...do it?"

I shook my head vigorously. "No! I'll only do *it* with Kalli. I already told all of you that."

"Kalli?" Mika asked.

Ulli sighed. "That's the name of his dead girlfriend."

"Ulli!" Marcelle scolded the girl. "We don't know that. She's just lost at the moment. Melvin is trying to get off the planet to find her."

"Oh, is that why?" Mika asked, a smile appearing on her face. "I can respect that. Are you ready to go?"

"Sure," I replied. "Can you tell me approximately where Atlantis is. I'm sure I can find it if I know where it's at."

She rubbed her chin. "Well, do you remember the place we went last time? That's on the coast of the Cosmic Ocean. There should only be one city under the sea. Normally, you'd have to charter a ferry to get down, but you might be able to teleport there directly."

Mika walked over to me, still a little red in the face. All three stood close as I wrapped my mana around all of us. This time, I didn't waste time in the void, scouring the ocean near the seaside town I'd visited. While the ocean was vast, it was also unpopulated. I saw the great city on the ocean bed, its single tower looking unnatural against the backdrop of an underwater mountain range. I zoomed in and selected a spot that didn't seem to be populated.

We appeared unnoticed in a dark alley only lit by ambient blue light that filtered through the sea. I grinned at the others and said, "It must not be very deep. The light gets through."

Marcelle rolled her eyes. "That's magic. Did you expect Atlantis to be completely in the dark. Look there."

I followed her finger to see a giant blue ball above the tower in the center of the underwater city. It radiated light that flooded the entire dome. People on the street didn't look at us and scurried away when we emerged from the alley. Mika laughed and said, "You sure picked a bad part of bad part of town to drop us in."

"How can you tell?" I asked, looking around for the first time. Most of the buildings seemed to be bars and hotels. "Okay, I get your point. So, what now?"

"Now, we need to find a place called The Purple Parrot," she explained. "When we get there, we need to order an extra salty oyster deluxe. That will get us in."

"In where?" Marcelle asked, folding her arms.

Mika eyed the older girl suspiciously. "Can we trust her?"

I smiled. "Sure, we can. At least, I hope."

It hadn't been my intent to doubt Marcelle, but it still leaked out in the end. She frowned. "The only thing I care about is your safety. Will you at least go as yourself this time?"

"Himself?" Mika asked. "Are you saying this isn't the real Melvin?"

"He's in disguise," Ulli giggled. "The real Mel looks a lot younger."

"Hey!" I grumbled. "I don't like the attention I get in my real form."

Mika nodded thoughtfully. "I'm torn. While I want to see what you look like, it'll be bad if we gather attention."

"Good point," I replied. "Sorry, Marcy. Incognito it is."

Marcelle sighed. "Just try to be careful."

"It'll be fine," Mika said. "Where we're going isn't dangerous."

"Then, why all the code words?" Marcelle asked, looking unconvinced.

Mika shrugged. "That's something you rich girls will never understand."

"I didn't start off rich," Marcelle replied, giving Mika a frosty look.

"Let's just go," I said, stepping between the two.

Marcelle sighed. "Fine. How do we get there?"

Mika shrugged. "I don't know. I've never been here before."

While the two of them bickered, Ulli walked over to an old man passing by. "Excuse me, Mister. Can you please tell me how to get to a place called The Purple Parrot?"

The old man laughed. "Oh, hoho. You're in the wrong part of town for that missy. How did you wind up over here? It's by the other sea wall, on the other side of the tower."

I tossed a glance at Marcelle. "Does The Creator have a tower here, too?"

She shrugged. "I don't know. I've never been here before either."

"No, no, no." The old man laughed. "The Creator never comes down here. The tower houses the magic that keeps this place from flooding. I don't think anybody lives in there."

"Interesting," I replied. It hadn't dawned on me to think about how the place worked. Part of me figured the system took care of things like that.

Having the tower to guide us, it was relatively easy to make our way through town. I could have teleported, but I wanted to check out the underwater city. It was interesting. We walked past structures made of coral and yards filled with seaweed, floating on unseen magic. The air was cool but humid, and water dripped from above, making me think the magical bubble had a leak.

Otherwise, I ran into similar businesses that I'd seen in Camelot. There were quite a few gift shops as well as multiple chain restaurants. I decided to stop by one of the gift shops when I saw an advertisement for a trident. Marcelle rolled her eyes when I walked up to the counter with the blueish green weapon on display.

Ulli squealed, "Buy it!"

"One, please," I announced.

The shopkeeper, a boy who looked to be about the same age as me, looked over my companions and sighed. "Sorry, you have to pay first."

I held out my hand. "Just give me the swiper thing."

"The reader?" he asked skeptically.

His eyes bulged when I touched the reader he provided, and it made a satisfied *ding*. He touched a separate reader to unlock the display and reached in to take it out. "I've worked here for a year, and nobody ever bought one of these. They are way too expensive."

I grinned, looking back at the girls. "I can afford it. Do any of you want anything?"

Marcelle shook her head, but Ulli and Mika started stacking souvenirs on the table. I watched with fascination as Ulli pointed at another item in the display case.

MERMAID SCALE
BECOME A MERMAID FOR A DAY
WARNING: THIS ITEM HAS MAGICAL PROPERTIES

I nodded enthusiastically. "We definitely want some of those. Marcy, do you want to be a mermaid?"

"Pass," she replied. However, she browsed the shelves and returned with a few books about Atlantis, as well as a T-shirt that read: "I visited Atlantis, and all I got was this lousy shirt."

Mika decided on a mermaid scale and found a magic puzzle box that she just had to have. I swiped the reader again and the boy behind the counter whistled. "Dude! Who are you?"

"Just some random guy," I replied, laughing.

The rest of the walk to the tower was uneventful. We looked in the window of every building we passed but nothing stood out like the trident. It took us about an hour until we got to the tower. It stretched well above the dome and was covered in moss.

The shimmering orb that lit up Atlantis actually came from somewhere high in the tower itself. I didn't see an entrance at ground level, so I assumed the old man was probably right that nobody occupied the structure. In any case, it was too slim to have much room inside anyway.

From there, we made our way to the sea wall. It was exactly what it sounded like. A road stood between a row of businesses and the edge of the dome beyond which stood the ocean. The pale blue light of the dome extended out into the water, and we could see various sea animals swimming around as we walked down the street. Toward the end of the row, we sat at the restaurant we were looking for.

PURPLE PARROT TAVERN
OPEN 24 HOURS DAILY

We walked in and approached a small stand manned by a woman in a skirt and business jacket. She smiled when she saw us. "Good afternoon, kids. Will your parents be joining you today?"

Not wanting to waste any time. I blurted, "I'd like to order an Extra Salty Oyster Deluxe."

[27]

"ARE YOU SURE ABOUT THAT, KID?" the woman asked, looking me up and down. "That's not a menu item, and it's quite spicy."

Spicy? Why couldn't things ever be simple? I looked back at Mika, who shrugged. The woman heaved a sigh and beckoned for us to follow her. "Very well. Have it your way. Come this way. We have special seating for guests like you."

We were led to a room in the back and sat around a filthy table. The hostess left before we could so much as order a glass of water. We waited in silence for several minutes before Marcelle whispered, "I don't like this."

"Me either," Ulli added. "It's dirty."

Mika rolled her eyes. "This is nothing. We had a flood once, and everything was covered in mud."

"I'm sorry," Marcelle said, looking guilty. "You must have had it rough. However, you have to admit, this room is not up to the same standards as the public tables."

I shrugged. "We didn't come here to eat. However, if the dirt is an issue, I can fix that."

I lit my inner fire and pushed a wall of flame out of my hands, devouring the scum and cobwebs that seemed to be everywhere in the room. Ulli and Marcelle were used to my tricks, but Mika wasn't. She dove out of the way as the flame raced past her. I gave the whole room a once-over, leaving it practically sparkling in my wake.

Right when Mika was taking her seat, a waiter in a fancy suit appeared with a covered platter. He set it on the table between us and smiled. "Bon appetite."

Like the host, the waiter retreated without saying anything else. We stared at the platter as if it were a trap. Tentatively, I reached out to grasp the lid.

"Careful!" Ulli urged as I slowly lifted it. Beneath was half a dozen oysters in a half-shell bathed in a buttery sauce.

"Try one," I said, pushing the tray toward Marcelle.

"Why me?" she asked, looking back and forth between me and the food.

"Because you like spicy food," I joked. "Besides, I can cure you if you get poisoned. It might be hard to cure myself if it's bad."

We were spared having to eat it when another woman in a black evening gown entered the room. She looked around and whistled appreciatively. "Did you clean in here?"

"He did," Ulli said, pointing an accusatory finger at me.

"Who told you to order the oysters?" the woman asked, ignoring Ulli's reply.

Mika stood to reply. "That would be my mom, Viola. She is the head of the coalition in the Camelot underbelly. She told me how to find you."

"Ah, that old crow," the woman replied. Viola hadn't seemed that old to me. "What can I do for you kids?"

That was my chance. "Viola says you might know of a way off Origin."

The woman laughed. "She was mistaken. Only The Creator can get on or off this rock. The planet is sealed. Even if you could survive the void, trying to slip past the barrier would be the equivalent of trying to pass through a blade."

"But my mom said you'd be able to help," Mika whined.

The woman gave a knowing smile. "If your goal is to leave Origin, then the answer is no. However, if you just wish to make a call, that's a different matter. I can help you contact someone on the outside. For a price, of course."

"How much?" I asked, thankful for my account balance. "I've got money."

The woman shook her head. "Oh, no. It's not going to be that easy. If you want me to use all the mana I've built up, you're going to have to put in some work."

"What kind of work?" Marcelle asked, looking suspicious.

The woman sat across from us and picked up an oyster. She held it up for a moment before slurping the contents from the shell. "The kind of work you're suited for. Magic.

"She never even gave us her name," Ulli muttered as we walked down the street toward the tower we passed earlier.

I sighed. "She did make a good point though. It's not like I could give her my real name. Not while I'm using this illusion."

"Do you think she knew?" Marcelle asked, looking worried.

It didn't matter if she knew. If she did, and I couldn't trust her, then my father already knew what I was up to. All I could do was keep moving forward and hopefully get in contact with Kalli. Realizing everyone was waiting for me to reply, I said, "I don't think so. Let's get this job done so she can pay up."

"Can you do the job?" Ulli asked.

I shrugged, looking around the undersea city. "It's going to be difficult without the system, but I have done similar things before."

The first challenge was getting an idea of how big Atlantis actually was. While I'd walked from one side to the other, it was actually much longer than it was wide. In the end, I stepped into the void to get a better look. Since time basically froze while I was in there, I left my companions in the street while I got the lay of the land.

The tower I'd seen earlier was almost dead center of Atlantis. Looking closely, I discovered a good chunk of the city had been reclaimed by the ocean. Remnants of buildings sat outside of the bubble, corroded and taken over by sea life. I dropped back out of the void in the same place I'd entered it, causing the three girls to jump out of the way.

"What was that?" Marcelle asked.

"I teleported," I replied. "I needed to get an idea of what we're up against."

"You flickered," Ulli said, getting up off the ground.

Marcelle ignored Ulli. "Did you get what you needed? Can you do it?"

"I think so," I said. "Part of Atlantis is underwater. If what that lady said is true, this tower is the key."

"If this is so important to Atlantis, shouldn't it be guarded?" Mika asked as we walked up to the sealed structure.

I reached out to touch it. Strong mana reacted the instant I made contact. It didn't repel me. Instead, it fed hungrily on the ambient mana that pulsed off me. So, I fed it.

The draw was similar to the time I summoned Kalli and it was all I could do to remain upright while I gave the tower what it wanted. I expected to see system messages telling me what was happening. That didn't happen because I was still blocked by my dad. However, a voice spoke in my head.

Do you wish to reclaim what was lost?

I didn't know how to interact with it. Was thought enough as it had been with the system? Not wanting to risk it, I said, "Yes."

This will be painful. Are you sure?

Was the system talking to me? Did it find a way to connect with me through mana when my father was doing everything he could to block it? I had to ask. "Yes, do it! But who are you?"

I am your connection to that which governs all. You can never be truly cut off. You are tied by blood. Her blood.

I wanted to think about it, but the system had other ideas. The mana stabbed into me, acting like a straw as it attempted to suck all of the life from me faster than my core could generate it. I vaguely felt the girls holding me up as my hand felt like it was anchored to the tower. I felt sick to my stomach as the process emptied me repeatedly. Then it was over, and darkness set in.

———

I found myself sitting by myself in the dream world. Once again, Kalli wasn't there. I still felt the connection. I even dreamed I felt her essence pushing through the void trying to reach me. What had I been doing? It was normal to forget a dream after suddenly waking up. Was it normal to forget what you did while you were awake if you suddenly fell asleep?

Then, I remembered. The tower. More importantly, I'd left Mika, Ulli, and Marcelle alone in Atlantis.

Wake up, wake up, wake up!

I flooded my body with mana, doing my best to rejuvenate myself. Hopefully, that would help me wake up. Then a voice spoke, "You don't need to rush things."

"Who said that?" I asked, looking around. A familiar feline woman lurked in the shadows of my dream. "Ugh, Aya, this is not the time for a tutorial."

"I'm not here to give you one," she replied, sauntering over to me. "It is time I told you more about what I actually am. You know my name is Aya, but that is just a nickname for what I actually am. I am an AI designed by a very special group of awakened called Technicians. I was infused into your core when you were very young to aid you on your journey."

"Wait just a second," I balked. "Are you saying you don't give tutorials to everyone?"

She stared at me and said nothing, waiting for me to digest what she just told me before moving on. When I thought about it, the only other person who had ever had a tutorial from Aya was Kalli. That had been because of her bond with me. Then again, that meant Aya was connected to her too. "Hey, do you know where Kalli is right now?"

"I'm sorry. I can't help with that," Aya replied curtly. "My primary function is to guide you so you can restore balance to the system."

"In case you didn't notice, I'm grounded," I replied. "Can you at least get a message to Kalli for me?"

She shook her head. "I apologize. My abilities cannot exceed your own. I am merely here to guide you."

"Well, guide me to Kalli, then!" I demanded.

Aya sighed, her tail swishing wildly behind her. "Solve the puzzle."

"What puzzle?" I asked, getting frustrated.

A smile appeared on her lips. "The one you've been focused on since your arrival on Origin."

"Can you at least wake me up?" I asked. "My friends need me."

"Your friends are safe," she replied. "I have shown myself to you to let you know the time is near. You must find a special artifact. The source of your father's power exists somewhere on Origin. Only you possess the power to claim it."

"What? Why?" I asked, completely flummoxed. "Why are you speaking in riddles? Just tell me what you want."

"Unfortunately, I wasn't designed to have answers," she replied sadly. "I was given to you to provide answers when the time is right in a way you can understand them. Originally, I did so with tutorials. Now, you need to know more."

"So, let me get this straight," I said, ticking off points on my fingers. "You can't help me get to Kalli. You want me to get an artifact, but you can't tell me what it is. And you can't tell me anything directly because you don't know what you want. Did I miss anything?"

"Yes," she replied, not bothered at all by my questions. "Time is of the essence. If the artifact gains any more mana, it will destroy everything."

"Oh, good," I replied, unable to control my laughter. "No pressure? Right?"

"I've said what needs to be said," Aya said with a straight face. "You may wake now."

———

I woke with a start, lying in the street with three concerned faces peering down at me. Ulli heaved a sigh of relief and announced, "He's alive!"

Mika looked up at the barrier overhead and asked, "Did it work?"

Marcelle laughed, looking off into the distance. "Yes, I think it did."

[28]

ATLANTIS HAD CHANGED. It was obvious from the moment we approached The Purple Parrot. It was no longer near the seawall. In fact, the seawall had receded quite a way into the distance. Just beyond the restaurant were the remnants of what had been underwater ruins.

Quite a few people had come out of the businesses and homes in the area to explore the phenomenon. We'd just taken a few steps into the ruins when someone spoke behind us, "I had a feeling you'd be able to pull it off."

"Who are you?" I asked, seeing the woman from The Purple Parrot. "And how did you know I could do it?"

She planted her hands on her hips, and a serene smile on her face. "I am a friend of a friend. You can call me Fortuna. As for how I knew, you wouldn't have ordered the extra salta oyster deluxe if at least one person didn't think you were worthy."

"Can I make that call now?" I asked, eager to get in touch with Kalli.

Fortuna sighed. "Are you sure you wouldn't rather explore the new Atlantis? I for one am quite eager to return to my old home. I still remember when the sea first reclaimed it. The barrier failed inch by

186

agonizing inch. There were a couple weeks where only half of my room was submerged."

I watched a few of the other Atlanteans as they splashed through what looked like tide pools. The part of me that enjoyed exploring paled in comparison to my need to find Kalli. I turned back toward the tavern and said, "I'd like to make that call, please."

———

It turned out, The Purple Parrot Tavern had a basement. Fortuna led us downstairs and through a storeroom to another room in the back. It looked like a one-bedroom apartment designed for the owner to live under the restaurant.

Fortuna sat the girls on a bench before guiding me to a large vanity with an obsidian mirror built into the wall. The mirror was fogged over as though someone had just taken a shower. Black smoke that reminded me of the candle seemed to hover around the frame, giving it a creepy appearance.

She motioned for me to sit in front of it and said, "Making calls between dimensions requires a lot of mana. You need to be absolutely certain who you wish to call because I won't be able to help you again for at least a month."

I smiled. "That's easy. Kalli is the only person I want to call. Just tell me what to do."

Fortuna hesitated. I had to ask her again, "Fortuna? How do I turn this thing on?"

She replied with a question, "Are you sure this is the person you wish to call? Is there not perhaps someone else?"

I turned to gape at her. Why would I want to contact anyone but Kalli? I shook my head. "No. I'm sure I want to call her."

I held my breath when she took an eternity to reply, "Very well. Tell me her full name and where she's at. It doesn't have to be exact. Just the planet will do."

"Well, the last place I saw her was on Gaia," I replied. "Does it matter if she might have been reincarnated?"

Fortuna replied, "That would matter quite a bit. If your friend passed away, she isn't the same person anymore. If she was reincarnated, you'd have to know her in that incarnation to call her. Furthermore, you cannot make calls to the afterlife, so if she went there, you're just out of luck. I have to ask you again, is there anyone else you wish to call."

"No, just Kalli," I doubled down, convinced all I needed to do was talk to her, to hear her voice. "Can you call her?"

She sighed. "Very well. Close your eyes and picture her. Then, say her full name. The mirror will do the rest."

I did as instructed, smiling as I envisioned Kalli's face. "Kalliphae Celestea Murphy."

When I opened my eyes, the fog had cleared, but all I saw was my own reflection looking back at me. Maybe the video wasn't working. "Kalli, are you there? Can you hear me?"

Fortuna rested a hand on my shoulder. "Sorry, kid. It didn't work. Don't worry, though. That doesn't necessarily mean she's dead. She might just not be on Gaia."

I sighed. The problem was I had no way of knowing where she was. That was why I hoped Fortuna could help. Then, it dawned on me. "Lavender! I'd like to call Lavender."

Fortuna shook her head sadly. "I hate to be the bearer of bad news, but I warned you. If you'd like to try again, come back in a month. We can make another call once the artifact has regenerated."

"Is this an artifact?" I asked, reaching out to touch it. "Perhaps I can…"

She smacked my hand away. "No! Absolutely not. Lord Tezcatlipoca is very touchy about who is allowed to touch the mirror. If you touch it, he might not let us make any calls at all."

"Lord who?" I asked, looking at the mirror with renewed interest. "If it just needs mana, I don't mind feeding it."

She sighed. "Mortal mana won't work. The god of communication himself provides the mana to make this work. There is another mirror, though. If you don't mind risking your life, The Creator also has a mirror that has a similar effect. It might even be more powerful."

"Is that so?" I replied, rubbing my chin. While I hadn't remembered seeing a mirror outside of the throne room, that didn't mean it wasn't there. I was eager to get back to the tower for once.

Fortuna took my hand and tugged me to my feet. "Now that we got that out of the way, would you like to explore the old city?"

I frowned, still staring at the mirror and the dark smoke that emanated off it. "Is there any way I can talk to Lord Tez, um, what's his name?"

"Tezcatlipoca," she replied. "And, no, you can't speak to him. He doesn't even speak to me. I inherited his mirror."

"You can see me, can't you?" I asked loudly, staring into the mirror. "There has to be something I can do to get you to help me."

When nobody responded, Fortuna said, "Like I said, you can't just talk to gods."

"Hold on a second," I replied, digging through my bag. "I just need to make a summoning circle, and we'll see about that."

I could have kicked myself for not being prepared. It was so easy to edit anything I needed that I never bothered to stock up on essentials, like a pen or duct tape. Fortunately, I found some leftover rice I'd thrown in there at some point. I spread the rice out in a rough summoning circle in front of the smoking mirror and sat in front of it. Clasping my hands together, I focused on the summoning ritual with a prayer. "Please summon the god of this mirror, Tezocal."

I felt the mana start to drain from me. While I'd come a long way from the two hundred mana I'd had when I summoned Kalli, the ritual still drained me rapidly. Once I bottomed out, it was a constant struggle to stay conscious. Fortunately, my mana regen had improved with my levels.

The ritual ended, and I sat there with my eyes closed trying to catch my breath. A deep voice echoed around me, "That is not how you pronounce Tezcatlipoca. Who are you, and why do you think you can summon me?"

I opened my eyes and realized I was no longer in Atlantis. The place I was in was surrounded by swirling light and looked familiar. I ignored his question and asked, "This is the void, isn't it? Do all gods live in the void?"

"I have summoned you to the ether," the voice replied. "I know not about this void you speak of. This realm exists outside of mortal comprehension."

"That's what my dad said about the void," I replied, smirking at the masked figure in front of me.

Tezcatlipoca had the appearance of a dark-skinned, scantily clad man wearing just a loin cloth over his well-toned body. He had a bone mask covering his face, which featured a plume of feathers. He squatted to get a better look at me. "Where you're at is irrelevant. What makes you think you have the right to summon me? You don't even worship me."

I shrugged. "I've summoned other gods in the past. Come on, Tezcat, I need a favor."

"It's Tezcatlipoca," the god corrected. "Do you mean to mock me by mispronouncing my name while asking for a favor with the same breath? Tell me why I don't smite you where you stand?"

"Can you do that?" I asked, standing up in front of the god. "This isn't my real body, is it? This is an astral projection, and you're trying to judge if I'm worthy."

"You are insolent," Tezcatlipoca replied. "That alone makes you unworthy. However, you are *his* son, so I may give you a reprieve. Unfortunately, I cannot grant your request. My mirror has rules, and one of those rules is only once per month."

"Can you at least tell me if she's alive?" I asked, my voice cracking.

He stood to his full height, suddenly towering over me again in the darkness. "Who? The girl you wished to call?"

He took a smaller smoky mirror out of a pocket in his loin cloth that shouldn't have been able to fit and held it up to his face. I craned my neck to catch a glimpse of Kalli's crimson hair in a storm of static like an old TV with a bad signal. The mirror went black, and he shook it.

I screamed, "Kalli! Can you hear me?"

"The connection is gone," Tezcatlipoca said, stashing the mirror back in his loin cloth. "You got your proof. Does this not satisfy you?"

"Is she alive?" I repeated.

He chuckled. "Of course, she is alive. My mirror cannot see the dead."

"Thanks, Tezcatlipoca," I replied, feeling genuine gratitude. At least I'd confirmed it. Kalli was alive. "Do you know any way to get off this planet?"

He shook his head. "I am a god of communication. I don't do travel."

"Can I call her in a month?" I asked, hoping the god could do what Fortuna could not.

He shook his head, causing the feathers to rustle on his mask. "As you can see, she is shielded from even me. It is beyond my power."

I sighed. "Well, thanks for trying."

"You're a peculiar one," the god muttered with a wave of his hand. That was the last thing I saw before he vanished into the void.

———

"Is something supposed to happen?" I heard Ulli whisper.

"Shh," Marcelle replied.

"I don't know," Mika whispered, ignoring Marcelle. "Has he ever summoned a god before?"

"Don't worry," Fortuna said, not bothering to lower her voice. "There is no danger of summoning that god. He's never come out before."

I opened my eyes. "You're right. He insisted on meeting me in the void."

All four of them stared at me. Marcelle found her voice first. "Are you saying you met that god with the long name?"

"Tezcatlipoca," Fortuna supplied helpfully. "You didn't go anywhere. Are you sure you didn't hallucinate?"

I yawned, still drained from the ritual. "I didn't, and he confirmed that Kalli is alive. I'll be back in a month to make another call. Do you need another favor before then?"

Fortuna's mouth fell open. "Um, I'll think of something. Did you actually meet him?"

"Yep," I replied, getting up to go. "He has a mirror of his own. It didn't work very well, though. Better than this one, I suppose. I'll check out the new part of town when I come back. For now, I need to get home to look into something."

While Fortuna seemed disappointed that I didn't want to stay, she seemed to understand. We accompanied her outside before finding a quiet area to teleport from. The first stop was Camelot to drop off Mika. By that point, all three girls were accustomed to holding their breath. We said our goodbyes, and I dropped Marcelle and Ulli off in my room. From there, I excused myself to the bathroom. Once I was alone, I teleported one more time.

[29]

I HADN'T PAID much attention to the artifacts outside of Merlin's throne room. Other than the ring I'd stolen, I never gave them much more than a passing glance. The first pedestal contained a dark mask with a red gem at the top. I was hesitant to touch it because of what had happened with the ring. The next two pedestals were empty. I frowned. I knew one of them contained the ring, but the other one...

Wasn't this where the mirror was?

I looked at the artifacts on the other side of the room. There were a pair of shoes with wings on them, a blood-stained sports bra, and even a blue wizard's hat with stars on it. None of them were what I was looking for. I resigned myself to the inevitable and pushed my way into the throne room. Merlin sat on his throne, looking bored as usual. He only looked up when I got close to him.

"Hi, Dad," I greeted him as casually as I could. "I've been curious about artifacts ever since you taught me how to make one. I noticed a few missing from the lobby out there. You don't store them somewhere else, do you?"

He yawned, looking at me with a bored expression on his face. "Finally into artifacts, are we? That's not a bad thing, but you're going to have a tough time attuning yourself to other people's property. I suggest you start giving some thought to what you'd like to make next. That wand is cute and all but hardly unique. Start thinking about making something with a specific use in mind."

"What about a mirror?" I'd blurted the question out before I had a chance to think it through. "Er, I mean, didn't there used to be a mirror out there?"

Merlin leaned forward on his throne and gave me a hard stare. "A mirror, huh? I can't say that I recall. Perhaps you are mistaking the glass cannon I used to own."

"A glass cannon?" I echoed, wondering if those were shaped like mirrors. "No, I'm pretty sure it was a mirror."

If he was hiding something, I couldn't tell from his expression. Finally, he came to a conclusion. "Fine, if you want to know about my artifacts, I'll show them to you."

He made a gripping motion with his right hand and the mask appeared in it. "This is The Mask of Avolette. I received it from an old friend several millennia ago. He imbued one of his quirks into it. Anyone who wears it is imbued with the strength of ages and the temperament to match. Another name for it is Mask of the Berserker."

I nodded, remembering the artifact armor and its Ruckus Mode that made me see red. Before I could comment, Merlin flicked his hand and the mask was replaced by winged boots. "These are called The Talaria of Mercury. It is said they were forged by the god Hephaestus. They grant the ability of flight even to the unawakened. They are pretty much useless to me as I can duplicate the effect with my magic."

"I can't fly," I began, wanting to try on the artifact.

Merlin laughed. "Can't you? You've already figured out the basics. You're only a few test flights away from actual flight."

He had a point. We'd gone over the aspects of wind elemental mana and how it could help me fly. I'd just never bothered to try it out. Something I would have to remedy in the future. Next, he brought out the blood-stained sports bra. He frowned when he held it up.

"This is a recent acquisition. It only became a relic because of a tragic series of events that happened to the wearer. It started out as a magic item when it was imbued with a certain kind of magic. Now, it possesses not only its old characteristics but also the means to connect two hearts across a great divide."

"Do you think I can contact Kalli with this?" I asked hopefully.

He shook his head, and the bra vanished. "No. I don't think that item will work for you."

"So, you admit she's not dead?" I asked hopefully.

Merlin flicked his wrist again, and the blue hat with the stars appeared in his hand. He smiled and held it out to me. "This is the hat I wore when I trained my last apprentice. Would you like to try it on?"

I blinked at the hat.

Why is he offering me this all of a sudden?

Still, there was no point looking a gift hat in the...brim? I reached out and accepted the offering. Almost immediately, I felt its mana wash over me, probing me as if to see whether I was worthy or not. Merlin frowned. "Peculiar. I didn't expect it to take to you like that. Go ahead, try it on."

I did as instructed, thinking I must look quite goofy wearing the hat with my jeans and T-shirt. The moment the hat touched my head, a matching blue robe materialized around my body. I jumped back, tugging at the silky blue material in an attempt to get it off. Merlin stood and walked around me. "Intriguing. This outfit will protect you while you wear it. I'm a little surprised it chose you."

"How do I take it off?" I asked, still trying to extricate myself.

Merlin chuckled. "Why would you want to do that? This is an improved version of the armor you used to wear. You do remember how it worked, don't you? Control it with a thought, and it will transform into whatever you see fit."

I closed my eyes and imagined the robe containing itself in a bracelet as the old armor had done when I didn't need it. Sure enough, the material melted off me and reformed around my left wrist. I was pleasantly surprised to discover the hat was also gone. Merlin nodded his approval as he sat back on his throne.

"Very good. Consider that my gift to you. It should protect you even better than the last one did."

"You made the other one, too, didn't you?" I asked, thinking about the black armor I'd accidentally bestowed to Rasputin's gut.

Merlin nodded. "That's correct. I made the black armor long ago during a dark period in my life. This one is a more recent creation, though I must admit I prefer the current one. It should suffice to keep you safe though."

"Thanks," I replied, realizing it was the first gift my father had ever given me. If I wasn't counting Marcelle and Ulli, that was. Then, I remembered the mirror. "Is that all your artifacts? Do you have any more?"

His expression darkened, and he clutched the armrest of the throne impatiently. "I have countless more. That doesn't mean I'm going to show them to you. I think it's time you called it a night."

He waved his hand, and I found myself pushed through the void and into my bedroom. Ulli squealed when I appeared in her private area. "I knew it! See Marcy, he wasn't taking forever in the bathroom. He teleported somewhere."

Marcelle made a noncommittal sound from somewhere in the distance. Ulli lowered her voice and whispered, "Why did you teleport back to my room? Do you need something?"

I shook my head, causing her to frown. So, I quickly backpedaled. "No, um, it's nothing like that. Dad sent me back, and I just popped out here."

"Oh," she sighed, still looking sad.

"Would you like to get dessert with me?" I offered, knowing Ulli loved sweets almost as much as I did.

She grinned. "Yes!"

———

I didn't get any privacy until much later that night when everyone went to bed. Of course, I had no intention of sleeping. I took out the black candle and looked at it.

Almost half left, huh?

I should have asked Dad if he had anymore evil candles. Without thinking too much about it, I lit the candle. As usual, the black smoke overwhelmed me, and I felt myself lose consciousness as I became the smoke.

———

I stood outside of a familiar cabin in the woods. While I'd never been there, I remembered it from Kalli's dreams. Worried that appearing as myself would traumatize the girl when younger me summoned her to Earth, I altered my face to the illusion I was using when I explored Origin. That combined with the blue robe I'd seen draped over the chair in her dream completed the ensemble.

No sooner had I completed the illusion than a pair emerged from the forest. I recognized the nun from the inn, but my attention was focused on her companion. While she had grown up a lot since the time I'd rescued her from Mardella, Kalli was unmistakable. I wanted to hug her so bad it hurt. However, she was a timid girl, probably eleven or twelve years old. She clasped her hands behind her back and ignored me by focusing her attention on the nun.

The nun gave her a pat on the backside and said, "Go on now. You asked for a master, and there one is. Introduce yourself properly."

She took a few steps forward, scowling back at the nun as she did so. I took the opportunity to try and break the ice. "Hello, little one. Have you awakened?"

Kalli turned her attention to me, looking me up and down. "You aren't much bigger than I am. Er, I mean, yes, I've awakened. My name is Kalliphae."

"Tell me what you can do," I said, ignoring her comment about my size.

She squeezed her eyes shut, and her face turned red. After a few seconds, she let out a deep breath. "I can't do it."

"It only happens when she's angry," the nun supplied helpfully. "She catches fire."

I smiled, remembering the time she did just that before punching Alex in the nose. Kalli scowled at me and grumbled, "It's not funny!"

I smiled at her, feeling affection despite myself. "Don't worry, Kalliphae. I promise, you're going to be an amazing pyromancer."

"Is that what I am?" she squealed. "Does that mean you'll teach me?"

"Of course," I replied. "I'll teach you everything I know."

The nun nodded at me. "I'll leave her in your hands, then. Please, see to it that she gets back to the monastery when you're done with her."

"Sure," I replied, trying to remember the spells she knew when I met her. Fortunately, there weren't many.

Feeling a bit more confident, Kalli walked past me toward the cabin. "Do you live out here?"

I shook my head. "No. This cabin is just here for our lessons. Feel free to treat it as your home away from home."

"But I don't have a home," she sighed with a sad look in her eyes.

I wanted to tell her everything. That a boy who loved her with all of his heart would summon her in just a few years. That her family was alive. That she was a princess. Most importantly, that she was loved. It broke my heart that I couldn't tell her anything. I whispered, "I'll show you everything, I promise."

She peeked back out of the cabin where she was already exploring. "Did you say something?"

I cleared my throat. "I was thinking we should get started. How would you like to learn your first magic spell?"

That did the trick. She squealed with excitement and bounced her way over to me. "Yes, please. What's it going to be? Do we start with fireballs? Please, let it be fireballs."

I held out a hand, palm up, and said a silent prayer that the magic worked for me.

"Bvizt."

A small ball of light, resembling a flickering flame, came to life in my hand. It didn't burn or smoke like a normal flame. It glowed silently in my hand. I held it out to Kalli, who reached out to touch it. Her hand passed harmlessly through the flame, causing it to flicker.

"This is a spell called Bvizt. It creates a ball of fire that isn't hot.

It's the safest spell you can learn and an excellent way to get control of your magic. Go ahead, give it a try."

She held out her hand and scrunched up her nose in concentration. "Bist!"

Nothing happened. She closed her eyes and tried again. "Bits!"

She opened her eyes and stared at her hand. "What am I doing wrong?"

I smiled. "Words of magic are a special language all their own. You need to understand the words to imbue them with magic. Let's start by teaching you to read and write the secret language of magic. Then, you can try again."

[30]

KALLI WAS A QUICK STUDY. She picked up the words of magic so quickly it made me jealous. It took everything in me not to jumpstart her core by connecting it to her mana channels. I had a strong feeling that doing so would change history. That by itself might change everything. While I desperately wanted Kalli to be stronger, I also didn't want to mess things up in a way that would make us not end up together.

She was adorable running around holding a glowing wisp over her head. "Look! I did it, I did it!"

I clapped politely and said, "Now, you need to do that a thousand more times until it becomes a part of you. Then, you'll be ready for the next spell."

———

I slept well that night, fulfilled after a fruitful day with Kalli. While I knew she was just a little girl from the past, being near her only reinforced how much I loved her. It was also the first time I didn't get caught using the candle. Feeling closer to Kalli than I had since I lost her, I pushed myself against the barrier that stood between us. The only thing I had to go by was the tether that still connected us. Confidence welled in me. I was going to break through. I just had to.

———

Kalli collapsed into bed after a long day of providing mana to the power grid. She'd passed the time by daydreaming about Melvin and how she longed to see him again. She was beginning to realize how much she missed his touch. A simple hug or the way he found to take her hand in his had seemed so trivial at the time. Now, she would give anything to touch him just one more time. Even sleeping was a chore without his warm back to snuggle up against. She shivered and clutched her pillow.

Somehow, inevitably, she drifted off to sleep. Like her bedroom, the dreamscape was a desolate world of isolation where even the dreams she once enjoyed as a child abandoned her. Remnants of Melvin abounded everything in the world they'd created together with their imaginations. She tugged hopelessly on the tether she still shared with him. Kalli knew he was alive somewhere beyond the darkness. That much she could feel. The problem was, she had no way of getting off Scrap.

Suddenly, something tugged back. That was new. Kalli raced along the connection to where it disappeared. The instant she got there she realized what was different. Melvin was there. Right there, just on the other side. She banged against it, screaming his name. *Melvin!*

The tether pinged back. Melvin was banging on the other side. He felt her. She knew it.

———

Kalli!

I'd heard her voice clear as day. The void felt like a wall, and Kalli was on the other side of it. Not somewhere in the distance but right there. I just needed to break down that wall. I renewed my efforts and threw myself against the barrier.

How is this keeping us apart?

There was no answer. However, I felt her banging on the other side of the barrier, desperately trying to break through. Suddenly, a voice spoke behind me, "Would you like some advice?"

I spun around. "Aya?"

———

Kalli blinked at the sudden appearance of the cat-girl. "Hey! Aren't you the person who runs the tutorials?"

Aya licked her hand as a cat would its paw. "Yes, I am the very same."

"I'm a little busy right now," Kalli said, pushing at the barrier and trying to feel Melvin again."

"I know," Aya replied. "That's why I'm here."

"Do you know a way to get to Mel?" Kalli asked hopefully while still probing for signs of Melvin.

Aya nodded. "That is correct. You both need to strengthen your bond."

"We already did," Kalli muttered. Even though she didn't have access to the system anymore, she knew the pledge was still in effect. She saw the physical manifestation of it in her core.

Aya floated around Kalli until she was between her and the barrier. Once she had her full attention, she explained, "You are currently at the fourth of the fifth known stages of mana bonding. The first is a common occurrence when two or more people form a group. You can feel each others's mana and physical bodies. The second is the marriage bond. You know it by its scientific label, mate. It's a deeper connection between two people, almost double that of the group connection.

"Beyond that is the third level. The two of you achieved this by swearing your lives to one another. This is a requirement to tether two souls together. That is why the connection cannot be cut, even by the most powerful of sorcerers. It is called Inseparable. The fourth stage is where you're currently at. You've opened your cores to one another and begun the process that will lead to the fifth and final known stage. This is known as Intertwined. To break the barrier keeping you apart, the two of you are going to have to become one."

"What is that called?" Kalli asked, wondering what it would feel like to be closer to Melvin than she already was.

"Unity," Aya replied. "If you do this, your cores will be one and the same. Separate only by your bodies."

"How do I do it?" Kalli asked, deciding she was all in.

———

"You have to open yourself to her fully," Aya explained as she floated across from me. "It is similar to what you've already done with your body to get to stage four. The only difference is you must open your soul to her."

"I want to do that," I announced while focusing on my core and willing it to accept Kalli.

It was then that I noticed that the mana from her tether always ended where it touched my core. It respectfully waited just outside of me without intruding on my life force. I opened myself and tugged on it. Rather than trying to force my way through the wall that separated us, I pulled her essence deeper into myself. All at once, the closeness I'd been craving washed over me. I felt her. All of her.

———

Kalli made the same connection at that very moment. It took a little more work to open herself, but that was only because she wasn't as experienced at manipulating her core as Melvin was. His essence bled into her, changing her core from the fireball it once was to a swirling star, still ablaze but also radiating a brilliant light. Along with the feeling came an overwhelming presence. They were together again.

———

Kalli!

Mel!

I closed my eyes in an attempt to blink away tears. It was too late, and I sobbed quietly from inside my core.

I missed you so much.

She was crying, too. *I know. Me, too.*

Somehow, we found ourselves back at the apex of our tether where we joined. The barrier that once barred our connection was now just minor inconvenience to be passed through with but a thought. We met in the middle, sometimes on her side, sometimes on mine. Our embrace was frantic and passionate. We cared about everything and nothing all at the same time. I loved her, and she loved me. That was all that mattered. Time stopped and the world froze as the only thing that mattered was each other. I was happy and totally satisfied to finally become one with Kalli.

———

I yawned as I woke up next to Kalli. She snored softly beside me in a bed made of fluff. Neither of us were awake, but we'd both fallen asleep in our dream. Unlike the previous times I'd done that, my spirit hadn't wandered away. Part of it knew it belonged to Kalli now. A golden ball of light danced in the air above us, hovering silently and providing the only light in the otherwise darkness.

"Kalli." I nudged her. "Look at that."

She stretched luxuriously, raising her arms above her head. Was she always so beautiful? She blushed as she sensed what I was thinking. I pointed at the light, and she smiled. "Don't you know what that is, silly?"

"No," I replied, looking at the light with renewed interest.

She giggled. "We made that last night. Did you forget the prophecy?"

I blinked, my mouth falling open for a second. "Is that a...?"

Kalli smacked me playfully. "Don't call her that. I think I'll call her…Sindra."

I sighed contentedly, looking at the twinkling golden light. There was a spark there. "How do you think this works? Will she be born in the real world?"

"Maybe," Kalli admitted. "I think we are looking at her core."

"Ahem," a voice called from the darkness.

Kalli shrieked and grabbed a handful of fluff to cover herself. Aya spoke again. "I'll give the two of you a moment. There is something we need to discuss."

One would think clothes weren't a necessity in a dream. However, when talking to an AI implanted in your subconscious to give tutorials, being properly attired was surprisingly important. Fortunately, Kalli and I quickly found our clothes and presented ourselves to Aya. Kalli folded her arms and asked in a rather annoyed voice, "What do you want?"

Aya gave us a smile that said she knew exactly what we'd been up to. "Congratulations on breaking the final barrier. While you now possess the ability to be together physically, I strongly urge you refrain from doing so."

"Why?" We both asked at once.

"While you would be reunited, you would still be trapped," Aya explained patiently. "Additionally, your father will know that his barrier has fallen and take steps to lock you both down. We have but a single chance to liberate the two of you, and it relies on neither of you acting rashly."

"So, what do we do?" I asked, frustrated that Aya was trying to prevent me from going straight to Kalli.

"Continue your quest," Aya replied. "You must find and gain control of the artifact. Your father will be unstoppable otherwise."

"I looked through all of his artifacts," I replied. "He even gave me one. They didn't seem all that special."

"What you seek is hidden," Aya said. "You must search for it."

"The mirror?" I guessed. "He says it doesn't exist, but I know I've seen it before. It doesn't matter now because I found Kalli. Just tell me what has to happen for us to be together."

"You must find the artifact," Aya insisted. "That is your only task. Everything else is already in motion."

"What about me?" Kalli asked. "I'm still stuck on Scrap."

"Scrap?" I asked. "What's that?"

Kalli sighed. "Your father Scrapped me! He threw me away here. It's a planet full of people he Scrapped. It's kind of like a prison but nice. People live their whole lives here, and nobody has ever escaped."

"Dad did that?" I asked, suddenly wanting to wake up and confront him. Then, I remembered Aya told me if he found out, he would make it so we couldn't be together. "Why would he do that?"

"I don't know," Kalli sighed. Aya also remained silent.

"What do we do next?" I wondered out loud. I'd asked the question before, but I didn't know how to go about finding an artifact. Did it even exist?

"Wake up!" Came the reply.

"What?" I asked.

Kalli glared at me. "I didn't say that. Who said that?"

"I got breakfast," the voice continued.

"Who is that?" Kalli asked again.

I groaned, deciding to wake up instead of answering.

[31]

"GOOD MORNING, ULLI!" I exclaimed with perhaps a little more enthusiasm than I'd meant to have.

Her smile dropped as I clutched her in an awkward hug. "Marcy, there's something wrong with Melvin today."

"What's wrong?" Marcelle called from her room, sounding disinterested.

Kalli's voice echoed in my head, causing my smile to widen to almost alarming proportions. *Do you want to tell me about these women in your bedroom?*

She wasn't mad. Not really. She now had full access to my memories, as I did to hers. I also knew the exact state of her emotions. Not only did I not have to worry about her affection level anymore, but I also didn't have to guess what kind of mood she was in. She knew everything about me, and I knew everything about her. Her affection was only matched by mine. We both sat in bed with big goofy grins on our faces. I said the thing we were both thinking.

We did it, Kalli.

She giggled to herself about the double meaning of my words. *Yeah, we did, and now nothing can keep us apart.*

I was so distracted by my private conversation that I almost didn't register Ulli trying to wiggle out of my arms. Next to me on the bed was a fallen plate laden with all kinds of meats and cheeses. I picked up a slice of green ham and popped it into my mouth. As usual, the meat was bursting with flavor. I chewed on it slowly, realizing I was sharing the experience with Kalli. Her stomach growled, and I felt that too.

You're lucky. I have to cook breakfast if I want to eat anything.

She crawled out of bed and freshened up before making her way to a crowded living room. Several children were awake before her and playing quietly. One of them looked up. "Morning, Kawwifay."

Kalli smiled as she yawned. "Good morning."

You have kids?

She rolled her eyes. *They're not mine. I'm just helping some friends out. They have to go to work early, so I make breakfast for their littles. Some of the other kids from the neighborhood also come here.*

I got out of bed, too, Ulli following me around like a worried hen. "Why are you so happy? It's weird."

"No reason," I replied, realizing that spilling the beans about my newfound closeness to Kalli could definitely get back to Merlin.

"What do you want to do today?" she asked, changing tactics.

I rubbed my chin. Part of me wanted to go back to sleep so I could be with Kalli again, but I knew that wouldn't work for a variety of reasons. Not only would Ulli and Marcelle freak out, but Kalli had a job to do and couldn't join me.

Then, there was my mission. I had to find the mirror Merlin was hiding from me. It had to be somewhere in the tower. Aya was adamant that it was critical that I find it. Now that I was reunited with Kalli, I could focus my intention on more important matters. Namely, how to break us out of our respective prisons.

"I think I'm going to explore the tower today," I replied, pulling off my shirt while I fished for a clean one in my bag.

You're awfully comfortable around those two.

Kalli had a point. She wasn't mad. It was amazing how relaxed she was with me. Being united was amazing.

It was awkward at first. Ulli and Marcy are great, though. I want to do what I can for them.

Kalli smiled. *I know.*

I took my time getting ready as I enjoyed watching Kalli make breakfast.

When did you learn to cook?

She stuck her tongue out at no one in particular, though I knew it was meant for me. *I've been able to cook since I was a little girl. Mary taught me. I just never needed to since you met me.*

Memories of a young Kalli fumbling around in the monastery kitchen under the watchful eye of a nun made me smile. Kalli blushed when she realized just how much I could see with the modified connection. Then, my mind went blank, almost like she'd turned off a television I'd been watching.

Good, I can turn it off, she announced with satisfaction.

I felt around in my core and quickly realized I could do it as well. While I still felt her within me, the information feeding through the tether was cut off. To do the same, all I had to do was pinch off the information feed before it bled out.

Kalli beamed at me when I pulled it off. *See! It's easy.*

So long as I never lose you again.

Warmth bubbled out from her. *Don't worry. You never will.*

Marcelle poked me. "You're right. There is something wrong with him. He's blushing. You're thinking about something naughty, aren't you Melvin?"

I poked her back. "Yeah, probably."

It was Marcelle's turn to blush. Then, I realized what I'd implied. "Not like that! I'm just happy. I'm allowed to be happy, right?"

Her expression softened, a smile forming on her lips. "Of course, you are. Where do you want to explore this time?"

"I don't know," I replied, heading toward the park. "I'll think about it while I do my morning workout."

Kalli was very interested in my daily routine. I made a point of showing off elemental mana-infused exercises. First, I infused electricity into my upper body while I did push-ups. Then, I used fire in my legs while I did squats.

Kalli pouted. *Even though I know how you do it, I'm still only good with fire.*

What about emotions?

I demonstrated by infusing passion alongside the fire to add a little more oomph to my legs. Kalli mimicked my morning routine but quickly wore herself out as her body wasn't used to it. She groaned, rubbing her arms. *I could really do with one of your massages right now.*

The kids under her care decided to join her, making a mockery of every exercise they tried. One boy, who was about five or six years old with sandy blond hair like mine, tried to do a push-up. He stuck his butt high in the air and looked back at Kalli through his legs. "Kalli! Kalli! Look at me. I'm doing it."

Kalli stopped herself just short of giggling and smiled at the boy. "Good job, Nelson. You're doing great."

I bit my tongue as I tried to stick it out at Kalli while doing jumping jacks.

Ugh. No, he's not!

Kalli demonstrated proper tongue sticking out etiquette by stopping her exercise before doing it. *Be nice, Melvin.*

Working out was so much fun with Kalli at my side. Everything was. My eyes watered as I realized how much I'd missed her. She wiped her eyes in sympathy, trying to hide it from the kids at the same time. Fortunately, Dad didn't show up for my training. While I did want to show him to Kalli, I needed a few days to work up to that.

When I was done exercising, I cleaned myself up with a quick flame wash. Kalli giggled. *You're only doing that because I'm watching. Don't tell me you just walked around all stinky after working out before this. Ew, you totally did, I can smell it.*

I shrugged.

I never really thought about it until now.

Kalli didn't use her own flame until she was safely out of range of the kids. I thought it was funny because she went full flaming angel mode in the middle of the street while walking to work. I walked through the tower as well, heading for a stairwell that I hadn't dared approach yet.

When we got there, Marcelle barred my path. "We can't go up there. The upper floors are off limits."

I walked around her. "I am his son, remember? Nothing is off limits to me."

She frowned but fell in line behind me. The next several floors were just duplicates of the lower one hundred floors. While slightly more glamorous than those below, the living conditions in the upper tower were pretty much the same.

Meanwhile, Kalli arrived at her place of work, which included a tiny cubicle with what looked like an electric chair sitting in front of a complicated panel of instruments. I knew what it was because Kalli did. The chair was connected to a very large mana battery that served as the power station for all of Scrap.

Kalli spent a large portion of her day feeding mana to the machine as fast as her body could regenerate it. It was good training for her core, constantly generating and pushing mana into the machine. Still, it was exhausting work. Watching, and feeling, what she was doing, I got an idea.

Wanna trade places?

Kalli blinked. ***What?***

I grinned mischievously.

You come over here, and I'll go over there and feed the machine for you.

Kalli was so shocked at my suggestion that she stopped feeding the machine for a second. ***Can we do that?***

I don't know how I knew, but I just knew we could. Our souls were interchangeable now. I gave hers a quick tug as I initiated the exchange. The next thing I knew, I was adjusting to an out of body experience on a strange planet. Kalli went through a similar culture shock as she suddenly found herself in my body.

She sent me a hasty warning. ***You'd better not touch anything while you're over there!***

I laughed, knowing full well what she meant. Kalli's laugh sounded like music to my ears, even though it sounded a little different coming from me.

I wouldn't dare!

Kalli resumed my explorations of the upper floors while I sunk myself into the task of feeding Scrap.

Let's see what this thing can do.

My core was still bigger than Kalli's, and it went with me when I transferred into Kalli's body. I rested my hands on the grip in front of the chair I was seated in. The porous material was filled with static energy that sucked at the air for ambient mana. Not wanting to let Kalli down, I started to feed the machine. It felt a bit like Zofia's mana battery but so much more advanced.

Meanwhile, Kalli was having a blast chatting up Marcelle and Ulli. I did my best to pay attention to the banter, but I was curious about the potential training I could do with the mega mana battery.

"There are so many delicious foods you haven't tried yet," Marcelle explained in reply to Kalli's question. "If you like, we can go to the dining hall after you're done here. You haven't been in forever, and Alfred misses you."

"Alfred?" Kalli asked, barely catching herself by going through my memories to find out who he was. "Oh, yeah. I'll definitely go see him."

I decided to step it up by infusing a little impatience into my mana coupled with electricity. I figured since it was a battery, why not use the most natural power in the world. My power flowed through the machine, connecting me through the battery and into the network.

I discovered that there were waystations with additional batteries as well as smaller ones in most homes. My mana touched all of them. The addition of both electricity and a compatible emotion increased my output exponentially. It was also easy to do. So easy that I was able to close my eyes and pay more attention to Kalli and the girls as they explored.

That was until I heard a voice, "Hey! Kalliphae. What's going on?"

My eyes shot open. "What? Who said that?"

It felt weird speaking in Kalli's voice. A pair of men burst into the room and looked at the monitors in front of me. I glanced at the screen they seemed fixated on and noticed a few of the gauges were redlining.

Energy Level: 128%

Energy Surplus: 962%

"What? How?" one of the men gasped as he stared at the screen.

Kalli echoed the sentiment in my head. *What did you do?*

I grinned.

I spiced up your mana.

Kalli groaned. *I hope you didn't break anything.*

Marcelle noticed her expression and sat Kalli down, asking if everything was okay. I had my own problems as the men leaned over the menu.

Do you want to change back?

Kalli nodded emphatically. *That's probably best. I really hope you didn't break it.*

[32]

EXPLORING WAS BORING. I was more interested in what Kalli was dealing with on Scrap. One of the men that had barged into the room was running a diagnostic on the control panel. "I don't get it. These readings can't be accurate."

"Is it bad?" Kalli asked. "I didn't break it, did I?"

The man turned around to gape at her. "No. It's not that. If these readings are to be believed, you just supplied all of Scrap with energy for at least a year. That can't be right, can it?"

Kalli stuck out her tongue. *Show off!*

I grinned sheepishly.

I missed you.

She smiled. *Me, too.*

"It's going to take us a while to check this out," the man continued. "We're going to have to inspect the whole grid to make sure this isn't a false reading. Otherwise, we have enough surplus that you won't have to come back for a while. Would you like me to look into other jobs you can do in the meantime? You'd be well within your rights to not take another job until you're needed here again."

Kalli shook her head. "I'll work. Let me know how I can help."

"Excellent," the other man replied. "Perhaps we can get you

training to be an engineer or a technician. Your fire magic will come in handy for both of those jobs."

I'll help.

Kalli smiled. I continued the climb as she went over her options with the two men. It turned out they were ultimately responsible for the infrastructure on Scrap while Kalli was more or less a hamster running in a wheel. With her doing the unthinkable, they saw untapped potential in her and were anxious to exploit it. I wasn't sure how I felt about that.

After about the fifth floor of entitled chosen women slamming doors in my face, I started ignoring them and sticking to the stairwell. My theory was there had to be something special on the top floor. We climbed another twenty floors before we had to stop.

Marcelle sat on the stairs, trying to catch her breath. "I need a break."

"I thought it would be Ulli who ran out of gas first," I teased.

Ulli laughed, flexing her arms in a bodybuilder pose. "I'm a dancer. I can climb circles around you."

"Wanna bet?" I asked, taking three steps at a time to get a head start.

She was quick to react, kicking off the wall as she flitted past me. Marcelle whined from below. "Come on, you two. Give me a break. My body isn't designed for all these stairs."

I was too caught up in the race to pay attention. I wasn't about to lose to Ulli. By the time I realized something was wrong, she was two flights above me. I wasn't sure how she was doing it, but she cleared entire floors in a single leap. It was getting so bad, there was only one way to win. I folded mana over myself and stepped into the void. Once inside, time slowed to a crawl, and I had plenty of time to plan for victory. Just as I approached Origin, Kalli reminded me I wasn't alone.

That's cheating, you know.

I froze, looking around in surprise.

That's strange. You can talk to me in here? I thought time was standing still.

Kalli giggled. *I'm a part of you, so if you can move, I can move.*

I tried to picture Kalli frozen on Scrap while internal Kalli talked to me in the void. She had other thoughts, nudging me toward another one of the orbs. *This one is Scrap. I don't know how I know, but I can feel myself there. If you wanted to come to me, all you'd have to do is go there.*

It was so tempting to do just that. I could be with Kalli in the blink of an eye. But Aya warned us not to do that. Dad would find out and ground us all over again. Then, there would be no escape. I had to get that mirror first. Returning my attention to the tower, I zoomed in on the stairwell. Ulli was only a few floors from the top. I decided to be practical. Winning the bet wasn't important.

I dropped out of the void right in front of Marcelle, who was just starting to ascend again. She gasped when she saw me, but I didn't give her time to complain, wrapping mana around both of us and pulling her back into the void with me. That time, I immediately dropped us just outside of the large door at the top of the stairs.

Ulli made it just in time to see me standing next to Marcelle, who was retching while desperately trying to catch her breath. She pouted. "You cheated!"

I gave her a sympathetic smile. "You're right. I had no clue you were that fast."

Ulli planted her hands on her hips. "It's part of my class. Since you cheated, I won the bet. That means you owe me a favor! I want you to take me on another date."

Another one? Kalli's hands were on her hips, too, as she walked down the street leading to her house. I could tell she wasn't mad. She had full access to my memories of the first date after all. *That girl has a crush on you. You better let her down easy.*

I know. She knows. I told her about you.

In answer to Ulli's question, I said, "Sure thing. Where do you want to go this time?"

She paused for a moment, a look of confusion on her face. "Wow, I didn't expect you to go along with it. Um, let me think about it. I'll tell you later."

Kalli laughed at me. *That wasn't letting her down at all.*
You can kiss me in front of her when you see me.
She scowled. *What makes you think I want to kiss you?*
You kissed me plenty last night.
That made Kalli giggle. *In your dreams!*
I laughed out loud, earning me a look from both Ulli and Marcelle.
Yeah, but it was a great dream.

————

The door at the top of the stairs was sealed. There was no doorknob or deadbolt. While we could plainly see the hinges where the door should open, there didn't seem to be any other way of entering. Marcelle and Ulli refused to help me find a way in.

Ulli backed away from the door and whispered, "Do you think that's The Creator's room?"

I laughed. "I certainly hope so. Otherwise, there was no purpose in coming all the way up here."

"You can't be serious," Marcelle said in an annoyed voice. "Are you trying to get us thrown out of the tower?"

"Hey, you wanted to come," I replied, shrugging. "Do you want me to take you back to my room?"

Ulli looked to Marcelle hopefully, but she shook her head. "No, we're here already. Besides, it'll probably be worse if you get caught, and he finds out you wandered off without us."

I decided that was good enough and ran my fingers along the crease in the door. Mana flowed out of me, which I hoped would give me an idea of what was on the other side. To my surprise, the door reacted and swung open. I stood there framed in the door, staring at a rather plain and very messy bedroom. It wasn't grand by any means unlike my room or the rooms of the tower maidens. A small cot rested in the corner, and the rest of the room was cluttered with shelves of exotic-looking items.

I scanned the room for mirror and, to my surprise, found three. The first was attached to the wall. It looked like a pane of glass that someone had clamped on because they wanted to see their reflection. I ruled that one out. The second was an ornate mirror framed in gold with colorful gemstones of every color. The final mirror was the one I remembered seeing in the artifact room. It was a simple wooden mirror with a dark brown flame.

I walked over and picked it up. Nothing happened. It was rather disappointing compared to the previous artifacts I'd encountered. It didn't accept me or attempt to bind itself to me. It felt as mundane as an ordinary household item. When I looked down at it, I was surprised. There was no reflection. I turned it over in my hand and held it up close to my face. There was nothing but an opaque glassy surface.

"Hello?" I spoke to the mirror. Ulli and Marcelle peeked over my shoulder, curious about what I was examining.

"Put that down!" a stern voice echoed through the room.

Marcelle squeaked and Ulli dropped to the floor. I looked down and realized she'd fainted. I set the mirror back where I'd found it and said, "Hi, Dad."

He glared at me. "Care to explain yourself? What are you doing in my bedroom?"

I shrugged. "I was looking for the mirror you said didn't exist."

"Why are you behaving like this?" Merlin asked. "Am I not treating you well enough?"

"You confined me to the planet," I countered, puffing my chest out to stand up to him. "I still don't see why I have to stay here. If you care about me, you should let me go find Kalli."

"I already told you," he growled. "She's dead. If I could bring her here, I'd have done it by now."

I was stunned. While I should have pieced things together when I discovered Kalli's whereabouts, hearing him after the fact drove it home. My father was a liar. His lies about Kalli made me second guess everything he'd told me since I met him. I'd trusted him about so many things. Would it kill me if I teleported off the planet? Was my mom missing? I asked the one question that seemed to matter.

"Are you using the system to destroy the universe?"

He frowned. "Who told you that?"

"Nobody," I blanched, trying to come up with a lie of my own. "It just seems like you're up to something."

Merlin sighed. "Is that what you think of me? The answer is no, I am not using the system to do anything of the sort. As I've explained to you at great length, I created the system to regulate the use of magic. You wouldn't like the alternative. Without some modulation, awakened can become too powerful. They are the ones you need to fear destroying the universe not the system."

I wanted to ask Merlin if he needed to be regulated but decided not to stir the pot. "So, why can't I leave Origin?"

For his credit, Merlin did seem pained by the decision. "Give me a little more time. Then, I'll let you go out. I promise. I'd also like to train you up a little more so you'll be ready to take over for me someday. I'd like to retire once I find your mother."

"What about the mirror?" I asked, glancing down at the strange artifact.

"That thing?" he asked. "Why are you so fixated on it?"

"It's cool!" It was the only thing I could think to say.

It took him a while, but he finally relented. "Fine. Just do your best not to break it."

———

"Why did you want that mirror?" Marcelle asked. She was still mad at me for getting her in trouble with The Creator. Ulli wasn't even talking to me.

I looked into the reflectionless mirror. "I don't know. Something told me it's important."

"Important enough to risk The Creator's wrath?" Marcelle asked.

"To me, he's just Dad," I replied, trying to force the mirror to reflect something with my mind. "I don't see why it's such a big deal. I told you that you didn't have to come."

Marcelle grunted and stormed off. Kalli spoke in her place, *you could be a little nicer. It wouldn't hurt.*

I sighed, flipping the mirror over again. Kalli was right. She always was. I had more important things to deal with, though. One was figuring out why the mirror was so important. I decided to try infusing it with mana.

[33]

A PAIR of red eyes appeared in the mirror, looking back at me. It was followed by a low ominous voice, "So, the offspring comes to seek me out. I see by your eyes that you have become corrupted."

"I have not!" I replied in an unintentionally loud voice.

Kalli was also curious about the mirror's proclamation. *Why would it say that?*

The mirror continued, "I see it in your eyes. The eyes of your kind never lie. Crimson means you allowed your inner hate to overwhelm you."

Kalli noticed my eye color for the first time. *What happened to your blue eye? It turned red.*

I frowned.

That happened right after I thought you died.

It was true. When I thought I'd lost her, I wanted to kill Rasputin all over again. However, it was just a fleeting thought. It wasn't like all the love in my heart died. Had it? Then again, I did make a proclamation that if I got Kalli back, I'd kill anyone who put her in danger. Kalli sensed my thought and said, *Please, don't kill. Not even for me. Not if you can help it.*

My heart sank, and I realized I'd made up my mind.

I can't lose you. Not again.

Kalli sighed. ***There are other ways.***

Focusing my attention back on the mirror, I asked, "What exactly do you do?"

The eyes glowed brightly. "I am the reflection that shows everything for what it truly is. Ask me a question, and I shan't lie."

"Why was I supposed to find you?" I asked, eager to get to the bottom of the mystery.

"Ask yourself that," the mirror reflected the question. "You sought me."

"I was told to," I replied. I couldn't say by who because Dad might be listening.

"You are mistaken," the mirror droned. "I am not the artifact you're looking for."

"What am I looking for, then?" I asked, flustered that I'd broken into Dad's room for nothing. "Can you at least tell me where to find the artifact I am looking for?"

The red eyes vanished. Kalli asked, ***Did you break it?***

I shrugged.

Maybe it's thinking.

The eyes returned a moment later, looking slightly dimmer. "The location is hidden. Even from me. You seek that which controls all. It is the base of your father's power and that which is both the beginning and the end. He without a doubt keeps it close. I used most of my stored mana seeking this for you. Please, allow me to recharge."

"Can I help you?" I asked. "I have mana."

The mirror shuddered. "For me, mana is knowledge. If I absorb your mana, all I will be able to reflect is you."

"Okay, take all the time you need," I replied, stuffing the mirror in my fanny pack. It wasn't like I needed it anymore. The main reason I wanted it was to find Kalli. Then, when Aya told me to find an artifact, I'd assumed it was the mirror I was after. Now, I had no clue what I was looking for.

Kalli had arrived at home during my adventure in Merlin's room. She was alone in the house, sitting on the couch with her eyes closed while she followed me through our connection. I grinned as an idea came to me.

Do you want to switch places and try dinner? It's really good.

Kalli smiled. *That sounds like fun, and I'd like to meet Alfred.*

So, we swapped places again. I found myself alone in the small house. It was still early in the day on Scrap. I knew because Kalli knew that the kids wouldn't be home from school for a while. Nobody expected her to be home either because she usually worked at the power plant all day.

Do you mind if explore?

Kalli stuck out her tongue, or was it my tongue? *Just don't do anything outrageous. I still have to explain how I pulled that stunt at the power plant.*

I laughed.

I'd never do anything outrageous.

I wrapped my mana around Kalli's body and jumped into the void. While Kalli didn't know how to teleport yet, I did. Being in her body allowed me to explore the orb that was Scrap. As usual, Kalli was in the void with me. *Hey! I said don't do anything outrageous, and the first thing you do is something you know I don't know how to do.*

I laughed.

I'm just exploring like I said I was going to.

I didn't have to worry about Kalli doing anything on Origin. While we were in the void, time flowed differently. I knew my physical body was frozen in my bedroom, and Kalli along with it. The Kalli that was with me was the same yet different. She was the Kalli that existed within me, though the experience would flow back into her once we emerged in reality.

Looking at Scrap, it was a fraction of the size of Origin. There were no oceans or large bodies of water. I couldn't tell where the planet got its water from. Or if it was even big enough to be called a planet. Maybe it was a small moon or a battle station. I zoomed in to see if there was anything inside of the planet. Unfortunately, while there were some caves underground, there was no hidden Imperial base. Kalli snickered at me as I explored. *Hurry up! I'm hungry.*

No, you're not. Time is literally standing still.

She added a sense of urgency in my mind. ***Still, I want to try that food. Pick a place already.***

I refocused my attention on the various structures on Scrap. For the most part, all I saw were rows of houses separated by a highway that circled the tiny planetoid. There were only a handful of places that were of any interest. I chose one of those. It was a cluster of buildings surrounding one of the planets only larger buildings. It appeared to be roughly twenty stories in height and entirely covered in glass. I appeared on the roof next to an access door.

Inside was another stairwell. I noticed Kalli started moving as well in my body, collecting Marcelle and Ulli on the way to dinner. Fortunately, she had access to my memories and had no issues finding the dining hall. On the way, she apologized to the girls, "I'm sorry about earlier. I didn't mean to get you in trouble with my father. I should have found another way without involving either of you."

My immediate reaction was to be mad at Kalli. She didn't need to apologize for me. I could do that on my own. Surprisingly, Marcelle spoke for the first time since storming off, "Apology accepted, but I'd appreciate it if you put at least a little thought about us into your actions. We don't have any choice when you do things like that. While he might not get mad at you, thing's won't be good for us if you ever leave."

"I won't abandon you," Kalli promised. I found myself agreeing with that sentiment.

"Do you promise?" Ulli squeaked, her voice barely audible.

Kalli smiled, putting a hand on her shoulder. "You have my word. Wherever we go, you go."

"We?" Marcelle asked, looking concerned.

Kalli gasped, a feminine sound I didn't usually make. "Oops, I meant wherever I go. Sorry, I'm just really hungry."

Marcelle raised an eyebrow but said nothing. I found myself walking down flights of stairs as Kalli entered the dining hall. They made their way to my private table where Achemes the chef was already wading through the other tables to get there. Kalli's mouth watered as she smelled the wonderful food we had every day in the tower. My stomach rumbled. Kalli's body was hungry.

I'm sorry I didn't get you anything to eat.

She giggled. *It's fine. You have to deal with the pain. I get to go on a free diet. Just make sure you take me home before you swap back.*

I poked my head into each floor as I descended. Most of the floors looked like offices. Some of the floors had an open floor plan and cubicles that were largely occupied. Others had private offices, most of which had their doors closed. I realized belatedly that I should have come in through the main entrance so I could see what the building actually was. Then I found the elevator.

Floor 1: Lobby
Floor 2: Reception
Floor 3: Day Care
Floor 4: Medical Wing
Flood 5: Spa and Fitness
Floor 6-10: News Officers
Floor 11-15: Research and Development
Floor 16-20: Governor's Offices

Armed with new information, I decided I didn't want to just barge in on the governor. I had no reason to disrupt anything. The fun option would be to check out the Spa, so I selected floor 5. The elevator descended smoothly. I supposed that had something to do with it being powered by magic.

DING.

The door slid open, and I stepped out. A woman in a white uniform smiled as I approached. "Good afternoon, Miss Kalliphae. Welcome to the Central building. Are you here to visit the spa? Step through the door on the left. I mutely did as instructed and walked down a narrow corridor to a changing room.

My eyes widened, and then my vision went black. When it returned, I found myself holding a drumstick of some exotic bird. Kalli had swapped us back by force. Judging from the lack of sensory perception from her end, she was blocking me again. Even though I knew the answer, I had to ask.

What happened? You changed back.

She growled at me. *Why did you walk into a room full of naked women? I wanted to eat that. You better keep the connection open so I can at least know what it tastes like.*

You can keep the connection open on your side, too, you know.

Once again, I already knew the answer. *No I can't! You'll be lucky if I ever let you use my body again.*

She blushed when I thought about various ways of using her body. *I didn't mean it like that!*

I sighed.

I know, but I can dream, right?

She laughed and replied, *No, you can't!*

Kalli made me try one of everything. She wanted to know what all the food tasted like, even the stuff I didn't like. While she kept her vision blocked, she did let me experience the soothing sensation of the spa as she soaked in mineral water. Everybody seemed to know who she was, and they all loved her. She had that effect on everybody. It was a skill I'd never developed. Kalli had some advice when I dwelled on it.

You could try being nicer to everyone.

I groaned.

I'm nice!

Kalli gave me a knowing smile. *How about you treat everyone like they were me?*

I thought about that, and she continued, *No! I don't want you to kiss everyone. Just try smiling and acting like you're happy when you see them. You have natural charm, when you choose to use it.*

I tried smiling at Ulli. She got a dreamy look in her eyes and smiled back. Kalli sighed. *Okay, maybe don't try smiling too much at that girl. She's lovesick.*

———

After dinner, I made plans for the next couple days. With no clear direction for the artifact I was looking for and having already found Kalli, we needed to come up with some things to do. Kalli planned on looking for another job, so I decided to show her around Origin during my free time. There was just one other thing I needed to explain. I hadn't really thought about it since I was reunited with her. She knew everything the moment it entered my mind.

Melvin, what is that candle? Did you travel in time?

[34]

I SAT on my bed preparing to take a trip into the past. Kalli was already tucked into bed back on Scrap but wasn't sleeping. All her attention was focused on me and, more importantly, the dark candle in my hand.

Are you sure you want to do this? I don't know where it's going to take me?

She huffed. *It's my past you're delving into. I think I have a right to be there.*

Okay, but be ready for it. Turning into smoke can be a little disorienting.

I wondered if a physical manifestation of Kalli would also be present when I went back in time. The moment I lit the candle, I evaporated into black smoke, which was sucked into the void. Before I knew it, the world rematerialized around me into a forest filled with tall trees and mossy green stones. In the distance, a young girl stood proudly holding a wisp of light. She was waiting for someone.

I felt Kalli's bubbly presence inside me. *Oh, Melvin! I know what happens today. Will you let me do it?*

Um, sure.

While I wasn't sure how Kalli was going to react to seeing herself, I sure wasn't expecting her to want to participate. I applied my usual illusion and relinquished control. Kalli smiled and strode from the forest with purpose. "Greetings, young Kalliphae. I see you've made progress. Today, I am going to teach you a spell that is one of my personal favorites. I think you will come to enjoy it as well."

"Will I be able to shoot a fireball?" Young Kalli asked with an eager look on her face.

"In due time," I heard my voice reply. "You must understand the importance of your training. Trying to bypass steps will only make your magic weaker. By the time I am done with you, you will wield fire like it's a part of your body."

To demonstrate what she was talking about, Kalli went full flame angel mode. It was an odd sensation being completely coated in fire. It flickered around me, covering every inch of my body. No, it was a part of my body, attached to my core through a million outlets in my mana channels. Kalli wielded it like an extension of her body. In that moment, she taught me something. I learned that just being able to wield all sorts of mana didn't mean I was a master of it. Not on the level Kalli was. I resigned myself to just how much I still had to learn.

Kalli grinned inwardly. *You should see my fireball now.*

The demonstration had the desired effect on young Kalli. The kid bounced up and down eagerly as Kalli walked her through the basics of the "**Pvruzth**" spell. It took young Kalli half a day to see any results. When it happened, it was so fast, I might have missed it if not for Kalli whispering in my ear, *Watch her left hand. She's about to make her first spark.*

Pride swelled within me as I watched the child swoon over her success. "Master! Did you see? Did you see? I did it. I made fire. Real fire. I felt the heat!"

"Well done," Kalli praised her. "Practice that until you can do it on demand. Once you can sustain the flame for more than a minute, I will teach you how to control the heat and smoke. Both are useful in the right circumstances, but a true pyromancer exercises exact control over every aspect of her flame."

———

Even though there was only one body, I felt like I spent hours that night sitting next to Kalli while she instructed herself on the proper use of magic. Little Kalli, as I was calling her, didn't make much progress. Kalli assured me it was all part of the process. *Us mortals don't just wake up one morning knowing exactly how to summon young maidens from other worlds. Some of us have to work at it.*

I'm pretty sure I screwed that spell up.

She giggled, which meant I giggled. Little Kalli looked up in confusion, and Kalli had to explain. "Sorry, I was just thinking about something funny."

"What was it, Master?" Little Kalli asked. "I want to know something funny."

"It was about a boy," Kalli admitted before catching herself and realizing she was me. "Err, I mean, one of the boys I taught in the past who did something funny."

It was my turn to laugh. Fortunately, I wasn't in control of my body at the moment. Kalli chose that moment to reply to me, *Are you saying you screwed up and meant to summon a different girl?*

I mock gasped, pretending to be appalled.

I would never!

It didn't matter. She knew I wouldn't change a thing just as I knew she was happy I messed up the spell. We sat in silence for a while and watched Little Kalli progress through her second spell. The little spark soon became a flame. Once she managed that, she squeezed her eyes shut and focused on making it stay. No matter how she tried, the flame always died after a few short seconds. She looked up imploringly. "This is hard. Can I try it inside where there's no wind?"

Kalli looked around. While there was a gentle breeze, it wasn't strong enough to even snuff out a match. "Sure, you can practice inside the cabin, but I forbid you to use your fire indoors outside of my direct supervision until you learn to control it."

"Oka-ay," Little Kalli chanted as she bounced to her feet.

We followed her in and sat in the lone chair that sat next to a cot. Little Kalli cast her spell, and the magic died once again. Then, she tried cupping her hand with the other one. That also failed. Her next test involved holding her breath. That ended theatrically when the fire winked out, and she started coughing violently.

Kalli was patient with her. "You are making a fundamental mistake. You've done well to generate the mana needed to generate fire. That isn't enough, though. Magic fire cannot survive on its own the same way regular fire can. You have to feed it constantly or it will die. When you speak the words, concentrate on the flow of your mana and will yourself to keep feeding it. I think we should go back outside. I'd hate to have to rebuild this cabin if you burn it down."

"I don't think I'm strong enough for that," Little Kalli muttered as she followed us outside.

———

It happened about an hour later. A great plume of fire erupted from the hapless girl as she expended all her mana in the spell. Kalli caught her and eased her to the ground. Little Kalli was unconscious. Kalli smiled at me as we carried her into the cabin.

I knew she was going to do that because I did it. Her next lesson is going to be learning to limit the flow, but that will have to wait for another day. It would be so much easier if you awakened her mana channels to give her full control, but I know why you can't. That's something special she needs to share with her you.

Her me?

Kalli stuck out her tongue, my tongue. *She has her own you. She doesn't get my you. You're mine!*

I'm confused!

We both laughed as a voice invaded the moment, "Marcy! He's doing it again. I think Melvin's on drugs!"

My eyes flashed open. The candle had gone out again, and Ulli was trying to pry it out of my hands. I quickly tugged it away and stashed it in my fanny pack just as Marcelle marched into the room. "What do you mean drugs?"

"He was sniffing black smoke from that candle," she announced. "I saw it come out of his nose."

"It's not a drug," I muttered. It took me a moment to realized that not only had Kalli relinquished my body, but she was also back on Scrap, stretching luxuriously in her bed.

She smiled when she felt my focus on her. *Good Morning. I slept good for the first time in a long time.*

My heart caught in my throat when I realized we'd stayed in the candle all night, and I wasn't going to be able to share a dream with her. Kalli laughed and sat up in bed. *Relax, we can dream together tomorrow. There's plenty of time. I'm not going anywhere anymore. Not even your father can stop us.*

With that thought in mind, I hopped out of bed, startling Ulli. Marcelle touched the back of her hand to my forehead. "He doesn't feel sick."

"He's not sick," Ulli complained. "He's high."

"I am not!" I groaned. "What I am is hungry. Let's go grab breakfast."

"See!" Ulli exclaimed triumphantly. "Now, he has the munchies."

"It's breakfast," I grumbled. "Am I not allowed to be hungry first thing in the morning?"

After grabbing a quick shower and freshening up, we made our way to the dining hall. Kalli let me stay in control as she had breakfast to make for the children in her house. As usual, their parents had gone off to work before she woke up.

Do you ever see them? It seems like their kids never see them either.

It reminded me of my mom. She had always worked three jobs, and the only reason I knew she'd come home on some nights was that the couch was slept on. Kalli sent feelings of warmth and affection to cheer me up.

Don't worry, Mel. We'll find your mother, and the kids do see their parents. They're around all the time on the weekends. Some of them work on the other side of the planet and don't come back till late. Some of the other older kids in the neighborhood pitch in to look out for them.

———

I stuffed myself during breakfast. Not because I wanted to but because Kalli wanted to try everything in one sitting. We started with a fruit smoothy with blue fruit that looked like strawberries but tasted more like bananas. Then Kalli had to try the orange one, and the green one. I was already not hungry when she saw the green omelets. After that, she wanted to try waffles with several different toppings. It was only when I threatened to puke that she finally relented but only after making me promise to come back for lunch.

Dealing with the stomachache turned into another form of training. I sat in the garden by myself and focused on the food in my stomach. While I had a basic understanding of how digestion worked, I'd never tried to help the process. I pushed mana into my stomach to see what would happen. There wasn't much room in there with all the food Kalli made me eat, so I immediately felt like I was going to be sick. I needed to introduce a little bit at a time and let it do its job. The problem was finding the right kind. An element like fire was out of the question unless I wanted to belch smoke and vomit ash. Just thinking about it made Kalli gag.

Ew, Mel. Stop thinking about gross things while I'm cooking. Sorry.

I focused on mana that would devour the food. Was that even an option? The answer was an emotion rather than an element. I made the mana hungry and let it trickle into my stomach and attack the food. The result was interesting. The food changed the mana, infusing it with a sort of life sustaining energy that I didn't normally generate. Once that mana fed, it returned to my mana stream to be replaced by more hungry mana. Before I knew it, the contents of my stomach were gone, and I was hungry again. While my mana was supercharged by the food, my physical body was not happy that I'd stolen all its sustenance.

I decided to try filling my stomach with the newly satisfied mana to see what happened. The hunger in my stomach was replaced by a warm satisfied feeling as my body went to work absorbing it. There wasn't even a need to digest it. I watched in awe as it made its way into my body through my intestines. Bits of mana found its way to my organs and muscles more naturally than when I force infused it. I also felt the effect on my brain, getting a lucid feeling that I normally associated with being in the zone.

Kalli noticed as well. *You're going to have to teach me that.*

I smiled.

Sure, but first you need to teach me something.

Kalli blinked in confusion. *Teach you what?*

I held out my hand and altered my mana to fire.

"Pvruzth."

[35]

KALLI COULDN'T STOP GIGGLING, and it made me very self-conscious. She covered her mouth with her hand in an attempt to control herself. *I'm sorry, Mel. It's just I've never seen anything you weren't naturally good at.*

I sighed. It wasn't that I wasn't good at it. I was probably better at making a flame angel than anyone except for Kalli. She was in a league of her own. While most pyromancers would have long moved onto more advanced spells, she'd internalized the flame hand spell and made it into something else entirely.

How come you never learned more spells?

She stuck her tongue out at no-one in particular. *It was probably because you summoned me before I could learn anything else. I always thought it was strange why my master chose me, a little girl from an orphanage, to teach magic to. It wasn't like I showed a lot of potential.*

I focused on calling the flame as close as possible to myself. While I was skilled at controlling the heat of the flame, it wasn't quite a part of me like it was for Kalli. With every flare of emotion, she wielded mana like an extension of herself. I felt a burning desire to do the same.

Kalli stopped what she was doing and rubbed her chin. ***Why don't you try to learn it with your natural element?***

She had a point. I was so caught up on copying her that I was trying to force an element that wasn't natural to me. Using fire required more concentration that took away from the core of the exercise. I snuffed out the fire in my soul and tried to focus on my natural element. There was always a little fire leftover that made me feel toasty inside because Kalli had taken up residence.

While my initial thought had been that my element was light, it was more than that. It was light in the same way that light contained every color of the spectrum. There were traces of every element buried deep within the mana that my core generated. That was why I could change it at will.

I wondered what my father's core was like. Had I inherited my multiple elements from him? What was my mom's core like? Was it a pebble like the unawakened I'd seen in the past or was it something special? Being that it was my mom, I just knew it had to be special. I closed my eyes and focused on letting it flow through me. Kalli did the same and nudged me with her mind, beckoning me to feel what she did. There was a fluid motion where mana burst out of her everywhere all at once. Little tendrils of fire danced, swaying back and forth while connected through deep roots that fed off her core.

I followed suit and pushed. Mana burst from me in a brilliant explosion, incinerating everything around me. The garden erupted into flame, and the ground below me turned to dust. I caught myself just in time and wrapped mana around myself, jumping into the void before I destroyed any more of the garden.

The void, unlike Merlin's tower, was made up of dark stuff and universes that seemed impervious to damage. I floated there for a long time, willing my natural essence not to devour everything it came into contact with. If Kalli's flame could stop burning, my mana could do the same. She encouraged me from within. Eventually, I managed to get the whole thing under control. It wasn't so simple as telling fire not to be hot. I had to do the same with all the elements. Water wasn't allowed to be wet, wind wasn't allowed to blow, etc. Corralling it gave me a sense of oneness with myself. I floated silently in the void with my legs crossed as my mana hummed around me like an aura.

"Trying something new today, are we?" Merlin asked.

I opened one eye to find him in the same pose, sitting cross-legged with a perfect aura of his own radiating out. He winked at me and continued, "What you've discovered is a form of meditation. Monks use it to refine their mana and find balance. The more practical side of the technique is that it teaches control. You've done well to teach yourself this. As I'm sure you're now painfully aware, our mana is complicated. Normally, it's a bad idea to try to be everything at once. However, if you master it, you can do anything. Even rule the universe."

I laughed nervously. "Is that something I want to do?"

"You had better," Merlin snapped. "You're my heir, remember? You need to be ready just as soon as I wrap up this project."

"What project?" I asked, hoping to get some insight into my dad's ambitions.

He frowned, his aura becoming unstable. He quickly pulled it back in to mask the slip. "I intend to find your mother and settle down."

"I can help with that," I replied. "I'm sure if you let me go back to Earth, I can—"

He cut me off. "That won't be necessary. Your training here is of greater importance. You must be ready to take your role when the time comes. I will not be able to mollycoddle you after I...after I...find your mother."

He was hiding something. That much was for sure. Was the mirror key to finding out what it was? Was I supposed to ask the mirror? I had so many questions, and Kalli had gone silent. She was listening, too, of course. I felt her. She just didn't have anything to say. Or was she scared of Merlin? I wouldn't blame her. I found him intimidating myself. He definitely wasn't a normal dad, not that I knew what that was.

Eventually, he stood and headed over to the sphere that was Origin. "Don't stay in here too long, son. This place has a tendency to mess with your mind."

Then he was gone, leaving me to continue the exercise. I'd managed to stop being a walking bomb, but I still didn't have the kind of control Kalli did. She guided me in my practice, offering feelings of support which helped me concentrate. *You don't have to do your whole body at once. Start with a finger, then move on to a hand.*

While she could have chastised me for being overly ambitious, she was patient, saying nothing when I messed up while praising me when I made progress. I realized she likely needed to advance her training more than I did, yet here she was talking me through a beginner level spell. Then again, I couldn't feel Kalli in the real world while I was in the void. It was another level of separation.

Kalli, can you feel yourself outside of here?

She blinked. I don't know how I knew she blinked since she didn't have a body. *Yes, and no. You see, everything you experience in here will pass to me when you return to reality. Similarly, everything I experience when I'm cut off will come to you. Remember, a piece of you is with her just like I'm with you.*

But what if you get in trouble?

Kalli giggled. *You're forgetting how the void works. Less than a second will pass while you're in here. That's why you never realized you were apart. I always realize it because I feel all the time you spend in here in an instant when you come out.*

Why didn't you say anything?

I was shocked that she kept such an important thing to herself. She smiled. *It wasn't important. Besides, I'm just happy that I'm not alone anymore.*

I knew exactly how she felt.

Do you think we can take our relationship to a sixth level? That way even this won't be able to keep us apart.

Kalli grinned. *You can always just take me with you.*

Good point.

I chose that moment to head back to the tower. After gaining enough control to not destroy anything, there was little benefit to staying in the void. I went over to Origin and focused on the tower where Merlin had already repaired the damage to the garden that I made. I dropped lightly to the ground and contacted Kalli.

I'm back.

She sighed. *I know. I was with you in there. Remember.*

I couldn't help but laugh.

No fair! Your inner me didn't tell me anything.

She shot a feeling of warmth through the connection. *Well, you were only gone for about a second. Your inner me already told you that.*

This is getting confusing.

Kalli laughed. *I know.*

———

"Take me to the library," I announced as I walked with Marcelle and Ulli after my morning workout.

"Sure," Marcelle replied. "The tower has several well-stocked repositories. If they're anything specific you'd like to research."

"Yes," I replied, hoping to surprise Kalli. "I'd like to look through some spell books."

Of course, Kalli already knew. Marcelle led me down quite a few floors. "The books on magic are actually on the lower levels. Tower maidens that make it up this high are usually interested in fiction rather than practical application."

"Yeah, romance novels," Ulli said, making a face.

Marcelle gave her a knowing look. "Yes, some of the more popular novels are more than a little risqué."

The library was on the twentieth floor. It consisted of old tomes with thick leather binding. I plucked one from the shelf and asked, "Are any of these available online?"

Ulli laughed. "See! I'm not the only one that thinks this is a little old-fashioned."

Marcelle rolled her eyes. "The bound volumes here in the tower are first editions. They were transcribed by great scholars of old and contain magic."

Mrs. Hodgins would love that. Scholars who are more ancient than she is.

Kalli scowled at my joke. *She's fifty-four. She isn't that old.*

I'd never thought about her exact age, but I must have known. Kalli knew, after all. It only took me a few minutes to find books on elemental magic. A bright red one stuck out.

Fire Magic for Beginners

Meanwhile, back at Lavender's house...

A great puff of steam erupted from a large machine. It looked like one of the first computers ever made. Massive, boxed components lined the walls filled with humming machinery attached to an even larger machine in the middle of the room by thick rubber tubes. Everything made noise. Some of it grinding, while others beeped.

Shara tapped a small hose that fed into the machine. A tiny flask dripped a small red liquid that she knew was her last sample of Kalli's blood. "If this fails, we're out of luck."

"It won't fail," Zofia announced. "It will do something, and that in itself is a success."

Joe nodded, running a hand over the machine. His eyes fogged over as though he was seeing something none of the others could. "It's working. So long as that's really Kalli's blood, it will work."

Lavender sat in a chair next to a door. It was a special door in the middle of the room, and it wasn't attached to anything. Anyone who knew Lavender knew how her doors worked. While it currently did nothing, once she applied an enchanted doorknob, it would open to some far-off place.

Wendy sat next to Lavender, sipping meticulously prepared tea. She'd offered some to the others but only Lavender and Joe accepted. Zofia refused to drink anything if she didn't know where it came from. Shara said she wasn't thirsty.

Suddenly, the machine let out a satisfying *ding!*

"Did it work?" Wendy asked, leaning forward in anticipation.

"Of course, it worked," Zofia scoffed.

"I can see it," Joe added, sliding open a tray and gingerly touching a shining red doorknob. "Whether or not we succeeded, my creation did its job."

"Our creation," Zofia corrected.

"You just programmed it," Joe replied with a scowl.

"It's not a competition," Wendy said, offering her boyfriend a sympathetic smile.

Shara laughed. "Of course, it is."

Surprisingly, Lavender laughed, too. "There's nothing wrong with a little healthy competition. That's what makes all of you so spectacular. Now, are you ready to be reunited with your friends?"

"Yes!" they all screamed in unison.

"Very well," Lavender grinned, pointing to the door. "Who wants to do the honors?"

Wendy stood up, taking the doorknob from Joe. "I might as well do something useful."

She took the knob over to the door and placed it in front of the hole. Like magic, it slipped into place with a *click*. Wendy took a deep breath while everyone gathered behind her and slowly eased the door open.

[36]

I SAT THERE in a daze staring at the fire magic book. My mind was elsewhere. More specifically, it was on Kalli, who stood dumbfounded in her house where several unexpected visitors had arrived.

Lavender stood framed in the doorway as Kalli was tackled by Wendy. Joe, Zofia, and Shara next to her watching awkwardly as the two girls struggled on the floor to compose themselves. I desperately wanted to teleport to them and escape through that door, but I remembered what Aya had told me. If I did that, Merlin would notice, and we would be trapped all over again. It was fine, though. Lavender was there, and she always had a plan.

Kalli read my mind and stared straight at Lavender. "You can't rescue me without Melvin. We need to find a way to free him from his father."

Lavender smiled and moved out of the way. Another person stepped through the door and smiled at Kalli.

Mom!

Kalli repeated my thought. "Mom!"

My mom smiled warmly at her. "You've become quite close to my son. Thank you so much for taking care of him."

"You're welcome," Kalli stammered, blushing furiously. "It was... my pleasure. I mean, I do love him. He loves me, too."

Lavender didn't mix words, her eyes baring down on both of us, even though there was no way she could see me. "This is very important. Have the two of you become one."

"We didn't have..." Kalli trailed off hopelessly, admitting. "Yes. We did."

"Excellent!" Lavender said, smiling for the first time since I could remember. "That will save us a lot of time."

Nobody heard Lavender but me, though. Everyone was too busy congratulating a very red Kalli for taking our relationship to the next level. I hoped it wasn't a problem that we had only been together in a dream. Otherwise, Lavender was in for a big disappointment.

Once the group let Kalli come up for air, Lavender started barking orders, "Get the equipment in here. Kalli, you need to get Melvin to find as safe a place as possible for us to hide when we get there. The tower isn't safe, as well as the majority of Origin. Foreigners from another world will stand out like sore thumbs. Melvin should know at least a few people who will sympathize with us."

Why are we hiding? Can't I just teleport over there and be done with it?

"He wants to know why he can't just come here?" Kalli translated.

Lavender quickly held up a hand. "No! He mustn't leave Origin. We cannot bridge that gap without the two of you. Your connection is the only way we will ever get onto Origin before tragedy strikes."

"Oh, no!" Kalli cried. "What kind of tragedy? Is something going to happen to Melvin?"

Lavender shook her head. "It isn't anything as simple as that. Merlin has built a machine that's been collecting mana for longer than any of you have been alive, and he intends to use it."

"What's wrong with that?" Joe asked, looking intrigued.

"That much mana must never be unleashed at once," Lavender explained. "Every time you cast a spell, there's feedback. Normally, you don't notice or just chalk it up as the way magic works. It's kind of like how you know fire is hot or water is wet. It's that gentle tug you feel when your mana enters the world. On a small scale, the effects on the world are negligible. However, with the amount of mana Merlin has accumulated, the feedback will be worlds shattering. Yes, entire worlds will be altered to an extent that they will be unrecognizable."

"Can't Melvin just warn him that could happen?" Kalli asked. "I'm sure there's a way to…"

"He knows," Lavender cut her off. "He doesn't care. He intends to cast this spell at any cost, even if the result is only the two of them surviving."

"Two of who?" Kalli asked, looking confused.

"She means me," my mom said glumly. "Merlin intends to use the mana he's gathered to make me immortal."

He what? Can't he do that with his own power?

I was dumbfounded. He'd talked to me about it. Kalli nodded for a moment before remembering she was my voice. "Melvin wants to know why Merlin can't just make his mom immortal with his own magic?"

"Because I won't let him," Mom replied, her brows furrowing. "We don't know exactly what he intends to do with the mana."

"Will it make her immortal?" Wendy asked.

"Nobody knows," Lavender said, shrugging. "I can't see what he plans to do or whether it succeeds, only the repercussions."

How can I stop him?

I still wasn't sure I wanted to do anything besides escaping with Kalli. He was my dad. What if Lavender was wrong? It was a given that she hadn't been wrong in the past but wasn't she guessing here?

Kalli found a better way of asking the question. "What do you want us to do?"

Lavender looked at Kalli, but I felt as though she were looking straight at me. "It is imperative that you find the artifact that controls the system."

"The mirror?" Kalli asked, echoing my thoughts.

"I don't know," Lavender admitted. "It could be a mirror."

"Well, Melvin has it in his bag," Kalli said. "Merlin let him borrow it."

"No, no, no, no!" Lavender barked, losing her cool. "He would never hand over such a valuable artifact. At least not willingly. It will likely be something he is very fond of or reluctant to let out of his sight."

"How will Mel get it from him if he keeps it in his bag?" Kalli asked.

"While he might do that, he can't for long," Lavender explained. "Control over the system relies on it existing. Putting it in a bag that warps reality would break his control over it. I am willing to bet he's keeping it out in the open."

Well, it's not the mirror, then.

Lavender continued, "Look for an object he doesn't let out of his sight. If you find something like that, it's likely the artifact."

What do I do once I find it? Destroy it?

Lavender's eyes widened when Kalli asked my question. "No! You mustn't. That would be catastrophic. Not only would that eliminate the system and disorient everyone in the known universe, but all of that mana would have to go somewhere. I'm afraid the feedback would be just as bad as trying use it all at once."

"So, what do you want Melvin to do?" Kalli asked, exasperated.

"I want him to attempt to claim control of it," Lavender said as though claiming someone else's artifact was as easy as calling shotgun on the front seat of a car. When she saw the look of horror on Kalli's face, she quickly added, "Don't worry, I have a plan."

———

"Origin to Melvin," Ulli said, waving her hand between me and the book. "Come back to us. You've been reading that same page for the last ten minutes."

I shook my head to clear my vision. Kalli was busy getting Lavender settled into Scrap. They didn't want to go back through the door to Earth because it might only last for a few crossings and would arouse suspicion. Instead, Kalli arranged housing for them as if they were newly dumped on the planet. Once in the new house, Lavender started placing enchantments on the place, and it vanished from Scrap.

"It was an interesting page," I lied, looking at the page with the safety warnings about how to use fire in a safe and responsible way. "Um, did you need something?"

Ulli shook her head. "I wanted to know if you needed any help. Maybe someone to practice with when you get done here?"

I blinked. "You want me to shoot fireballs at you?"

"Not *at* me, silly," she giggled. "There has to be some way I can help, right?"

I shrugged. "Actually, after this, I think I want to go back to Camelot and check in with Mika. There's something I need to ask her."

"Mika again?" Ulli asked, her face reddening. "Can I go?"

"Sure," I replied, not wanting to arouse suspicion.

———

We left the library and found a quiet place to teleport from. Not wanting to surprise anyone in the underground settlement, we arrived just outside of the tunnel that led there. That meant I had to walk past the guards to get in. My favorite guard, Jasper, the man with the spear, barred our path with a smirk on his face. "I don't suppose you told anybody you were coming today?"

"Nope," I replied, trying to match his demeanor. "Are we required to down here?"

"I don't know," he said smugly. "On account of the fact that nobody who doesn't live here ever visits. Except for you, that is."

"Can you just tell Mika we're here to see her," Marcelle asked, not wanting to waste time with male bravado.

Jasper looked over his shoulder and another guard ran off. He turned his attention back to Marcelle and said, "She's not here, right now."

"Can I see Viola, then," I asked.

He frowned. "She's very busy. Why do you need to see her?"

"It's personal," I replied.

"Wait here," he replied, leaving two guards as he left.

———

An hour later, Ulli tapped me on the shoulder. "I don't think he's coming back."

I jumped as I'd been invested in a conversation between Kalli and Wendy. It was weird not being there in person, but Kalli absolutely refused to switch bodies when our mutual friends were involved. When I asked why, she just gave me a simple reply. *They would notice, and that would be so embarrassing.*

Before I got a chance to answer Ulli, someone tapped me on the shoulder. "What are you doing here?"

"Mika!" I exclaimed, flashing her a smile. "We came to see you, and I need to talk to your mom."

"You always need something when you drop by," she sighed. "At least you're never boring. Why are you waiting out here, though?"

"We were instructed not to let them in," one of the guards explained.

"Who told you that?" Mika asked.

"Jasper," the guard replied. "He told us to keep them here until they go away."

Mika rolled her eyes. "You do realize you're only out here to guard for anything dangerous, right? Not visitors."

The guard stammered, "But we had orders."

Mika rolled her eyes and took me by the hand. I felt Kalli's jealousy at her forwardness. *Why is everyone you know over there a girl?*

Mika frog-marched us past the guards and into the main hall. From there, she slowed down and asked, "So, what brings you here today?"

"I need to ask you and your mom something," I explained. "In private."

———

Viola actually was busy. It took another hour for her to free herself up to see us. In the meantime, I decided to visit the infirmary and see who I could heal. Fortunately, the only patient turned out to be Ollie, and just for a scraped knee. I patched him up in no-time flat and sent him on his way. After that, I struck up a conversation with one of the nurses. "So, how many people that live down here are actually F Ranked?"

She gave me a knowing smile. "Everyone who chooses to live here ends up F Ranked eventually. As you know, we only maintain our ranks when we are useful to society. Even highly skilled people can't maintain a decent rank if they spend all their time helping the less fortunate. That's why we end up with our own communities. Nobody cries foul so long as we don't cause waves.

There had to be a better way to go about ranking people. I didn't have time to ask more questions because Viola arrived. "Hello, Melvin. Sorry for the wait. What can I do for you today?"

[37]

"I NEED a secure place that even The Creator can't find," I stated.

Viola raised an eyebrow. "What for?"

"I don't think I can say," I replied.

She sighed. "I appreciate everything you've done for us but I'm afraid I can't put my people at risk without knowing what it's for. I know it may seem like we are defying the system by living down here, but that's not the case."

On the other side of our connection, Kalli was translating everything that we were saying to a very interested Lavender. She chose that moment to interrupt. "Tell her the Lavender Witch is coming to Origin."

I repeated what she said, and Viola gasped. "You know the Lavender Witch?"

I grinned. "Yeah, we go way back."

It was true. I'd met Lavender the first week I awakened. Viola was impressed. "Of course, I know of the legend of the Lavender Witch. The question is, how do I know this is real?"

After Kalli translated for me, I parroted Lavender's response, "She will explain everything when she arrives. Until then, there is nothing to fear from taking me to one of your safe rooms."

"How do you know about…" she trailed off. "Never mind. I will do what I can. Give me a couple days."

Does that work?

Kalli replied even though I didn't need her to. *She says that'll be fine.*

As usual, Viola insisted we stay for lunch. Kalli laughed when she saw what was served. *This reminds me of a good day at the orphanage. Every now and then, someone managed to catch a raquirrel, and we had meat for dinner.*

I tasted the gamey meat, wondering what it must have been like growing up in an orphanage on a medieval planet. Mom and I hadn't had much, but at least we had McDonalds. After eating, I was eager to get home. Kalli giggled. *You just want to sleep so you can dream with me. There's no need to rush. I'm not going to bed for a few hours because I'm catching up with everybody.*

Part of me was jealous. However, it wasn't like I couldn't be there. Kalli went out of her way to include me in the conversation. The only thing I couldn't do was have a private conversation with Joe. It was difficult for Kalli as well because she didn't want to block me out, so she couldn't have any alone time with Wendy either.

Shara was quiet. Years of being isolated on Blood Moon had taken their toll. I was partially responsible for that because of what happened with her mother. Zofia was also quiet, but for very different reasons. She had a tablet in her hand, which she hacked at furiously. When Kalli asked what she was working on, she replied with an annoyed look. "You have no idea how difficult it is bringing a feudal kingdom up to the modern age. Negotiating with the adventurers' guild alone is a huge pain."

"We've been building Celestea and Meltopia from the ground up," Kalli said. "If I can give you any advice, I'd be more than happy to."

Zofia rolled her eyes. "Thanks for the offer but I'll have to pass.

The administrator has a vision for Dabia. One that will make it very prosperous."

Kalli rubbed her chin, disregarding Zofia's rejection. "You know, we need to establish the adventurer's guild in our land. Do you think you can introduce me to the leader of yours when we get back?"

"I guess," Zofia muttered, a look on her face like she'd tasted something sour. "You won't like their rules though."

"What do you mean? Kalli asked.

Zofia scoffed. "They act like they are above us. Did you know they don't respect borders or private property? A couple adventurers just barged into the castle claiming to be on a quest. They didn't agree to leave until my men were forced to pull guns on them. Such tacky weapons. I hate having to rely on them."

"You can make better weapons now, right?" Joe asked. "Those PINGs of yours are interesting."

Zofia rolled her eyes. "You can't expect me to assign one of those to every gate guard, can you? Crude weapons are much easier to buy at a discount and hand out. Besides, I'm the only one in the TGB who can create mana batteries. It's a pain."

"We can help with that!" Kalli volunteered.

"I'm going to hold you to that, "Zofia replied, a hint of a smile appearing on her face. "Maybe you can help me negotiate with the guild, too."

Lavender gave her a knowing smile. "There are things you can do to protect your interests. As a way of thanking you for your help here, I'll teach you some simple enchantments to help hide your facilities from low-level adventurers."

"What about high-level ones?" Zofia asked, raising an eyebrow.

Lavender laughed. "I'm afraid the only answer for that is to grow stronger. There is only so much I'm willing to protect you from, especially considering what we both know about your ambitions."

Zofia turned away, her face reddening at the accusation. Kalli noticed the air of awkwardness and changed the subject. "So, what do we have to do on this end once Melvin finds a safe place for us on Origin?"

Lavender nodded to Joe and Zofia. "These two need to find a way to make a portal through your bond to get through the barrier around Origin. While it is possible to strong-arm your way through by other means, there is no way to do that without alerting Merlin."

"Right," Joe said as he rummaged through a toolbox. "This is going to be a bit more complicated than using a blood portal."

"A blood portal?" Kalli asked.

Shara looked interested in the conversation for the first time. "That's right. We used your blood to form a portal that led right to you. I don't know how they did it, but it had something to do with the fact that there was residual mana in your blood."

Lavender nodded. "Rasputin used a similar tactic to follow Melvin to Gaia. Traces of mana are left behind when you teleport. He opened a portal at that spot you left Earth from and followed its trail through the void. Using mana from Kalli's blood was a lot trickier, but these two managed to find a way."

Joe nodded. "I invented a device that tracked your mana signature. Zofia boosted the signal so it could track inter-dimensionally. I still don't know how she did that."

"The laws of the universe are bendable," Zofia said with a yawn, as though the topic bored her. "We already cracked this code when we broke through to Gaia. Using a similar technique, I allowed the mana to point the portal device in the direction of its creator. I'm fairly certain this invention can track anyone."

"If you have their blood," Joe pointed out.

"Fresh blood," Shara added. "Mana doesn't last in blood forever. You're lucky I'm an expert at preserving my samples. Normally, there wouldn't be any traces of the owner after just a day or two."

"How long will it take for us to get to Origin?" Kalli asked.

Lavender let out a long sigh. "I'm afraid you can't go."

———

We were both frustrated by the revelation that we still couldn't be together even after Lavender showed up to rescue us. It turned out that

Kalli had to stay behind or everyone would be trapped on Origin with me. The idea was to get Lavender to Origin, find the artifact, and somehow get Merlin, the most powerful man in the known universe, to part with it willingly. If Lavender had more to her plan than that, she wasn't letting on.

Ulli and Marcelle were starting to get worried about me. I looked up to find Ulli a few inches from my face. "That's the third time you've spaced out today. If you count the time you got high on the candle, that is."

"I did not…" I started to say.

"Then what is going on with you?" Marcelle asked. "We're close enough to know when you're acting weird. Weirder than normal. Putting the candle thing aside, you spaced out in the library and now. It's like your brain was in another place."

"I'm sorry," I replied. "I just have a lot on my mind."

"Is there anything you'd like to talk to us about?" Marcelle asked softly.

I stared at a fork full of meat and tried desperately to think of something. In the end, I said, "I think I need to be alone so I can think things through."

Both girls looked sad. Marcelle forced a smile onto her face and said, "Very well. We will give you some space. Just remember, your safety and wellbeing are our responsibility, too. Try to keep that in mind."

———

I sat on my bed when we got home. It was still several hours from the time when Kalli would be able to sleep, so I decided to go for a walk.

Marcelle got up the moment I moved toward the door. I stopped her with a raised hand. "I'm going for a walk. I'll probably end up stopping by Dad's throne room."

"Understood," she replied. "Will you join us for dinner?"

I groaned at the thought of more food. I'd already stuffed myself during breakfast and had a large lunch. Now, they were already preparing for dinner. Even Kalli was excited about it. How had I become a lightweight eater? I vowed to train harder when it came to my Food Fu and gave a noncommittal reply. "I'll let you know when I'm hungry."

The walk to the throne room didn't take long at all. I only paused for a few seconds to look at the artifacts outside of his chamber. Nothing had changed since the last time I was there, and none of them looked like what Lavender was looking for.

As usual, he was sitting on his throne when I arrived. This time, he looked up before I got there. "Good afternoon, son. What can I do for you?"

I looked around the room. Outside of the alcoves filled with women in frilly dresses, the throne room was fairly devoid of furniture. The only thing in the long room was a gold embroidered red carpet leading to a simple throne. Well, I called it a throne. It was actually a high-backed wooden chair with a comfy looking red cushion and ornately carved lions' claws for arm rests. Beside the chair was a table heaped with delicious-looking fruits and cheeses. Normally, Merlin had one or two of his women fanning and feeding him. Today, he was alone.

He cleared his throat to get my attention. I looked up sheepishly and said, "Sorry, I was exploring the tower and ended up here. Why don't you decorate this room more. Doesn't sitting there alone get boring?"

He looked around at the alcoves. Waves of gasping and swooning followed wherever he looked. That just made Merlin groan. "As you can see, I'm never alone."

"Yeah, but you can put up a TV or something for entertainment, right?" I replied. "If this was my room, I'd add a pool table and several screens. Do they have sports on Origin?"

He rubbed his chin. "There is a game I used to watch called The S.I.M.P. Games. Unfortunately, recent years haven't been that exciting. Several years ago, one of the players managed to awaken himself and caused a lot of drama. Now, *that* was entertainment."

I gaped at him. "What kind of sport is a simp game?"

He chuckled. "No, not simp, it's spelt S.I.M.P., and it stands for, well, I forget what it stands for. That doesn't really matter. The idea behind it is they pay unawakened to play a game. I think on Earth, they call this reality TV."

"Do you make them all live in the same house?" I asked.

Merlin laughed again, amused by my question. "I guess you can call it that. Every year we choose a different planet to bring the players to. Most of them have never been off their home world. We try to use players from different worlds in different years. The interesting year used Earth for most of the players. They went to Gaia as a matter of fact."

"Do I know any of them?" I asked, curious that he was mentioning both of the worlds I'd been to.

Merlin rubbed his chin. "I don't know. Have you been to Albion?"

"You mean the city from the sword?" I asked, remembering the inscription on my Excalibur replica.

"The very same," Merlin replied, clapping. "You've either done some research on me, or you're very familiar with Arthurian lore."

I decided to change tactics. Perhaps Merlin controlled the system with a personal item. "Can I see your wand?"

He frowned. "Look, son. You're not ready for an artifact like that."

I sighed, and took one last look around before heading back to my room.

[38]

I RUSHED THROUGH DINNER, much to Kalli's dismay. She couldn't argue that either of us were hungry. She'd just eaten, and I was still stuffed from the breakfast. Still, I humored her by trying a few desserts before shuffling off to bed. Ulli caught my arm as I ducked under the curtain leading to my room. "No playing with that candle tonight!"

"I'm going straight to bed," I promised with a yawn.

The problem with falling asleep is you can never do it when you want to. We tossed and turned restlessly for about an hour before finally nodding off. The first thing I noticed in the dream world wasn't Kalli. It was the golden ball of light that seemed to be growing.

What was it that you named her? Sindra?

Kalli scoffed. *Please, tell me you didn't forget the name of your future daughter.*

How do you know it's a girl? Isn't that a biological thing?

She rolled her eyes. *I can tell. It's a mother thing.*

We followed the light while it zipped from one place to another, sometimes on my side of the bond, and sometimes on Kalli's. If there was a wall that had been keeping us apart, Sindra didn't seem to notice.

After a while, we wound up in the bed made of fluff. I snuggled up to her and asked, "Did you make this bed?"

Eye eyes widened as she looked at me. "No. I thought you did."

I picked up a ball of fluff, watching it dissipate in my hands. "That's strange. I wonder where it came from."

Kalli giggled. "We needed a bed, and one appeared. Isn't that how dreams work?"

"What if I need a toilet?" I asked with a smirk on my face.

"Don't even think about it," Kalli muttered, shoving me playfully.

Just as falling asleep had taken forever, spending the night in Kalli's arms went by way too fast. I woke up earlier than usual. I tried to fall back asleep, but it was no use. We were up for the day.

Kalli laughed at me as she stretched luxuriously in her bed. *Don't worry about sleep so much. You're only anxious because we've been apart for so long. After a few nights, it will feel normal.*

I grumbled as I got up and made my way to the bathroom. To my surprise, Marcelle was already up and standing watch by the door. The only sign of Ulli was snoring coming from her room. Kalli and I chatted while we went about our morning routines.

What are you going to do today?

She yawned. *I'm going to see if Lavender needs any help, and then maybe look for another job. I don't want to sit around all day. Especially if I can't come to Origin. How about you?*

That was a good question. What was I going to do? I was at the mercy of Viola when it came to finding a safe room. While I could pop over and ask her if she was ready, it hadn't been a full day yet. I knew I still needed to search for the artifact, but I was running out of places to look.

I decided to start the day with some exercise. After making my way to the park, I went through elemental and emotional training while trying to think of various things Merlin might use as a system encompassing artifact. Did he use a computer? That would be the most logical place to keep one. Or perhaps a smart phone?

Getting an idea, I took out the M-Phone. "PAA? Are you in there? Do you have access to the network on this planet?"

The tinny voice of the phone responded, "Unfamiliar network detected. Attempting to connect. Connection successful."

"Excellent," I said to myself before turning my attention back to PAA. "Can you get me a list of all documented artifacts on Origin?"

"Generating," PAA droned, and a list appeared on the screen.

It was a lot longer than I expected it would be with twenty-three pages of results. After going through a few pages, I noticed a problem. "Can you sort by ownership?"

"Yes," PAA replied, altering the menu. "Do you have a specific owner in mind?"

"Yes!" I bellowed. "Give me Merlin."

"Error," PAA droned in its emotionless voice. "No records found."

The image on the screen mirrored what I'd just heard in bold red print. I scratched my head, trying to think of a way to get the data I needed. Taking out the artifact mirror I'd borrowed from Merlin, I asked, "Can you scan this and tell me about it?"

A red laser emitted from the top of the M-Phone and scanned the mirror. The phone beeped, and PAA announced its findings, "Unknown artifact detected. Unknown power. Owner is unknown. Would you like to go on record as the owner of this artifact?"

Another dead end. I sighed, holding my head in my hands as I tried desperately to think. Kalli offered a suggestion, *Ask it about the system.*

"What can you tell me about the system?" I asked, wondering if PAA would know about the existence of an artifact.

"More information is needed to answer that question," PAA replied diligently. "Please, specify which system you are referring to."

"*The* system," I said. "The one that governs everybody's classes and skills."

A wall of text appeared on the screen with PAA giving a brief summary. "The existence of the system has been widely debated over the years. Compared to computers and modern-day video games, there have been reports of people seeing or hearing illusions of various forms containing information about their current state of being. Not much can be confirmed as the information is typically private, and no two people seem to be alike."

"Is there a central computer or artifact that governs the system?" I asked hopefully.

PAA emitted a grinding sound. "There is no information on a computer or artifact in relation to the system."

"Where can I learn more about the system?" I asked.

Another list populated the screen. "There are a series of bibliographies of scholars and historians who have documented their experiences with the system. Some have even gone so far as to research the ways in which famous awakened appeared to interact with the system."

I suddenly had another idea. "Do you have any books written by Merlin?"

Again, a list of books appeared on the screen.

Books Written by Merlin

Wordless Spellcasting
Manashift
Creating a Legend
Vivien

My eyes gravitated to the last entry on the list. "Mom?"

What did Dad write about her? I had to know. "Where do I find these books?"

"The closest library to you is in the tower," PAA responded. "Or you can download a digital copy."

I grinned, looking at the options. "I'd like an audio book, please."

"Purchased," PAA responded, sounding slightly more excited than usual. "Downloading now. Download complete."

"Wow, that was fast," I laughed, clicking the title to start the book. "How fast is your download speed?"

"You are logged onto the tower's intranet," PAA explained. "No faster connection exists on Origin. All data is stored internally for use by tower maidens and guests of The Creator."

A flourish of music flooded the garden as the book started playing. Merlin's voice began narrating his book. "The name of this book is

Vivien, written by Merlin. It has been confirmed that the actual Merlin wrote this book. Chapter one, when I first met her. It was the year 29672. By this point in my life, I had already grown to my full potential and taken many lovers. I'd given a handful of them the gift of immortality. I would come to regret this very much over the coming generations. Vivien was different than any girl I ever met."

I skipped ahead a few tracks. "It was only after her fifth death that I realized I had a problem."

Still not enough. I skipped further. "The only logical conclusion I could come up is that women are not logical. Not this one in any case. No matter how many times I attempted to bestow the gift, she refused every time. It became a game to me, finding her in her latest incarnation and making her fall for me all over again."

Skip. "My love for her is purer than any emotion I've had in my life. Perhaps I can convince her to pass the veil and ascend to the other side. I will give up this immortal frame to be with her in that case. Life is meaningless without her."

I scrolled all the way to the end of the book. Merlin didn't say anything about the system or his plan to win my mother. It was a tribute to her that read like a diary. I downloaded the other books he'd written to peruse later.

Meanwhile, on Scrap...

Kalli spent a good part of the morning with Wendy. They made breakfast together while Joe and Zofia worked on a new portal generator. Or at least that's what she thought they were doing. They didn't take out tools to tinker with their creation. Instead, they ran their hands over the bulky machines with their eyes closed.

Wendy explained the process. "They are feeling the insides of those things with their magic. Joe's gift allows him to create physical gadgets. Zofia's specialty is programming them. Together, I think they can make anything."

"And Shara?" Kalli asked, glancing at the gothic blonde woman with dark red eyeshadow who was sitting in the corner watching.

"Oh, she's done for now," Wendy explained. "She's our blood specialist. She's how we got to you. Since there's no more blood to deal with, she's just waiting for when Lavender needs her again."

"Will she?" Kalli asked, looking around for Lavender who seemed to be missing.

"Lavender wouldn't have brought her if she wasn't needed for something," Wendy said, tasting the tea she was brewing. "The same goes for me. Right now, I'm just doing what I can to help but I'm sure there will be something for me to do later."

"For starters, you refused to let me go alone," Joe pointed out, his eyes still closed.

"That's right," Wendy said. "I still think I'll be useful before this is all said and done with though."

"You will, honey," Joe said. "I wouldn't trust anyone else to have my back."

Kalli was struggling to keep up with two conversations. Melvin had taken out his phone and was researching the system. She offered some thoughts while also trying to keep her conversation going with Wendy. When breakfast was ready, they had to force Joe and Zofia to take a break. Breakfast on Scrap was a far simpler affair than it was on Origin. They didn't have much meat, so a lot of the things they ate were managrown substitutes. It tasted so similar to real meat that Kalli wondered why people still ate meat on the other worlds.

"Some habits are harder to break than others," Lavender explained. "Many people swear there is a distinct difference in the flavor and the unawakened don't have access to mana."

After a quick breakfast, Kalli set off with Wendy to present herself at the job office. People greeted her on the street with a sort of reverence she wasn't used to. Word had spread that she singlehandedly powered the entire planet for a year, in a single afternoon. It took her a lot longer to get to the capital building than it did Melvin. When she finally got there, a receptionist met her at the door. "Greetings, Miss Kalliphae. You're expected. Please, proceed to the top floor."

Kalli gaped at the receptionist. "The top floor? I just came here to get another job. Isn't that the reserved for VIPs?"

The receptionist smiled. "Yes, it is, and that's exactly what you are. Go on up. I'm sure they will give you a job."

Nobody mentioned Wendy, who quietly accompanied Kalli into the elevator. She whispered to Kalli as the elevator ascended. "What's on the top floor?"

Kalli whispered back. "The governor's office."

[39]

"PAA, Give me the schematics for the tower." I said, holding the M-Phone up to my face.

The digital assistant sprang to life. "Generating the layout of all known areas of Merlin's Tower. Many areas are either restricted or not currently mapped. Pro tip, I can populate the map as you explore."

"Well, that's something," I said, hopping to my feet.

I started for the exit of the garden with my head buried in the map. Marcelle fell in beside me as I passed her. "Where are you going?"

"Exploring," I said, heading for the stairwell.

"Again?" she asked, sounding exasperated.

I held up the map. "This time I have a better idea of where I'm going. Don't worry, we aren't going to Merlin's room again."

She flinched when I said his name. I knew they all knew Dad as The Creator, but I didn't care. He wasn't that to me. Unless I thought of the fact that he spawned me, but who counts that? We ascended a few floors before walking down a long hallway.

"What's over here?" Marcelle asked.

"Storage," I replied, pointing to a room on the map.

As usual, the women on the upper floors went out of their way to ignore me. Some theatrically closed the doors to their bedrooms when they saw me approach. I rolled my eyes and quickened the pace, speaking to Marcelle in a loud voice that I knew would infuriate the women, "I wonder what they did to make it up to this floor. It's not like Dad's chosen anyone since I was born."

Marcelle stiffened, whispering her reply. "I don't know, but do you think you can keep it down? Or are you trying to make all of them hate you?"

I laughed. "I don't think any of them like me anyway. My presence here is a threat to them. Have you seen how they all look at me in the throne room?"

Marcelle stared at me. "No. It's pretty hard to focus in the presence of The Creator."

No matter how I tried to look at him as an intimidating presence, all I saw was my father. At least how that was how I always pictured him being. Maybe I was mad because he was never in my life growing up. Everything would have been so different if he'd just been around. I could have grown up rich. Kalli interrupted my thoughts. *Is that really what you wanted? Your home with your mother felt cozy to me.*

A big house would have been cozier.

Kalli sighed. *I would have settled for that hut in the middle of nowhere if it meant I could have grown up with my parents. I'd give anything to have them back now.*

I'd nearly forgotten what happened to Kalli's parents. While I was bonding with my father, Kalli had lost both of her parents. I could tell she was also worried about her sister. One of the first questions she'd asked Lavender was about Shiviria and how she was doing. In Kalli's absence and with the death of her parents made public, Shiv had been declared Queen of Celestea. Like Kalli, she decided to buck tradition and keep her first name. It was bad enough being Shiv Celestea Celestea without adding a third Celestea for good measure at the beginning.

Kalli giggled as she watched me try to sort through Celestean naming conventions. *If Mother were still alive, I'm sure Shiv would have done it just to make her happy. I probably would agree to it if it brought her back.*

Does that mean I'd have to be Melvin Celestea?

She stuck her tongue out. *Would that be a problem?*

Marcelle nudged me to get my attention. I looked up from my map. "What?"

She pointed at a rather beat up door that seemed out of place on the otherwise pristine floor. "We're here."

———

The door wasn't locked, which didn't bode well for what I hoped to find inside. There was no light in the cluttered room, so I was forced to make a ball of light to illuminate the room.

"What is this place?" Marcelle asked, wrinkled her nose in disgust as she ran a finger across a dust covered table.

"I don't know," I admitted. "The map wasn't very specific. It just says Storage M."

"Do you think these are more of The Creator's belongings?" Marcelle asked. "Because I do not want to get caught in one of his private rooms again.

I laughed. "Judging by the dust on everything, I don't think anybody has come in here in quite a while."

While we looked around, a small group of women gathered just outside of the room. I heard them whispering while I looked around.

"That's his son, right?"

"Yeah. Do you think he'll try to claim us?"

"Nonsense! We're the select few. The Creator told us so."

"Not in a very long time."

"Relax," I called over my shoulder loud enough for them to hear. "I'm not interested in any of you."

Several of the women gasped and walked away. I'd just opened a drawer when someone spoke behind me, "What makes you think you're so special? You're not the first of his children to come here. You know that, right?"

I turned to look at her. It was my turn to gasp when I saw the woman. She was a tall version of my mom. The similarities were obvious, right down to the way she groomed her hair. I sighed and turned back to the drawer. "I guess Dad has a type."

"What is that supposed to mean?" she growled.

"It means you look almost exactly like my mom," I replied, not sure why I was explaining myself to a stranger.

When she didn't reply, I looked over my shoulder to find her wiping tears from her eyes. "Look, I'm sorry. I didn't mean anything by it. I'm sure you have lots of qualities he finds attractive."

I would have told her she was beautiful, but Kalli was listening. Besides, every woman in the tower was. Kalli just sighed. *You can tell girls they are beautiful. I don't mind. Not like that anyway.*

It was too late, though. The moment to cheer her up had passed. She marched over and stood in my face. "What are you doing in here anyway? What is all this junk?"

"I don't know," I replied. "That's why I came up here to check it out. Didn't you ever notice this room before?"

She shrugged. "I always thought it was an unused bedroom and never thought twice about it."

"I'm Melvin by the way," I said, realizing I didn't know any of the women in the tower outside of Ulli and Marcelle. "What's your name?"

She smiled for the first time since I met her. It made me feel like I was home again. "My name is Debra, but you can call me Debbie or Deb. All my friends do."

I nodded absentmindedly as I continued to search the drawer. I picked up a tiny blanket and shook it. A cloud of dust blossomed out, causing all of us to cough. Deb took a step back and covered her mouth with the collar of her shirt. "A little warning would have been nice."

"Sorry," I said while still choking.

I almost put the blanket back before I noticed it was embroidered.

Melvin

I stared at it for a long moment. Marcelle leaned in to examine it. "You don't suppose that's…"

"Mine," I finished. "I don't remember it, but I wouldn't, would I?"

I set the blanket on the table and started rummaging again. There were all sorts of random things in the drawers that might have belonged to a baby or young child. I placed my hand against a painted handprint on a piece of paper. There was also a rattle and a tiny shoe.

In the bottom of the drawer was a faded photo. In it was a picture of my mom when she was much younger. She was clearly pregnant and standing beside Merlin, who looked no different than he was today. It was the first time I'd seen the two of them together. "I guess I really am his son."

"Were you not sure before?" Deb asked, looking surprised.

"It's not that," I replied. "It's just that I've never seen a picture of my whole family together. Mom never kept any pictures with Dad in them."

"Oh," she replied. "That's kind of sad. At least you're here now. You have to feel pretty special to know you're The Creator's son."

I gave her my most rebellious grin. "Not really. What makes me feel special is that I'm my mom's son. I'm sure Merlin would agree."

Both Deb and Marcelle gasped when I said his name. "You know, his name isn't going to bite you."

"But it's so informal," Deb gasped.

I laughed. "Aren't you trying to date him? You don't hope to be Mrs. The Creator, do you?"

She scowled at me. "No! But, still, you can't just call him by his name. Nobody does."

"I do," I pointed out. "Maybe if he's extra nice, I'll call him Dad. "One thing I definitely won't be calling him is The Creator. He didn't come up with that himself, did he?"

"No," Deb shook her head rapidly. "He did not. They teach us about him in school. Everyone knows the polite way to refer to him is as The Creator since he created the system, which allows us to be awakened."

"Did you ask him?" I asked.

She shook her head quietly. "I've never spoken with him."

"Wait," I said, stopping to look at her. "I thought you were one of the select few up here on the upper floors. Aren't you on the short list or something?"

Deb sighed. "He hardly says two words to any of us, and that's usually just to ask for favors."

I raised an eyebrow at her. "Favors?"

"Not that," she said, trying to suppress a laugh. "Usually just to feed him or dote on him. He seems to enjoy that. I'm only allowed to go down there once a month. We have a rotation."

Melvin! It was Kalli's voice in my head. She urgently pointed at the machine Joe and Zofia were working on. It was glowing. *I think it's ready. You need to find a safe place for the portal.*

I took a moment to put the blanket and the picture in my bag.

I'll get right on it.

I turned to Deb and Marcelle. "I need to go back to Camelot for a bit. I'll be back in time for dinner."

"Wait!" Marcelle roared, grabbing my arm. "You can't go without me. It's not safe."

Deb also took a step forward, though she didn't touch me. "Do you mind if I join you for dinner. I'd like to ask you more about The Cre... I mean, about your father."

"Sure," I replied. "The more the merrier."

Without waiting for her to reply, I folded mana over Marcelle and myself.

———

I didn't waste time in the void even though it was standing still. I zoomed in on the underground until I found Viola and appeared right in front of her. Fortunately, she wasn't doing anything private. Unfortunately, she screamed and dove out of the way.

"Don't do that!" she said, clutching her chest. "I see why Mika complained when you teleported into her room."

"Sorry," I replied. "I didn't have time to play with Jasper this time. Did you secure a safe room? It's time. They are ready."

She smiled. "Yes. It's ready. I hope she knows what she's doing. If we get caught, it will be the end. For all of us."

I grinned back. "What could possibly go wrong?"

[40]

"THIS WOULD BE SO MUCH EASIER if you'd just tell me where we're going so I can teleport," I whined as Viola led us through the countryside riding animals she called Crast.

"There is a reason we can't teleport," Viola replied. "Teleportation leaves behind a trail that can be tracked. You're going to have to refrain from teleporting directly to places from here on out. While I accept the risk that comes with helping you out, I do not want to extend that risk to my people."

"I understand," I sighed, shifting my weight in an attempt to get comfortable.

Viola slowed her Crast until she was riding beside me. "Don't you have mounts in your world?"

"Yeah," I replied. "But I've never ridden one. My mom couldn't afford to send me to camp, so the closest I ever got to riding is when I rode a dog when I was three. It didn't end well. I fell off. At least that's what my mom tells me."

"Your friend isn't having any problems," Viola said, nodding toward Marcelle, who looked like she'd been riding all her life.

Mika also accompanied us. Viola didn't allow anyone else from the underground to come along, even though Jasper insisted he needed to keep her safe from me. The Sun was starting to set by the time we arrived. We rode through a small town nestled up against a cluster of hills. She stopped at a shed that looked out of place. It sat suspiciously close to a large hill with no other structures around it. "This is it. Come with me, and I'll show you how to get in."

I expected her to unlock the door but instead she walked around behind the shed and pointed out a crooked slat on the rear panel. Once she straightened it out, I heard something click followed by a grinding sound. We then walked away from the shed and Viola led us down a path through the hills.

"A cave?" I asked, as I saw it looming in the distance. "Why did you pull that switch if we were going somewhere else?"

"You'll see," she said with a coy smile.

The cave was pitch-black, so I summoned a ball of light, which floated just above my head. The path through the cave wound so much that I wasn't sure which direction we were going. There were also multiple forks, with side tunnels leading off into the darkness. I lost track of all the lefts and rights we took by the time Viola smiled and said, "Here we are. This room is usually sealed off. That switch you saw topside opens the door."

It wasn't so much of a door as it was a boulder. I had no clue how something that heavy could move just by pulling a simple switch. Once we were all inside the room, Viola flipped a similar switch to the one on the shed and the boulder slid back into place. The only thing missing was a magic sound to inform us we'd unlocked a secret room.

"Here you go. One fully equipped safe room, complete with its own water supply, Viola Said, pointing to a cave off to the side where the sounds of running water could be heard in the distance from an underground stream or something. "So, I've been curious since you told me. How are you going to get around the blockade on this planet and summon the Lavender Witch?"

"I don't know," I admitted, also informing Kalli that we were ready through our bond.

Kalli wasted no time telling Lavender. The enchanter smiled and said, "Now, we are going to need the two of you to take a nap."

A nap? How is that supposed to help? Besides, I can't fall asleep in the middle of the day.

Kalli had already made herself comfortable on a cot positioned in the middle of the room with all the machinery. I looked around, and there was nothing for me to sleep on but the pebble strewn floor. Fortunately, I still had my bottle of Cradle in my bag. I took it out and found a suitable rock. After spraying it generously, I sank into the most comfortable bed outside of our dreamland fluff. Kalli could tell that my bed was better, so she pouted. ***That's not fair!***

I'll be sure to get you a bottle when we're together again.

"What are you doing?" Marcelle asked, tapping her foot anxiously. "We really shouldn't stay out all night. Ulli will worry."

"I apparently need to sleep to make this work," I explained. "I don't know why, but Lavender usually isn't wrong."

The women made themselves comfortable while I tried to fall asleep.

———

"I can't sleep with you staring at me," I grumbled, glaring at Marcelle.

She looked away. "Sorry."

Mika giggled and stood up. "I'm going to check out that water source and find a place to pee."

Viola pointed to another cave. "The toilet is down there."

"Oh, good," Mika replied, scuffling off in the other direction. "I hate it when I have to squat. Thanks."

———

"Finally!" I cheered when I finally materialized in the dream world. "I think I got performance anxiety and all I was trying to do was fall asleep."

"You made it!" Kalli exclaimed, throwing her arms around me. "I've been here for hours."

272

"No, you haven't," I replied. "It only took me ten minutes to fall asleep after you did."

"Are you sure?" Kalli asked.

"No," I admitted. "I fell asleep and lost count."

She giggled and took my hand as we walked around our shared dream watching the golden ball of light as it fluttered about. I noticed something strange about it. "Did it grow?"

Kalli nodded. "Of course, she did. She's a growing girl."

"But she doesn't have a body," I said, wondering what made her grow.

"It's our mana," Kalli explained. "She's feeding on it."

"So, what do we do now that we're here?" I asked.

Kalli shrugged. "Lavender didn't say. She said sleeping would be enough."

"So, normal bedtime activities?" I asked.

Kalli raised an eyebrow. "Is that all you think about?"

I kissed her gently. "It's not all. I think of other things, too."

"Like what?" She didn't let me answer the question as she wrapped her arms around me to kiss me.

We were so busy making out that I almost didn't hear it. A strange sound came from the other side of the dream. Kalli's side. She looked alarmed as well, clutching me tighter as she looked off in the direction of the barrier between our souls. "Did you hear that?"

"Yeah," I said. "Do you think we should go check it out?"

She shuddered. "I don't know. There hasn't ever been anything in here with us before. Besides Sin, that is."

As if responding to her name, the golden ball of light shot off toward the sound. Kalli screamed and reached out. "No! Sindra, you mustn't. Come back."

I was on my feet in a heartbeat, chasing my brain baby through the barrier with Kalli hot on my tail. We flew through the barrier with little resistance and ran directly into Lavender. The impact sent us all tumbling to the ground while Sin circled overheard.

"What?" I stammered. "How?"

Lavender climbed to her feet, dusting herself off. "This is the only way to get to Origin. The two of you created a bridge through the ether that transcends time and space."

"We *what?*" Kalli asked, looking confused.

Lavender chuckled, offering Kalli a hand to help her up. "You created shared space through your bond. We aren't in your heads like you think we are. We are in the space between space. It's where you go when you dream and why dreams seem real. It's usually a personal space where you can dream about anything, but I'm special. I can enter dreams and influence the world in here."

"You're going to change our dreams?" I asked.

"No," she replied, shaking her head. "I just came to give you this."

She pressed a doorknob into each of our hands. They glowed for a moment before fading into a shower of sparkles. Where they had been, a tiny tattoo of an open door appeared on the palms of our hands.

"What does this do?" Kalli asked, rubbing the tattoo to see if it would come off.

"This is special magic. You can transform doors into gateways. I use them to travel through the cosmos, but the two of you can use them to get to each other. It's less restrictive than normal teleportation, and it leaves no sign of your passing. Other than the door, that is. When you wake up, I want you to find a door and press your hand to the door-knob. Think of Kalli, and only Kalli, and infuse the knob with mana. The door will open a rift that will lead you to one another. That is how we are going to get to Origin."

"That sounds easy enough," I said.

Kalli nodded as well. Lavender placed a finger to each of our fore-heads and said, "Wake up!"

———

I woke with a start, causing Mika to jump. Was she leaning over me? I rubbed the sleep from my eyes and struggled to sit up in on the ultra-comfy rock. Kalli woke at the same moment, also groggy from the abrupt ending of our dream. Lavender sat cross-legged next to her, looking as though she had been meditating. She opened her eyes slowly and said, "Everybody get ready. I have delivered the doorknobs."

Is that what Joe was working on? Magic doorknobs?

Kalli shrugged. *They looked like real doorknobs when they came out of the machine. I think Lavender did something to them.*

I stretched before getting up and looking around. "I need a door."

Viola looked at me as though I'd gone insane. "Don't worry. The boulder blocking the entrance is secure."

"No!" I said, cutting off any further explanations. "I need an actual physical door. One with a doorknob preferably."

She pointed toward the cave I'd seen Mika walk into earlier. "The bathroom has one. Sort of."

I walked down the hall with three women in tow. Viola was right. It was only sort of a door. A large wooden barricade had been erected to block off what I assumed was the toilet. It was secured to the wall with twine. While it didn't have a doorknob, it did have a handle. I prayed that would work and reached out for it.

Kalli had a much easier time finding a door. The building she had designated for her friends had plenty of them. She chose one of the bedroom doors and also placed her hand on it.

Even though we both knew it couldn't happen right away, we had the same thought. We wanted to be reunited. The doors glowed on both sides. Then, it faded and looked like a makeshift outhouse again. I took a deep breath and pulled it open.

[41]

THERE SHE WAS, inches away from me. Kalli stood on the other side of the door on another planet in, for all I knew, another dimension. But there she was right in front of me. In that moment, I didn't care about Lavender's warning. We both surged forward at the same moment and met in the doorway. Her face was wet. Was she crying, or was it me? We didn't kiss in that moment. We just hugged and held each other tight. I didn't want anyone to pry us apart ever again.

Lavender gave us time, waiting patiently while the others fidgeted uncomfortably. Even though we stayed that way for a long time, it still felt way too soon when I was forced to let her go. Kalli stepped back, and Lavender passed through the portal, followed by Wendy, Joe, Zofia, Shara, and my mom.

I immediately threw myself into her arms when I saw her. "Mom!"

She sobbed, clutching me so tight I couldn't breathe. "I'm here. Sorry I had to go away for a while. Lavender said it was the only way."

I felt my eyes water as Lavender held the door open for Viola. "You and your daughter should leave Origin. It isn't safe for you at the moment."

"Go on, dear," Viola said, giving Mika a pat on the backside.

Mika spun and glared at her mom. "No way! I'm not going through without you. Either you come with me, or I'm staying. Besides, who's going to look out for the others if we leave?"

Viola sighed. "I'm not asking. Go through the door. I'll take care of everyone. You can come back once it's over."

"But, Mom…" she stammered the oh so familiar whine as Viola gently sent her through the door.

Kalli patted her on the shoulder. "I know how you feel. Trust Melvin. He won't let anyone get hurt."

Lavender closed the door before she could change their mind. "Okay, now that we're on this side, there are some things we need to go over. First, I need to have a private word with your friend here."

She nodded to Marcelle and walked into the other room. Marcelle cast me a furtive glance before following. That left me with everyone else congregated next to the bathroom.

"So," I said nervously. "I missed you guys."

Wendy smiled and hugged me. "We missed you, too. I'm glad you're all right."

Joe grinned at me when Wendy let me go, offering me his hand to shake. "Yeah, how did you go and end up here?"

"I teleported," I replied. "I think Dad had something to do with it. Whenever I teleport the old way, I end up outside of his throne room."

"Wait a second," Joe said, refusing to let my hand go. "There's a lot to unpack there. First off, he has a throne? Is your dad the king or something? Second, what do you mean the old way? Do you have a new way of teleporting?"

I grinned, folding mana around myself. It took a lot longer to demonstrate from my end than it did for Joe. For me, I had to float through the void over to Origin, find the hiding place, and drop myself right in front of Joe.

He gasped when I appeared in front of him. "What? How?"

Lavender chose that moment to return. "Weren't you warned about teleporting in and out of here?"

"Yeah," I admitted reluctantly, reclaiming my hand from a startled Joe. "Since I both left and returned here, there really isn't much to trace though, right?"

Lavender sighed. "Hasn't your father taken you to the void yet? You left traces in there as well. If he were to go in there right now with the intention of finding you, it would lead him straight here."

"Oh," I replied, worried I'd just got everyone caught.

She waved my fear away. "It should be fine. The residual trace doesn't last long. If he didn't know you were in there, it's unlikely that he will find us. No more teleporting, though."

I agreed, and we followed Lavender back to the main room to find a rather subdued looking Marcelle sitting in the corner. She refused to make eye contact with any of us. I wanted to know what Lavender said to her but decided it would have to wait until later. I led Mom over to the rock and motioned for her to sit down. "Try this. It's soft."

She frowned at me until I demonstrated by sinking into the rock. Then, she sat next to me. "Ah, magic. I should have known."

Lavender cleared her throat to get our attention. "Okay, everybody. I've spent several lifetimes to get us to this moment. As some of you know, I am what is known on Earth as a Fate. That means I am cursed with visions of the future. I call it a curse because I am limited in what I can do about what I see. The role was passed on to me from the previous Fate some two thousand years ago. She explained to me that it is of paramount importance that I can never talk about what I see or do anything to try and thwart it. Otherwise, it will change, and never in the way intended."

"Wait a second," Joe said, holding up a hand. "Aren't you talking about it now? Isn't that going to change everything?"

Lavender gave Joe a knowing smile. "Good point. In this case, I saw myself having this discussion. In reality, I'm a wild card. It's impossible to tell what my actions will do to the future. Because of my knowledge, everything I do has at least some impact. The reason I am acting now is because I know inaction will have world ending consequences. Any alternative is better than what I've seen."

"Can't we just talk to Merlin?" I asked. "I'm sure we can convince him to see reason. Especially Mom…"

She cut me off. "While I see your point, I assure you, my brother will not be persuaded, even by Vivien. Oh, I'm sorry, your name is

Samantha. I've known you in so many incarnations. Anyhow, even Sam can't persuade Merlin not to do what he is planning. He is desperate, and desperate people are not prone to reason."

"What do you need us to do?" Wendy asked.

She smiled at Wendy. "I brought all of you here because you have a role to play. Melvin still hasn't found the artifact that controls the system, but I'm sure he's made progress."

I took out the picture of Mom and Dad together. "Well, I can tell you where it's not. The problem is I still don't know what I'm looking for. He spends most of his time in the throne room, but that room is empty. There is no decor whatsoever."

Lavender closed her eyes and didn't say anything. We stood in silence for a while before Zofia spoke. "I think we should capture him and worry about whatever you're looking for later. If we know he's going to cause this apocalypse, taking him out of the equation will stop it, right?"

Lavender's eyes shot open. "There are items in the throne room."

"Really?" I asked. Lavender said it as though she'd been there. " Where? Are they invisible."

Lavender chuckled. "Think. What's he sitting on? What does he eat off? The relic can be anything. Your next quest will be to touch everything and see if you can interact with it."

"Will he let me do that?" I asked, a grin forming on my face at the mention of the word quest.

"No," Lavender replied. "That's why I brought Sam. She will be the perfect bait to lure him out of the tower."

I stared blankly at her. Did Lavender mean to put my mom in harm's way just to get a crack at Merlin. Sure, one life wasn't as important as the entire universe, but I wasn't about to let her risk my mom. I was about to speak up when Lavender continued. "Don't worry. The primary reason I selected Sam for this job is because she is the last person Merlin will ever hurt. Additionally, I have no intention of having her deal with him on her own. It will be a trap, and I will be there to confront him."

"Can you handle him?" Shara asked, looking skeptical.

"No," Lavender replied softly. "This isn't about stopping him. Not while he's in control of the system. It is, by far, the greatest concentration of mana in existence. He would only need a fraction of that to wipe out Origin and all of us along with it. The only thing stopping him from doing that is Sam."

"What about me?" I asked. "I'm his son."

Lavender sighed. "I don't know how to put this. While I know he's shown you affection, he's using you. You were drawn to Origin to lure your mother here."

"He's using me as bait?" I asked, pulling away from my mom in shock. "Dad says he's training me to be his successor. He wants to retire and settle down with Mom."

"Yes, that is all true," Lavender replied. "He's used you to lure her here so he can do just that. The part that's missing is what he intends to do in between. If we let him get his hands on Sam, he will perform a ritual he believes will make her immortal. Melvin, do you remember how it felt to contain Quetzalcoatl in your core?"

"Yeah, I think so," I said, trying to remember exactly what it felt like. "I remember feeling stuffed, like I'd eaten so much I was about to burst."

"Yes," she said, smiling. "And that was only about fifty thousand mana. The mana contained in the system at this very moment is in the millions. While your core may be able to contain it, there is no way your body will. The force of the ritual will rip a mortal body apart."

"What if he has a plan?" I asked. There was no way Dad would let Mom die. "Maybe he will make her a new body or something. I made one for Maya and Nir Vana."

"Melvin," Lavender sighed when she said my name. "You weren't creating anything. Humans can't create living things. Not even Manipulators. This is going to be hard to hear but, when you summoned those bodies, the system found them for you. Three people died to draw your friends from the ring."

"Three?" I asked, shocked beyond belief. "I only summoned two bodies."

Lavender took a deep breath and said, "You messed up the first time. By the time you deleted that body, its original owner had passed over."

"Why didn't you tell me any of this before?" I asked, my voice cracking. Even Dad didn't tell me about the people I'd killed when he explained how Manipulation worked. "I would have never used the magic like that if anyone warned me."

"I'm sorry," she said in a low voice. "As I explained. I can't reveal what I see. If I say something and you change everything, the entire future becomes hazy. You have no idea how difficult it is to stay silent when I know people are going to die."

"You knew Stefanie was going to die!" I exclaimed.

Wendy gasped. Joe held her and glared at Lavender. "That's cold. Real cold."

Lavender shook her head sadly. "That's just one of a thousand painful decisions I've been forced to make over the years. The Fates are not allowed to intervene. I am truly sorry for the loss of your friend."

"It was my fault," I muttered, feeling the loss all over again.

Mom hugged me, pulling me close. "No, it wasn't. That was an impossible situation. You can't blame yourself."

"You know about that?" I asked, turning to stare at her.

She nodded. "I've been watching you ever since you went to The Academy. I'm sorry I couldn't contact you. You needed space to grow."

I sighed, closing my eyes and holding her tight. "I was worried something happened to you."

She smiled. "Did you use the candle I left you?"

Lavender tutted at my mom. "The candle was meant for you. This is another example of how I can't influence the future. I intended that candle to allow your mother to visit her past lives with Merlin and perhaps persuade him to alter his course. Instead, she gave it to you and brought about this reality."

"What changed?" I asked out of curiosity.

"Without that candle," she replied, looking me straight in my eyes. "You never would have met Kalliphae."

"I would have summoned her," I replied. "I did that before the candle."

Lavender chuckled. "Your use of that candle influenced fate. Actually, if you trace it back far enough, I influenced fate and drew the two of you together. By giving your mother that candle, I enabled her to give it to you. In turn, you used it and formed a connection with Kalliphae before you summoned her. Magic isn't linear, so it doesn't matter that you technically did all of that after the fact. Historically speaking, it occurred several years before you met her."

"I'm confused," I said, rubbing my temples.

"We all are," Joe added.

"I get it," Zofia said, looking smug.

"Sure, you do," Shara replied, laughing.

"That's the wonderful thing about the future," Lavender said. "It happens whether you understand it or not."

[42]

"I don't like this plan," Joe grumbled with his arms folded as he watched us prepared to depart.

"Sorry," Shara said with a smirk. "You're the odd man out."

"I'm the only man," Joe grumbled before glancing at me. "Oh, sorry Melvin. You know what I mean."

Wendy gave Joe a kiss on the cheek. "Don't worry, honey. We are going to be fine. We won't do anything until you confirm he is out of the tower."

"It still sucks that I can't join the group," I grumbled.

Whatever Merlin did to me to prevent me from accessing the system was also blocking me from joining groups. Fortunately, even he couldn't prevent my bond with Kalli. Not anymore. Therefore, we had to play a complex game of telephone. Lavender was in the group and also had a way of communicating with Kalli. In turn, Kalli talked to me and relayed information to the group through Lavender. It wasn't ideal but it worked.

"Promise me you'll keep her safe," Joe said, grabbing my arms.

"You have nothing to worry about," Marcelle huffed, prying Joe off me. "Nobody is allowed to harm a tower maiden. They will be treated with every due respect. There is some work involved but I think the three of them can manage."

"Work?" Zofia asked, raising an eyebrow.

Marcelle huffed. "Technically, you don't have to do anything but then you'll never get off the first floor. You're latecomers as it is. Most of the girls down there are much younger than you."

"Won't we stick out?" Wendy asked.

Marcelle shook her head. "No. It's been expected that Melvin would bring some girls back to the tower ever since he arrived. If anything, it took longer than expected."

"Hey!" I grumbled. "I'm not like my father. I don't collect women."

"Good boy," Shara said, patting me on the head.

"I'm also not a dog," I barked, causing everyone to laugh.

"Come on, let's go," Marcelle said from the door, beckoning for us to follow. "People are going to start wondering where you are if you don't return soon."

By people, I knew she meant Ulli. She was going to be mad at me for excluding her on my latest adventure out of the tower. Viola led us through the cave, explaining the route as we went. "Remember, first you go up two floors. Then, you go down twice. There are some turns to remember. Go left here, and then right at the next intersection. Once you get to this point, look for the letters on the wall. First you follow the B path. Then the A path. After that it's the B path again and, finally, the A path. After that you're back at the start. That's it. Simple, right?"

"Is that supposed to be a joke?" I asked, raising an eyebrow at her.

Viola winked at me. "That's how I remember the way."

"That does that sound familiar?" I asked, scratching my head.

"That can't be a coincidence." Joe laughed, looking down at his notes. "Up, up, down, down, left, right, left, right, B, A, B, A, start?"

Viola laughed. "Mika came up with it. She says she got it from one of her favorite video games."

"Really?" I asked. "We'll have to play sometime."

"I'm sure she'd like that," Viola replied.

———

We left Joe and Viola to return to Mom and Lavender back at the hideout. Normally, I'd teleport back to the tower, but today was different. This time we had to come from someplace other than Camelot where we could say I picked up some girls. It felt tacky, but it was the best way to get them in without any unwanted scrutiny.

The walk took the remainder of the day. We bypassed the little town outside of the hideout and headed for a nearby town. There, we found a small restaurant and sat down for a snack.

"So, how are you, Melvin?" Wendy asked. It felt like the first time we'd been able to slow down since they arrived. "Does your father treat you well?"

"Yeah," I replied. "He's okay. He teaches me things."

"The Creator is benevolent," Marcelle said. She had looked troubled ever since her conversation with Lavender.

"Are you okay?" I asked, placing a hand on top of hers.

Marcelle flinched. "Today has been a lot to take in. I'm still not sure if we're doing the right thing. I trust you, though."

"If it makes you feel any better, I'm not sure either," I replied, giving her hand a little squeeze. "Lavender is a good person, so I think we can trust her."

"More than your father?" Marcelle asked.

"I don't know," I said slowly. "I know I'm going to have to make a decision at some point. I just… I just…"

Wendy smiled. "Just focus on one thing at a time. We can worry about the rest when the time comes."

"Is there going to be a test?" Zofia asked, looking at the menu. "I'm not sure about this tower girl thing. It's not really my thing."

Marcelle chuckled. "Normally, yes. You'd have to be referred by your hometown and then go through several interviews followed by orientation trials to even be considered. Fortunately, you have The Creator's son's recommendation, so you get to bypass all of that."

Shara rolled her eyes. "I guess that makes us The Creator's son's chosen."

"This is going to be fun," Wendy said, sipping tea that made out of a glass of water.

"Order anything you like," I said. "It's on me."

"Are you really The Creator's son?" the waitress asked, giving me an appraising look. "I wouldn't mind being your chosen if you're looking to start a family."

Marcelle stood suddenly. "You will not address The Creator's son so informally, and he is not taking applications. If you want to go to the tower, you know how to apply."

The waitress looked stricken. "I-I'm so sorry. I didn't mean to offend..."

"Relax," I said softly. "I don't mind you asking at all. Marcy, please be nice. If you want to go to the tower that bad, of course you can come."

What? I felt Kalli's apprehension rising.

Relax! It makes sense to bring extra women along. That way Wendy, Zofia, and Shara will be even safer.

Kalli blinked. *Oh, that makes sense. Sorry.*

I smiled, secretly pleased that she was jealous. Kalli blushed. Once word got out that I was choosing women to take back to the tower, the tiny restaurant was overrun. So many women showed up that I was forced to meet with them at a booth in the back while a line formed out the door. They ranged in age from twelve to thirty. Every woman who thought she had a chance threw her hat in the ring.

"Are you sure you want to leave your family?" I asked one of the younger ones.

She nodded, her hands fidgeting in front of her. "I don't know if I want to get married right away, but I'd like to live in the tower."

"Are your parents okay with it?" I asked.

She looked over her shoulder and motioned to a couple in the parking lot, who started waving frantically. Cars in the small town we were in were not the flying variety. Just the plain old standard ones we had back on Earth. I guessed that was life in a small town.

Out of curiosity, I asked, "What rank are you?"

She frowned, her eyes tearing up. "I'm D rank, but I'm sure I can do better if you give me a chance. I'm a hard worker. You'll see."

"Don't worry," I replied. "You can come. In fact, everyone here can come."

I counted twenty-two girls. It didn't matter how old or young they were because I wasn't interested in any of them, only Kalli. Having that thought reassured her, and we shared a moment where everyone else just went away. Kalli ignored the children and their parents around her, and I ignored the bustling crowd that was pressing in around me. It felt like I could reach out and touch her even though we were worlds apart.

Just then, Marcelle led Zofia, Wendy, and Shara who struggled to make their way through the crowd. "Are you ready to go?"

I nodded, standing up and clearing a path for them. She frowned. "So, who did you select?"

"All of them," I crooned with a lopsided grin.

"All...of...them?" she asked, taking the crowd in for the first time.

"Yep," I replied. "Shall we teleport back to the tower?"

"I guess," she muttered, looking visibly upset with me for the first time since I'd met her.

"Everyone, gather around," I called out. "And hold your breath."

———

At least half of the women didn't listen and wound up doubled over on the bottom floor of the tower retching. Marcelle sighed and walked over to a device on the wall. She picked it up and spoke in a soft tone. Once she returned, she called out to the others, "Come this way, ladies. The administrators are preparing an orientation where you will receive your room assignments. You will all be placed on the first floor for the time being. Over the course of the next week, you will be evaluated and reassigned to a more appropriate floor. Enjoy yourselves. You've made it to the tower."

She spun on her heels and marched to the elevator. I followed and whispered, "What about Wendy, Zofia, and Shara? Can we take them back to my room?"

Marcelle glared at me but spoke quietly so only I could hear, "Do you want them to stand out? The whole idea of bringing all these women was for them to blend in, right?"

"Why are you so mad?" I asked. "You understand what we're doing, right? Lavender told you…"

She covered my mouth with a finger. "I get it, and I won't do anything to mess it up, but I don't have to like it. You just cheapened everything I've achieved in my life."

Without waiting for me, Marcelle stepped into the elevator and punched a button. It closed with a hiss, leaving me to stare at the door.

I'll never understand women.

Kalli rolled her eyes. *You do realize I'm a woman, right?"*

I stepped into the void and, my heart caught in my chest. Merlin stood there looking at me. "Are you fun, son?"

I tried not to look guilty. "Maybe a little."

He stood next to the orb that represented Origin and zoomed into the first floor of the tower where I'd just left. Attendants made their way there and were busy mopping up the barf from the floor while others guided the crowd of women into a large room. Merlin turned to stare at me. "I get having a little fun, but what exactly is this? It looks like you brought every eligible woman from the town of Middler to the tower. Do you even like any of them?"

"Sure," I replied. "Some of them were nice."

"But why?" He sighed. "I don't get it. Do you intend to court all of them?"

Fortunately, I'd prepared an answer for that particular question. "I wanted to give them a better life. I invited the waitress to the tower and, the next thing I knew, the whole town was there. It's hard to turn anyone down. How do you do it?"

To my surprise, Merlin laughed. "I don't. The solution is simple. If you want a selection of the best women on Origin brought to the tower, you tell a recruiter what you're looking for. They have an extensive testing system to make sure only the finest women who meet your exact criteria are brought to the tower. Would you like me to get rid of these women for you?"

"Can they stay?" I asked, trying to sound sincere, and not like I was up to something.

Merlin sighed again. "Fine. Just promise me something. Don't do that again."

[43]

"THIS IS CONVENIENT," I said as I waltzed over to the elevator.

Ulli scowled. "What is? Having dozens of new women to fawn over you?"

Marcelle had rubbed off on her, and now both of them were mad at me. If I didn't have Kalli's presence in my mind, I probably would have been depressed living with two women who weren't speaking to me.

"You know you don't have to come, right?" I muttered, punching the elevator call button repeatedly and hoping it would hurry up.

"Oh, no you don't!" she exclaimed, stomping her foot on the ground. "That's how we got into this mess. If I'd been there, I would have shooed them all off before they could even make that indecent proposal. Besides, some of them are so old. Even older than Marcy."

"Did you hear that, Marcy?" I said, looking over Ulli's shoulder and causing her to jump. "She called you old."

Ulli spun on the spot, looking guilty. When she figured out I was messing with her, she rounded on me again. "That was mean!"

"So was calling Marcy old," I replied.

DING.

The elevator arrived with its familiar sound, and I stepped on with

Ulli storming in behind me. While Lavender had explained things to Marcelle, we decided it was for the best to keep Ulli in the dark. From her perspective, I'd officially decided to start dating. It was a little out of character for me, considering I'd done nothing but swoon over Kalli since I met her.

"You know I'm not trying to replace you," I said after riding in silence for several minutes. "Either of you."

She sighed. "I know but it's just a painful reminder that you didn't choose either of us. Just when I'd come to accept my role here you invite all these women, and now, I don't even have that anymore. It's frustrating."

"I didn't invite them to replace you," I said, choosing my words carefully and hoping Kalli wouldn't misinterpret them. "I brought them here so they can have a better life. You are still important to me."

Ulli didn't say anything until we made it to the bottom floor. When we got there, she tugged the sleeve of my shirt. "Can I be your first woman?"

"What?" I asked, startled by the question. "Kalli is my first...I mean only woman."

"Not like that," she giggled. "I mean your first tower woman. Or second. Marcy should be first. I don't mind her. Just, please..."

I knew what she wanted. Ulli didn't want to be lumped in with the new girls on the first floor. I patted her on the head and smiled. "You can be first woman. If anyone asks any questions, just remind them whose room you sleep in."

She beamed at me, all semblance of being upset gone from her face. When the doors slid open, she skipped out, heading toward the common room on the first floor. I followed close behind, letting her take the lead.

"Listen up, everyone," Ulli called over the din in the crowded room. "Lord Melvin is here to do an evaluation."

Was I? I just wanted to see Wendy and the gang, not perform a surprise inspection on a bunch of level one girls. Outside of the newcomers, all the girls on the first floor looked like little kids. I wasn't sure what the minimum age to be given tower access was but the majority of them looked to be around ten years old.

The common room was loaded with fun things to do. Easels lined one wall with paintings in various forms of completion attached. Several of the girls had board games set up on long tables and were fully engaged playing them. They looked up at Ulli with mild irritation on their faces. I spotted Wendy in the corner showing off her magic by making a wind dervish around an open book. The younger girls gathered around, clapping excitedly as the book fluttered like the core of a living thing.

She saw me and walked over, leaving the dervish as the center of attention. "Good morning, Melvin."

I smiled. "Good morning. Did you sleep well?"

She yawned reflexively. "Yes. The rooms are quite nice here. They are evaluating the younger girls today, so Shara and I are free."

"What about Zofia?" I asked. "Isn't she older than both of you?"

Wendy giggled. "You've seen her. She got tired of telling everyone she isn't a kid, so she gave up and went with it. In any case, she will be free tomorrow."

"Would you like a tour?" I asked, looking around for Shara.

"Sure," Wendy replied, turning to grab her bag.

Ulli cleared her throat, and I turned back to her. "Oh, right. This is Ullrisa Cypress. Her friends call her Ulli. She's my, um, first girl."

Wendy looked at her with a mischievous smile on her face. "Is that so? It's a pleasure to meet you, Ulli."

"You can call me Ullrisa," Ulli announced coldly. "Melvin gave me my surname!"

"Is that so?" Wendy repeated, putting her bubbly friendliness on display.

"Where's Shara?" I asked, looking around and not spotting any sign of the blond hemamancer.

Wendy giggled profusely. "She's more vampire than she cares to admit. She went to bed about an hour ago."

"Oh," I replied, watching the wind dervish dance around while

Wendy's attention was focused on me. "I guess we should let her sleep then. Um, how are you doing that?"

"What?" she asked. "Oh, him? That's a Kamaitachi. You know, a wind spirit."

"It's alive?" I asked. "Did you bring it with you from Earth?"

She smiled at me as though I were an ignorant child. "Spiritual creatures like Kamaitachi or gods can't pass between worlds. I thought you knew that. This Kamaitachi is from this world. I don't know what they are called here."

"What happens if you leave it here?" I asked.

Wendy shrugged. "I don't know. She might stay and play, or she might fizzle out. Wind can be unpredictable like that."

"Are you done chatting?" Ulli asked. I turned to find she'd somehow found and assembled a good chunk of the women from Midler. "You already know Lord Melvin. My name is Ullrisa Cypress, and as Lord Melvin's first girl, I am in charge. If you have any questions or need anything, you come to me. The first thing we are going to do is line you up for inspection. Lord Melvin is going to…"

"Can you handle that for me, Ulli?" I asked, taking a step back. While I'd brought the women to the tower, the last thing I wanted to do was *inspect* them.

She frowned before ultimately sighing. "Ugh, fine. Everyone, line up."

I didn't waste any time, and grabbed Wendy, wrapping mana around us and stepping into the void. Inside the relative darkness surrounded by planetary spheres, I took a moment to examine Wendy. First, I poked her on the nose. "Wake up!"

Kalli scolded me. *Stop messing with her. You know she's frozen in here.*

I sighed.

I was wondering if there's a way to wake someone up.

Kalli affirmed what I was already thinking. *She's frozen, not asleep.*

Giving up on the idea, I picked a place about halfway up the tower and reappeared. Wendy blinked and looked around the quiet hallway. "Where are we?"

"Floor forty-seven, I think," I replied. "I just wanted to get away from all the chaos."

She nodded. "So, what now?"

That was where I was stumped. While I knew I needed to find the artifact, I still didn't know what it was. Lavender wanted me to scour the throne room but only after they'd lured Merlin from the tower. I looked up at Wendy who was still waiting for an answer. "Have you heard anything from the other end?"

We both knew that talking openly was dangerous. Merlin could have any number of people listening to me. Mentioning keywords such as Lavender or my mom was dangerous. I just had to hope Merlin hadn't tracked me closely enough to remember Wendy. She closed her eyes for a few moments before shaking her head. "They're still getting ready."

"Well, would you like a tour, then?" I asked, realizing we had time to burn.

She smiled and nodded. "Sure, that sounds like fun."

———

It felt like there were three of us on an outing while I showed off the tower's amenities to Wendy. Kalli didn't leave us alone for a single minute. While it had been ages since The Academy, I knew she had been jealous of Wendy in the past. She giggled when we remembered the experience with Alex. I was jealous of him at first, but he ended bringing us together by trying to push me away. What had been jealousy quickly turned to gratitude, not that I'd ever tell him that. Kalli felt nothing but affection for Wendy, too.

Rather than teleporting, we took the elevator, stopping a few times so I could show her how the living conditions changed the higher we got in the tower. While the lower floors contained small rooms and large common areas, the upper middle floors had much larger rooms and smaller common areas that were more adult-themed. We passed by one room where a group of women sat huddled around a viewing screen, watching a familiar show.

"What's that?" Wendy asked.

I watched for a few seconds before laughing. "It's a game the rich play where they sponsor someone to go to another world and do quests. I think they call it the *Simpleton Games* or something. Ulli says they used people from Earth several years ago. It looks like this year is from planet Quackalot. Do you remember the Pouldarians?"

"Yes!" Wendy replied, stifling a giggle. "I had Mr. McDucken-Stein's class, too, you know."

"Oh, right," I replied. "I forgot."

Next, we made our way up to my floor. I dragged Wendy over to the restaurant, intent on showing her the finest dining on Origin. Kalli drooled as the appetizers were brought out. I sighed and decided to be the gentleman.

Do you want to switch?

Kalli looked at Mika, who she was alone with at the moment, before deciding. ***Yes! But just while you eat.***

The next thing I knew, I was sitting in awkward silence with Mika. She was still mad at her mother. I could tell by the way she sat stiffly, staring at the closed door that used to be a portal.

"It's going to be okay," I said softly "You know that, right?"

She glared up at me. "You can't know that. Mother doesn't take care of herself. Without me there, she's going to get herself killed. I don't want the last thing I said to her to be in anger."

"It won't be," I replied. "Lavender will make sure she's safe. With any luck, she's already gone back to Camelot."

"You don't know my mom," Mika said, tears forming in her eyes. "She will put herself in the middle of it. She has a bit of a hero complex."

I wanted to point out that Mika was doing the same thing, but she probably wouldn't listen. Besides, she was stuck on this side of the door unless Lavender bothered to open it again. I looked at the door-knob. It couldn't be that simple to open, could it?

Just when I was about to get up to check, Kalli gasped. Merlin appeared behind me at the dining hall. ***Melvin! Switch back. Hurry.***

———

"Can I help you, Pops?" I asked, craning my neck to look up at him.

Merlin tutted, but otherwise didn't react to the nickname. "Showing off for your new girlfriend? I don't think we've met. I'm Merlin."

Wendy stiffened, spluttering as she struggled to swallow a meatball and answer at the same time. Giving up, she picked up one of her several cups of tea and took a long sip to calm herself.

She then stood and curtsied so naturally I would have sworn she'd practiced for the occasion. "Hello, my Lord. My name is Wendy Haruko. It's a pleasure to make your acquaintance."

I was surprised. Merlin had caught me off guard, and I was fairly certain I would have messed up if I were her. One thing I noticed that was odd, was that Wendy didn't use her real last name. Surely, Merlin would notice that.

However, he didn't seem to and continued, "My son has excellent taste. I hope the two of you are happy together. As a matter of fact, Kiddo, how about you take the next week off and spend some time with your new lady friend here. You already seem to be aware of your credit line, so go have fun. Live a little."

Then, in true Merlin fashion, his voice amplified, and he said, "Dinner is on the house tonight. Everyone, eat to your heart's content. We're celebrating young love and lasting connections."

He left to a chorus of cheers.

[44]

I FELL ASLEEP EARLY that night. Both Kalli and I were frustrated to be cut off from whatever Lavender was up to. Neither of us could be in the group. Kalli because she was on another world, and me because of the parental block. That left us out of the loop. To top it off, Marcelle and Ulli were still frosty with me while Mika was terrible company because she was upset at her mom.

"Fancy meeting you here," Kalli said with a smile as I floated over to her half of the dream.

I held my arms out to hug her. "Hi, Princess."

She shrieked and flitted away from me, acting as though she were running from a stalker. The only thing that gave her away was the laughter as she snorted trying to hold it in. "Shoo, you! Oh, and I'm not a princess. I'm a queen."

"Not anymore," I reminded her, sticking my tongue out. "Your sister took your place after you got Scrapped."

She stopped backpedaling, allowing me to catch her and turning serious in an instant. "You're right. I hope she's doing well. I wish I could be there for her."

"She's fine," I said, wrapping my arms around her. "You heard

Lavender. She has plenty of people to help her. I'm sure they told her we're alive, so she won't worry."

"I hope so," Kalli sighed, kissing me softly. "So, what should we do today?"

I rummaged through my bag. It was strange to have a bag in my dream, but I didn't question it. Most everything I had access to in the waking world was available to me in there. Whether it was because I knew I had it or if there was an actual connection was beyond me. The only item that seemed to be affected when I used it in the dream was the black candle. Kalli nodded the moment she saw it. "Yes! I think I know the dream that's coming next."

"You do?" I asked, noticing the candle only seemed to have a single use left.

"Yeah," she said, looking a little sad. "This is the only time my master was cruel to me. I know why he did it now, so I'll do it."

"Why?" I asked, not wanting to hurt any version of Kalli.

She smiled. "It was the day he let me go. The day you summoned me."

"Oh," was all I could say.

Kalli gave me a warm smile. "I was so mad when you summoned me but also relieved. I think if my master had told me we'd work it out, I would have run away from you. It was because I had nowhere to go that I ultimately accepted a blundering boy summoning me."

My face burned as I remembered how arrogant I was to think I could summon someone just because I read about it in a book. Kalli took pity on me. "If you weren't that boy, I never would have met you. Then, I'd probably be dead now, or worse. It's kind of embarrassing to think Lavender saw all of this in advance. I wonder if she knows how it's going to end."

"I don't know," I admitted, wishing she would tell us and be done with it. "So, are you ready?"

Kalli held up a finger and a spark of flame emerged. "I'm as ready as I'll ever be."

I held out the candle, and she gently touched the wick. The flame flickered to life and black smoke erupted. Next thing I knew we were in a hut. Kalli's voice caressed my ear. *Give me control.*

I applied the illusion of Kalli's master and relinquished control just in time for a frantic young Kalli to burst through the door. She was holding a piece of parchment and had tears in her eyes. "Master! It's terrible. I need your help. You need to take me away from this place. Very far away."

Kalli sighed. "Show me what you've got there, little one."

Young Kalli did as instructed. It was an amendment to her contract with the Hellquist's. I wanted to laugh.

You did have a copy of the contract.

Kalli sighed. *No. My master took it with him.*

She took a deep breath and said, "This is a part of your destiny. You are about to embark on an adventure that will forever change your life. While I cannot interfere in what is about to happen, I assure you that you have no need to fear. Embrace your fate. Remember this always. You are special."

Before either of us had a chance to gauge young Kalli's reaction, the candle went out. The next thing I knew, we were staring at each other back in the dream. Kalli wiped a tear from her eye and said, "There, it's done."

"Do you think she took it okay?" I asked, my heart breaking for her.

Kalli laughed so forcefully that I thought she was making fun of me. "Well, right about now, she's sprinting through the forest thinking her last hope abandoned her. Then, she's going to stumble and fall down a hill, and some boy is going to summon her to a strange world. I think she's going to be more than okay. Especially now that she realizes that her master never abandoned her. Because I am my master."

"That's kind of poetic," I replied. "I'm glad we strengthened our bond. I would have made a terrible master."

"That's right," she grinned. "But you don't make a half-bad boyfriend."

———

I groaned as I found myself suddenly awake.

Aww, the dream was just getting good.

Better luck tomorrow night. Kalli snickered but I could tell she was frustrated as well. Something had rocked us out of the dream and neither of us were sure what it was. I looked around my room in the darkness. Ulli snoring was all I could hear. If Marcelle was in the room, she was fast asleep.

I got up and made my way to the bathroom. It was still the middle of the night. Things were the same on Kalli's side. She woke up alone in her bedroom. It was still dark outside. Of course, it was always dark on Scrap.

Come to think of it, it's always day on Origin. I wonder if these two planets are linked somehow.

Kalli shrugged. *I hadn't noticed. You only let me have control when we're in the tower. You can't tell if it's day or night in there.*

She had a point. Unless I was out in the garden, there were no windows in the tower. We both did our business and went back to our rooms. Kalli lay in her bed and had a thought. *Do you think your father sleeps on his throne?*

I immediately knew what she wanted to do.

I don't know. Maybe. You want me to go check, don't you?

She smiled. *It can't hurt.*

I agreed, and after a quick check on Ulli and Marcelle, I tiptoed out the door. We decided not to teleport just in case Merlin tracked that. Halfway there, it dawned on me just how much the tower was starting to feel like home. I never got lost anymore, and I had no problem strolling through the place in my pajamas.

The instant I opened the door to the throne room, I knew something was different. What I always thought was natural light coming in through windows high overheard was gone. Looking up, I saw nothing but barren walls where the windows once were. If not for my ability to see in the dark, I could have been blind. There only light in the room was a faint glow from the table beside the throne.

I crept through the vast room while keeping watch on the alcoves I passed along the way. All of them were empty, their occupants retired for the night. I wondered if Merlin was asleep on the cot in that tiny room at the top of the tower, or perhaps he was caught in the embrace of one of the upper tower maidens.

I pushed those thoughts from my mind as I approached the glow. It turned out to be the mysterious grapes I'd asked my father for when I first arrived.

I didn't know they glowed.

Kalli smirked. *You want to eat one, don't you?*

While the thought had crossed my mind, I didn't want to admit it even though I knew she knew.

No, but it might be the artifact Lavender is looking for.

I reached into the bowl, taking a handful of the glowing fruit. They looked like regular grapes, if they were radioactive that was. Of course, I was familiar with the effect. Kalli and I made something similar happen to a bowl of noodles and a chicken nugget. Did Dad infuse his food with mana? Was I about to find out what his mana tasted like? The thought made my stomach lurch. Curiosity won out in the end, and I popped one into my mouth. My eyes immediately watered, and my face puckered up. Kalli winced in sympathy.

Ahh, it's sour!

She groaned. *I know, I can taste it, too.*

Dropping the rest of the fruit, I picked up the bowl. Though well crafted, it felt like a normal bowl. Even pushing mana into it had no discernible effect. I was just about to put it down when a low voice made my spine crawl, "Ah hah. I caught you with your hand in the grime bowl!"

I spun on the spot to find Merlin sitting on his throne. Was he there the whole time? I didn't put it past him to have an invisibility skill. "I don't know what's gotten into you, but I'm disappointed to catch you sneaking around in here. I need to be able to trust you or I'm going to have to revoke your tower privileges. Can I trust you, son?"

"Of course, you can trust me," I blurted the words out, trying desperately to make up an excuse that didn't involve looking for forbidden artifacts. "You wouldn't give me a grape, er, what did you call it...a grime, and I wanted to know what they taste like."

"Well, now you know," he replied. "You could have asked Achemes. He can make you anything your heart desires, even these. Now, how to make sure you don't do this again? I think I'm going to ban you from this room for now. If you need me, call my name. I'll hear it and come. Understood?"

"But I…" I tried to object but, with a wave of his hand, I found myself sprawled on my bed.

Kalli sighed. *That didn't go well, and we didn't even find anything.*

I smiled. Kalli was wrong.

I learned two things. First, he knows my room layout, so he's either been here or he can see me in here. Otherwise, I doubt he could have dropped me on my bed after Ulli rearranged the room. The second is, he doesn't want me in the throne room.

Kalli frowned, seemingly oblivious to the obvious thing we discovered. *Even if he's hiding something, now we'll never find it.*

I think that's why Lavender is here. I'm pretty sure he just gave away that the artifact is that chair. He also has some way of telling if someone enters the throne room. We're going to have to wait for Lavender to put her plan in motion before we can try again.

She sighed. *What are we supposed to do until then. I hate all this waiting.*

At least we're together.

―――

It was still early, but I decided to head downstairs and see if any of the girls wanted to grab breakfast. Since Merlin believed I'd already chosen favorites, it wasn't suspicious when I only invited Wendy, Shara, and Zofia. I made sure to wake Marcelle and Ulli before heading down. They were already mad, and there was no sense making them madder.

Ulli surprised me by flying out of bed when I mentioned getting breakfast with the girls. I chuckled as I watched her race to the bathroom. "Don't you usually sleep in?"

"Not today!" she called over her shoulder, already starting to shuck her nightgown as the door slammed shut.

Marcelle was more subdued, stretching her arms above her head. "What's gotten into you two today? It's early."

"Nothing," I replied guiltily. "Just an early morning breakfast."

"Sure, it is," she muttered, giving me the stink-eye. "You're clearly up to something. It's a good thing you have me to make sure you don't get into too much trouble."

[45]

"So, do you have a plan?" Wendy asked as we exited the breakfast hall.

"Yes," I replied with a chuckle. "It's called operation wait for you know who."

We all knew who I meant. The girls had the added luxury of being in Lavender's party. So far, all I could glean was that it wasn't time yet. Since I assumed the artifact was still in the throne room, we needed to come up with a plan to get in through now that Merlin had banished me.

"What are we supposed to do in the meantime?" Zofia asked, folding her arms.

"You could do what you normally do in the morning," Marcelle suggested, winking at me.

Shara seemed interested all of a sudden. "What's that?"

Ulli raised her hand excitedly. "That's easy. Every morning after breakfast, it's training in the garden."

I couldn't help but crack a smile. Ulli was happy again. Wendy smiled, too. "Let's do that."

"Are there any places to do Alchemy in the tower?" Shara asked, glancing at Marcelle.

Marcelle frowned. "Hmm, I'm not sure. There are some workshops on the upper floors, but I don't know if any of the women in the tower study alchemy. You can request one, of course, if there isn't. Would you like me to check?"

"Can you?" Shara asked with a hopeful look on her face.

I nodded, wondering what she was up to. "I'm sure Marcelle can work something out for you."

Not to be left out, Zofia asked, "What other kinds of facilities do you have here? I'd like to see what the technology is like?"

"Fi-ine," Ulli groaned, sagging slightly. "I'll take you to a holo lab."

"What's that?" I asked. That was something I hadn't seen either.

Wendy tugged at my sleeve. "No, mister. You're all mine. I want to see what your training looks like. I'll have you know I've been training pretty hard myself, and there's something I want to show you."

Ulli glared at Wendy but allowed herself to be led off by Zofia. Marcelle gave me a stiff bow even though her expression told me she didn't appreciate being dismissed. She spun on her heels and led Shara in the other direction.

Once we were alone, Wendy stopped to grin at me. "Don't worry. They both have things they need to do. I want to show you that I've been busy too since we've been apart."

"I can't wait to see," I replied, offering her my hand to lead her to the park.

It didn't take long to get there as it was relatively close to the dining hall. Merlin had already repaired the damage I did the last time I trained. We made our way over to the clearing, and I sat down.

Wendy took a seat directly across from me and waited expectantly. "How do you normally train?"

"Do you want me to do my normal routine or teach you something specific?" I asked, not sure where to start.

She smiled. "Dealer's choice. Do whatever you want for now. I have something to show you after."

"Okay," I replied, trying to decide what would be most impressive.

While I'd practiced a lot since arriving in Origin, most of it had been internal.

Perhaps she will be impressed if I make her an artifact.

Kalli crinkled her nose. *No! I mean, do something else. I was kind of hoping you'd make me the next artifact.*

She had a point. Not only did I want to make something special for her, but it would also take too long. It took me a while to figure out the best mana to feed Kalli's first wand. Merlin said it should have taken me a lot longer to figure out.

"Have you ever infused your muscles with elemental mana?" I asked, wondering what kind of training Wendy had done since I last saw her.

She shook her head, still giving me that same smile from the first time I met her. It was a breezy sort of smile that gave me butterflies in my stomach. She shook me out of my reverie when she replied. "No. I've never done that before. Well, not exactly."

What did that mean? It didn't matter, I stood, and she followed suit. "Okay, I'm going to start with something simple. I'm going to infuse fire into my legs and jump."

Focusing an element into my mana was becoming second nature, so I added some emotion to give it an extra boost. Passion seemed to pair well with fire. It worked for Kalli. Kalli giggled at the thought, earning her a glare from Mika who was reading a book right next to her.

Why don't you go do something, Kalli?

She sighed. *I feel like something is about to happen, so I can't be distracted when it does.*

I also had a bad feeling. If only there was a way to ask what Lavender was doing without being overheard. If Wendy knew anything, she wasn't telling. I decided to focus and leapt into the air. Passion infused fire was a bit more powerful than I expected. My muscles exploded like tightly bound coils, launching me high into the air above the park. Even though the top of the tower was so high it passed through the clouds, I didn't come close to passing through them.

Being airborne gave me an excellent view of the surface outside of the tower. The ruins looked small, like shrubs surrounding a great oak tree. In the distance, I saw clusters of buildings on the horizon that I assumed must be one of the nearby towns that I hadn't visited.

A green blur startled me, and I looked up to see Wendy sail past me. I infused my body with wind mana as I plummeted back to the surface. That slowed my fall, but Wendy still descended slower. I waited a few seconds until she nimbly touched down beside me. "Wind works better for that."

"Did you infuse your body, too?" I asked, stunned that she outdid me at my own skill.

She giggled. "No. I can't do that. At least not until you teach me."

"Then, how…?" I asked, trailing off as I couldn't even figure out what to ask.

Wendy waved her arms around and a gentle breeze caressed my cheek. "Did you forget that I'm an aeromancer?"

"No," I replied. "But, wow, that's impressive. Were you able to do that before?"

Wendy sighed. "Oh, come on. You've already seen me do stuff like that. Do you remember when we jumped off the roof and floated to the ground? This and that are the same thing. The thing you did back then shocked me. I thought I knew everything, and you went and became the wind."

That took me back. It had been an accident. I was trying to become one with the wind and ended up doing it literally. I'd traveled halfway across Los Angeles before I managed to re-solidify and land on the roof of a skyscraper. "That surprised me."

"Do you think you can do it again?" Wendy asked.

I frowned, my brows furrowing as I tried to remember how it felt. Wendy shifted her weight from one foot to another as if she had to pee and was trying to hold it. "Watch this. Maybe it will jog your memory."

She disintegrated right in front of me, turning into a cloud that caught on the breeze she'd created and swirled around me. Even though I couldn't see her, I heard her voice in my ears. "This is how it's done."

"What? Wow," was all I could say.

I had to squeeze my eyes shut to get the proper feel for it. First, I infused my entire body with wind mana. Then I focused on the memory and willed my essence to ride the wind. As it turned out, the wind was Wendy. Soon enough, I felt my feet leave the ground. Actually, I didn't have feet anymore. Not really. Wendy danced and swirled around me. Her voice was everywhere and took on a musical texture, like wind whistling between the trees. "You have to be careful when you do this with another person. Whatever you do, don't become one with the other breeze."

"Why?" I whistled back.

She giggled, sounding kind of like a wind chime. "Because that's how wind gods make babies."

I gasped, which came out as a gust of wind and intentionally flowed farther away from Wendy. She giggled again and followed me. "Don't worry. I won't be careless enough to let that happen. I was just warning you in case you decide to become wind with any other wind sprites. I don't think Kalli would mind if you became fire with her, though."

Kalli's voice echoed in my ears like an explosion, *I would very much mind if you did that!* She must have felt my sadness because she added. *At least not until we're older.*

———

Wendy and I explored all around the outside of the tower. We even flowed through the ruins at the base. As Marcelle had warned me, it was littered with people who lived in the ruins. While they didn't seem dangerous, I was wind at the time. It might be different if I decided to march past their homes with several unawakened women in tow.

The outside of the tower wasn't very special. It was surrounded by a shimmering barrier, though I had no clue what it was for. The barrier extended far beyond the ruins, as though Merlin was defending against an attack that might come from one of the distant cities. The upper floors of the tower had no windows, even though I'd seen them from the interior. Perhaps they were all like the throne room where the windows disappeared when Merlin turned out the lights.

"We can use this form to sneak around," Wendy explained. "Lavender says Merlin can track normal teleportation because it leaves behind a trail and goes through the void."

"Did she teach you how to use this magic?" I asked, still wondering how she figured it out.

Wendy giggled again. "There's something I never told you about myself. I'm the daughter of Fujin, the Japanese goddess of the wind. I've always had a strong affinity for the wind. I figured out how to do this after watching you do it. The thing I could never figure out was how you did it in the first place. I guess that had something to do with your dad."

As soon as she said it, I immediately wondered if Merlin could do the same thing. Or if he'd seen us do it and was somehow following us. There was wind that always buffeted the tower, but I had no reason to believe that it was Merlin.

"This is how we are going to infiltrate the throne room," Wendy went on. "Lavender is almost ready to spring the trap."

"What are we waiting for?" I asked. "Let's get this over with so I can see Kalli again."

"Easy, Tiger," Wendy said. "Zofia and Shara both have jobs to do if we're going to get through the lock Merlin put on the door. Then you will have a small window to figure out the lock on the system. Everything is going to rely on you figuring it out. Even Lavender doesn't know if it's possible."

"Then, why are we doing it?"

Wendy's breeze turned cold. "Because everything will end if we don't."

[46]

"IT'S A GHOST!" Tower maidens shrieked as they fled a phantom gust of wind that blustered through the halls.

Wendy was having fun while we got lost looking for the computer lab. "What did that girl call it, the holo room?"

I laughed. "Do you mean Ulli? Yeah, that's what she called it."

"Why don't you know where it is?" she asked.

"I've never been there." A quick way to find it would have been to teleport and take my time locating Ulli through the void. I agreed not to do that, though, so the only way of finding it was to look around the old-fashioned way. Well, except for the wind. I could have asked for directions, but who thinks about that when you can blast through the halls as twin gusts of wind. It took us a lot longer to find it that way, but it was also much more fun. Our constant laughter made us sound like wailing ghosts everywhere we went.

It turned out that the holo lab was twenty floors below the floor I lived on. Glass doors somehow detected us even though we were wind and slid open long enough for us to both pass. Ulli looked up in surprise when a gust of wind blew in through the door. I decided to tease her and flowed in circles around her like a private mini-tornado. She pumped her arms in a panic as she danced around the room, managing to move away from the computer terminals. At least, I thought they were computers. While had display displayed information, it floated in the air above a workstation Zofia was seated at.

She ignored us and hammered away at several control panels at once. Ulli started hyperventilating, so I returned to normal. She gasped as Wendy did the same. "You jerk! I thought you were some kind of evil spirit, and why didn't you help me, Zofia?"

Zofia tilted her head to the side but kept typing. "What? Did something happen? Kinda busy here."

"You seriously didn't feel...?" She stamped her foot as she spoke. "Ugh, never mind! What are you guys doing here? Did something happen?"

"No," I replied. "Actually, we just came to see what Zofia is working on and if we can help."

Zofia snorted, not bothering to look at us either. "Fat chance of that. Did you even know that there is an electronic security system that covers the tower and the buildings outside? It tracks everyone in here and records their activities?"

Ulli gaped at her. "It does? Really? Everything we do?"

"Everything," Zofia replied dryly. "Even how long you spend on the toilet."

"That's disgusting," Ulli grumbled. "What is that information even used for?"

Zofia shrugged. "I don't think anybody looks at that specific data. There're definitely no cameras in the bathrooms. Trust me, I checked. That might help with the mission by the way."

"What mission?" Ulli asked, eyeing me suspiciously.

"That's not important," I replied. "It's an inside joke between me and Zofia."

Ulli raised an eyebrow. "What could she possibly want to do in the bathroom with Zofia?"

Fortunately, Wendy saved us with her reply. "Have you seen the size of the bath in Melvin's room?"

A smile settled on Ulli's face. "Yeah, I have. Melvin lets me use it whenever I want."

"What do you need from us?" I asked, wanting to get the conversation back on track. "Is there anything we can do to help?"

Zofia chuckled. "Not unless you can magic Joe in somehow. Then again, I don't really need him for what I'm trying to do. It looks like your dad had someone set this up but doesn't bother maintaining it. I've already been able to disable the audio and video in this room by replaying the feed on a loop. When the time comes, I should be able to do that elsewhere. I've already set up a worm, so I should be able to control everything from my room back on the twenty-third floor."

"You got assigned to the twenty-third floor?" Ulli asked in shock. "It took me nearly a year to make it that high when I was your age."

"I'm older than you," Zofia muttered as her cheeks puffed out in a pout that made her look even younger.

Ulli looked to me for conformation, and I nodded. "Yeah, she's in her twenties. Can you show us where Marcy took Shara? I need to talk to her next."

"No! Someone needs to stay here with Zofia," Ulli replied. "You'll have to wait until I find…"

"I can stay," Wendy volunteered with a friendly smile.

"No!" Ulli barked. "I mean, someone needs to watch you, too. Um, fine. You do know how to get back to your room, right, Zofia? You go down the hall and take the elev—"

"Yeah, yeah, I know," Zofia replied, waving her off. "I'll be able to concentrate more once you're gone anyway."

————

Ulli rounded on me once we were out of earshot of Zofia. "I'm not sure she should be doing that. The Creator isn't going to like it very much if he catches her. She might even be thrown out, and I don't even want to think about what that would mean for her family."

I winked at her. "Don't worry, I'll protect her. Besides, she doesn't have any family."

Ulli gasped and looked down. "Oh! I'm sorry. I didn't know."

While I wasn't sure if the TGB agent had family, it wasn't a lie that she didn't have family on Origin. The lab, it turned out, was in the basement. I looked around as we stepped out of the elevator. We had to walk to a second elevator after the first dumped us on the first floor. "I didn't know we had a basement. Why doesn't the main elevator go down?"

Ulli rolled her eyes. "This floor is mainly for storage and infrastructure. It makes sense that the public can't come down here. Normally, you need a special pass to come, but we have all access as you're chosen."

"That's convenient," I replied. "Why were you nervous when we visited Merlin's room, then?"

Ulli spluttered, cursing a few times as she bit her tongue. "Ugh, nobody is supposed to go there. Not without invitation. That's common sense."

"Right," I replied, laughing at the obvious joke. "So, where are Shara and Marcy?"

"Over this way," she replied. "At least, I think. I've never actually visited the place."

We passed by a series of large doors as we walked through the winding halls of the tower's underbelly. Ulli took out a map as we went. "It looks like the tower has five sub-basements, so there are more floors beneath this one. The alchemy lab was placed down here so it can be closer to where the toxic chemicals are stored. There are several sections of the lab where you have to wear protective equipment."

I looked over at the map. None of the information was listed there. "How do you know that?"

She grinned. "I looked it up in the holo lab once I found out Marcy was taking your friend down here. Also, that Zofia is quite moody."

Wendy giggled. "She is an acquired taste, that one."

We arrived at the lab to find most of the lights out. The only section lit up was in the far corner where Shara and Marcelle hunched over a desk. From the looks of things, Shara made herself right at home in the massive lab.

When they heard us, both girls turned. Shara started toward me, speaking excitedly. "Perfect timing. I'm going to need a sample of your blood."

I started backpedaling and ran right into Wendy. Our legs tangled, and we ended up in a heap on the floor. Kalli giggled back on Scrap, earning another glare from Mika. Before I could recover, Shara was on me. I felt a pinch on my arm, and blood shot out of me. I looked up to find Shara threading a string of it straight from my vein into a vial she held in her other hand. It filled quickly, much too fast for a normal blood draw. Once it was full, she withdrew another and repeated the process. She did that until she possessed four full vials of my blood.

It looked like way too much. Part of my brain wanted to be dizzy even though my body recovered from the loss almost instantaneously. "Hey! Won't I die if you take that much?"

Shara raised an eyebrow. "I don't know? Will you?"

"Maybe!" I grumbled.

She sighed. "Why don't you try standing up. If that doesn't work, do some of that chosen one magic to revitalize yourself."

She was right, of course. In the time it took me to complain, I had completely recovered. I unceremoniously dusted myself off and climbed to my feet, turning to offer Wendy a hand. She stood behind me with an amused look. "That was interesting. You're remarkably heavier than you look."

"I know," I grumbled, my mind flashing back to the way the kids in high school teased me about my weight. "I've always been that way. I used to think it was odd, but it probably has something to do with magic."

Wendy rubbed her chin for a moment. "That's probably true. I've always been light for my size. It must be the wind."

Shara had already walked back to the table and was connecting one of the vials to a tube by the time we walked over there. I watched it flow into several beakers before asking, "What is this exactly, and why do you need my blood?"

"I'm making you a master key," she replied, grinning from ear to ear. "Since you share your father's blood, this should help you."

"In other words," Ulli said with a sigh. "You're going to enable him to get in even more trouble."

"Don't worry about it," Marcelle said in a low voice. "He's agreed to leave us out of it this time. He's just looking for a special toy."

"Oh!" Ulli shrieked, piecing things together. "That's what you were doing in his room. Looking for some toy? Wow, you really are his son."

"Uh, yeah," I muttered, not sure how else to answer. Having Ulli out of the loop was kind of a pain. We stood back and watched Shara work for a while until I became impatient. "Can I do anything to help?"

She looked back over her shoulders. "I don't know. I'd hate to be responsible if something blows up and you get killed...or worse."

"What's worse than death?" Ulli asked Marcelle.

Marcelle leaned closer but we heard her anyway because she wasn't trying to hide her comment. "She could accidentally turn you into Melvin."

I groaned as the girls scooted a healthy distance from me. Even Shara laughed. "Relax, it's not anything quite so gruesome. The blood can cause your body to mutate though. You don't want three arms by any chance, do you?"

"What about you?" I asked, ignoring the raging laughter behind me. "What if you get deformed. At least let me help shield you or something."

Shara held up a hand to stop me as I edged forward. "Don't worry about me. I have immunities to blood. Most spells and compounds that use it as a base can't affect me. I've also developed an immunity to the attack that killed my mother. Not that I'd ever bite you, of course. I'm not a vampire."

"That's good to know," I replied slowly, wondering if Shara held a grudge after all. "You know, if I had it to do again, I would have tried something else."

"It's fine," she said, waving me off. "Mother made her choice. I built up immunity because I knew I had an inherent weakness. It's just self-preservation. That's all. Nothing against you personally. Wait, this is almost done. Hold on, I think your blood is going to take. Perfect, there we go. Would you like the rest of this blood back?"

I looked at the vials in her hand and shook my head. "No, thanks. That's okay. You keep it."

She grinned, and they disappeared into her cloak so fast I was positive she planned the whole thing. We watched as Shara methodically cleaned the equipment, explaining as she went. "It's very important to sterilize everything after each use. A small contaminant can corrupt the end result in unexpected ways."

Once she was done, we walked together to the elevator. Shara pressed a small cylinder into my hand and whispered, "You're going to need this when the time is right."

I looked at her. "When will that be?"

"She said you'd know."

[47]

NOTHING HAPPENED FOR THREE DAYS. Going about my normal routine without teleporting or leaving the tower was mind numbing. I tried to focus on Kalli and what she was doing, but she was just as bored as me. Wendy, Zofia, and Shara made themselves scarce, too, probably because they didn't want to attract too much attention to the fact that we knew each other. Merlin was true to his word and didn't drop in on me at all. I walked over to the throne room once and discovered the doors were sealed tight. There was no way I could investigate them without alerting him.

Marcelle and Ulli were acting weird too. I wasn't sure if I should be concerned but I woke up one morning and neither of them were there. The next time I saw them, they whispered while casting nervous glances my way.

I wanted to talk to Ulli by herself but, the moment Marcelle left, she made a bee line for the bathroom. "Sorry, Melvin. Gotta go."

I knew they were up to something but couldn't do much about it. Lavender chose that moment to make her move. The door between worlds burst open, and she looked straight at Kalli while speaking to me. "Melvin. It's time. Merlin has left the tower and is coming for your mother. Meet Wendy and find a way to the relic.

Where are they?

Lavender replied, knowing my reply before Kalli translated. "She will meet you at the elevator. Do not teleport."

I left Ulli in the bathroom and sprinted for the door. The elevator dinged right when I arrived, and Wendy stepped out. She was with Shara.

"Where's Zofia?" I asked, wondering if they left her behind.

"She's in her room," Wendy replied hurrying past me into the hall. "She's monitoring us from her computer."

"Okay," I replied, leading them to the stairwell.

"I thought the throne was on this level," Wendy said as we ascended to the next floor.

"It is," I replied. "But the door is sealed. Don't worry, I have an idea."

It wasn't perfect. I'd never had a chance to see if my theory was true. I burst in through the first door I came to on the next floor. It was right above the throne room. A woman in a red nightgown jumped out of her chair. "M-my Lord? This is highly irregular. I'm The Chosen…"

"I know," I replied, waving her off. "I need to borrow your stairs real quick."

"But…" she stammered.

I ignored her and raced over to a winding stairwell on the far side of the room.

If she has a way of contacting him, this is totally going to backfire.

Kalli started pacing. *Be careful, Mel.*

It would be easier if I knew what Merlin was doing. Wendy and Shara looked worried, but neither of them said anything. All I could do was hurry.

At the bottom of the stairs, was one of the alcoves that normally connected to the throne room. Only, there was a problem. A wall stood between the tiny nook and the vast throne room that hadn't been there before. Did it grow when Merlin was out of the tower? I was positive it hadn't been there when I snuck in the other night. That could only mean one thing. Merlin sealed off the alcoves before he left. He knew I intended to break in again.

"Now what?" Wendy asked.

I shrugged and turned to face them. "I don't know. Maybe try the front door?"

She shook her head. "No. Zofia says that's a bad idea."

"Why?" I asked. "I know it's locked. But we can…"

"It's guarded?" Shara mumbled, sounded as though she didn't believe what she was saying.

"By who?" I asked, realizing I'd never seen any guards in the tower before.

Wendy looked horrified when she replied. "Not a who. A what. It appears your father has a dragon."

"We need to get through this wall then," I replied. "Zofia, can you tell if any of the alcoves are open?"

I couldn't interact with Zofia from outside the group but I knew she could hear me through the group.

"They're all sealed," Wendy replied for her. "We're going to have to break the wall down. Also, Zofia doesn't have eyes in the throne room. There's either no cameras or she's being blocked."

"Keep me posted on that dragon," I replied, walking back to the wall. "We're in trouble if it gets into the throne room."

While it was a solid wall, it didn't feel particularly special. There was no mana imbued in it. I closed my eyes and probed it with mana. The wall was designed to seal off the throne room. Was it meant to keep me out? No. It clearly wasn't. Did he not realize I'd make another attempt on the throne? The whole thing screamed trap.

"Be ready for anything," I whispered, glancing over my shoulder to make sure nobody was spying on us above.

Once imbued with my mana, the walls parted as though they were liquid. I could tell by feel that they were made of dense metal, probably lead or something similar. The throne room was bathed in darkness, with only dim light behind me leaking in. I stepped into the throne room, feeling exposed in the large space. From the subtly sounds behind me, I knew Wendy and Shara were at my back.

We tiptoed slowly, stopping every few feet to watch a shadow that appeared to be moving on the throne. While I could see the entirety of the room, the condensed darkness around the throne played tricks with my eyes. Was someone sitting there?

"Identify yourself," a deep voice bellowed so loud it echoed throughout the chamber.

"I'm Melvin Murphy," I replied, puffing my chest out. "I'm the son of The Crea… I'm the son of Merlin!"

"You are not yet worthy" the voice boomed. "Prepare to prove yourself."

I looked over my shoulder at Wendy. "Did Lavender give you any advice for me?"

She shook her head rapidly. A siren went off in the background and glowing red eyes appeared behind the throne.

"Hold on a sec, guys," Zofia's voice boomed somewhere in the distance. "I think I can help."

A second pair of red eyes appeared just above where Zofia's voice came from.

"What do we do?" Shara asked. "Make a run for the throne?"

I shook my head, eyes still locked on the shadow above the throne. "There's something there. I think it will kill us if we don't deal with whatever that thing is first."

"I don't see anything," Wendy said, standing beside a pair of wind dervishes she'd summoned.

"I don't know how to explain it," I replied. "It's a living shadow."

The first set of red eyes slowly made its way to the throne. There was a metallic clink every time it took a step. When I finally managed to make out what it was, I gasped. A shimmering black robot blended perfectly with the darkness. All except for the glowing red eyes. It was roughly humanoid in shape, with two massive arms and legs. It was so huge it stood nearly twice as tall as I was.

"We have to fight a pair of those?" Shara asked, gasping. "I sincerely doubt they have blood."

I gulped, looking at the eyes in the back of the room. "I take the front, you two take the back?"

"There's no need for that," Zofia's voice echoed again. "I'm controlling that one. Just back me up."

A beam of light shot out of the darkness directly toward the black robot. Its hips swiveled on the spot, raising a plated arm to absorb the blast. Sparks flew in every direction, lighting up the room. That silhouetted a being of pure darkness that sat on the throne with the same bored posture Merlin usually had. It reminded me of a shadow boss in one of the video games I played.

The dark robots didn't let me focus on the shadow boss for long. A maelstrom roared to life at my side as Wendy prepared powerful magic. I looked for Shara, but she'd vanished into the darkness. If I wasn't preoccupied by the monsters in front of me, I'd probably have wondered if she was taking after her mother after all.

While Zofia's robot was putting up a good fight, it was obvious that she didn't know how to control her robot as well as the one she was fighting. The other one transformed one of its arms into a sword that was long enough to be a lance. It lashed out at the other robot while still blocking laser beams with its plated arm. Zofia tried to dodge but the blade went right through its torso. Sparks shot out and it staggered as it attempted to extricate itself.

By that point, Wendy's storm had built up to a proper mini-tornado. She sent it at the enemy robot with a swish of her hand. It struggled to remove its blade from the other's chest as it tried to deflect the tornado with its arm just as it had the laser beam. The wind ignored the obstruction and slammed into the robot full force, knocking it off balance.

Realizing I wasn't helping, I held up my hand and shot a jet of flame at the monster. If I had access to the system, I would have chanted Kalli's favorite spell, "**Pvruzth.**" Instead, I closed my eyes and willed the fire to be hot enough to melt metal.

Wendy's tornado helped my flame, feeding it and fanning it around the robot. If machines needed to breathe, we would have suffocated to death. Aside from turning red, it didn't melt. It didn't even stop working. The robot ignored us and used its second hand to brace itself so it could pull the sword out of the other robot.

Zofia swore like a sailor through the speaker as she struggled to make the fallen machine respond before eventually giving up. "I'm sorry, guys. You're on your own for now. I'll see what other defense systems I can access."

"This isn't working," Wendy said as she tugged me back. It was impossible to tell if our attacks were doing anything more than annoying the massive robot.

I redoubled my efforts, adding an electrical element to my mana and naming the new attack for good measure. "Thunderous Arson!"

The robot staggered and stopped advancing, its sword arm transforming into something else that looked like a cannon. Wendy let her storm dissipate and levitated, two tiny tornados forming under her feet.

"What are you going to do?" I stammered between clenched teeth. "I can barely hold this thing off."

"Give me some time," she shouted to be heard over her storms which sounded like jet engines. "I have an idea."

I held up my other hand, pushing more mana into the attack in an attempt to make up for the lack of Wendy. Zofia had gone silent since her robot went offline.

Use rage! Kalli barked through our bond. *Add a storm of emotions to your, um, storm.*

Becoming enraged on command was difficult. I wondered how the big green guy from the comics did it. Kalli helped by picturing Rasputin. That did the trick. I saw an image of Kalli exploding and an unhealthy rage flooded through me. The power of my attack grew as I poured raw emotion into it. The inferno was no longer able to contain the electricity, and it lashed out, striking the walls and ceiling in random strikes of lightning.

Wendy yelped from above as one of the lightning bolts struck close by but managed to call out a custom spell of her own. "Downburst!"

I felt the wall of pressure as wind plummeted off Wendy and slammed into the robot. Its legs buckled and it fell to its knees, parts of its armor peeling off under the force of the wind. I used the opening to force my attack inside. The electric flame vanished for a moment. Then it glowed from everywhere before bursting out in a spectacular explosion.

[48]

THE THRONE ROOM lit up in a brilliant explosion. I flattened myself to the ground, curling myself into a ball as the shockwave hit.

Wendy let out a squeak as she was thrown into the ceiling by the force of the blast. She descended slowly, still having the presence of mind to lighten her body. I rushed over and probed her with my mana for injuries. Though she was battered and disoriented, nothing stuck out as life-threatening.

"Not bad," the voice of the shadow said. Its baritone voice sounded nothing at all like Merlin. "I don't know if I'd call that a pass, but at least you didn't fail."

I climbed to my feet, dusting myself off before reaching down to offer Wendy a hand. She coughed a few times before accepting the help. "I hope that's all the fighting we have to do."

"Me, too," I grunted, wondering what was going to happen next. A flash of blonde hair just behind the shadow behind the throne caught my attention.

If she wants to be an assassin, it will probably be a good idea to dye her hair.

Kalli cleared her throat, noticing my bad habit of getting distracted in life-or-death situations. *Focus, Melvin.*

I took her advice and addressed the shadow, "If we didn't pass, what's next?"

"Come closer," the shadow beckoned. "Prove your worth."

"What are you?" I asked before correcting myself. "*Who* are you?"

"I am what I am," it replied. "I am a specter of the past, tied to an artifact. I know you are his son, but that doesn't equate to worthiness. Step forth and be judged."

"Are you Merlin's shadow?" I asked, feeling like I was stepping into a trap when my legs started walking on their own. "Did you tell him I'm here?"

"I answer to no one," the shadow replied, standing in front of the throne with its arms crossed. "I alone choose who is worthy to lay claim to the throne. The fate of the cosmos depends upon it."

"Is the throne the artifact?" I asked, moving a little faster as I was suddenly in full agreement with my legs.

"The throne is the throne," the shadow replied, bending down to stroke the arm of the chair. "That which lies within can take any form depending on its master. The current owner chooses to use it to lord over all. Is that also your intention?"

"I haven't thought about it," I admitted, wondering what I'd do with ultimate power.

"Give me your hand," the shadow said, reaching out when I stopped in front of it. "Submit yourself."

I wondered if I was making a major mistake, but something told me I wouldn't win in a fight. The moment I made contact with the shadow, I felt something invade my body. The shadow was inside of me. It swirled around my core and prodded it, testing for a reaction.

I vaguely sensed both Shara and Wendy as they made contact with the shadow. Whatever attacks they threw at it were nullified as they were sucked in the same way I was. Before I knew it, the three of us stood before the shadow like children standing meekly before their parents. The shadow said nothing as it carried out its test. Kalli said something in the background, but it sounded very far away.

Then, it was over. The shadow let go of my hand and said nothing.

It ignored me as it continued whatever it was doing to Wendy and Shara. I reached out to grab the tentacles.

"Do not interfere!" It boomed, stopping me in my tracks. "No harm will come to your friends. Not unless they continue to be aggressive."

I had a strange feeling it would be pointless to attack. Perhaps I sensed its power, or maybe it planted the thought in my head. I wondered why it allowed Merlin to control the artifact in the first place. Surely, it was more powerful than him.

It released Shara first. "Unworthy. While you come from prestigious stock, you lack ambition."

Then, it let Wendy go. "It has been long since I encountered a demi-god. Unfortunately, you are lacking as well."

"What about me?" I whispered, wondering why the shadow didn't say anything when it let me go. "Am I worthy?"

The shadow stared at me for a long time before replying, "I see something in you. You are much like your father. However, something is missing, and I cannot allow you to attempt to claim the artifact as you currently are."

"But there's no time," Wendy said. "Lavender can't hold him off. He will be back, and then it will be too late."

"Alas, you are probably correct," the shadow said, sitting on the throne again. "There is no shame in conceding defeat, though many argue otherwise."

"No," Lavender spoke in a firm voice that startled me. She emerged from a door that appeared several feet behind me and strode to my side. "Now is the time. I see now why I couldn't see beyond this day. A Tuatha De Danann still exists. Ancient magic is at play here."

"Welcome, Gwenddydd," the shadow said, not at all surprised that a voluptuous woman just stepped out of a door-shaped portal. Then again, he was a shadow creature himself. Or a Tuatha thing Lavender said he was. "Do you wish to be tested?"

She shook her head. "You already know I'm not worthy. I need you to test Melvin again. He is the one. I have seen it."

"The result will be the same," the shadow droned, sounding bored. "You have the gift of sight. Surely, you have seen at least this much."

Lavender flapped her arms, looking panicked for the first time since I'd known her. "That is not possible. You know what will happen if he fails. Surely there must be a—"

She stopped and rubbed her chin while turning to me. "Listen carefully, Melvin. All bets are off. You must do whatever it takes to claim the artifact. Do you have the ring with you?"

"Yes," I replied, running my finger over the invisible artifact on my finger that Lavender had hidden. "It's no use, though. Only Mardella and a couple of princesses—"

She cut me off. "Now is the time to use it."

I looked at the shadow. "Do you want me to—"

Lavender cut me off again. "No! The Tuatha De Danann do not have souls as we do. They are guardians. You need to figure out how to become worthy while I buy you some more time."

"Time?" I asked. "What do you mean?"

"He's coming," she gasped, sweat appearing on her brow. "Also, don't blame your friend. She only betrayed you because I manipulated her."

"Who betrayed me?" I asked, thoroughly confused.

I didn't have a chance to figure out what she meant because Merlin chose that moment to appear. He looked like the wizard of legend, decked out in a full wizard's robe with a hat to match. It wasn't the blue one. He'd given that to me. This one was dark red and pinstriped. It was like someone did a marketing campaign to make Merlin 2.0.

Lightning arced across the room as Merlin gathered power into a multicolored ball. He glared at Lavender and shouted, "Gwen! I've gone to a great deal of trouble to flush you out over the years, and you dare to appear here in my home! Do not expect any mercy from me. Not this time!"

"Dear brother," Lavender replied, producing a gnarled staff and pointing it at Merlin, "I prayed this day would never come."

"Nonsense!" Merlin screamed. "You were always jealous of me. Of what I have become."

"You let your infatuation warp you," Lavender said, roots growing from the staff and into the ground. "Surely, you can see that she now fears you."

"Leave Vivien out of this," Merlin snarled, launching his attack from the wand he refused to let me touch. Half fire and half water, a ball of plasma shot toward us.

The only thing that stood between me and sure death was Lavender. Roots shot up through the concrete floor of the throne room and intercepted Merlin's attack. They ripped through the floor in an instant where a flash of light signified Merlin's attack had exploded. I wondered vaguely if any of the tower maidens on the floor below us were injured. There was no time to think about that though. Lavender was buying me time, and I needed to spend it wisely.

"What does this blood thing do?" I asked, taking out the cylinder that Shara made.

Shara shrugged. "It's a bio key. Lavender said you will need it to form the connection."

I held the cylinder up to the shadow that was looking intently at me while ignoring the battle raging around us. "Does this change anything?"

It reached out and touched it. "This means nothing to me."

I looked back and forth between Wendy and Shara. "Do you think I should drink it or something?"

Wendy shrugged and Shara shook her head. "No. That wouldn't do anything. That's made out of the refined mana in your blood."

What was missing? I suddenly realized what was missing.

Kalli! Where are you?

I don't know if there was distortion from the shadow, or if I'd somehow tuned her out, but I vaguely recalled Kalli saying something, and then going quiet. When she didn't reply, I focused on her. She had her eyes squeezed shut and was focusing really hard. Then, she vanished. It was only for a brief moment and part of me knew where she was.

Then, she appeared in front of me breathing heavily. Memories of her getting the hang of the void crashed into me as she came back to me in an instant. Now, you could probably write a book about the proper way to greet your lover in a war zone, but I can tell you from experience, none of that matters when you see your girlfriend for the first time in months. Kalli threw her arms around me, and we embraced, holding each other so tight that it almost hurt.

I don't care if we're trapped here, she said, a fierce look of determination on her face. *I am not going to let you die.*

I wasn't worried about getting off Origin either. The die was cast the moment Lavender set foot on the planet. If Merlin was going to blow up the universe, he had to be stopped. Beyond that, the only thing that mattered was that we were together, and Origin was as good a place as any for that.

"You are now complete," the shade said softly. Nothing of us noticed the shadow as it approached and touched us. "The two of you together are worthy to claim the artifact. Do you wish to proceed? I must warn you that rejection equals death."

[49]

"YOU WILL NOT RELINQUISH THAT THRONE!" Merlin shouted at the top of his lungs as the shadow stood and stepped aside. "Stand your ground, Dagda."

The shadow nodded to us. "You must choose your own free will. Acceptance will equal a life of servitude, while rejection will result in death. Do not make this decision lightly."

Kalli and I looked at one another and nodded. In truth, we'd already decided to trust Lavender. While I cared about my dad, I'd only just met him. If Lavender was convinced the world was going to end, I wasn't about to doubt her. Not only that, but Mom was on her side.

As one, we knelt before the throne and touched it together.

Welcome...
Scanning Users

Melvin Murphy
Bloodline M

Kalliphae Murphy

Bloodline M

Sindra Murphy
Bloodline M

Bloodline Accepted.
Access Granted
Commencing Synchronization Process...

We froze as a jolt of mana surged from the throne and into our bodies. Not that we wanted to, of course. We were stuck, tethered by the mana that pulsed straight through to our cores. It was a terrible spot to be in with the battle still raging around us. Neither side appeared to have the upper hand at the moment and a stray spell was all it would take to end things for us very quickly.

My focus was drawn back to my core as an icy sensation started to creep into me. The system wasn't stopping with just a simple scan. Kalli and I convulsed. Something was wrong.

I vaguely heard Merlin over the sound of rushing mana. "Give up, child! There is nobody in existence who can contain the system but me."

The problem was, I couldn't give up if I wanted to. Once the system started synchronizing, there was very little we could do except go along for the ride. I couldn't even access the blood vial that was locked in my other hand. Wendy and Shara hovered off to the side, neither brave enough to get too close or make contact with either of us.

Merlin pointed his wand at me. "Last chance, boy! Stop what you're doing or face the consequences."

Lavender materialized between us. It was at that moment that I realized she could teleport. She's always used the doors, so I'd concluded that she used it as a workaround.

Sparks exploded off Lavender as she blocked whatever Merlin had cast at us. At least I thought it was Lavender.

Did her hair turn gray?

When Kalli didn't answer right away, I turned my head to look at her. She was more frozen than I was, sweating profusely as she strug-gled with the mana coming from the system. She was usually so strong that it was easy to forget that she didn't have the same mana pool as I did. Focusing on our bond, I allowed mana to flow freely from her side.

Kalli sighed in relief and locked eyes with me. *You need to focus. The shadow said this might kill us.*

She was right. I'd let my bad habit of being distracted by the world, well, distract me. While we were still in danger, I was going to have to trust my friends to keep us safe.

Mana flowed at a constant rate from the throne to my body, trav-eling through my mana channels and into my core. Outside of Kalli, foreign mana hadn't ever penetrated so deeply before. My vision blurred as my consciousness was sucked inside of myself. The interior of my core looked very similar to the dream realm where Kalli and I spent our nights. While she wasn't with me, I felt her on the other side of the tether. It was no longer barricaded over on Scrap. The tether felt like a long string that stretched from my house to Kalli's.

Mana flooded the room around me, causing the environment to sparkle with ambient energy. It spread up and down the tether, connecting us in a more profound way. The golden ball of light that represented our coupling shimmered as it sped back and forth from one end of the tether to the other, seemingly oblivious to the mana that coursed through it.

It accumulated on my side far faster than it had on Kalli's. While she had grown immensely since I'd known her, her core was far smaller than mine. The imbalance caused mana to travel over to my side in waves. The golden light rode the waves over and over, sailing back to Kalli's side just in time to ride a fresh wave back to my side again.

If I didn't know any better, I'd say Sin was playing with the mana.

Kalli grunted. *Is this painful at all for you? I feel like I'm being stretched out, and not in a good way.*

It's not too bad, and look at the bright side. After this, you'll probably be able to store a lot more mana. Imagine how big your flames will be then.

I felt her discomfort through our bond and tugged at the tether to open it up a bit and allow more mana to pass into me. While I wanted to go bring Kalli over to my side where she would be more comfortable, I realized that wasn't possible. She couldn't escape her core. It was what defined her.

Initialization Complete...

Welcome to The System...

Registering New Superuser: Melvin Murphy
Registering New Superuser: Kalliphae Murphy
Registering New Superuser: Sindra Murphy

Would you like to assign an artifact? Y/N

Mana Remaining: 23,058,023,455
Mana Absorbed: 122,122

It stopped.

I heaved a sigh of relief, immediately floating over to Kalli to make sure she was okay. She smiled and accepted my embrace when I arrived. A glance at the golden ball of light told me Sindra was okay as well. She continued to race around our combined cores, paying little attention to the ambient mana in the air.

Kalli clung to me, her eyes still affixed to the system menu. *There's so much more mana. What are we going to do with it?*

She was right, I had no clue. That was the mana Lavender was worried was going to destroy the universe. I wondered how Merlin ever expected my mom to absorb all of it. There was no way I could let him try.

Do you think we can take it slowly?

Kalli burped for effect. *I don't know about you, but I'm stuffed.*

A scream reminded me that the battle was still raging out in the real world. I pulled myself out of my core to find my hand still stuck to the throne. Whatever it was doing, it hadn't let go. It was Wendy who'd screamed. She lay on the floor nearby with several smoking holes in her shirt. Lavender stood between her and Merlin as she waved a staff above her head. Brilliant light shone above us before crashing down on Merlin in the form of pink rays. Merlin did a summersault as he dodged. I realized he was infusing his muscles at a far more expert level than I'd ever mastered.

Part of me was still torn. While I believed in Lavender, Merlin was still my dad. I didn't want to see him die or anything. Could we find a way for everyone to survive this? Perhaps that's why it was our job to nullify the system. Once that was out of the way, they would have nothing left to fight over.

I gave my hand another tug, feeling it start to come free even though the throne didn't want to let go. It felt as though I were a chunk of metal fighting against a powerful magnet. Kalli saw what I was doing and tried as well.

"That won't work," the shadow said, still standing idly by the throne.

"Why not?" I asked, tugging harder and feeling my hand start to come free. "I'm almost…"

"You need to follow the prompts," the shadow continued. "Choose a new artifact for the system or you will never have full control."

"A new one?" I asked, tugging even harder.

Connection Lost!
Registration Paused.
Re-establish contact to continue…

We both flew back at the same moment. Somewhere in the distance, Lavender screamed. "No! You mustn't give up."

Suddenly, Merlin was between us and the throne. He had a frantic look in his eyes. "I'd hate to think you betrayed me, son."

His eyes narrowed as he sat in the chair. I looked around frantically for Lavender and found her on her knees about twenty feet away. Wendy had yet to get up, and Shara was nowhere to be found. Merlin ignored them all as his eyes closed on his throne. "Hmm, I see. You could have ruined everything. Tell me, what do you know about the system?"

"I know you plan on using it to destroy the universe," I replied, saying a silent prayer that he would deny it.

"Is that what she told you?" he asked, glancing over at Lavender who glared at him in silence. "Did she tell you how she knows that? Or that her visions have a greater chance of not coming true if she acts on them? For all she knows, the world will end if I don't do this."

"Have you ever asked Mom what she wants?" I asked, causing Merlin to flinch.

"You don't know your mother," he growled. "Not like I do."

"That's hilarious coming from you," Mom's voice echoed through the hall.

"Viv?" Merlin cried out, standing abruptly. "Where are you?"

"Never you mind," she replied. "If you knew me, you'd have never left. I don't want eternal life or anything to do with power. All I want is to enjoy what I have with the people I love. You know, to live my best life. I told you I'm perfectly fine with Melvin being special and enjoying your lifestyle. Why wouldn't you just stay with me? You never stay with me. Not once in all the lives we've lived together."

"You remember?" Merlin asked, sounding out of breath. "You never said…"

"I remember everything," Mom said, sounding equally exasperated. "Yet, I fall in love with you every time. If you'd just get out of your own head and let yourself be happy, maybe we could be together."

Suddenly, Merlin vanished. I knew from experience that he'd located Mom and was teleporting to her. Lavender rose to her feet and shouted at me, "Melvin! Now, go for the throne. Finish the process!"

"Then what?" I asked. "How are we supposed to control that much mana if even Merlin can't do it?"

She shrugged with a sigh. "That, I don't know. All I know is that you can, and you will. The universe depends on it."

Just then, Merlin reappeared with Mom and Joe. He threw Joe to the floor while he sat Mom gently on the throne. Lavender raised her wand, but it vanished into thin air and a metal cage appeared around her.

Merlin chuckled and waved his hand theatrically. "This could have all been avoided. How long have you been hiding her from me, dear sister? None of this had to be difficult."

I forced myself to my feet and stared him down. "Why are you doing this? You heard Mom. She doesn't want this. Any of it. Why don't you settle down and enjoy the quiet life with her? Maybe even move her in here."

I didn't mention the tower full of women. Hopefully, he would have the good sense to clear them out if he invited Mom over. Either that or move to a tiny house by the sea and adopt a few cats. Mom would enjoy that. Merlin sighed. "I didn't know it was her. By the time I realized it, Grenddydd had already hidden you both from me."

"You abandoned us," I said, wanting to cry but deciding that wasn't a good idea before a potential fight. "We lived in the same place all my life and you never came back."

Merlin turned to look at Mom. "Tell me, my love, were you aware of my sister's treachery? Did you knowingly deceive our son?"

[50]

"Yes," Mom replied, looking straight at me. "Merlin was unstable. Once I had you, I knew I had to keep you safe from him. At least until you were old enough to know the truth. So, I spoke to Lavender, and we came up with a plan to protect you until you were old enough to fulfill your destiny. I trust you to make the right decision, whatever that ends up being."

I gaped at her. How could she say that with a straight face? On the one hand, I was thrilled that Mom trusted me. Isn't that what all kids want? On the other, it was way too much responsibility for one kid to manage. I didn't want to be the guy who blew up the universe. Since when was that cool?

Lavender spoke from her cage. "This day has been etched in destiny since long before you were born. It's either the day Merlin destroys everything or the day that you save it. One of those things will happen."

"You're mistaken, Lavender Witch," Merlin spat, glaring at her. "You've always meddled even though your predecessor told you not to. Every time you get involved, calamity follows. Do you remember the Dark Ages?"

Lavender sighed. "You were just as much to blame for that as I was. He was your apprentice."

I looked back at my friends as Merlin and Lavender argued. Wendy was up but nursing her left arm. Joe seemed to be okay, but Shara was still missing. Kalli was right next to me and had just gotten her breath back.

I checked the system for access and pulled up Merlin's menu.

Name: Merlin Wyllt
Class: System Administrator
Level: ???
Affection Level: Blocked

At least I still had access, but I was unsure how that would help. Mom stood. She only came up to Merlin's chest but seemed to tower over him with her hands on her hips. I always thought of it as her superpower. Whenever she was angry, she could make me feel like I was about an inch tall without saying a word.

"Do you love me?" she asked, staring him down. "I mean, do you truly love me?"

Merlin wasn't backing down, though. "Of course, I do. Which is why I have to do this. You could never understand how it feels to watch you die."

She sighed. "If you love me as you say you do, you would never do anything to me against my will. I do not want this. Not if the risk is destroying everything."

"That won't happen!" Merlin shouted. "I won't allow it."

"You can't control everything," Lavender said.

"Watch me," Merlin growled, strutting around Mom and behind the throne.

He began chanting a spell I didn't recognize. Runes lit up on the floor in a dull red glow. Mom fell back against the throne and let out a yelp. I jumped to my feet to rush to her, but that magnet was back at work again, pushing me away from the throne.

I tried to DELETE the runes, and then the throne itself. Nothing worked. Everything in the room was protected. Even Lavender's cage. Mom sat restlessly on the throne while Merlin circled the room while continuing to chant.

I looked over at Joe and Wendy to see if they had any ideas, but they were all sprawled out on the floor, struggling to get to their feet. The only two of us who were standing were me and Kalli, but we couldn't get close enough to Mom or the throne to do anything at all.

Lavender ??? has invited you to join a group.

I blinked. Of course! I had system access. I could join groups again. Through my bond, I noticed Kalli had also received an invite.

You have joined the group.
Kalliphae Murphy has joined the group.

Listen carefully and don't think a word.

I turned to stare at Lavender. She stood in the cage, gripping the bars with a look of determination on her face. Merlin was so wrapped up in his ritual that he didn't pay any attention to anything else. I thought that was a little arrogant of him considering he didn't bother to lock any of us up. Just Lavender.

She continued, *I am going to buy you a small window to get to the throne. The two of you must complete the registration process.*

I pushed against the field that kept me from the throne.

I know, but where do you put that much mana? It's in the billions now. Won't setting it loose destroy the universe?

Lavender closed her eyes. *Not exactly. The ritual he's performing on the system is what will cause the apocalypse. You must assign an artifact and remove the mana from the equation. Preferably something he can't access. I don't know the answer, but I am confident you will.*

I wanted to ask so many more questions, but Lavender didn't wait. The bars of her cage frosted over. She thrust her hand out, and the frozen metal shattered, shards conveniently flying straight at Merlin. He ducked under his cloak just in time to not get peppered with the sharp slivers of metal.

In that moment of distraction, Lavender was gone. She reappeared in front of the throne and grabbed Mom by the wrists, hoisting her off the throne. Mom yelped and Lavender folded mana over herself. Only she didn't vanish. She flickered for a second, and Merlin appeared beside her, grabbing her by the throat. "No, you don't! Not this time."

Lavender clutched at his hands, unable to pry them off. Instead, she leaned into Merlin, kicking off the ground and jumping. They both flew back into the darkness, leaving Mom behind.

Go now! Lavender's voice sounded strained, even through group chat. *I won't be able to hold him for long.*

What is the blood key for? Kalli asked in desperation as we both lunched for the throne.

Mom stood there, not moving, as we each grasped an arm of the tall-backed throne. It looked as though she'd been stunned.

Would you like to assign an artifact? Y/N?

The system waited patiently for us to make a decision. What could we use? Where could we put over a billion mana? Would the system accept my fanny pack? Perhps the blood key? We tried some of the options as we came up with them.

Error: Fanny Pack of Nil space cannot contain mana.
Error: Blood Key [Melvin Murphy] not compatible

What else was there? The void? The artifact I made out of Kalli's wand? Wendy screamed at me. *Hurry! Lavender's dying!*

Error: The Void cannot be used like that.
Error: Kalliphae's training wand not compatible.

I groaned and tried to pull away from the throne so I could think. It was no good. I was still stuck to the throne.

CRUNCH!

Wendy and Shara screamed, and our eyes were drawn to Lavender, whose head was bent at an unnatural angle. A strong wave of conviction came from Kalli, focusing my mind back to our task. ***You know what we have to do, Mel.***

The sad truth was, I did know. There was only one choice. There had only ever been one choice.

But we'll die!

She let out a slow sigh. ***At least we're together.***

At the same time, we focused on the menu and assigned an artifact.

Option Accepted...
Preparing for data transfer...

A jolt went through us like someone flipped the switch while we were connected to a battery. Mana flooded through us, disregarding the fact that we were already filled to capacity. I reached out for Kalli, who did the same, and we clasped hands. I felt nothing at that moment but love. It was a pressure that welled up inside of me and had been desperate to break loose since the day I met her. I told myself that the pain I felt was just the build-up to the bliss we would feel when we could finally be together.

Kalli squeezed my hand. ***I wish I could have spent forever with you.***

You will. I don't care where you go after this. I will follow you.

She squeezed her eyes shut, and I did mine as well. My thoughts became fuzzy as I wondered what would happen to the leftover mana after we exploded. Surely, we couldn't absorb billions of mana. Not before it killed us. Would there still be enough left over for Merlin to destroy everything with? Was there a chance he could succeed and make Mom immortal? Perhaps Lavender was wrong? Then, I remembered Lavender was dead, and my heart broke.

Something else broke at that same moment. We both felt it. Something inside of us ruptured and mana began pouring through the gap like water through the side of a punctured swimming pool. It was going somewhere and neither of us knew where. I thought my existence would cease to exist at that point but, instead, I felt something else. Relief.

I heaved a sigh and pulled my consciousness within, trying to figure out what was happening. Instinctively, I knew Kalli was still alive, though neither knew for how long.

One look from inside told us that mana was flooding through our cores down the tether that connected us. Only it was flowing from both sides and disappearing into the wall gap us. Rather than the barrier that had been there when we were separated by Merlin, the golden light shone like the sun as it fed on the mana like a hungry infant.

"No! Don't eat that!" Kalli screamed as she launched herself toward the light.

I rushed over from my side, and we met at Sindra. For the first time since we created her, she didn't attempt to evade our touch. She pulsed happily as mana flooded into her from both sides.

"How is she doing that?" I asked, running my hand through the mana as it passed.

Kalli shrugged. "I don't know, but I think Lavender foresaw this."

"What do you mean?" I asked.

Kalli blushed. "She was a little too interested in whether or not we did it."

"Oh, right," I replied, feeling a little embarrassed that I hadn't noticed Lavender's interest in our love life at the time. "Do you think she knew Sin could do this?"

"Sin? I like that," Kalli replied with a smile. "Do you think she can handle all the mana?"

"I don't think we have a choice," I replied. "It's either that or we die."

"Or worse," Kalli said. "The whole universe blows up."

"Or that," I conceded.

It felt like an eternity passed as Sindra absorbed all the mana from the system. While the ball of golden light grew, it wasn't nearly as big as I thought it should be with over a billion mana.

Just as it began, the process ended with a system notification.

System Transfer Complete...

[51]

IT WAS QUIET, too quiet. We floated next to the golden orb in complete silence after the rushing water sound of the mana was long gone. Both of us stared at the orb, wondering if we'd caused lasting damage to our future child. While thinking of a glowing ball of light as my daughter was silly, I felt an unmistakable bond.

Oh, no! Kalli squeaked in shock. We both felt it before the message appeared.

Lavender ??? has perished.
Lavender ??? has left the group.

There was no time to worry about Sindra. We jumped back to our bodies. It seemed that time slowed down while we were in dream space. Merlin knelt over Lavender who he gently lowered to the ground. He whispered as he closed her eyes with his hands. "You can rest now, Sister. I'll show you. I'm right."

Kalli removed her hand from the throne, and I did the same. The magnetic attraction was gone. For once, the throne was just a chair. Mom looked down at me and whispered, "Did you do it?"

I nodded in silence. Merlin acted as if nothing happened and rose to his feet. "Now that we got the distraction out of the way, why don't we continue? Honey, if you'd be so kind as you take your place on the throne."

Mom sighed. "I haven't been your honey for sixteen years. Not since you abandoned us."

How was she so calm? Merlin just murdered the most powerful person I knew, and she wasn't even batting an eye. Merlin ignored the jab and went back to work on the ritual. It was different, though. The runes changed color. What had once been shimmering blue had turned a dim red. Merlin frowned before rushing over to the throne, which Mom had decided to sit on again.

"What have you done?" he bellowed, rounding on me and grasping my shoulders. "Give it back! You aren't going to like what I do if you don't."

"Let him go!" Kalli screamed, jumping on him and clinging to his neck while emblazoned in green flame.

Merlin growled and released me to grasp at Kalli. He flung her over his head, sending her flying into the darkness. I wasted no time, folding mana over myself and stepping into the void. My intention had been to teleport to Kalli and catch her, but Merlin followed me into the void space.

"I'm not going to say it again," he bellowed, lunging at me. "Give it back!"

Not having time to choose a location, I dropped out of the void and found myself outside the tower in the ruins. A rustling noise told me I'd probably startled someone with my sudden appearance. Merlin dropped out right in front of me, having taken his time in the void where time didn't flow to locate me.

He reached out for me, but Kalli appeared between us. She wrapped mana around us, and we vanished. Rather than taking me to the void, we reappeared instantly, only this time in Lavender's underground hideout.

I looked around for any sign of Merlin while Kalli rubbed her arm. "He won't find this place. Lavender masked it."

"We shouldn't underestimate him," I replied, reaching out to probe her arm with my mana. "We need to rescue the others."

Kalli shook her head, sighing in relief when I found the fracture in her arm and began mending it. "No. It doesn't matter. Merlin won't stop. We have to deal with him first. Somehow…"

She was right, we may have dealt with the system, but Merlin was still a very real threat. He wouldn't stop until he figured out what we had done with the accumulated mana. The hideout was abandoned. We looked around for Viola, but the only thing left was Lavender's inter-dimensional door.

"Should we hide on Scrap?" I asked, realizing Mika was probably on the other side of the door.

Kalli shook her head. "We can't run away. Your mom and all our friends would pay for it. Like it or not, we have to face him."

Having time to think for the first time since entering the throne room, I took out the blood key again. Why had Lavender insisted on Shara making it in the first place? Thinking of her name reminded me that she was in a group with us and could answer for herself.

Shara? Wendy? Are you there?

Wendy replied, *We're here.*

Can you guys escape through the door you came from?

She sighed. *No. It was destroyed by Merlin in the fight.*

I groaned. They were trapped. We were going to have to come back for them, but first, we needed a plan.

Shara, I need to know why you made this blood key. Did Lavender say anything when she asked you to make it?

Shara took a little while to answer. Her voice sounded shaken. *Um, I'm sorry, I can't believe she's gone. Lavender said Kalli would understand what to do with it.*

Kalli reached over and took the vial out of my hands. While she'd watched Shara make it, she'd been on Scrap at the time. For all I could tell, it was just a normal vial of blood. I inspected it to confirm.

Item: Blood Cipher (Melvin Murphy)
Components: Blood, Mana, Essence of M

Item Rank: B
Item Level: 1
Item Owner: Murphy

Kalli clasped her hands around it and closed her eyes. While it wasn't visible to the eye, I felt her mana seep out and surround the vial. She scrunched her nose in frustration when the glass didn't allow mana through and fumbled with the cork stopper until she managed to remove it. There was a strong reaction the moment her mana came into contact with mine. I'd seen it before back on Earth. At the time, I thought it was just the result of combining our particular flavors in food, but seeing it again reminded me that I'd seen it somewhat recently as well. Our combined mana in my blood took on a golden glow that reminded me of the ball of golden light in our dream space. It was the same color as Sindra.

I couldn't help but laugh at the thought.

Well, that's another way of combining our mana.

Kalli glared at me, but I could tell she wasn't upset. *That's our future daughter you're talking about. Sin is more than just a combination of our mana. Much more.*

Kalli was right, of course, and she knew it.

Item: Master User Key
Components: Blood, Mana, Pure Essence
Item Rank: S
Item Level: 1
Item Owner: Murphy

The question was, what to do with it? My first thought was to drink it but the idea of drinking blood made my stomach turn. Not to mention that was the path to vampirism. Kalli and I had both been plagued with nightmares for months about the whole vampire thing. Then, there was Shara. I was pretty sure she would have a fit if we announced we were vampires all of a sudden.

If it wasn't food, there was only one thing left. Kalli and I nodded to each other before sitting down and turning our thoughts inward.

Hey, Kalli. Since when have we been able to do this without sleeping?

She shrugged. *I don't know. You did it so I knew I could, too.*

Wait, I thought you did it first.

We both tried to think back and wound up laughing. Neither of us could remember. The golden orb had been floating between our cores for a while since absorbing all the mana from the system. It floated over to us when we both appeared on my side of the dream, waiting intently as we looked at the vial of golden liquid as if it expected us to do something.

Kalli pulled the stopper again. The liquid bubbled out of the vial as though we were in outer space. Normally, I'd find that strange but we were in a dream at the moment so it didn't count. The bubbles of golden mana stretched out into a long string that sought out the orb. It shimmered brightly when it made contact. Two wispy tendrils stretched out toward us.

I looked at Kalli apprehensively, and she nodded, reaching out to take one. The moment I took mine, I felt a static shock and an explosion of colors erupted into me. Then a voice spoke that was neither mine nor Kalli's. *I was hoping I would get to meet the two of you in this form.*

I was confused. Kalli seemed to understand something I didn't. *Hello, Sindra. My precious one.*

I gaped at the little golden ball.

Wait a second. Aren't you supposed to make baby sounds before you sound like a college grad?

Sindra bobbed up and down, seemingly excited. *That would be true if I was a baby. However, what you don't realize, is that human tendencies are tied to the flesh. Here, I am a concept, the result of your combined essences. Don't worry. When I am born, you will still be able to enjoy the full experience of being my mommy and daddy.*

Kalli frowned. *How do you know all of this?*

The artifact you bound me to is a wealth of knowledge. It

contains more data than any one person can absorb in a thousand lifetimes.

It was my turn to be confused.

Are you saying you know everything the system knows?

Sindra bobbed from side to side. *I actually know very little. It's just that I have access to all this information in real time. I believe the effect will minimize when I am born. The human brain isn't designed to process all of this.*

Kalli reached out to stroke the ball of golden light. It floated into her, and she giggled as the raw energy made her fingers tingle. *Do you think you can help us defeat Merlin?*

Yes! Sindra replied, a projection of light appearing in front of her. *There is a message in the system for you two about that.*

The light defined itself as a woman in a dazzling red dress. I recognized it as the dress Lavender was wearing the day we met her. She smiled and took a few steps toward us. "Hello, children. I'm sorry you had to witness my death. It hasn't been easy for me, and I've known about it for nearly a century. Before you try, I cannot answer any questions. Too many words make the future unstable.

I am glad you were able to figure out the key. With it, you strengthened your bond and prevented Merlin from taking the system by force. It will also give you the tools you need for the battle yet to come. I wish I could help you with that, but my visions stopped when I died. This is all I can do. You have everything you need to survive. Remember, use the ring if you can't bring yourself to kill your father."

Then, she vanished. We stared off into space for a while before Sindra spoke again. *That is all she left. There are several other entities, but I don't think they will be of any use. I believe you've met Aya.*

I jumped at the mention of her name.

Oh! The tutorial cat. Do you think there's a tutorial on how to beat Merlin?

Kalli slapped my arm playfully. *Be serious, Melvin. I don't know about beating him, but we need to rescue our friends and your mom.*

I smiled.

Yeah! You're right.

[52]

So, how are we going to do this?

I was at a loss. We'd managed to steal the system from Merlin and flee to safety but also abandoned Mom and all our friends in the process. Not only that, but Merlin would hunt us to the ends of the universe to get it back.

Kalli planted her hands on her hips in a Superman pose. *I'll tell you how we're going to do this. Together. He may be powerful, but he's still just one man, and mortal, right?*

I sighed.

I'm pretty sure he's mortal. Are you saying we should kill him?

Kalli shrugged. *I don't know. What if he kills someone else? Like your mom.*

She had a point. I didn't want anyone else to die. Still, that had to be the last option. Unless Kalli was in danger. I knew exactly what to do in that case. Kalli sensed my thoughts and walked over to kiss me. *No! I don't want you walking down that path. Not even for me.*

While I tried to hide it from her, I'd already made up my mind. Defending Kalli was the same to me as self-defense. I'd die without her. That part of me understood how Merlin felt about my mom. The only difference was that if Kalli chose to live out her life and die, I'd follow her into the unknown, not live forever and try to make her do something she didn't want.

Kalli cleared her throat to get my attention. *I can see what you're thinking. You know that, right?*

I nodded but folded my arms defiantly.

I know. I was just thinking about what we have to do. We have one big advantage. Merlin accidentally showed it to me when he blocked me from the system. I'm going to activate parental locks on him. It won't shut him down but, hopefully, it gives us enough of an edge to stop him somehow.

Kalli giggled. *That's actually a good idea. We need to see what we can do with the system now that we have control. Also, do you think we have access to all that mana?*

I started flipping through menus trying to figure it out.

I don't know, but there's a lot of stuff here.

I expected Kalli to lean over my shoulder and watch as I worked, but she surprised me. She pulled up her own menu and started flipping through spells. *That's strange. Most of the spells are grayed out. Oh, never mind. I see. I can only use spells that somewhat match my element. I can use Wind, Fire, and Earth, but Water, Ice, Electricity, Light, and Dark are grayed out.*

I went to the spell section as well. Nothing was grayed out. It made sense in a way since my core was made up of non-aspected mana. While I'd originally mistaken it for the light element, Merlin made it clear that our family mana was unique in that regard.

Scrolling through the list, I noticed that most of the spells were difficult to pronounce, most of them barely words. Then, something odd caught my eye.

Kalli, look at the Earth spells. Do they look odd to you?

Kalli looked down the list and giggled. *That's silly. Do you think somebody changed them? Who says words like Pew!*

A rock the size of a bullet whistled past my face. I felt the shock-wave ripple across my cheek as it passed.

Whoa! You almost hit me.

Kalli rushed over to examine my face. She'd felt it through the bond. ***Oh, my gods, Mel! I'm so sorry. I didn't know I was going to launch a rock at you.***

I shrugged, laughing the adrenaline out of my system.

Yeah, I guess we need to be careful with those words. It's obvious someone simplified them to make them easier to say.

After familiarizing ourselves with new spells, Kalli and I took time to practice editing and world-building. Both would come in handy in the fight against Merlin. While we had effectively cut him off from the system, he already demonstrated to me that he was more than formidable without it. He probably even knew quite a few World Magic spells.

At the time when we had cast it, Kalli and I didn't understand World Magic or where it drew its mana from. We just knew the Celestea castle on Luna held quite a bit of it. With the loss of system mana, we could only hope that Merlin didn't have another reserve somewhere. That was probably too much to ask.

The next question was how to draw Merlin out of hiding.

He's probably waiting in the void for us to try and teleport.

Kalli smiled. ***We already know how to get around that. Wendy taught you.***

She was right. I'd practiced becoming the wind and knew I could get back to the tower that way in a matter of hours.

But what about you? I don't think I can carry you that way.

Her smile twisted in a most sinister fashion. Suddenly, Kalli started flaming. It was nothing new. I'd seen her do it on multiple occasions when she was excited about something. Only, this time, she didn't stop. Her body warped under the flame, looking like a heat haze illusion before ultimately disintegrating.

I heard her giggle as the flame wrapped itself around me. ***Hurry up and change so we can go. We need to hurry so Merlin doesn't have a chance to come up with a plan of his own.***

While I could have experimented with another element, I didn't have time for that. I quickly became the wind and flowed alongside Kalli. We exploded out of the hideout, quickly blasting through the twists and turns. As wind and fire, it was much easier to find the exit.

We just followed the air pressure and were quickly released from the mountain with an explosive gasp.

While we never lost contact with each other, Kalli and I were very careful not to fully combine while traveling to the tower. Wendy had warned us. The journey took two hours once we got high enough to catch a friendly breeze. I worried about the barrier as we approached the tower, but it didn't seem to be a problem. Either Merlin had forgotten to block me, or he couldn't block his own blood without blocking himself. Or perhaps it was a trap.

Kalli agreed. **He's probably waiting for us. We need to be ready for anything.**

I decided to ask the others.

Hey, guys, we're here. Any sign of Merlin yet?

Joe replied for the group, *Not yet. We've moved into the alcove, but it's locked from above. I'm pretty sure I can break through if needed. We were just waiting to see what you're going to do. Also, there's the matter of Lavender.*

He looked down at the lifeless form of Lavender. It was left unspoken, but it was fairly obvious they couldn't sneak through the tower hauling a body. She was going to have to be left behind. Knowing where they were helped me come up with a plan. We entered through the park on the throne level of the tower as I gave my instructions.

Break the door and head for the elevator. Make your way to the first floor and leave the tower. We will meet you on the way.

Staying in our elemental forms, we flowed along the walls, trying to look like an innocent backdraft as we made our way toward the elevator. Could it be possible that Merlin was unaware of us? We'd just caught sight of everyone when he made his move. Merlin appeared behind Mom and wrapped his arms around her. Before anybody had a chance to object, he was gone.

Mom!

Even though I knew he was baiting me, I had no choice but to follow.

Kalli, wait here. I've got to rescue her.

Merlin was waiting as I appeared in the void. He paced around my mom, who was frozen. "You know, she'd be able to defend herself if she'd just let me awaken her."

"Why didn't you just awaken her?" I asked, wondering why Merlin opted for the nuclear route when there was a much simpler option. "It's not like she could have stopped you."

He laughed. "Have you ever tried to awaken the unwilling?"

I paused, thinking back to the many people I'd awakened. While many of them didn't know what awakening was, I'd explained to all of them what I was doing. Merlin took the answer from the expression on my face and went on. "It isn't pretty. You might even say it's torture. A core that doesn't want to be awakened or that's awakened by force becomes warped. In some cases, it even implodes and that's a fate worse than death. You obviously wouldn't want that for your mother, would you?"

At that moment, Kalli appeared at my side. Merlin scowled at the two of us. "Okay, enough conversation. I'm going to make this simple. Give back the artifact, and I'll return your mother to you."

"You wouldn't dare hurt her," Kalli said, folding her arms. "You love her."

He looked at Mom before answering, "That is true. I do love her. However, I've loved her through many lives. If she dies today, I'll just wait for her to respawn again. When you're as old as I am, time is but water dripping in a bucket. You, on the other hand, only get one mother. She won't be the same when she comes back. That bond will be lost."

"You're sick!" Kalli said, her voice dripping with anger.

"Enough!" Merlin screamed, a vein throbbing on his forehead. "Do we have a deal?"

"No," I heard myself saying the word as though I was someone else. "I can't sacrifice the universe, not even for Mom."

"So be it!" He sighed, holding out his wand. "Then I have no further use for you."

An arc of flame shot out faster than I could react. Just as it was about to hit me, something slammed into my side, knocking me out of the way. Kalli yelped as the attack hit her square in the chest. At that moment, I saw red. Even the prospect of Merlin murdering my mom didn't enrage me like the thought of him hurting Kalli.

Before I knew it, Kalli's training wand was in my hand and pointed at Merlin. I didn't bother feeding the wand any element and just let my natural mana blast through. Merlin hid behind Mom, forcing me to pull the attack back at the last second. By that point, Kalli was on her feet, aiming her own wand at Merlin and letting out a torrent of flames at the wizard. He dove behind Origin to evade Kalli's attack.

Instead of pursuing her attack, Kalli pulled back the flame and lunged for Mom. *I'll come back as soon as I can.*

Then, they both vanished, dropping out of the void. Merlin stepped out from behind Origin and glared at me. "You cannot hide her from me."

Then he vanished, too. I don't know how I knew, but I knew he went to where Mom and Kalli were. I focused on Kalli through the bond and dropped out of the void just in time to see the two of them square off. Merlin appeared behind Kalli, and black smoke shot out of his wand. She began coughing and sputtering as the smoke wrapped itself around her body.

I targeted the smoke and edited it.

DELETE!

Fortunately for me, magic was defined as an item. Merlin's eyes widened as his attack was nullified. He didn't waste any time rounding on me. Shards of ice shot out of his wand. I held up my hands to block the attack.

[53]

THE ATTACK NEVER CAME. A brick wall created by Kalli materialized out of thin air to intercept it. I teleported to her side and cast the first spell that came to mind.

"*Pew!*"

A rock the size of a baseball shot off my wand and into Merlin. His robe ballooned out to soften the blow. It still hit him with considerable force, causing him to wheeze and stagger backward. I raised my wand to cast another spell, but he waved his wand and suddenly I was frozen again.

He waved the wand theatrically. "Tricks like this are also possible with magic. Sorry, it's come to this, but you've left me no choice."

I could tell Kalli was also paralyzed as he stalked toward me. The next shot out of his wand was a stream of blue plasma which I was powerless to stop. The force of the impact knocked the wind out of me and seared itself into my midsection. I went down in a heap, fearing the attack had gone straight through me, taking vital organs out along with it.

Melvin! Kalli shrieked, rushing to get in front of me.

Looking down, I realized what happened. While my shirt had been incinerated, the armor Merlin gave me absorbed the worst of the attack.

All I felt was the impact and some of the heat. In a moment of fear, Kalli managed to break free of the paralysis and rush to my side. Either that or Merlin couldn't do two things at once. That made me think. We could do two things at a time, and we could do them seamlessly.

Rising to my feet, I pointed my wand at Kalli and sent as much flame as I could muster at her. She reached out a hand to collect it, allowing it to form into a great ball of fire while flashing her most Kalli-like glare at Merlin and editing a tiny pebble on the ground in front of him. It expanded into a massive wooden doll, sending Merlin flying into the air. At the same time, I edited a portion of the ceiling.

Item: One Ton Boulder (Edited)
Components: Rock, Dirt
Item Rank: D
Item Level: 1
Item Owner: Murphy

It shuddered and broke free. Watching the boulder fall made it sink in that we were back in Lavender's hideout. Merlin looked up at the last second and just managed to propel himself out of the way before the boulder crashed into the ground, kicking up a cloud of debris.

He landed across the room from us and swished his wand in the air again. The tightness returned, and we found ourselves paralyzed again. Rather than following up with an immediate attack, Merlin closed his eyes and began chanting.

"Quedious Mikka Oddulous Rai."

Mana accumulated at the tip of his wand, causing it to take on a distinctly green hue. His eyes closed as he focused mana from some unknown source. Even while paralyzed we still had full access to the system. Between the two of us, we edited more items in an attempt to break free from his control.

Merlin laughed and a barrier appeared around him, deflecting the feeble attacks. There was only one thing inside of the barrier with him. Mom. She rose to her feet behind Merlin, and he cast her a sidelong glance as mana continued to accumulate on the tip of his wand.

"I'm sorry, my love," he whispered to her. "I can't let anything stand between us anymore, not even our son."

Merlin gasped as a slender hand reached out and grasped the tip of his wand. Her hand withered before he could do anything about it. Horror filled me as the green light invaded Mom's unawakened body. I felt the paralysis slip again as Merlin dropped his wand and caught her. Kalli and I both rushed over as Merlin clutched her.

"Why would you do this?" he cried out, tears running down his cheeks. "You can't take World Magic inside of yourself. It will damage your soul."

Mom reached out to me with a shriveled hand that had turned so black it appeared gangrenous. I instinctively took it, not caring if her affliction might spread to me.

Looking over Merlin's shoulder, Mom squeezed my hand. "Do it. It's the only way."

Unable to control myself, I began sobbing and pushed mana through the ring and into Mom. Her hand dropped as her soul was sucked into the ring. Merlin stiffened as well, his body touching hers and also caught in the magic of the ring. I continued to push mana into the ring until I was certain both of them were firmly trapped. Mom's body continued to blacken, and the World Magic continued to rampage through her body.

Kalli pushed past me and took Mom's body in her arms. Before I knew it, she'd vanished with her. Realizing there was only one place they could have gone, I left Merlin where he'd fallen and followed them into the void.

Just like the last time, Mom's body was a statue in there. The World Magic paused as well, only extending halfway up her arms and legs. Relief washed over me as I realized there might still be hope.

Did you manage to put their souls in the ring? Kalli asked, giving me time to compose myself.

I held my hand with the ring up, reaching out for Kalli with the other.

There's only one way to know.

A heated argument was well under way by the time we arrived in the ring.

"I was doing this for your own good!" Merlin roared through the door in the second cell. "If you hadn't been so stubborn, I never would have had to resort to such extreme measures."

"If you'd respected my decision, you could have gone on to lord over creation to your heart's content," Mom countered from the first cell.

If anybody else was paying attention, they weren't being obvious about it. Once I saw Mom's face poking out of the slat in the first door, I opened it and let her out.

She hugged me and smiled. "Good job, Melvin. I knew you'd make the right decision. It's over now."

"Not yet!" I cried. "It's not over until we save you. Your body is... Your body..."

I couldn't bring myself to finish the sentence, so Kalli took over for me. "Your body is just fine, Mrs. Murphy. I brought it to the void where time doesn't flow. It's safe until we can figure out a way to..."

Mom cut Kalli off with a finger to her lips. "Call me Sam, sweetheart. Or Mom. Are you two far along enough in your relationship to call me Mom yet? That isn't important now. You two saved the important bits. See, my soul is just fine."

She twirled for emphasis.

"It's not the same," I replied, feeling like Mom wasn't taking this seriously. "I need you out there."

She ran her hand across my cheek. "You don't need me anymore, honey. I raised you and that was enough. You're strong. Even if you don't see me again in this life, there's always the next one."

"What about our daughter?" I asked, taking Kalli's hand in mine. "Surely, Sindra is going to need her grandma around as she grows up."

Mom laughed. "Well, then. She'll just have to visit me. Or I can borrow a body. There are options."

"We can't do that," I said, remembering what Lavender told me about editing bodies. "Someone would have to die for that."

Mom shook her head and pointed over her shoulder toward the cell Merlin was in. "It seems to me you have a spare body lying around that isn't in use. While inhabiting an awakened body will take some getting used to, I'll do it for my grandbabies."

"Grandbabies?" Kalli asked hesitantly. "I only agreed to one. Not plural."

Mom smiled. "It's fine, dear. You can go at your own pace. I'm in no rush."

"Um, okay," Kalli replied, mollycoddled for the moment.

"I never agreed to let anyone use my body!" Merlin shouted from his cell.

Mom walked over to the slat where he was glaring at us from the darkness. "Listen here. You wanted to spend eternity with me, and I'm in here with you. At least for now. But I'm warning you, if you keep acting like a jerk, I'm going to reincarnate, and you'll never see me again. Don't think you found me all those times. I let you every single time."

Kalli leaned over and bumped me with her shoulder. *Your mom is a badass!*

I smiled weakly, still hurting that she was okay with being virtually dead.

Don't I know it?

Kalli wrapped her arms around me, sensing my turmoil. *It's going to be okay, Mel.*

Tears streamed down her cheeks as she reassured me. She remembered that her own parents also died. I squeezed her back, kissing her wet cheek.

It's going to be okay for both of us. Now that this is over, we can go find your parents, too.

She smiled. *I'd like that.*

Just as we turned to leave, Merlin's frantic voice called after us. "Hey! Don't forget to preserve my body."

"Don't worry," I replied over my shoulder. "Mom's gonna need it.

We'll throw you in the void, too."

"No!" He nearly screamed. "You can't store things in there. We aren't the only ones with access."

That gave me pause. I stopped and walked back to his cell with Kalli. Mom stepped aside to let us see him.

"What do you mean we aren't the only ones?"

Merlin looked down the hall toward the other cells. "The fact that you stole my ring and how quiet it is in here, tells me that you let the other prisoners out. That means you let my father go. I hate to break it to you, kid, but he's a far bigger threat than I ever was."

"Your dad?" I asked, gaping at Merlin. "Which one?"

"Malric," he drawled the name. "I don't know how you figured out how to get in here, but letting him out might as well have doomed the universe. It was a miracle that I got him in here in the first place."

"What about Longinus?" I asked, remembering the other man who had offered help with our corruption in exchange for his freedom.

"That old monk?" he asked with a chuckle. "That guy was too cocky for his own good and challenged me to a duel. After I defeated him, he swore he would never stop challenging me, so I put him in timeout. I suppose you released him as well?"

"Yeah," I replied, crossing my arms. "And Nir Vana."

Merlin chuckled. "I would have thought you of all people would keep her locked up with your moral convictions. That was one naughty little minx. She destroyed souls to prolong her life."

"How did she destroy them?" I asked, second-guessing myself once again.

He let go of the bars. "Did you ever wonder how she managed to live so long? It wasn't just the fresh bodies. She fed on the souls of others. I can't imagine her not doing it again, even if you promised her otherwise. Reincarnation will not be kind to her after what she's done."

"She made a contract with me," I balked. "A magic one."

Merlin sighed. "Well, maybe she will behave. If the penalty for doing otherwise is severe enough."

"She'll die," Kalli said softly.

"That might do it," Merlin said.

[54]

ONE BENEFIT to defeating Merlin and offering to preserve his body was that he gave me access to the tower's treasure vault. He wanted me to only grab a special preservation bag, but he wasn't exactly around to stop me from claiming everything. While the bag wasn't designed for dead bodies, it was more than up to the task of preserving them. We returned to the void first to safeguard Mom's body. She said she didn't need it anymore, but I was determined to fix her up so she at least had a comfortable option when she wanted to visit the mortal world. Merlin's body was more of an afterthought, but he had a point, it was healthy, and Mom could use it whenever she wanted. She even had his blessing.

The rest of the treasure room was even more impressive. Merlin had been holding out on me. There were more artifacts than I could count, sprinkled over five floors that weren't on any map. The entrance was in the back of the tiny room at the top of the tower I'd thought was Merlin's bedroom, hidden behind an old wardrobe. It seemed as though Merlin was a hoarder of magic items and weaponry.

While it was true, he also had his fair share of gold and other items of monetary value, he seemed far fonder of collecting items created by powerful awakened of the past. There was documentation to go along with almost everything, including the ones he kept on display by the throne room.

Merlin asked us not to show his treasure to anyone else, but I decided to anyway. They had risked their lives for us. Joe and Zofia ran around the room excitedly when we got there.

"Do you realize what this means?" Joe asked, holding up a handful of jewels. "This means we don't have to worry about the future. Ever! Our kid's kid's kids will be well taken care of."

"Yeah," I laughed. "I'm pretty sure we're set for life without all this treasure. Did I tell you that I have an unlimited bank account?"

Joe frowned. "Does that work back on Earth? Wait, you aren't going to live here, are you?"

"I haven't thought about it," I admitted, sharing a glance with Kalli. "Kalli wants to go back to Gaia, at least for a little while. I think we're going to have a home on Earth too. Unfortunately, defeating Merlin is probably going to throw both Origin and Scrap into chaos, so I think we're going have to spend some time here as well."

"I can help with that," Zofia said, marching over to us with a handful of tech she'd found. "For the right price, of course."

"Of course," I replied. She's been particularly helpful in the aftermath of the fight against Merlin. Not only did she secure the tower by locking all the rooms during the battle, but she made sure information got out to all of the tower maidens that they were safe once the fight was over.

When we returned to the throne floor, we found Marcelle waiting for us on her hands and knees. The sight of her reminded me that she'd vanished right before Merlin left the tower.

"Where did you go?" I asked, wondering if she'd betrayed us.

Kalli stepped in front of me and placed a soothing hand on my arm. ***Relax, Mel. Let her explain.***

Looking down, I could see Marcelle was shaking. I sighed and knelt in front of her. "Relax, it's over now."

She didn't look up. "I'm sorry, Lord Melvin. I've betrayed you. But I have a reason. Will you please hear me out?"

I extended my hand to help her up. "I will. Come, stand up. There's no need to kneel. I'm not going to be the new Creator."

Marcelle sighed and accepted my hand, climbing shakily to her feet. The words flew out of her mouth so fast it seemed like she was worried she was only allowed a single breath. "I'm sorry I told Merlin everything. Lavender told me to. She said it wouldn't be a betrayal, but I forgot it would be a betrayal to you. I'm so sorry. Can you ever forgive me?"

"Wait a second," I replied, trying to steady the woman who looked on the verge of passing out. "Calm down. What exactly did Lavender say to you?"

She didn't say anything for a minute while Kalli and I walked her to a chair. After taking a moment to calm down, she told her story. "Lavender could tell I was nervous when she stepped through that magic door. I was loyal to you, I swear, but she insisted that informing The Creator was the thing that would help you the most. When he found out she was here with your mother, he instructed me not to tell you he knew. He then made me show him where I'd seen her. Only I didn't. She gave me a map and showed me this valley. It wasn't too far away, so I had no issues bringing him there. I got the feeling Lavender lived here on Origin before by the way she described things."

I shrugged. "She was old. Maybe she had."

"Anyway, she was waiting for us with another woman," she continued. "I think The Creator called her Sam."

"That was my mom," I replied, frowning at the thought of her blackened body. "She's dead. Sort of."

"Sort of?" Marcelle asked, sounding taken aback. "Ahem, she and Lavender ran into some caves along the valley, and The Creator tried to chase them. He teleported a few times to catch them, but all I could see was him blinking in and out in the same place. Then, he ran after them, and I didn't see him again. After that, I waited for a bit, and then walked to a town to call for a ride."

"Alfred?" I asked, earning a nod from the girl.

She sighed. "You were the first one I looked for when I returned. I am so sorry I didn't tell you about it before. She told me not to tell you but I knew it was wrong. I've betrayed you, and I don't expect you to forgive me."

I was torn. In a way, she had betrayed me. But if I looked at it through the warped glasses of Lavender's scheming, her part of the plan was to betray all of us. She was the ultimate bait that lured Merlin into the trap.

I gave her what I hoped was a reassuring smile. "Don't worry about it. As I said, it's all over now. No hard feelings."

"Am I still one of your chosen ones?" she asked quietly.

Kalli answered for me, perhaps a little too enthusiastically. "No! I mean, he doesn't need that. There are no more chosen ones."

"Don't worry, though," I reassured her. "We're not kicking anybody out. It's going to take some time, but I intend to make sure everyone in the tower...no, on Origin, is well taken care of."

"And Scrap," Kalli added. "Don't forget Scrap."

I laughed. "Yes. We're going to take care of all the worlds."

"What do you intend to do about the dragon?" Zofia asked, flicking a thumb over her shoulder in the direction of the throne room. "You didn't forget about the fire-breathing dragon, did you?"

"Did it breathe fire?" I asked, hiding behind Kalli. She was fireproof.

"Don't they all?" Zofia asked, rolling her eyes.

Wendy shrugged after everybody else failed to say anything. "I don't know. We've only met that one dragon with you, Mel."

"It did breathe fire," Joe added. "Sort of."

Shara whistled. "Are you guys always in trouble like this? I can't believe I'd ever miss the safety of the Blood Moon. And that place is filled with murderers and thieves."

"I'm going to go alone," I announced as I came to a decision. "I can teleport out quickly if it tries to attack me."

"Not without me," Kalli said, clutching my arm. "Don't forget who's fireproof."

"And me," Wendy hastily added. "I'm not about to let you both die after coming this far."

"Here we go again," Joe sighed, taking something that looked like a laser gun out of his bag.

Zofia started toward the elevator. "Fine, why not. I'm headed to the holo lab to see if I can help."

While we had fought a dragon god in the past, there was no telling if Merlin's dragon was more powerful or not. We ultimately decided to let Kalli scout ahead in her fire form. I held my breath and watched through her eyes as she slowly floated around the corner toward the locked throne room doors.

"This is a surprise," a rumbling voice echoed through the halls.

The dragon's glowing blue eyes stared at Kalli as she wafted into the room. "I take your continued existence to mean that you defeated the great and powerful Merlin. Worry not, mortals. I mean you no harm. My only reason for being here was to detain a couple of children."

I shouted from down the hall. "Are you saying he asked you to babysit us?"

The dragon roared with laughter. "Call it what you will. I did my job, and you didn't enter through this door. I consider my debt to the old man paid."

"So, you'll leave us be?" Kalli asked, inspecting the dragon for good measure.

Name: Livyatan
Class: Primordial Fire-Breathing Sea Serpent
Level: 162
Affection Level: Honor Bound

"I have no quarrel with you, mortal," Livyatan replied, yawning for emphasis. "You are with the boy who revived the tower in Atlantis. I suppose I owe you a debt now as well."

Deciding it was safe, I joined Kalli in the room. "I'm Melvin, and this is my girlfriend, Kalli."

"I think I'm a little more than that," Kalli scoffed, acting offended as she materialized beside me.

"Sorry," I replied, laughing for the first time in what felt like ages. "This is my fiancé, Kalli."

"Better," she replied. "It's a pleasure to meet you, Levy."

"Levy, huh?" the dragon repeated, roaring with laughter. "It's been eons since I've had a nickname. Perhaps the new generation won't be as boring as the last. Alas, I must get back to the sea. I dry out if I'm away too long."

I thought he was going to teleport, but the dragon floated off the ground and proceeded to fly down the hall toward the park. When he had gone, Joe, Wendy, and Shara walked around the corner.

"Is it safe to come out?" Joe asked, looking a little sheepish. "Don't get me wrong, I would've fought with you, but we wanted to see what would happen first. I'm glad it worked out and nobody died."

We made our way back to the locked throne room door. It appeared Merlin used some kind of a magic seal on it. Fortunately, we had skills to deal with that.

DELETE!

With the door out of the way, we returned to the throne room. Or at least what was left of it. The walls were lined with pockmarks that told the tale of Merlin's clash with Lavender. When we got to the alcove where Joe left her body, we discovered it was gone. In its place was the shadow from the throne.

"Welcome back, conquering heroes," it said in a monotone voice. "If you are here in search of the body of Gwenddydd, you have come in vain. Her body and soul have been reclaimed by the Mountains of Nocht."

Tears streamed down my face as reality finally set in. Lavender was truly gone.

[55]

THE SHADOW GAVE us a few minutes to compose ourselves. It never dawned on me that leaving the body behind would result in someone absconding with it.

"Can we visit her?" Kalli asked, wiping her eyes on her sleeve.

The shadow shook its head. "Only those with the blessing of sight may come to the mountain and, then again, only once they've risen above the mortal plane."

"Okay," I replied, lacking anything better to say as I grabbed Kalli's hand for comfort.

We walked over to the throne to see if we missed anything when we liberated the artifact. The shadow followed. Joe gave it the side-eye. "Um, it's following you."

"Is there something else?" Kalli asked, looking hopeful. "Did she leave a message for us?"

Again, it shook its head. "I am bound to the artifact. Where you go, I go. That is how it has always been and how it always will be."

"Wait, what?" I asked, looking at the creepy shadow. "You can't just follow us around for the rest of our lives."

It only seemed to have one body gesture as it shook its head again. "I will pass with the artifact when she is born."

"No!" Kalli screamed. "You can't. You'll scare her."

"She will grow accustomed to my presence," the shadow replied. "I will be with her all her life. She will come to know me as her shadow. Or Tuatha if you must give me a name."

"Shadows don't usually follow you around..." I hedged when I realized that's exactly what shadows did. "Er, I mean, they don't walk around, and they certainly don't talk."

The shadow melted into the floor. It was dark still in the throne room, so I wasn't sure if it dissipated or went into my or Kalli's shadow. We felt it as a warm sensation in the darkness which was the only proof it was still with us.

Is this acceptable? the voice echoed in our ears in a similar way to group chat. I knew we were the only ones that could hear it.

"That works," I replied, looking nervously at Kalli.

Does it work for you?

She sighed. *I guess there isn't much we can do about it. Too bad it doesn't fight. I'd feel better if I knew it was a bodyguard for Sin.*

The voice heard Kalli through MateChat. **I am a protector of the relic. No harm will come to her in my presence.**

———

Ulli was furious. We'd locked her in her room after Marcelle abandoned her. She flew at us when we entered the room, before skidding to a halt when she saw all the people with me.

Her eyes locked on Kalli, who was holding my hand at the moment. "Um, who's this?"

"This is Kalli," I announced, holding her hand up like a trophy. "The one I've been telling you about."

She gaped at her. "What? How? I thought she was dead or something?"

Marcelle stepped in, placing a hand on Ulli's shoulder. "Calm down, Ulli. A lot happened this morning. Everything is about to change."

"Please, don't kick me out," Ulli pleaded, pushing past Marcelle to throw herself at my feet. "I don't care if I'm the other woman. I don't care—"

She ran out of words and knelt, looking at the floor. I held out my other hand to her, which she took and let me help her up. She still refused to look at me.

"Relax, Ulli," Kalli said softly. "Nobody is going to be kicked out."

It took a while for her to calm down, especially when she found out that The Creator was gone. It was becoming more and more clear that we were going to need to make an announcement to all the tower maidens about the future of the tower. Rumors were starting to go around as the upper-floor women returned to their alcoves to find the throne room in desolation.

"I think I can help with that," Zofia announced through a speaker built into the wall. I looked around for cameras, wondering just how much surveillance Dad had in my room.

"What do you have in mind?" Kalli asked, pushing past my discomfort to communicate with Zofia.

"There are a couple of options," Zofia explained. "But the best one will probably be to record something and broadcast it through tower vision. That will take over any screen in the tower and display your message."

So, that's what I did. We took to the throne room to make the broadcast. That way the women in the alcoves could be in direct attendance while at the same time serving as a symbol of my coming into power. It wasn't that I wanted to rule, but we needed some semblance of order to prevent pandemonium in the power vacuum left behind by Merlin.

"Greetings, ladies of the tower. My name is Melvin, and I am the son of Merlin, The Creator. Due to circumstances beyond his control, Merlin has been forced to leave Origin. Rest assured, this will not change your current lifestyle in any way except for the fact that you aren't grooming yourselves to be potential wives for anyone. In fact, you are free to find love elsewhere if you wish. The same goes for any other goals you may have. Live your best life!"

The thought of Mom's catchphrase brought a tear to my eye. I coughed and wiped my eyes while pretending to cover my mouth.

"My door is always open should you have any thoughts or concerns. My goal is to leave Origin a better place than I found it. While I won't always be on the planet, my two assistants will do everything they can to support you in my absence. In case you don't know them by name, they are Marcelle Barlow and Ullrisa Cypress. I trust them both implicitly."

Marcelle stiffened when she heard her name. I wondered if she still blamed herself for betraying me. Part me of agreed. She could have at least told me. However, I really needed to get off Origin, and they were the best choices to take charge, at least for me. Viola might make a more mature leader in the long run, but I needed to talk to her and set up some kind of election.

That reminded me. I motioned to the camera for Zofia to cut the stream before turning back to the others. "We need to figure out what happened to Viola and go tell Mika. She's probably out of her mind with worry."

"She went to Hideout B," Joe said from the back of the group. "Don't you remember I was there?"

"Why didn't she come with you?" I asked, remembering Joe showing up with Mom and Lavender when the fight broke out.

"She couldn't add anything to the fight," he replied. "Lavender wanted to keep her safe."

"What about Mom?" I barked. "She didn't add anything, and she died because she was here. Who kept her safe?"

For Joe's part, he at least looked guilty. "Look, man, I couldn't stop her even if I wanted to. Lavender said she was necessary to make sure the universe didn't end, and your mom insisted on coming to make sure you were safe. What was I supposed to do? Make a cage and toss her in?"

I sighed. "I guess not. Can you take us to Hideout B?"

Joe nodded. "Sure, provided to take me back to Hideout A so I can get my bearings."

I glanced at Kalli, who'd teleported straight there during the fight with Merlin. She nodded.

I've never teleported so many people before, though, she confided in me through MateChat. *Can you help me?*

Sure.

Everyone I intended to take was already in the throne room except Zofia. She assured us through the intercom. "You guys go ahead. There are some more things I want to look into here in the holo lab."

"I'm going to stay as well," Marcelle announced. "I'm sure some people are going to have questions, so I'm going to wait here and do what I can."

"I appreciate it," I said, turning to Ulli. "What about you? Would you like to come?"

Ulli folded her arms, a look on her face like she'd eaten something sour. "I'm still a little upset that you left me out last time. I'm coming."

———

Getting to Hideout B was ridiculously easy. Instead of heading down the path with A marked on the wall, we continued down B. Viola opened the door as we arrived, welcoming us into a cozy little room that looked like it was designed just for one person.

"Did you succeed?" she asked, giving us a look of concern.

"Yes," I replied, not knowing what else to say.

"I see," she sighed. "I suppose that means Lavender is dead. We will mourn her."

"And my mom!" I grumbled, mad that people kept glossing over that fact.

Viola sighed. "And your mother, though Lavender told me she won't be lost forever. There is still a way to see her again."

"I know that," I replied, wondering just what Viola thought her comment meant. "I'd still prefer her in the realm of the living."

She held up her hands to placate me. "I understand. I'm sorry if I came across as insensitive. Bear in mind I still have no idea what happened. You're going to have to fill me in, but first, would it be possible to take me to Mika? She must be worried out of her mind."

It was a short walk back to Hideout A where the door was. Mika jumped to her feet and rushed at us the moment we opened it. When she saw her mother, she flew into her arms, crying loudly and ignoring everyone else in the room.

Viola patted her head softly and said, "There, there. It's all over now."

We waited in awkward silence while Mika cried herself out. When she emerged from her mother's shoulder, her face was red.

I quickly edited a tissue and handed it to her, which she blew her nose into loudly.

"Thanks!" she said, handing it back.

DELETE!

I was so happy to have that skill again. Hopefully, it didn't still have snot on it wherever it ended up.

Mika stared at her hand where the tissue had just vanished before shrugging. "So, what happens now? Is the universe safe?"

"It is," Kalli said. "Now, we have some business to take care of back on my home planet. We were hoping Viola and you could help out with Origin while were gone."

"What do you mean?" Mika asked, looking at her mom in confusion.

I smiled. "With The Creator gone, there is going to be a power vacuum. While I'm prepared to take responsibility for that, I'd rather the planet not fall into chaos during the transition. I'm going to need help informing the different cities as well as coming up with a solution for the local government system. I'd like to revamp the ranking system at the very least."

"That's a tall order," Viola said. "I moved underground to avoid politics like that. I do know some people, though, so I'll see what I can do."

"If you're going to change things, I'd like to be involved," Mika said, stepping past her mom.

"You will be," I assured her.

"What will you guys do?" Kalli asked, looking at Joe, Wendy, and Shara.

"I need to get home," Shara announced. "And just so you know, I may be calling in the favor you now owe me sooner rather than later. The vampire war you started is going to happen sooner or later. Try to get stronger before that happens. I doubt the other vampiric families will be friendly like my mom or Merlin was."

"You considered that friendly?" I asked. "You realized he just killed Lavender and destroyed my mother's body, right?"

Shara laughed. "You haven't seen anything yet."

"I think we are going to stick around with you two for a while," Joe said, breaking up the pending argument between me and Shara. "The only thing we have to do back home is wedding planning."

"Wedding plan…" Wendy started, her breath catching in her throat when she turned to find Joe on one knee holding a ring in his hand. "But, how? When. Did you ask my…?"

"Because I love you," Joe replied. "Since the first time I met you, and yes, I asked your father. It wasn't easy when he spends so much time up in the clouds, but I managed to get a minute with him while you were packing to come here."

"I can't believe this," Wendy said, dancing with Kalli.

"Um," Joe stammered, still on his knee. "Will you—?"

"Yes!" Wendy exclaimed. "A thousand times, yes!"

[56]

THE REUNION between Kalli and Shiv melted my heart. The young girl flew off the throne, tossing her tiara to the floor before throwing herself into Kalli's arms all while sobbing loudly. Her attendants made a point of looking distracted and letting the sisters have the moment. I decided to escort Shara back to the portal that led to Blood Moon. She offered to show herself out, but I refused to take no for an answer. She's done so much for us.

"We're bad luck for each other," she said as she opened the door leading home.

"What do you mean?" I asked, wondering if she thought I was making a pass at her.

Shara laughed. "Well, the first time we met, my mom died, and now yours has. I'd hate to think what might happen if we ever meet again."

"It wasn't your fault," I replied. "Besides, if it wasn't for you, I'd still be trapped on Origin."

"It wasn't your fault either, you know," she said, resting a hand on my shoulder. "Daddy told me the things she did to stay alive so long."

It was a strange feeling. When I'd met her, she was a hyper kid, and here she was older than me. She gave me a sad look and hugged me before turning to leave.

"I'm sure we will meet again," I called after her, not wanting it to be goodbye forever.

"I'd like that," she whispered as the door slipped shut.

———

After Shara left, I checked in with Sylvia. She wasn't fazed at all by the news that Lavender had died.

"I already knew," she sighed. "We said our goodbyes. That's why she trained me in the first place. The day you saved my life, you set this future into motion."

"What else happens in the future?" I asked, hoping the kid would be more forthcoming than her predecessor had been.

Sylvia giggled and shoved me playfully. "You know I can't tell you that. Think about it. If I told you you'd live happily ever after, you'd do something to screw it up. But if I told you something bad would happen, you'd probably make it worse by trying to stop it."

I chuckled. "Life as a Fate must be tough."

"You have no idea," she replied, looking much older at that moment. "All of my dreams are nightmares now. I don't remember the last time I had a regular one."

"Do you need me to save the universe again?" I asked, wanting to help out somehow.

Sylvia laughed. "I'm sure you'll rise to the occasion when the time comes. Just—"

"Just what?" I asked, realizing she'd been about to tell me something.

She looked up thoughtfully. "Well, take care of your daughter. She is going to need you. She is, um, special."

I knew Sin was going to be special. However, I didn't like the way Sylvia said it. I didn't press her to elaborate. The last thing I wanted was to accidentally trigger another apocalypse by asking a Fate too many questions.

———

While I was on Earth, I decided to visit Mrs. Hodgins. With Mom and Lavender gone, the old Scholar from the library was as close to family as I had left. While I could have just teleported, I decided to call my old friend Mac.

"Melvin, is that you, buddy?" His voice reeked of excitement when he answered the phone.

"Hey, Mac. Can I get a lift?"

"Sure!" He yelled so loud I had to pull the phone back from my ear. "I'll be right there."

It took him about an hour to get there from wherever he was. I spent that time catching up with Sylvia and Eddie, who were now living alone in Lavender's house like an underaged married couple.

Sylvia was happy to see me while Eddie blamed me for Lavender's death. He spent most of the time with his back to me and when he did speak to me, it was usually short answers. Sylvia, on the other hand, acted like she'd aged a hundred years. She sat me down to tea and lectured me about the importance of being a responsible administrator for the system.

When Mac arrived, he wanted to know all about my adventures during the drive. He also told me about his life. It turned out, the Humcab made him somewhat of a celebrity in the taxi circuit.

"They're a two-week waiting list to get a ride in this bad boy," he explained. "I had to cancel three appointments just to pick you up."

"Don't worry. I'll pay for it," I replied, rummaging through my fanny pack for something of value.

"Don't even think about it," Mac replied, not looking back at me. "Your money's no good here. Any time you need a ride, it's on the house."

I didn't bother telling him I could teleport, but I did tell him about the adventures Kalli and I went on, only leaving out the parts of the story where we nearly died. There were way too many of those. He continued to make chitchat, and I found my attention starting to wander over to a conversation Wendy and Kalli were having back on Gaia.

"What? You, too?" Wendy swooned when Kalli told her the news of our engagement.

"Yeah," Kalli replied. "Though he didn't exactly propose. I sort of blurted it out to Father when we discussed something Mother said. Mel did make me a diamond for my ring though."

"He didn't propose?" Wendy asked in disbelief.

Kalli blushed. While we had discussed marrying many times, it was more of a forgone conclusion than any question I actually asked. Back when I confessed to her, I'd been terrified of her saying no even though we were already formed the mate bond. Only a short while later, I deepened the bond by adding a conditional contract, vowing to die instantly should I ever stop loving her. That was where Inseparable was born.

Then, on Gaia, we'd become intertwined in an effort to share our innermost feelings. The final step came when we were separated by Merlin. Our souls merged. That one was called Unity. Now it was hard to tell where she ended and I began. Or was it where I ended? I couldn't keep track anymore.

Kalli giggled. ***Stop pondering our bond. You're making me laugh over here.***

I was spared having to apologize when Mac said, "We're here."

Walking up to the door, I wasn't quite sure what I was going to say to Mrs. Hodgins. So much had happened since the last time I saw her, so many people had died. How did I tell her about Mom and Lavender? Or about the universe almost ending.

It was all a moot point because the moment I walked into the room, Kalli chose that moment to switch with me, and I found myself in her body staring at a puzzled Wendy.

"Are you okay?" Wendy asked.

I must have been making a face. Nobody knew we could switch places but us. Kalli wasted no time hugging a bewildered Mrs. Hodgins. I was never that affectionate. She was going to give us away. Wendy repeated the question.

"Um, yeah I'm fine," I replied, trying to come up with an excuse. "Mel did something silly that caught me off-guard."

It was so weird hearing Kalli's voice come out of my mouth. She sounded totally different from her perspective.

Wendy giggled. "Yeah, Joe does that to me, too. You said Melvin made you a ring? Where is it?"

I rubbed the back of my head as I thought about it.

Yeah, Kalli. Where is the ring we made?

Kalli stopped chatting with Mrs. Hodgins as she thought about it.

Um, uh oh, Mel. We gave the diamond to Daddy.

That was a problem. It could be literally anywhere.

I know! We should ask him what he did with it.

The suggestion set off a chain reaction of events. I watched in shocked silence as Kalli told Mrs. Hodgins she had to go. Then, the shocked expression on Wendy's face when I suddenly appeared next to them. What followed was an insistent tugging sensation as Kalli urgently requested her body back.

Once we were situated, she grabbed me. "Okay! Let's go."

I stood there slack-jawed while my mind caught up to Kalli. "What? Oh, you want to go see your parents. I think I have an idea."

Wendy gaped at us. "Um, what's going on? Why is Melvin here?"

Kalli gave her that smile that always disarmed me whenever she used it. It appeared to have the same effect on Wendy because she just shrugged. "Fine. Go with him, but you owe me some answers when you get back."

"You'll get them for sure," Kalli replied, grabbing my shirt. "Are you ready, Mel?"

Being one with me had its perks and Kalli immediately knew what I had in mind. Not waiting for me to answer, she wrapped mana around us and teleported.

Once we were alone in the void, she rounded on me. "Okay, where do we go next? You sounded so sure of yourself."

I smiled. The first time I went to Luna was without Kalli. She hadn't experienced the afterlife like I had. I knew Elysiana could take us there. The question was, would she?

Looking at planets other than Origin was a new experience in the void. I was tempted to wander around, looking at other locations sprinkled in the distance I'd never been to. However, Kalli's sense of urgency won out, and I went to Luna. Structures around the planet told me the Ancients were hard at work rebuilding their lost civilization.

I selected the Lunar version of Celestea Castle, and we appeared in the throne room. Unlike the previous times I'd visited, it was vacant. The darkened room was well-maintained even though it didn't serve a purpose.

Taking a guess, I spoke out loud. "Um, are any gods around today?"

The shadows came to life and a shade appeared in front of me. "Welcome back, Lord Melvin. Why do you request an audience today?"

"We need to visit the afterlife," I explained while Kalli squeezed my arm excitedly.

"I'm afraid that isn't possible," the shade replied. "While the Goddess of Death did escort you in the past, it was because your friend did not belong. Unfortunately, you have no business in the—"

The shade was cut off when my shadow came to life. Tuatha grew until he towered over the shade. "Please, fetch your master. The new lord of the system requests an audience."

The shade froze, either speechless or unable to reply. I was about to ask if we broke it when the gods appeared. They came out in force, all seven Gaian gods.

Jagriel floated over to me, puffing his chest out. "You dare make demands of my—"

Tuatha floated in front of me. "Silence, Jagriel, God of Destruction. You are in the presence of he who can erase you at a whim. I suggest you pay some respect."

To my surprise, the god knelt. "I apologize, my Lord. I did not know he had ascended."

When the other gods also fell to their knees, I started to wonder just how much power the system had over them.

Tuatha seemed to read my mind. **They pay homage to me. My**

existence predates them. Fear not, they will obey you all the same. Make your request.

"Please, take me to my parents," Kalli blurted, not waiting for me to say anything.

Elysiana rose, casting a glance back at Jagriel before approaching us. "Very well. Please, prepare for some disorientation. Passage into the afterlife can be somewhat jarring for mortals with bodies."

I tried to remember if I'd felt sick the last time, but I was too focused on Stefanie at the time. Judging from the look in Kalli's eyes, I figured the last thing she was worried about was her stomach.

"We're ready," I told the goddess, giving Kalli's hand a squeeze for reassurance.

We faded more than teleported before reappearing outdoors in a valley filled with fog that came up to our waist. Elysiana stopped Kalli as she started to walk forward. "No. You cannot cross completely over. You won't want to come back. Wait here for them to come to you."

[57]

As Elysiana said, a pair of figures appeared out of the fog and approached. Kalli whimpered as her parents drew close. They stopped just out of arm's reach.

"Thank the gods you're alive!" Celestea exclaimed with a sad smile on her face. "We feared the worst when you vanished from Gaia."

Tears trickled down Kalli's face. "It's not fair. I only just got you back."

"I know, sweetheart," Charles said, taking a step closer. "Knowing you're alive and happy means the world to us."

"But I don't want to lose you," Kalli sobbed, reaching out for her father. "Can I visit you here?"

"That isn't a good idea," Celestea said softly. "This isn't a place for the living."

"She's right," Elysiana added. "The allure of the unknown is strong in this place. Every time you visit, you lose a piece of yourself."

"What can we do?" I asked, looking to the goddess for answers.

She shrugged. "This is why I don't like bringing people here. Eventually, you will be reunited. That is the way of things."

"I don't want to wait," Kalli sobbed.

"I know, sweetheart," Celestea said. "But you have to. We lived our lives. It's time for you to live yours."

"Live your best life," I whispered the mantra so quietly that nobody should have heard.

Kalli heard me through our bond though, and she knew where it came from. She smiled through the pain and nodded. "I will, Mother. Just you watch."

Before we left, I pulled Charles aside. "Excuse me, sir. There's something I need to ask you."

"What?" he asked, raising an eyebrow. "I've already given my blessing for you to marry my daughter. What else is there?"

"The ring," I replied in a low voice. "Do you know where it is?"

"Oh, that," he said with a smile. "I sure do."

––––––––

Figuring out which planet to live on wasn't as big of a deal as I thought it was going to be. Most of the magic doors were already in place, and our bedrooms became an inter-dimensional hub. There were three of them. Our old room in Celestea Castle on Gaia refused to let anyone else sleep there. Not even Shiv.

We still had the bedroom Lavender assigned to us back at her house. We technically didn't need that one, but it was a convenient way to get to Earth when we didn't feel like teleporting. The last room was the one I had shared with Marcelle and Ulli back on Origin. Kalli wanted to add another one on Scrap, but she'd lived with another family during her stay, so we decided to add a door in the Governor's office.

ENTERING WORLD EDITOR MODE
NEW WORLD UNDER YOUR CONTROL DETECTED
WOULD YOU LIKE TO ADD ORIGIN TO YOUR EMPIRE?
Y/N?

I expected the first one and quickly added the planet. It was strange adding a whole planet. The only thing I could think of was that they previously belonged to Merlin and had gone up for grabs. I quickly added Scrap and Gaia when they popped up. The next one surprised me.

WOULD YOU LIKE TO ADD EARTH TO YOUR EMPIRE? Y/N?

I hesitated. Surely the governments on Earth would object to me claiming the whole planet for the Meltopian Empire. Would they even know? I clicked **YES**. I mean, why not, right?

WOULD YOU LIKE TO ADD POULDARIA TO YOUR EMPIRE? Y/N?

The name rang a bell, but I couldn't remember where I'd heard it before. Kalli remembered. *Isn't that Mr. McDuckenStein's home world?*

It went on like that for hours. Thousands of notifications crossed my vision as planets previously ruled over by my father presented themselves to me.

Do you think anyone on any of these planets will care that they are now part of the empire?

Kalli shrugged. *I don't know. It was different on Gaia. We only added towns when we were there. So, of course, they knew.*

The question soon answered itself when an attendant I didn't know about introduced himself to me. He entered the throne room with an entourage.

"Greetings, my Lord. My name is Evander," he said with a bow. "I was your father's chief council. If you'll permit me, I'd like to introduce you to some of the key people who run things here in the tower."

Name: Evander Cevast
Class: Savante
Leve: 57

Affection Level: Loyal

"How come I've never heard of you?" I asked, looking past him at the long line of people. "Any of you?"

He flashed a smile that I found a little condescending. "It is our job to not stand out. We have been here the entire time."

I looked over the crowd behind him but only recognized one of them. Achemes, the chef, stood proudly in his white uniform near the back of the line. I heaved a sigh as I realized I was going to have to get to know quite a few people if I wanted to run an entire planet.

"Do you guys represent Scrap as well?" I asked, wondering how Merlin managed the other planet.

Evander shook his head. "The staff you see before you are responsible for operations here in the tower. Every city has its own internal government that answers directly to you. If you wish, I will handle the day-to-day affairs as I did for your father and report to you."

"I have someone for that," I replied, thinking of Marcelle. "I'd like you to report to her. As for the rest of you, keep doing what you've been doing. My goal is to disrupt as few things as possible."

While it was still my goal to do away with the people-ranking system, I didn't want to announce that publicly until I had a viable alternative in place. For that, I needed Viola.

"Very good, my Lord," Evander said, clapping his hands. "Please, have your chosen representative contact me, and I'll make sure she has everything she needs."

———

Gaia was a hot mess. The planet had been thrown into disarray with so many royal deaths caused by Rasputin. With Kalli also presumed dead, Shiv had been made Queen. While she officially adopted the regal name Queen Celestea, we still called her Shiv. She liked it that way.

The Kingdom of Dabia was redefined as The Technocracy of Dabia run by President Administrator Zofia. Zofia liked when I suggested she was Supreme President Administrator Zofia until I pointed out that also made her the SPAZ of TOD.

The High House of Solitair was more or less back to normal with Maya back on the scene. While the majority of the citizens of the volcanic city had fled to other planets, it still housed most of the high-levels on Gaia.

The new colony of ancients on Luna formalized their new government as the Elven Federation. It never dawned on me that the magical beings trapped for so many years beneath the machine in the Lunar castle were elves. On second glance, I did notice their ears were slightly pointier than usual. We encountered a problem when they started doing commerce with Gaia. They gained access through the portal in Celestea Castle. That meant all business from Luna passed through my bathroom. We corrected the problem by moving the Luna door to the newly established Lunar Embassy located just outside of the castle.

In fact, we established embassies for every sovereign nation on the planet. That included Celestea, Solitair, Dabia, Vestaria, Albion, and Meltopia. While I was still the emperor of Meltopia it became the banner for all beastmen who lived on the continent. However, there were a pair of continents to the north between Dabia and Solitair.

One was covered in forest and was home to Mardella and Alariel. We'd visited them at their cabin, as well as the castle where Alariel's grandmother did her dark experiments in the basement. While I heard there were other towns on the continent, I hadn't been to any.

Albion was another unknown country. The first time I heard of it was when I saw the embassy. There, I discovered that the continent used to be nothing but ruins. That was until a man from Earth showed up. He called himself Alexander the Great. Some humans and several races of beastmen chose to migrate from Dabia and set up a nation with him. Albion was also known to have more dungeons than anywhere else on Gaia.

Back on Earth, Sylvia and Eddie were the most impacted by the loss of Lavender. Not only was she their teacher, but she also raised them. Considering both were still children, we decided the best thing to do was move Mrs. Hodgins into the house. That way they would at least have adult supervision. Eddie was approaching the age where he could start going to school. While he still spent time with his family, he'd come to call Lavender's house home. That wasn't about to change even with Lavender gone.

Sylvia's situation was different. She was a newly trained fate. That meant a couple of things. First, she couldn't attend school like normal awakened teens. There were no classes for her. The other thing was, she couldn't go home to her family. If word got out that she had the gift, there would be no end to people trying to exploit her. Her family couldn't live with her either.

"I know what will happen if I live with them," she explained. "And I always want to remember them as the loving parents they were before I got my powers, not what they may become when they realize what I can do."

I wanted to argue that parents weren't like that, but I could only imagine the possible futures the kid could see. Being awakened also added the fact that she would likely outlive her family by several lifetimes. That was something I might have had to go through with my mom if she hadn't ended up in the ring with my dad.

———

"What next?" Kalli whispered as she snuggled up next to me in bed.

We'd taken to talking out loud. We'd grown so used to talking in our heads all day that hearing each other's voices when we were alone together somehow felt more intimate.

"I don't know," I replied. "We can do anything. What do you want to do?"

She sighed. "Well, there are so many things we are going to have to do. We're responsible for hundreds of worlds now. That means we should probably go there. Also, we need to help Shiv get Celestea up and running."

I laughed. "Those are things we have to do, but what do *you* want to do?"

Kalli frowned, shifting in my arms to look at me. "You know, I never put much thought into it. I mean, I know I want to be with you, to reunite when we were apart, but I never put much thought into what I want after that."

"Do you want to have Sindra?" I asked, feeling a tinge of excitement at the suggestion.

Kalli's face scrunched up in a scowl. "You just want to *make* her. Kids are a lot of work, and that isn't even counting being pregnant. You know what, I do know what I want to do. Let's get married. I want to throw a big party and invite all our friends. Maybe Joe and Wendy can get married, too. They said they wanted to."

I smiled. "Nothing will make me happier."

———

It didn't take long to find the jeweler that Charles told me about. He offered his condolences for the loss of Kalli's parents the moment he saw me.

"Do you mind coming with me?" he asked, motioning toward a small shop behind him. "There is something the king asked me to make. I'm not sure if it was supposed to be a surprise."

I allowed him to guide me into his shop, not telling him that I already knew what he made. He brought it out from the back, resting on a satin purple cushion.

Item: Mana Diamond Engagement Ring
Components: Mana, Carbon, White Gold
Item Rank: S
Item Level: 1
Item Owner: Murphy

While I would have loved to surprise Kalli, there was no way to do so with our bond. Intense emotion flooded through me, and I found myself crying as I held it up to the light.

"Is everything okay, my Lord?" he asked, looking nervous.

"No. I mean yes, everything is fine," I spluttered. "We're just...I mean, I'm just happy."

He still looked confused when he offered me a smile. "Excellent. I wish the two of you every happiness. You deserve it."

———

We showed Mom the ring first. Kalli and I visited her in the ring, ignoring Merlin in the other cell when he asked to see it, too.

"I'm so happy for you both," Mom said as she held Kalli's hand. "I knew this day would come from the moment I met you."

Kalli blushed. "Really?"

"Of course," Mom replied, beaming at her. "He shows me a smile I've never seen when he talks about you. A man can't smile like that for just anyone."

I wondered if Merlin had a smile like that just for Mom. There was no way I was going to ask either of them. Before we left, Mom said her famous phrase. "Live your best lives, you two."

"Don't worry, Mom," we replied. "We will."

THANK YOU FOR READING ACCIDENTAL ORIGIN

WE HOPE you enjoyed it as much as we enjoyed bringing it to you. We just wanted to take a moment to encourage you to review the book. Follow this link: **The Accidental Origin** to be directed to the book's Amazon product page to leave your review.

Every review helps further the author's reach and, ultimately, helps them continue writing fantastic books for us all to enjoy.

———

Also in series:
The Accidental Summoning
The Accidental Education
The Accidental Contract
The Accidental Corruption
The Accidental Origin

Check out the series here! (tap or scan)

———

Want to discuss our books with other readers and even the authors? Join our Discord server today and be a part of the Aethon community.

Facebook | Instagram | Twitter | Website

You can also join our non-spam mailing list by visiting www.subscribepage.com/AethonReadersGroup and never miss out on future releases. You'll also receive three full books completely Free as our thanks to you.

Looking for more great books?

Everybody wants a second shot at life... Few get that restart. Chosen by roaming angels and sent off to another world full of magic and cultivation, where they can live in ways that could only be dreamed of on earth. Where the only thing that dictated their fate was power. Anyone who met Chance would have agreed that he deserved it more than most. Life isn't that easy. Just like everything else, there are rules and regulations—and Chance didn't make the cut. Not until a lucky encounter gets him a one-way ticket to his future. A world where he can make something of himself. If only he hadn't landed in the middle of an endless maze full of monsters salivating for his life. Isolated and lost, the only thing Chance has to work with is his strange, luck-based magic and his determination to finally live a life worth living. Fortunately, he has a whole lot of good Karma built up. **Don't miss the next hit Progression Fantasy Cultivation series from Actus, bestselling author of *Blackmist* & *Cleaver's Edge*. Join the adventure of a Karmic Cultivator in a brutal new world who refuses to compromise his values on his quest to grow stronger. Sometimes, luck isn't all it's cracked up to be.**

Get Weaving Virtue Now!

———

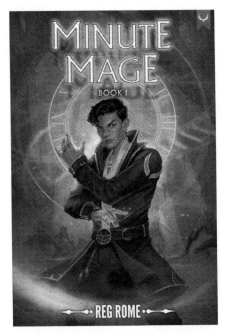

———

Some seek power. Some seek justice. Others seek to root out the filth lurking in the darkest of corners. Spot was summoned from his comfortable charging pad and familiar floors to a world of magic and intrigue. But after the flight of his new patrons, he is left alone to care for a filthy castle. During his quest to keep this new home clean, Spot will face demons, foreign armies, and his arch nemesis, the dreaded stairs. All those who stand before him will be swept away. Those who follow his spotless trail will find enlightenment, purity, and a world on its knees. **Follow this wholesome vacuum on his quest to power in *All the Dust that Falls*, a hilarious new Isekai LitRPG that will make you question what it means to be a hero. Or if heroes even need limbs, or mouths, or... you get it.**

Get All the Dust that Falls Now!

———

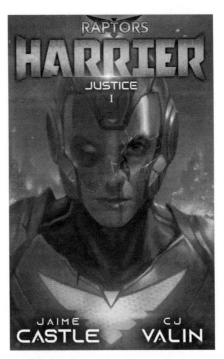

For all our LitRPG books, visit our website.